TARNISH

THE

VEIL

SINS OF THE VEIL WATCHERS

BOOK ONE

C. L. CROSS

Copyright © 2025 C. L Cross
All rights reserved.

No part of this publication may be reproduced, distributed, or transmitted in any form or by any means, including photocopying, recording, or other electronic or mechanical methods, without prior written permission of the author, except as permitted by U.K. copyright law.

The story, all names, characters, and incidents portrayed in this production are a work of the author's imagination. Any identification with actual persons, places, and events is coincidental.

ISBN: 9798284602126

Book Cover by ambientpixelstudios

For the quiet little girl with a big dream.

You did it.

The following transcript contains secrets belonging to the Order of Hunters that have been published against the Council's wishes with one objective: truth.

With this text, this anonymous author prays history judges the central figures of these historical events on facts and not the words of the victors.

CHAPTER ONE

Hunting is not a career option, but a calling. To swear the oath and take the brand is to promise a life in the dark, forsaking the stability of oneself for humanity's security. A Hunter will live, breathe, and die by the Code.

Henri Lupine's founding speech to the Order of Hunters.

Most folks said the monster skulking at the apex of Scafell Pike was a modern myth. Some blamed the escaped lynx for Keswick's missing hikers and campers, while fewer, still, accused the solitary butcher of acquiring a taste beyond the conventional.

Erika knew better.

She shouldn't have found it funny that the resident 'crazy lady' of the Stag's Antlers almost hit home with her conspiracies. Not that the poor butcher did anything—sometimes quiet people were just quiet people—but her morbidity struck truth in its tricky little bullseye, the reality a similar premise, a similar *corruption*.

Two hikers disappeared almost a year ago. A fortnight later, a dog-walker uncovered a half-eaten corpse at the base's riverbed. Every month since, at least one brave—or stupid—soul vanished from the mountainside.

All roads pointed towards one particular monster.

Propped on the barstool, Erika swallowed her answer with a sip of her latte as laughter shook the pub's four ancient regulars—and its rickety pillars. It was quaint, but the Stag's Antlers needed a serious refurb.

Tarnish the Veil

When cutting off Crazy Lady—a.k.a. the local drunk—the barman confessed a thought that his brother must have been taken by the legendary beast while hiking overnight with two friends. The trio left at midday, after a heavy lunch, last Saturday. Night blanketed the hills two days later, and nobody had heard from them since. The barman's brother was too experienced to lose his way; his friends too loyal to leave him in trouble. Local police dismissed them as reckless young lads who'd return when their hangovers subsided. Fucking ignorant, as per.

Erika's conversation with the barman soured when the subject turned personal. *Who are you?* he asked. *Why are you so interested in local folklore? What's that mark on your collarbone?* Of course, Erika kept her answers brief: *just a tourist, I read a book about it once, it's just a tattoo.* Same old, same old. The frustrated barman threatened to fling her out with Crazy Lady, but the fact that police called him delusional, yet this *girl* believed him, was enough for the barman to surrender a circled map. *My brother is all I have,* he said.

How could she turn him down after that?

With Dad certain of the Selene Pack's whereabouts—again—he sent Erika on her way late afternoon—alone. Erika hid the lump in her throat with a curt nod, reminding herself that she was used to tracking beasts—she'd been doing it since Mum was taken.

Erika wondered what her mum would think when Dad pushed her out of the door tonight with an arsenal and the order to *kill it and don't die*. Pretty meagre instructions for her first lone hunt, but Dad's training prepared her for nothing short of success.

She could do this. She was ready.

Erika ascended the mountain, trudging through the western woods for around an hour before discovering a clearing stinking of burnt timber and stale cider. The setting sun broke through overhead branches in a kaleidoscopic explosion, igniting aluminium wrappers, paper tobacco packets, and crushed beer cans. The hikers had a fun night, it seemed, with crackling fires and music in the midst of a monster's hunting ground. Ignorant idiots? Yes, but they didn't know any better. As far as they were concerned, the wendigo ceased to exist when the bedtime stories vanished and adult logic settled in.

How ironic.

From camp, Erika found a trail: deep prints reminiscent of human feet leading deeper into the dark. She clambered over arthritic undergrowth to face the mouth of a cave, releasing a breath in a cloud before her lips. The air was brisk on the mountainside, but the thought of what lurked within is what made her shiver.

According to the Hunter's Codex, wendigos favoured cold and secluded hideaways like this where they could stash their prey. A crude refrigerator, if you will. If any of the hikers were alive, they were within.

She'd hunted dozens of times before this. Still, her heart thundered at the prospect of crossing the cave's threshold without her father's whispered guidance. If not for possible survivors, she would have set a trap at the mouth and waited for it to emerge, but every minute she waited for the beast to spring could have been the hikers' last. Human deaths brought attention the Order was not inclined to deal with. Besides, burning bodies was Erika's least favourite job.

She unfastened the torch from her belt, switched it on, and stepped inside, silently reciting the words of the Order. *I am the warden in the shadows. The light in the—*

Erika angled her torch downwards at a thick splash. Blood smothered—no, *coated*—her battered boots. Her mouth dried, her tongue laced with iron. Chances were, she was returning from the cave with two—maybe less—survivors. Shit, wendigos shouldn't have even wandered this far from the peak in December, and this was the third sighting in four months. Corruptions should not have been so common.

With the implications at the back of her mind, she pushed on, following the crimson trail, her stomach contorting at what she'd find at the end of it.

Because she knew what she'd see. The outcome was always the same.

Her pupils adjusted, but it pained her to keep them pointed at the abyss ahead to avoid any surprises, and not to look too long at the vicious claw marks scarring the cave walls. She let herself wonder if it was the wendigo or its victims that made them, then stashed away the thoughts as she often did. Thoughts like those could kill you as much as a wrong step.

I am the warden in the shadows. The light in the dark...

Then she heard it—the wet crunch of flesh and bone. Her blood chilled as she turned a corner and covered the torch's bulb, approaching a fork in the tunnel system.

The beast hunched over a hiker's body, grey skin thinning over the sharp bumps of its curved spine with every movement. It ripped into the hiker's chest, hollowing him out, pouring innards onto the stone floor in a cacophony of vile, merciless sounds. *Rip. Squelch. Rip.* It was hard for Erika to imagine the wendigos as humans once.

But the wendigo *was* human—one of two students who sought to climb the pike after finishing university six months back, if Dad's research was correct. Somewhere, it all went wrong, the boys got stuck, and one of the two gave in to *the hunger*. Although one still drew breath, two boys died that day. Corruption by gluttony could never be satiated.

The acidic stench forced bile up Erika's throat. In its frenzy, the wendigo failed to notice she was there, watching in the shadows, completely still.

The monster was near-blind. So long as Erika's light pointed away from it, the wendigo would not see her, but if it turned around, it would charge. Having to carry a weapon and a torch was a huge disadvantage here.

That was why they hunted at night. That was why they belonged in the dark.

A pained sob reverberated through the walls, coming from the right-hand tunnel. Erika bit back a sigh of relief, hoping, for selfish reasons, that it was the bartender's brother. She hadn't met any of the other hikers' families and did not intend to. You never forgot the face who mouthed the words that shattered your world.

The wendigo paid no attention to the hiker's cries. Why would it? It had its prey—there was no need for it to worry. This was Erika's chance to gain the upper hand.

She estimated the distance from her spot at the fork entrance to the tunnel on her right: around ten metres. She counted again—still ten metres. That was all it took to get from where she was and where she needed to be. She would find the survivor first and deal with the creature later.

Fuck, this was risky.

The light in the dark. The shield at humanity's back…

Eyes on the wendigo, she sidestepped for the tunnel's mouth, slow, calculated, and careful. If the wendigo turned around, if she needed to—

Stop.

Fortune favoured the monstrous tonight.

The stone was so small it became invisible in the dark, but the sound was there. It skipped diagonally across the cavern under the force of Erika's boot. Dad always said, *Watch your feet!*

She flipped the torch off before the wendigo could turn around.

Engulfed by the darkness, she waited.

The tunnel was perhaps two large steps away, but running was not an option. Wendigos were renowned for their speed, and stumbling blindly through its maze was surely a signature for her death warrant. It was a mistake so stupid of a Hunter to make that, if that were to happen, even her father would refuse her funeral invitation. She wouldn't attend either, if that were possible.

Erika made one mistake, but she would not make another. She would wait. She was patient.

Nails scratched stone, and the ragged breathing grew louder. Louder. *Louder.* Until the scratching stopped—until the wendigo stared at her, mere inches from her face.

Dad's help would have been appreciated *right* about now.

Her lashes fluttered as the icy air caressed her, sliding its way through her fastened coat and into her chest and heart. The smell… God, the *smell*. Bile gathered, and her stomach flipped again and again until—

It growled—an odd sound, partly human, like a child pretending to be a wolf. Erika craved just a few deep gasps to steady her nerves, but that was impossible. Every breath was short and shallow, timed and savoured.

Another ragged breath, and the stench augmented. The monster almost touched her now. It knew something was there, but could not pinpoint predator or prey. Wendigos were lone creatures, you see. *Nothing* was a friend to them.

If it focused on her face, it would not see her hands. Erika slipped one into her deepest coat pocket, gently removing a copper coin. It waxed the rough callouses on her palm.

Keep it steady. Keep it steady.

She was a good shot. She could do this.

She waited for the pungent breath, then released the coin with a sharp flick of her index finger and thumb.

The creature startled at the coin bouncing off the opposite cave wall. It scuttled after it with a hiss, leaving its prey—those dead *and* alive—behind.

Erika dared to let out a gasp.

She had maybe a minute to reach the survivors and made haste rushing down the tunnel, switching on her torch.

Slumped against the cave wall, a body in his arms and a bloody, blue coat draped over him, was one of the missing hikers. He sobbed into his friend's chest—another hiker—and bolstered his cries as he saw Erika enter.

"You need to get out! Haven't you seen that thing? How have you not been—"

Erika pressed a finger to her lips. "Is he alive?"

The hiker gulped, then mimicked her hushed tone. "Yes, but he's been bleeding out for hours. Fell unconscious... I don't know how long ago."

Erika nodded and knelt, pressing the back of her hand to the hiker's forehead. "His temperature's high. He'll need treatment the moment we get out."

The hiker gawped. "G-get out? Are you daft? That thing is—"

Erika clamped his mouth, nearly slamming him into the rock behind. She hated this part of the Hunt: the people. Monsters didn't question you.

She hissed through her teeth, "I came here to get you out. I can't do that if you draw that thing here and it kills me first."

The hiker stilled. She let go and he released a breath. "Who are you?"

She picked the coat off the unconscious hiker. Wool lining. *Flammable enough.* She had her own jacket—a corduroy-collared, olive-green thing she rarely took off, but, quite frankly, it was costly, and Initiates didn't get expenses from the Order.

The hiker tilted his head. "A name, at least?"

Erika fumbled around her pockets for matches and found a small, opened pack, willing his silence.

"Mine's Joshua," he said. "What's yours?"

She checked the matchbox: six left. It was enough. She met Joshua's eyes for only a moment. In the torchlight, his gaunt bone structure and mousy hair reminded her of the bartender she met earlier. "Erika," she replied.

She examined the size of his friend: too big for either of them to carry alone. There was no way she could get him and Joshua past the wendigo undetected, especially when she made a slip-up of her own earlier. Joshua's missteps would end all three of them in seconds. If they were hoping to escape, the creature had to die.

"I'm going to kill that thing." Joshua's baby-blue eyes bulged. "And I need you to help me."

"Me? But I can't... I don't know how... Why do *you* know how?"

"You don't need to fight it. The wendigo—the creature out there—sees things based on movement. It can see *me* in the dark, but I can't see *it*." She dumped the coat and matchbox in his hands. "I'll attack first. While I do that, you need to light this on fire and throw it in the middle of the cavern so I can see what I'm doing."

"Okay." His mouth tugged in a half-smile. "But you know, this is my favourite jacket."

She glowered. "Just make sure it burns before you throw it."

He rolled his eyes. Erika had no interest in getting to know the people she saved. If the hunt went wrong and something happened to poor Joshua, moving on had to be swift. No mourning on the job.

Erika unbuttoned her coat, reaching for the flare guns strapped to the halter at her chest. As eager as she was to bring the crossbow to the mountain, her favourite weapon was useless against wendigos. Arrows could slow them down, but only fire granted a more permanent ending.

Joshua watched as she checked the guns' contents, slack-jawed. "Who... Who did you say you worked for, again?"

Erika brushed rogue strands of ash-blonde from her brow and gave Joshua a slight smile. "I didn't."

They were ready. At least, *she* was.

"When you light the coat, hang back and keep still. Let me do my job."

Joshua didn't argue. "I understand."

With an encouraging nod, Erika gripped her guns and stormed the cavern.

Tarnish the Veil

A scarlet flare shot across the cave and singed the wendigo's arm. It screeched, backing up as Joshua ignited the coat and launched it below its dirty feet.

Then it roared, the sound an expulsion of two voices; one that of a maddened bear, the other a man trapped in a body twisted by desperation.

Erika winced, unable to block her ears. The wendigo darted around the fire and slung a clawed hand for her abdomen. She leapt back, careful with her feet, dodging slashing hands ready to cut like blades. It was faster than her, and she would eventually tire from all this dodging.

She grabbed a knife from inside her coat and countered one of the wendigo's strikes, jabbing the blade into its gnarly bicep.

It roared and tossed Erika away like a rag doll, her flare guns flying free.

Erika slammed into the wall. It was angry now. *Very* angry.

Joshua retreated into the tunnel and watched from the sidelines, obeying Erika's order to be still.

She reached for her flares, then paused—they were nowhere to be found.

Either of them.

CHAPTER TWO

In accordance with the Treaty of the Four Worlds, members of the Quadruple Supernatural Alliance, defined as arcanes, vampires, lychans, and Hunters, are to coexist equally. Threats to the peace or security of any species face severe punishment at the Alliance's discretion.

The Hunter's Codex, Chapter I.

The wendigo prowled around the burning coat, orange flames licking its dead skin, turning it a glowing, threatening red as it growled. Erika's hands scrambled along the cave floor for any signs of the guns hidden in shadow.

An *actual* light in the dark would have been fucking useful right now!

Joshua jumped into the cavern, running straight for the flare behind the wendigo.

He didn't stop when Erika yelled. He called her name and kicked the gun in her direction as the wendigo spun around, screaming in his face.

I am the shield at humanity's back. I am the Order of Hunters…

Long fingers wrapped around Joshua's neck and lifted him off the ground. His legs locked straight as he choked, gasping for air.

Erika snatched the gun and fired.

And I will endure.

The flare ripped through the wendigo's skull with a shriek and a crackle. Sparks flew out of the back of its neck and ricocheted off the cave wall.

It flung Joshua towards Erika. As he hit the floor with a grunt, he scurried back, reaching blindly for Erika's arm.

Erika rose to her feet and nudged a pale Joshua to back away as the creature screamed and burst into flames. It collapsed in a fiery heap on the floor, limbs crackling like firewood until they turned to ash, black blood staining the cave forevermore.

Liam, the third hiker, was unconscious while Erika and Joshua lugged him together from the cave and towards camp: the last place Joshua recalled having phone signal. Following a short call to the mountain rescue team, and Erika demanding Joshua's secrecy about the wendigo, an air-ambulance landed in a nearby clearing.

"Why not?" he persisted, the ambulance's propellers, muffling his voice. The paramedics tended to Liam a few yards ahead. Joshua had only a few cuts and bruises, and Erika refused any attention at all. "Shouldn't we be yelling about wendigos from the mountaintops?"

"No."

Humanity had always been fragile. It needed protecting, not educating, against the evil lurking in its shadows. Encountering entities humanity could not understand ended only in two ways: control or mass extinction.

The Quadruple Alliance, the Treaty, the Order—they all protected *everyone* against that.

"Imagine the outcry if this were to get out," Erika carried on. "The innocents that would be harmed."

"Innocents were harmed today! Not knowing what was out there made us helpless."

Erika reached for her neck, stunned at the absence of the necklace she forgot she no longer wore. As a Hunter, she was not only responsible for the protection of mankind but the safety and secrecy of the Alliance: the arcanes, the lychans, the vampires. To keep those select few protected, all had to be hidden from humanity. Even if they made it difficult.

Joshua retired his argument when Erika refused to change her answer. She even ensured a subtle threat to *find him again* if word of the wendigo got out. He was to tell others they fell from the southern cliffside. If authorities pressured them, he was to contact Erika, who would take the matter further with the Order's Council. Their contract with the arcanes had a clean-up team on standby, but they seldom used it—memory erasure toed a narrow moral line.

The rescue team escorted the pair back to the village while Liam received medical treatment. They would never find the burnt body of the wendigo's first victim, so Erika took the signet ring from his little finger for Joshua to give to the family. She did not ask for his name.

After a thank-you from the bartender—Joshua's brother, she learned—Erika wished them both luck in their recoveries and began her ten-minute walk to the dusty log cabin she and Dad called home for the hunt.

It was messy, but she'd done it—her first lone hunt as an Initiate. Nothing more than what was expected of a Lupine.

Trekking to the cabin through roadside woodland, Erika sank her teeth into a hefty club sandwich from a garage near The Stag's Antlers. Dad packed for convenience more than anything else, so their meals for the week had been *unsatisfactory*, to say the least. Fearing her taste buds had taken a dip, Erika craved something different to spark them back to life. She bought Dad a cheese sandwich, figuring he needed *some* nutrition aside from instant noodle cups and dry crackers. A chill scattered down Erika's spine when an icy wind blustered through amber foliage overhead, yet a spring hastened her step. Even if he didn't say it, Dad would be proud of her tonight. With the wendigo gone, she prayed they'd be leaving the cabin in the morning, if not now.

Kicking off a hunting career at sixteen had her accustomed to sleeping in hovels—cabins, caravans, tents and even the car—but she drew the line at safety hazards with rotting floorboards and nasty little spiders, the ones with the massive backsides fit to burst and release thousands of spawn onto Erika's pillow.

Being in a foul mood the day Dad announced their accommodation, Erika threatened to turn the car around and leave him. When he told her to stop complaining and do it, she caved. She never *really* wanted him to be alone. *Don't make idle threats*, Dad said. *Stick to your word.* A true Lupine would put the job above comfort, he might as well have said. She'd been miserable all week but kept her mouth shut, longing for a night at Diana's to bask in a hot shower and watch a film or two with Ollie and the twins. The thought of Diana's hot chocolate tickled Erika's tongue with every passing day.

When she approached the woodland's edge, a sour taste replaced the phantom sweetness.

A Mercedes A-Class, black and glossed like spilt ink, cornered the cabin, lining itself parallel to Erika's sooty Ford Fiesta on the driveway. As far as she was aware, only Erika's closest family members—Diana and the twins—knew their location, and this was not Diana's pick-up.

Dad had no friends. Something was wrong

Erika scanned the windows as a shape cut through the cabin's light. Then another.

She ducked, crouching behind a thorned shrub. Surely, Dad would tell her of any visitors due to drop by. Neither of them liked surprises. The people inside were unwanted, and that made them enemies.

Rushing in was not an option. She tread carefully on her approach, treating it the same as any other hunt. *Assess. Plan. Execute.*

Erika weaved around the undergrowth for cover, homing in on the cabin. There was just one way in and out—the front door beyond the porch—then two windows flanking the entrance, the others boarded up. The scene within melded into view as she climbed the damp decking. She held her breath when it creaked.

"Don't make this harder for yourself, Christopher. Where are the others?"

Erika flattened against the cabin's exterior. Beneath the windows, she could not see clearly, but heard the woman's voice perfectly, whimsical and harsh as a gust of wind. To stay hidden, this angle had to do for now.

"We parted ways after the ritual," Dad said, steady and sure as he often was. "I haven't seen any of them in years."

"Lies," the woman hissed. "All you people do is lie."

"Lia—"

"Don't 'Lia' me. You lost that right after what you did."

"I did my duty. It's not my fault you stood in the way of it."

Erika swallowed. She had always been the more prominent negotiator within their father-daughter duo.

Lia softened her tone. "Oh, but I'm not playing your games anymore. I'm not playing *any* childish games now. You must have spoken to at least one of the twelve. Tell me where they are."

Dad groaned. "I. Don't. Know."

Erika clutched the dilapidated windowsill and risked a look, tilting her head back so she could see the upper bodies of everyone in the room.

Five faces scowled at the centre where her father knelt, only his shaggy brunette head visible. The apparent leader, Lia, looked middle-aged (perhaps only a few years younger than Dad), clad in a black jumper and trousers like the rest of her group, with contrasting red hair resting upon her shoulders, twisted and wild as a fiery brazier. A golden pendant hung from her neck, bearing a symbol Erika struggled to recognise from a distance, with an unmistakable white jewel etched into the pattern. It captured the light in a way only syphons do, the Aura air-magic swirling through the stone, bound to its wearer.

An arcane.

This was *bad*.

Erika spotted her duffel bag in the far corner of the cabin. Containing only a few essentials, her nylon, green bag went everywhere with her besides hunts, if she could help it. Within it, folded into a compact, pocket-sized box, was the crossbow she trusted with her life—rightfully so on many occasions. If she could kick off into a decent sprint to get to it...

Across the room, Dad caught her eye. His lips pressed together, tight in silent instruction. *Get down.*

She did—just as Lia spoke again. "Your daughter hunts with you?"

Dad kept silent. Erika held her breath—Lia spotted the bag. "She's old enough to hunt now, isn't she? What is she, twenty-something? Twenty-one—"

"Twenty-two." Dad sighed his words. He understood the threat as well as Erika, but she was no damsel in distress. She wouldn't go *anywhere* with them willingly.

"I see," said Lia. "Well, I'm sure she'll be back soon. We might as well get comfortable." The arcanes snickered. *Not in that cabin,* Erika thought.

"She's not coming back!" Dad insisted. "We argued. I told her to go after her last hunt. To leave."

A subtle warning to run—to leave *him*. But no Lupine would ever be left alone. Not while Erika drew breath.

"Really, Christopher? I thought I told you to stop *lying.*"

The wind picked up, but the air turned thin. A smell tickled Erika's nose, prickling her arms as the syphon around Lia's neck glowed. Erika sucked in a gasp. *No. No, no.*

Lia's voice darkened. "Do you think me a fool? She left her things, her car—"

"That's my—"

"That is *her* car, Christopher, don't tell me otherwise. She's coming back. And she'll be back soon, I imagine."

"She's not—"

Dad choked as a gale carried magic's scent around the cabin, smoky and warm like an incinerated firework.

It took all Erika's willpower to keep low and steady herself against the cabin wall. *He won't die*, she assured herself. Lia needed him for *something*.

Fuck, arcanes were *Alliance*. Never had Erika seen one violate the Treaty like this. Not with her mind intact, at least.

Erika's calloused fingers splintered the windowsill. She never imagined assessing an arcane as an enemy, but there she was. She peeled her eyes to identify the syphons on each of Lia's companions, but they could have been anything—necklaces, rings, bracelets, belts, even earrings if they fancied it. Were all of them even arcanes? If just one were a vampire or lychan, her artery surely would have been torn out by now. They would have heard her.

Dad gasped as Lia's hold on him eased. She did no damage, but this was only a warning. *Think, Erika…*

Lia's voice soothed, her resonance almost mothering. "Tell me where the Hunters are, Chris. I won't even look at your daughter if I don't have to."

She could look while Erika's arrow lodged between her eyes.

Dad raised his chin. "This is madness, even for you. Your cult was banished before. Do you think your Divines will be so kind if you take another shot at this? If not for my family, do it for yours. Your son won't want this for you."

Clever. An impromptu brief the same as any other hunt. Only there was no space for Erika's questions now.

Lia was an arcane—a cultist. The Divines were not on her side. She had a son that Erika could use, but involving innocents was not her style. She also had a syphon, yet no coven. That meant she found a way to steal it back. *Unless…*

No. Only Divines could bestow syphons. They bound the wearer to their Divine, uniting the coven. The bottom line of Erika's training was *no coven, no syphon.* Lia stole it.

"My son knows the cost of the ritual," Lia declared. "Does your daughter?"

Worn floorboards creaked beneath the weight of her father's silence.

"I see. Interesting. Then I'll give you a choice. Tell me where the Hunters are, and we will leave before your daughter returns."

Dad's mouth clamped shut in a few long minutes of protest. Wind gathered, chilling Erika to the bone. Her hand found the flare gun in her pocket, closing around the hilt.

Impatient, Lia snarled, and magic circled the cabin, Dad crouched in the storm's eye. He winced, his jaw forced open, shoulders pulsating as the arcane drew air from his lungs with a slow, careful wrist movement, reeling it in on an invisible thread.

He choked. Louder. *Louder.*

Like a shotgun, Erika threw her body towards the door.

CHAPTER THREE

Hunters are, first and foremost, detectives. One who lacks evidence awaits a terrible fate in the court of life and death.

The Hunter's Codex, Chapter III.

"STOP!"

Erika froze, still crouched below the window but a few inches closer to the door. Dad was breathless. His mossy eyes flitted towards her from inside the cabin, begging her to stop.

She couldn't just *leave him*.

"Losing your nerve, Lupine?" Lia taunted. "If you find that difficult, just imagine what's going to happen when your daughter—"

"Parkview Tower. Room 432. Edinburgh."

The Hunt begins.

Erika silently rehearsed the information as Lia's mouth opened and closed, flustered at the ease of her interrogation.

Oh, but it would not be so easy. In no life would Christopher Lupine sell out a Hunter. Lia thought he had given up, but his fight waited outside, grasping a flare, ready to defend her Hunters—her family—in whatever way necessary.

Lia combed the room, meeting flashes of united white smiles. "Five to go. Now get in the car."

"You think—"

"Get in the car, Chris. Unless you want your daughter to meet Felix."

Lia gestured to a burly arcane. Felix controlled the room from the corner with his astonishing size. Inky tattoos sprouted from his sleeves and collar, rounding at his bald head and halting upon a heavy brow. Judging from his animalistic grin and the rounding biceps crossing his woollen shirt, Erika decided against interacting with the beastly figure. Arcanes were best fought up close, but Felix would break her in half.

Footsteps chorused, and Erika dropped off the decking. She pressed into the damp mud beneath the shrubs and weeds growing against the cabin, scraping her palms on branches and thorns, wrecking her nails with dirt.

Lia's smug grin headed the pack, followed by Dad, flanked by Felix and a blonde male. Bringing up the rear was a far younger, tall, and slender brunette woman with dark skin, who drew a flirtatious finger down the blonde's back, giddy at Christopher Lupine's vulnerability.

Erika's fingertips dug into the dirt. She wanted to lash out—to wipe the smiles off their faces; show them they hadn't beaten a Lupine just yet. But she was not stupid. She kept quiet, kept low. As she did with the wendigo, she needed a strategy.

Only Dad always *told* her the strategy.

They reached the Mercedes where Felix pushed on Dad's skull, shoving him in the backseat before the blonde male slid in beside him, the brunette entering from the other side.

When the final male—a long, ebony-haired, arcane with the eyes of an undertaker—tried to enter the passenger seat, Lia took his arm. "Not you, Percy. Go to Edinburgh. See what awaits us there."

"Yes, ma'am."

Percy took two strides back and disappeared in a cloud of tenebrous smoke and ash. A Shadow Traveller, Erika realised. *For fuck's sake.*

With Percy gone, Felix leaned in close to Lia. "And the girl?"

Lia shrugged. "She's no more than a child. What can she do against a dozen witches?"

Erika's nails raked the soil. Did she wish to see the wendigo for reference?

Hang on. Lia called her band *witches*. That term hadn't been used by the Alliance since before the Treaty—before the Covens. Not in a positive light, anyway.

And there were *a dozen* of them.

"What if she comes after her father?" Felix pressed, his voice broad northern and gravelly. "You know how loyal this lot are."

Another shrug from Lia. "And you know how the ritual works. If she wishes to endanger herself, she can be kept as a spare. And if her father doesn't cooperate then—" she glanced at Dad, her hazel glare icing over, "—she might prove the better replacement."

Erika held her breath. *A bloodline ritual.* She studied them years ago but never imagined encountering blood magic beyond manic renegades.

For Blood Witches to unite in such a way, they had to be desperate. Desperate for her father's blood, her blood.

Ollie's blood.

Arcanes did not need blood as vampires did to survive, but if one dared to break Treaty law and seek out the most coveted magic source, the power became too tempting, too *euphoric*. Power was the arcane's drug.

Lia and Felix packed themselves into the car and set off down the gravel. Light shrank between the trees, taking the cult, and Dad, out of sight. Erika fought every instinct to not charge after them.

She waited twenty seconds after they passed the tree line. Thirty.

Certain they were gone, Erika dragged herself from the undergrowth and stretched her limbs.

For the first time, she began the Hunt alone. Dad always found the Supernatural. *He* tracked it down. *He* briefed her. Now, it was up to her. It all was.

She took a breath. She managed a wendigo—a monster. Arcanes were the closest supernatural beings to humans. They thought like her. How bad could they *really* be?

It didn't matter how far they went because she would succeed and bring Dad back. Lupines would never quit—especially on each other.

The arcanes flipped the cabin upside down, desperately searching for *something*. Erika's new mauve travel cushions, a gift from Dad, were all but shredded, thrown across the living room over the loose pages of her father's journal. Glass shards blinked beneath her torchlight, and Erika found no sign of the tumblers she bought for hunting trips. Those possessions were the little parts of home she carried, working in hovels such as this, and this 'cult' destroyed them. Insensitive bastards.

She lit the candlestick on the coffee table with one of her matches and checked her bag first. The nylon rustled, and her nerves eased when her arm resisted the mallard-green duffel. She exhaled a sigh when she felt the hard, square body of her folded-up crossbow.

If the arcanes spotted what a prize this weapon was, surely it would no longer be in her possession, and Erika might as well have lost an arm. She left it behind because the weapon was no use against a wendigo. To arcanes, however, an arrow to the chest would prove just as deadly as it would to any human.

Everything else was accounted for: Grandpa's journal, the bamboo hairbrush, a handful of makeup, spare change, basic toiletries, and a phone charger. Besides the crossbow and small quiver of spare arrows, it was the simplest assortment of things. It almost made her seem like a normal twenty-something-year-old. What a thought that was.

Just one thing was missing.

Erika dragged her hands across the bag's floor, feeling for the silver chain until panic sent her frantic. *Where is it? Where is it? Where is—*

Her fingertips buzzed—she found it. She fell back onto the floorboards, weighed down by shame. Her fingers looped around the delicate silver chain and its pointed clear quartz. It felt so comfortable in her palm, but it had not sat close to her heart in months. She wondered whether its identical counterpart had been neglected just as much, or as little.

Neglected or not, she still held onto it and dropped the chain and the memories that came with it into her bag.

Dad's journal was next. Almost every page had been ripped from the binding, leaving the faded black leather cover naked, pushed underneath the rotten sofa to soak up the dust and mould.

Once grabbed and ordered somewhat correctly, Erika flicked through the pages, careful not to let them float away.

Hunters kept journals in their prime to record, educate, and remind themselves of their findings. With only two hundred years of Supernatural cooperation, contemporary Hunters had the best understanding in the history of their profession. Even so, every species held their secrets. Every hunt was a learning curve to uncover what the Alliance may have hidden—or not yet discovered. No-one truly knew what lurked both within and outside the Veil, and Erika was unsure if she ever wanted to find out. The demonic stragglers and corruptions sprouting on her side were terrifying enough.

From his journal writings, she discovered Dad came across arcanes only once on a hunt, putting down a crazed renegade for endangering her mum. The Order criticised him for being impulsive, but he would do anything to protect her. Would *have*, anyway.

But that didn't matter, because the writings were lies. Dad excluded his entry on this 'Lia' and her so-called cult. He'd told Erika more than one story of putting down an arcane, yet his pages encased only the brutal hunts of rogue lychans and recounts of General assignments. When Erika started her own journal, *nothing* would be omitted.

She closed the book with a sigh and slid it into her pack. All she had were a few hints and an address. Not much, but enough to start the hunt.

Grabbing her father's things as well as her own, she stepped outside the cabin for the final time and tipped her head up at the sky. Pitch black now with grey, grumbling clouds that tightened her chest, it warned her from setting off for Edinburgh.

But she had to go. Dad needed her.

If anyone knew of Dad's more covert hunts, it was Diana. Calling her in the car was no use. It was of no concern to Erika—Diana had always been the type to switch off her phone when busy—but the cult's threats did make her wonder.

She called again, then tried Ollie. Before she could try Florence, the signal cut out, then she entered roads she deemed too dangerous to use a phone on.

She was two hours away—if she followed the speed limits. She'd go to Diana's first. Then she would hunt.

CHAPTER FOUR

The Order's founding is, ultimately, attributed to three Hunter families: the Hopkins', the Stearnes, and the Lupines.

A Hunter's History by Alexei Arwood, Chapter Three.

Rain burst through the darkened sky as Erika drove through York, her knuckles whitening while she strained to see the winding country roads ahead. She passed markers signalling the end of her journey: her secondary school's green gates, the magnolia beds at the second-last roundabout, the convenience shop selling pick and mix around the corner from Diana's. In normal circumstances, she'd be grinning from ear to ear, but every red light had her tapping her nails. Her school gates blackened beneath the storm clouds, dirt piled in place of magnolias, and Mr Milburn's graffitied shutters rattled closed.

She pulled up the tarmac mound behind Diana's decade-old, green pickup and yanked back the handbrake. She switched off the engine and snatched Dad's journal from the passenger seat on her way out.

She fumbled with the keys, slammed the door, secured all three locks behind her, and called Diana's name. She charged into the kitchen, breath heavy, trailing rainwater on the black and white tiles. She found her aunt sitting at the table, the bank's logo lighting up her laptop, and a steaming mug of coffee beside her. Erika's eyes grazed over the kitchen knife beside the cup, and Diana's hand on the back of the chair, ready to stand.

Her eyes softened, and then her jaw dropped at the state of Erika frozen in the doorway, covered in mud, shoes still red with the hiker's blood.

"Erika, you're soaked." Diana leapt to her feet.

"Lia," Erika croaked. "Who's Lia?"

Diana paled. "I think you'd better sit down."

"Dad's ex?"

Diana covered her mouth with a fist and nodded. "Aurelia."

Already, Erika had told her about the cult and Dad's abduction. Diana gave little in return beyond *that* bombshell.

"Diana, please," she begged. "You must know something about the cult or the ritual."

Diana stared at nothing in particular. Her shoulders clenched and relaxed with every passing second beneath her fleeced, white dressing gown. "I know there *was* a ritual, but your father would not tell me anything more. We never hunted together. Ever."

"Will contacting the Divines do any good?"

She shook her head again. "Too much paperwork and red tape. And no phones there, remember? We'd have to trek to Stryga, and that would take time."

A seven-hour car journey and a less-than-conventional ferry ride. Of course, the arcanes *had* to isolate themselves on an island *and* be inherent technophobes. "Time Dad doesn't have."

Erika snatched her car keys from the table, and Diana rose. "You're going to Edinburgh?"

"It's the only lead I have." Erika buttoned up her coat. "The Shadow Traveller will already be there."

"Then it's likely the Hunter is already missing."

Erika glanced at her dirt-rimmed nails. If she leapt to Dad's defence, would he be safe, or would she be dead? "Maybe."

Diana pondered for a moment, then shook her head. "No. No way are you doing that drive tonight."

"I have to! Dad's the one at risk here, not me. I'm already unprepared as it is." With just one lead and no clue of what the hunt entailed, time ticked on.

"That's exactly why you should stay. Look at you! You're exhausted and covered in blood, dirt, and God knows what else. You need food, sleep, and a shower."

Stone-faced, Erika released her shoulders in a sigh. "I need to begin this hunt. Now. Is the ammo still in the garage?"

"Yes, but… Just…" Diana chased her out of the kitchen. "*Slow down*, please. You said it yourself: you're unprepared for this, and you're alone. Imagine what could happen! For all you know, you could be springing a trap, playing right into their hands."

"But I can't just—"

As Erika whirred, Diana's glassy green eyes made her heart steady. She had these *looks*. Not all of them were nice, but all made her listen.

Her aunt's head shook slowly. "I can't watch any more of this family sprint off for a hunt. Not after Freddie." Erika's eyes grazed over an empty kitchen chair—the one with the antlers carved into the uncomfortable headrest.

"You can handle this, Erika, I know you can. But the last time this family ignored my pleas to take a break, we lost another member."

The tug to not disappoint Diana, to make her life as easy as possible, was strong, but Erika's will to protect her family was stronger. She would do it for all of them, just as they would for her if they could. Even if they didn't like it.

"I'm not Freddie," she claimed. "Dad needs me, and I'm sure he's relying on me to help him."

She tugged her ponytail from underneath her collar, tightening it. "I'm going. Tonight."

"Tonight?"

She spun, having been too preoccupied to notice footsteps on the stairs. Ollie reached the bottom step and blocked the doorway, head tilted to one side with quiet anger flaring in his bright blue irises, fawn hair wet and clinging to his forehead, his cheeks flushed.

Erika *tried* to look happy to see him. She *was* happy to see him. But it had been a month since she last paid her brother a visit, missing a promised cinema trip and two football matches. For the last week, she thought about how to make it up to him when she returned home, and now she was here, ready to leave again without even saying 'hello.'

In her defence, she wasn't *meant* to be there.

"Ollie." At this distance, their heights matched. She met him at eye level from the hallway. "You're taller."

"And you're leaving again." Ollie approached, and Erika backed into the kitchen. His bare feet tapped the tiles. "You've just got back, haven't you?"

Erika swallowed. "I needed to pick something up for Dad's work. It was urgent."

"And you have to go back the same night because…?"

"Because Dad asked me to."

The same excuse every time. No wonder Ollie stopped texting Dad.

Ollie flicked his brows. They were thick. Wild. "Work over family again. It's fine. I get it."

Even if it was justified, he didn't have to be a brat.

"Ollie," Diana scolded. "Your sister's working very hard at the moment."

"I should think so. Just look at her!" He gestured to Erika's figure, the mud, the blood. "What even happened to you?"

Erika blinked. "I—"

"Fell," Diana answered. "She fell."

"In what? A swamp?"

"I was on a walk," Erika went on. "The path turned boggy and I slipped."

Diana smiled. So forced, so fake. She made it look real. "But she's fine now!"

"Fine enough to leave right now, apparently." He half-rolled his eyes, turning to return upstairs. "I won't stop you."

Erika groaned and crossed the doorway. "Ollie—"

"Leave him." Diana hooked her arm. "He'll cool down in a bit."

Erika staggered back to the kitchen and slid into a chair, grunting as her bruised shoulder blade hit the corner. Certain Ollie was upstairs, she looked to Diana, massaging her injury from the wendigo. "He's grown so much in a few months."

"He's fifteen. They shoot up quickly at that age. Like bloody trees, those boys are."

"That doesn't help, Diana."

"I'm only warning you. As he grows up, he'll suss out who was there for him and who wasn't."

"But I've been here! Just not physically, lately."

Diana lowered into her seat—the antlered one. She used to sit close to the door. She reached across the table to squeeze Erika's hand. "I know that. He doesn't."

"But if I could just—"

"No."

Erika snatched her hand away. "Why not? At his age, I was training for my first hunt. It's not fair on him."

"He—" Diana bit her tongue. Her aunt's stance on the matter always frustrated Erika. Despite being the strong woman she was, she struggled to hold her ground when the same topic revolved back around again and again. If she was honest, Erika was convinced Diana would wholeheartedly agree with her own opinion and let Ollie know the truth.

If it wasn't for her father's command.

"He can't know," Diana said. "Not yet."

"Why?"

Diana shook her head, ending the discussion. "It's for his protection."

She echoed the same words since Ollie learned to talk. *Ollie isn't ready. This is our secret: Lupine to Lupine.*

But he would never be ready. Even now, he still had no idea what awaited him.

Erika grew up engulfed in the supernatural world, told tales of her ancestors, horror stories of the monsters prowling in the dark: legends of arcanes, lychans, vampires, and their Hunters. From the day she began training, a dream took flight to visit Oblivion's Watch and complete her initiation trials. At eighteen, she did just that.

Ollie had no such childhood. The youngest Lupine lived as normal a life as possible with a family of supernatural Hunters. He attended the same school he enrolled in at three years old, joined the football team, and met up with the same friends he had held since nursery. The eight years separating the Lupine siblings split their lives completely, one being enlightened, fighting in the dark, the other clueless, living in daylight. Out of the few remaining Lupines, Ollie was the lone member to live that way.

Lupines led the Hunters to their initial glory. Now, they remained few in numbers, left with one General, a retiree, and a twenty-two-year-old Initiate to pick off poltergeists and pests at the Council's will.

Erika did not notice Diana stand until she squeezed her shoulder in passing. "I'll run you a bath."

CHAPTER FIVE

Hunting is a balance of strength and wisdom. Should the scale tip either way, a timely death awaits the unworthy.

Philip Lupine's Journal, Second Edition.

Exhaustion stapled Erika to the kitchen chair until the bath filled. Diana was right. Straining herself to track down the cult after hunting the wendigo was dangerous. Stupid, even.

Edinburgh's Hunter was gone, but the lead would still be there in the morning. As Aurelia said, they needed twelve Hunters. They needed five more—four if they'd already seized the one in Edinburgh. Erika had time. She needed to recharge.

Her muscles cheered when she slipped into the steaming bathwater. She splashed her face before lying in the effervescence, rubbing the contours, ridges, and pores along her skin. She sought to ease her mind, soak in the lavender bubbles, and regenerate every cell in her body, but failed miserably. Every time she closed her eyes to breathe in the bathing oils, she saw the cult succeed—saw the air pulled from Dad's lungs until he could breathe no more. Steam turned to smoke in her nostrils, eucalyptus to sage.

Water ran down her arm, and she jolted. It dripped onto the hands she dangled over the tub's edge. *Just water. It's just water.*

Soaked and scrubbed, Erika pulled the plug and dragged herself from the tub, tugging the white cotton towel off the radiator to wrap around her body, hugging it close.

She never called it hers, but the spare bedroom at Diana's was the closest thing to her own bedroom. She tried to get Erika to paint it once, but she refused. Diana painted them a wisteria purple, softened by the sandy carpet, decorated with framed pressed flowers, faux ivory furniture, knitted blankets, and a vase of fortnightly-replaced wildflowers. Those were perhaps the only things she would have chosen. Florence called them weeds, but wildflowers were delicately beautiful. Not extravagant like the roses or tulips lining the porch, but elegant in their uncontrolled, subtle way.

The room had always been cold, and the first week of December pushed an even sharper draft in. Erika shifted aside the short, thin pyjama sets in the dresser and pulled on a fleeced pair of cream joggers and a white t-shirt. She brushed through wet hair and, looking in the vanity mirror, caught sight of her duffel bag at the foot of the bed, car keys cheekily left on top.

She sighed. This was her last chance at comfort for a while, but she had to prepare for the journey ahead. Diana acknowledged this, it seemed.

She flung open the wardrobe doors and rummaged through the piles and hangers of clothes she left behind, grabbing what she needed: a few t-shirts, jeans, underwear, and a jumper in case the temperature took an unprecedented dip. It had been a warmer Winter than usual, but the Northernmost regions held a brisker forecast.

She folded the clothes atop the empty pearl vanity for now. In the morning, she'd take them to the car when the rain stopped instead of wasting the lovely oils and creams scenting her skin.

The door creaked.

Ollie was in his room. Mugs clanged downstairs as Diana made the drink she promised.

Erika's hand hovered over the pile of fabric, brows knitting together.

Asthmatic gasps made her grin, and she almost burst into laughter when an oblivious reflection of the pink pyjama-wearing stalker crept in behind her.

Erika spun to catch the flying palm, flipped the figure over her shoulder, and slammed her into the floor with a thud.

Florence arched her back. The silk of her mauve pyjamas hissed with her. "How'd you know?"

"Psychic powers."

"You didn't have to throw me on the ground."

With a smile, Erika gripped her cousin's soft hand and dragged her up, Florence's forehead nearly bumping her nose. "That was a consequence. You need to learn what that is."

Florence yawned and stretched her arms. She was more toned than the last time she saw her. No quieter, though. "God, you sound like Uncle Chris."

Erika winced, playing it off with a smile. "Ouch. Someone's upset."

"*Someone* is in pain!"

Erika pouted. "Aw, I didn't realise you got so old and decrepit! Is that a grey hair?" Florence swatted her reaching hand away, making her cackle.

With a frowned stare in the mirror, Florence combed her glossy curls with slender fingers, then let out a sigh before picking up the bamboo brush Erika had just put down. Naturally, her hair was darker than Erika's; still ash-blonde but not as pale. She began highlighting it at sixteen, and the cousins now passed as sisters, the only remnants of

Freddie Mullein's hair colour found in her twin brother. If not for Erika's age, both girls could have easily been Diana's daughters.

"I've been practising, you know? But Alfie says I'm not very subtle."

Erika snorted. "You're not."

Florence side-eyed her and turned back to the mirror. "Better than Alfie, though. He doesn't even try."

"I wasn't aware this was a competition." Erika folded her arms. "The kid's in bed now, isn't he?"

Florence continued to brush. "He spends all day, every day, reading those stupid books in the loft as if a demon would turn up and demand a duel of wits instead of killing him on the spot."

That girl had his life from the womb.

Erika shuffled past her cousin, heading for the wardrobe. Florence pursed her lips when Erika set a pair of trainers next to the pile of clothes. "You're leaving tomorrow, aren't you?"

"I almost left tonight," Erika admitted. "Your mum convinced me to stay."

"Thank God she did. You'd be in deep shit if you left without a catch-up."

Erika snorted a laugh. "You don't scare me like your mum does. You don't have the look."

"I'll get it! One day."

Erika disagreed, but she would never kill her cousin's dreams.

With an exasperated sigh, Florence flopped backwards on the bed. The blankets creased, and the satin throw pillows rolled to the carpet. "Can I go with you?"

Erika threw the pillow at her cousin's chest. "No."

"Please! I'm so bored. I promise I've been training non-stop since I left school—I almost have abs now! Even before that, I've been working hard to become a—"

Erika smacked a finger to her lips and shushed her. Pointing to the converted loft room upstairs reminded her to keep quiet.

"I don't know much about this job," Erika confessed. "This could be more serious than even I know. I can't take you with me into unknown danger, especially without Dad."

"If it's so dangerous, why are you going alone?"

Erika felt Alfie's glare before he spoke. She turned to meet the green eyes matching his twin and mother, narrowed behind thick, square rims, waiting for the reply he already knew.

Erika crossed her arms. "I can handle it."

"Right." He mimicked her stance. Fortunately for him, he inherited Diana's Lupine stare, though Erika knew better than to be wary of it. "And what *exactly* are you handling?"

He knew she had no idea. He must have talked to his mum already. "My own business."

"*Family* business. Which means I can help."

"Can you, hell. Neither of you have ever fought a Supernatural, never mind an entire arcane cult."

Florence's eyes bulged in morbid curiosity. "There's a *cult?*"

"Actually, we have," said Alfie. "Remember that demon in the shed?"

She did. Trying to convince Ollie that a rat put a hole in the ceiling was an awkward one, especially when it was on fire.

Erika sighed. "Yes, I remember the demon in the shed. But it wasn't the two of you that killed it."

"I don't remember it being *you*, either," Alfie retorted.

Erika glared at them both. "I killed a wendigo today. I'll cope just fine."

Florence whistled under her breath as Erika selected a few pairs of socks from the drawers beneath the wardrobe, including a fluffy, patterned set for sleeping.

"Wow, a wendigo…" Florence's stare turned blank. "What is it?"

Erika slammed the drawer. "This is *exactly* why you two aren't coming."

"I'm not as thick as Florence!" Alfie exclaimed. Florence gasped.

"You're also not as strong as her," Erika reminded him. "How many runs have you been on this week, Alfie?"

He frowned. "One."

"Because he missed the bus," Florence uttered.

"Florence hates cardio as well!"

"I have asthma!"

"See?" Erika gestured at them both with the socks. "You're not ready."

She tossed the bed socks on top of the pile. *Perfect shot.* Alfie scrunched his nose at the owls printed on them. "You can't do this hunt with just one person."

"I never said I was going alone."

She was, but she never *said* it.

Alfie's lip quirked. "Uncle Chris is missing, and you have no friends. It's obvious you're going alone."

Erika fell beside Florence, scowling. "You know, I came here to relax for the night. Not to be told I sound like my dad and have no friends."

Florence tilted her head. "You *do* sound like your dad and have no friends."

Erika opened and closed her mouth, stuttering. "I have… friends."

Florence snickered. "You have *a friend.*"

"That you've spoken with in the last two weeks?" Alfie added.

Erika counted in her head: one, two… six weeks since the last text.

Dammit.

"Alright, but I sound nothing like my dad."

Florence laughed, forcing a deep, gravelly accent sounding *vaguely* like Christopher Lupine. *"You need to learn the consequences of your actions."*

Alfie joined, *"It's my business. I'll deal with it."*

"You are not ready for the trials ahead."

"Be quiet, twins! Why are you so stupid?"

They laughed hysterically, convinced they had the voice nailed perfectly. When Erika picked up the vase, they ran.

The twins scurried out of the room and Erika shut the door. She picked up her phone: no new notifications since this afternoon. The most recent texts were from Dad telling her to remember her flares for the wendigo. The other messages were gossip from Diana, outfit pictures from Florence, and a too-formal check-in text to Ollie that he never replied to. Another, the text she remembered as being from six weeks ago (which turned out to be ten), was from Pete.

Bumping into each other was completely unexpected—he jokingly called it fate, but had a nice time seeing her again and wished to do it more often. Her reply was short, blunt, and detached as though a robot had written it, but she would obey Dad's wishes. Their recent meeting was completely unbeknownst to him, but she hated putting on a cold front when she missed Pete terribly.

Dad warned her against getting close to people for three reasons. The first: they could betray you. Second, they could change you, make you weak. And the third?

Well, they could break your heart.

The temptation was too great, so she put the phone away beside the winking quartz in her bag

She could not fight the temptation to loop its chain around her neck.

CHAPTER SIX

Initiation means sacrificing your old family for a new one. As such, hunting is an inherited honour passed on to the most trusted descendants. It is rare for outsiders to embrace such a commitment.

The Hunter's Codex, Chapter I.

Diana greeted her downstairs with a steaming mug of hot chocolate, a plate of ginger biscuits, and a smile bright enough to light up the room.

Erika snorted. "Some might call this bribery."

"It *is* bribery. If you stay, you can drink it."

She joined her aunt at the table and wrapped her hands around the mug. "I think the pyjamas give away that I plan on staying. I'd look ridiculous taking on a cult dressed like this."

They sipped hot chocolate together, and the topic spun to Diana's most recent first date.

"You climbed out the window? Diana, that's horrible!"

"He was a pig! His hand managed to *accidentally* brush my thigh eight times before the main course. And he suggested a *coffee* at his flat within half an hour. I would have swilled him with my wine, but it was too good to waste. He paid for that, at least."

Erika choked on a marshmallow. "Don't ever change, Diana."

Diana's smile faded as she tapped the table. "I don't know why I even bother dating anymore." Erika leaned in and tipped her head. "Not all of them are as bad as that. Some men are lovely, but…"

"They're not Freddie."

She shook her head. "No-one can replace your uncle. We met young and fell quickly. Your grandpa disapproved, but I told him to stuff it." Erika exhaled a laugh. "Maybe you should think about doing that with—"

"No."

"He's a lovely boy, Erika."

"I know. But Dad thinks I should keep my distance."

Diana leaned in. Her hand found the quartz dangling over the table. "And what do you think?"

Erika closed the cold quartz in her palm. Little things reminded her of him every day. Green October foliage, the taste of lime and tequila, warmth from her blanket as it tickled her nape. But when she worked—when she defeated demons, passed trials, earned praise from senior Hunters—she remembered what she could lose. Diana had a beautiful relationship with Freddie, but she put that relationship first. She married young, had children young, and when Freddie died, she was forced to retire young. Erika adored Diana for the sacrifices she made, but she couldn't live like that. Not when she had worked so hard to be the only Lupine Hunter of the next generation.

Erika let go of the quartz and sipped her drink. "I think he's right."

They stilled as Ollie drifted through the kitchen, pouring a glass of water.

Erika waited for him to turn the tap off, realising he was not going to speak first. "Are you going to bed?"

Ollie sipped his water, looking through the window, gripping the sink. "Yes."

"Oh." She shouldn't have expected anything else—it was close to midnight already. "Then... goodnight."

Ollie released the sink and scratched his fringe, shiny with moonlight. "Yeah. Night."

Erika recalled better conversations with her brother. She combed her drying hair from her face. The ash-blonde appeared brown while damp.

Diana craned her neck to look around the doorframe, watching Ollie disappear upstairs. "He's started asking more questions," she whispered.

Erika frowned. "Questions?"

"About you and Chris. Why you're always away, what you *actually* do for work. That whole private investigator story has been showing a lot of holes lately. He's getting suspicious about all of us."

She knew the story wouldn't work forever. To Ollie, their dad was a private investigator, and Erika was his apprentice. It let them get away with not disclosing details about their careers, but the sketchiness of it all, the mystery surrounding Uncle Freddie's death, the ban on entering the garage...

"I'd be asking questions if I were him, too. He doesn't know *anything.*"

"That's how it has to be," Diana reminded her. "He used to just be curious, but..."

The shadow crossing her features unsettled Erika. *"But?"*

"He's not just curious anymore. He's angry at us."

"He's a teenager. All teenagers are angry at their families for whatever reason."

Diana shook her head. "No. Ollie's worse. He's short-tempered and frustrated at nothing. He needs his dad and his sister around."

"I can't just drop everything. He and I are all that's left hunting in this family—"

"I know, I know." She held up a soothing hand. "That's why I wanted to ask a favour."

Erika sipped her hot chocolate again—still scolding hot, creamy, and sweet. "What is it?"

"Take the twins with you."

Erika coughed up her drink. "Not you, too."

"Have they talked to you?"

"They asked if they could come with me."

"And?"

Erika gawked. *As if this was up for debate!* "Absolutely not."

"Why?"

She rolled her eyes. "You can tell they're your children."

"They've been desperate to hunt with you and Chris for years, but your father won't give them a chance."

"This hunt is not the time to learn on the job, Diana. Dad could die if I fail."

"So could you."

Erika's hands closed tighter around her mug. She had Dad's training. The twins did not. "I'll be fine."

Diana was not so easily convinced. "I'd feel more comfortable if you took them with you. There's safety in numbers."

"I've been on so many—"

"Please." When Diana blinked, her eyes shimmered. "They're desperate. *I'm* desperate. They want to hunt—to be like their father." And mother, Erika imagined. Diana Lupine was no small name back in the day.

"We were a family of great Hunters once." She settled a hand on her mug, the one scarred with a vampire's bite. "Lupines were a driving force in forming the Order centuries ago, and now, well—" she gestured to herself and Erika, "—now all that is left is us and your father."

Erika learned firsthand the weight of carrying the Lupine legacy. Every man from the Lupine bloodline held the position of Councillor since its formation around two hundred years ago. Until her grandpa, that was. Since then, the name and the family had shrunk. Tragedy stunted them into normalcy.

"That is exactly why it's my responsibility to bring him back," Erika argued. "And I can't do my job properly if I'm babysitting."

"Just give them a chance. Please, that's all I ask. It's a risk, I know, but Florence is strong, Alfie's smart. And if this works out, our family can grow stronger."

Erika slouched and pursed her lips. Diana had never been a big advocate for growing the Lupine name, even giving it up when she got married to spite her father.

Maybe she was starting to panic about it. Or maybe she was desperate for her children to connect with the family, those living and those not.

Perhaps it was something else.

Checking the twins were not in earshot, Erika leaned in, hushing her voice. "Are you still getting help from the Order?"

Diana checked as well. "I am, but costs are always going up. There's always something more that needs buying or fixing, and a Hunter retiring in her late twenties doesn't warrant much of a pension, I'm afraid."

"What about Freddie's?"

"Flies out on bills."

"His will?"

"That's for the twins. I won't take from their savings."

"Have you told Dad? We could send you more this month."

Diana forced a smile. "You're a young woman, Erika, and you earn your own money. Keep it."

Erika crossed her arms and sat back in her chair. Diana didn't bring up the conversation about money, but she had gotten her own way from it. If the twins started hunting, they could earn. Erika didn't want this for them. Alfie was smart enough to do whatever he desired, and Florence surely could have found another passion. Neither were really cut out for the balance of strength and wisdom that hunting required.

But Diana needed this

"Fine." *But she wouldn't make this easy.* "If they're not ready by ten, I'm leaving without them."

Diana leapt to her feet and squealed. "Thank you! They'll be so excited to hear that."

"Give them a full briefing. Perhaps you'll scare them into backing out."

Diana scowled at Erika's wicked grin. "I'll talk to them now. You—" she clicked her fingers, "—get some sleep."

"Yes, sir."

Erika finished her hot chocolate in one gulp and was ushered upstairs by Diana. She brushed her teeth, then stopped at the stairs to Alfie and Ollie's shared loft room, calling a 'goodnight' to her brother.

He didn't answer.

Chest tight, she shut herself in her room and climbed beneath the freezing bedsheets, pulling the heavy, white, decorative blanket over her curled-up body.

Thoughts of the day spiralled like a hurricane. *The hiker's corpse. The wendigo. Dad. Aurelia. The Shadow Traveller. Felix. The family income. Ollie.* It took a while for her to settle. It did not matter how tired she was.

She drifted off after some hours, still just as on edge as she was driving there. Her eyes shut, then opened again to rhythmic tapping on the window.

She prayed to whatever gods existed that it was just the rain eager to get inside.

CHAPTER SEVEN

All hunts concerning Alliance Supernaturals must be approved by the Council. Should a Hunter undertake such a hunt without permission, they must convince the Council and relevant Supernatural authorities that they acted in the interest of upholding the Treaty and were unable to seek out the Council due to time sensitivities or the inability to contact them.

The Treaty of the Four Worlds, Section 5, Paragraph 5.

When morning arrived, Erika and Diana packed the car while the twins willed themselves awake at around eight. The pair packed the night before, leaving their bags by the front door, and neither needed their mum to wake them, for once.

"I told you they're eager," Diana said, hoisting up Alfie's backpack. The nylon edges were sharp, stuffed with books.

Erika grabbed Florence's duffel. Makeup clattered within. "We'll see."

The early winter sun peeked over a glassy horizon beyond jagged lines of bricked houses. Smoky tendrils expelled from Erika's lips, and the frosted grass crunched beneath her boots. Christmas was coming. January's dark nights would soon follow.

And they were *dark, dark* nights. If wendigos and demons were common now, the coming weeks would be rough.

Erika dropped the bags to open the boot.

"Do you have enough weapons?" Diana wondered.

Tarnish the Veil

Erika checked the street, then lifted the fabric compartment on the boot's base, unveiling the stash Dad instructed her to maintain. Since his own car was written-off months ago, Erika's Ford had become the primary vehicle for their hunting trips. Her only rule was she would always drive. She wouldn't be caught sitting in the passenger seat of her own car.

Diana smiled at the arsenal, ranging from a few poisons and explosives to blades and guns of all shapes and sizes. Erika restocked on ammo from the garage half an hour ago. "Such a Lupine. And your crossbow?"

Erika tapped her pocket. "Always close."

Diana gazed through the deep khaki cotton. "God, I love that thing."

"You could get your own," Erika hinted.

She shook her head. "My hunting days are over, I imagine."

Diana's sigh made Erika squeeze her shoulder. Beneath the wool were solid traces of experience in the field. Diana was too young to be sidelined, but her children, and her brother's children, came first. Erika wondered whether she would return to work when Ollie was old enough, or if the lack of practice had rusted her skills and tarnished her confidence.

It was a shame. Grandpa had called her a prodigy.

The twins managed to be ready just in time for a hearty breakfast. It was large, even by Diana's standards, every plate stacked high with crispy bacon, sunny fried eggs, juicy sausages, grilled tomatoes, saucy beans, and golden, crunchy toast. Only Alfie's differed from the rest with his vegetarian alternatives.

Erika *never* neglected eating before a hunt. At the end of the day, food was fuel, and who knew when she would next have a break? She filled herself to the brim, chugged a mug of coffee, brushed her teeth, and ushered the twins outside within twenty minutes. Poor Alfie barely made it out the door when Florence shouldered him into the shrubs, announcing her claim of the front seat.

Erika took a long, steadying breath in the doorway.

Silent, Ollie followed them outside. Diana said he didn't react much to the twins' departure. He nodded as though he expected it, somehow.

Erika turned as she reached the car and noticed Ollie's expression falling. She thought he would have gotten used to this by now. Then again, did she really want him to have such low expectations of her?

"Will you be gone long?" he asked.

Erika shared an uncertain glance with Diana, who shrugged in silent apology. "I'm not sure, if I'm honest. But I promise, when I come back, I'll be home for a while."

"You always say that."

Dad's stance on Ollie made it so Erika lived two lives: one of normalcy and the other extraordinary. Most Hunters picked one. She fought for both.

"Hey." She tapped his chin with a smile. "I'll miss you, you know?"

"You always say *that* as well."

"And I mean it. When I get back, we'll go somewhere nice, I promise. Wherever you want. We could see that film you wanted to watch."

"No longer in cinemas."

"Then maybe we could go to the arcade?"

"I don't care. I just want you home."

Whenever Erika asked what he'd like to do on their days together, Ollie jumped straight to the cinema, the arcade, the beach—sometimes all three if he felt bold. Erika gave him everything: the film, the games, the ice cream, the hot chips they shared on the pier.

He didn't ask for special treatment, now. He begged for the bare minimum.

She knew Dad would be furious when she said, "Two weeks. I can promise two weeks at home after this."

Ollie's eyes lit up. "Really?"

"Really."

Dad asked to be consulted before she took leave, but he could hunt alone if he was so desperate. Erika hated the thought of it, but he could prioritise simpler jobs from the Council until she returned. This could be his Christmas present to her if he wanted.

If he made it to Christmas.

"Thank you," Ollie replied. "Then I guess I'll see you soon. Hopefully."

Erika's smile strained. The path ahead was treacherous, cloaked in mist and blood. "Hopefully," she echoed.

She hugged him tight. Every hunt was a risk, she knew that, but not having Dad fighting at her side or uttering advice strained her confidence. This hunt was a test she had not prepared for.

Diana patted Florence's pockets, "Inhaler," pointed to Alfie, "glasses," and stepped back. "Okay. Flo, do you have enough—"

"You don't have to say it, Mum. Yes, I'm stocked up just in case."

"Okay, good. Then…" She choked, breathing in the sight of them both. Florence made a poor choice in her white, fleeced quarter-zip, but took her mother's advice in sticking to black, breathable gym leggings and Diana's old hiking boots. She applied a reasonable amount of makeup to her under-eyes and acne scars, and let her beach waves flow free, a few black hair ties cuffing her wrists.

Alfie made far more practical decisions in his grey cargos and tightly laced hiking boots, matching his mother's, though Erika noticed that he drowned in the oak-brown, faux leather and sheepskin jacket. Her heart ached to know whose initials were stitched into the tag. He kept his glasses. Contacts never agreed with him.

Diana squeezed them. She brushed Florence's hair from her eyes and kissed Alfie's cheek before releasing them and moving on to Erika. She couldn't remember the last hug she had, and accepted it more than the twins.

"Bring them back," Diana whispered. "Bring them back like I know you can."

Erika clenched her fists as she squeezed. "I will. Promise."

Diana inhaled when she stepped back. Ollie's glance shifted her way for a second, but a distracting smile from Erika made him look back, away from Diana's tears.

She slid into the driver's seat, and Ollie grumbled to Diana. She could not hear them with the door shut, but he didn't look pleased. Neither did Diana. Her retort triggered a weak smile in return and both waved the car off, disappearing in the wintry mist.

The car swerved to a skull-shattering roar. Erika looped the wheel as she scoured the neighbourhood for an incoming attack.

She stopped looking when Florence smacked the volume button on the radio. "Sorry! This won't—"

Erika jabbed it, forcing the car into silence—apart from Alfie's hysterical laughter.

Florence gulped at Erika's glare and turned to look out the window, watching the quiet familiarity of the neighbourhood houses roll by.

Erika glanced in the rear-view mirror. It wasn't too late to turn back yet. She could have easily taken the next right turn and looped back around, leaving the twins on their mother's doorstep without another word.

Yet, she bit the bullet and kept on driving. It was not until she merged onto the motorway that Florence turned up the music and Alfie raised his legs onto the backseat. *For Diana,* she reminded herself when her patience wore thin. She owed *everything* to Diana.

CHAPTER EIGHT

The Hunter's Mark is a symbol of resilience and loyalty. Trust its bearer as you do the Code.

The Hunter's Codex, Chapter I.

Room 432. Parkview Tower. Edinburgh.

They made it. The location was easy to find on the city's outskirts—the journey itself just as simple. Clouds circled overhead for almost the entire four hours, with fog submerging the Ford's wheels on the motorway.

Erika parked behind the red-bricked block of flats just past two in the afternoon. Despite their large breakfast, the twins, mainly Florence, pined for something more. She would admit they spent most of breakfast pushing their food around the plate.

"That was four hours ago," Florence whinged. "We're starving."

Erika huffed a sigh as she turned off the engine. "I'll look into this lead, then we'll go for food, if we must."

Florence tutted. "*If we must*. God forbid we're hungry."

"*I?*" Alfie echoed. "Aren't we all going inside?"

"No." Erika unbuckled her seatbelt. "I don't know what's in that building."

"All the better reason to go as a group."

"All the better reason to keep you from harm's way," Erika corrected.

She tossed Alfie her car keys. "Lock yourselves inside. I shouldn't be long."

"And if you are?" Florence pressed. Already, she got comfortable in taking off her seatbelt and stretched her legs.

"If I'm any longer than fifteen minutes, I'll text. If I don't text—" She paused. If it were Dad or even Diana in their position, she would have asked that they went in after her. Since it was the twins… "Call me. Worst case scenario, you drive away."

Florence paled. "I can't drive."

"She wasn't talking to you," Alfie snapped.

Erika had just enough time to snatch the travel-sized quiver from the glove compartment and slam the door shut before the twins' argument kicked into full swing.

She clipped the quiver inside her coat and zipped it up, the crossbow folded up in her pocket just in case.

The receptionist pointed her in the direction of Room 432. Ordinarily, it was difficult to slip into residential flats or hotels, but a warm smile and the excuse of visiting a family member as a birthday surprise let her in just fine. It always amazed, and concerned, Erika just how trusting some people could be. Percy likely got in just as easily.

The elevator chimed, and the doors rattled open on the fourth floor. No cameras blinked on the ceiling.

Erika armed herself.

She scanned the corridor and flipped up her hood before taking the little box from her pocket. With a flick of a thumb over the latch, the wings of the crossbow spread into full flight. She unzipped her coat to take an arrow from the quiver and nocked it in the bow.

The floorboards creaked beneath her boots as she walked.

The room held something—even a hint to where Dad could be or what the cult wanted. He led her there. If Dad was anything, he was not a time-waster.

Erika counted the rusting gold numbers as they flitted by, *410, 411, 412,* all of them broken or chipped in some way.

She pressed on through the festering smell of decades without efficient heating or ventilation, passing ugly, painted walls hued in yellow, smudged with fingerprints. She cringed at the crunching carpet of red and gold swirls, trying to ignore the brown, human-shaped stain in the centre.

She passed more doors. *Room 428, 429, 430.* Knowing she was close, she raised the crossbow to her chin, the arrow's silver tip locked on every target that caught her eye.

She reached for the handle, then froze. The door swayed an inch forward and back. As suspected, the arcanes had got there first, breaking the lock with a force only magic could attain without leaving a bootprint on the door.

She nudged the ebony door with the crossbow, letting it fall open.

Books, journals, and scrap paper littered the wooden floorboards from one side of the living room to the other. They stirred in disorganised piles while burgundy curtains flapped in the breeze from the open window facing the door, just above the wooden desk. A gust slammed the door behind Erika.

She backed in a circle to get a feel of the room. There were few indications of an actual home in a Hunter's dwelling. Most spent their lives on the move, making it difficult to put down roots, and possessions only weighed them down. Erika never let herself think about how she'd decorate a home of her own if she ever found one.

The biggest bedroom had little left in it: a few piles of masculine button-ups atop the chestnut dresser, but no weapons or hunting journals—only a book of baking recipes Erika recognised from Diana's kitchen windowsill.

She turned towards the second bedroom, stopping when paper crumpled beneath her boots in the doorway.

Curiosity picked it up; realisation quirked her lips. *Waltz of the Flowers.* It used to be her favourite piece to play while Dad was out hunting—when Erika wasn't old enough to join him. The violin slept in the cupboard under the stairs at Diana's now, collecting dust.

The piece was different to hers, transposed for a piano. Erika poked her head into the second bedroom, spotting the plug-in keyboard on the floor, and smiled.

Her joy faded. The bedsheets were crumpled, the pillows thinned with age like the first. Two people—perhaps two Hunters—lived there.

Was this Hunter part of the ritual, too? If so, the arcanes were further ahead than Erika imagined. Another possibility was the Hunter was not involved in any way and was simply absent… or dead.

Erika accompanied Dad on pretty much every hunt since she turned sixteen. Even if she made no money from the hunts until she passed her trials, she rejoiced, always despising her school days when she would be left behind at Diana's to study and train. It was common for Hunter parents and children to stick together, usually until one passed away or the child became a General. If that was the case for this pairing, the Hunter taken for the ritual had a son, judging from the clothes left behind.

Erika fell back on her heel into the living room. The Hunter had to have something: a journal, a box, a... *trunk*.

Disguised beneath the television, a robust walnut trunk hid in plain sight, untouched by the cult and, until now, Erika. She pushed the upturned desk chair to one side, then heaved the television onto the frayed rug, crushing papers beneath it, and reached for the lock. Having no key, she removed a pair of hair pins from her coat pocket and picked it—*thank you, Dad, for the training*.

The lock clicked and she threw open the lid, meeting a wide collection of muted colours in the form of journals, vials, salts, weapons, and ammunition.

A smile tugged Erika's lips. "Found you."

As she reached for the closest worn journal, the door whined.

Her steady hand hovered over the frayed spine as a gun loaded behind her, breaking the silence that nothing but the wind tried to fill.

She took no chances.

She rose and spun around to face her foe, crossbow lifted to eye-level, meeting the scope of a shotgun.

CHAPTER NINE

Tractatori: the manipulators. A branch of witchcraft affinities permitting the individual to bend an element to their will.

To Hunt a Witch: A Hunter's Guide, by UNKNOWN. Chapter III: Tractatori.

The gunman's frame cast a long shadow over Erika with broad shoulders and contours on his arms, chest, and legs. The man was trained. In a one-on-one brawl, weapons excluded, Erika imagined he'd win on natural strength alone. She had to keep him at arm's length—get that gun from his hands, if possible.

With brown eyes deep enough to match the walnut trunk open at Erika's feet, he frowned, skimming them between the arrow's tip and her scowling face as if wondering which was the sharper weapon.

"Tell me your name," he said. His voice was low, threatening with a hint of panic and a gentle Scottish twang.

"You first," Erika retorted.

"I asked first."

"I was here first."

"This is *my* home."

"This is—sorry, what?"

Erika glanced between the two bedrooms, the trunk, then back to the gunman. He was young, she realised, maybe her age or slightly older. It was unlikely he was involved in the ritual himself, so perhaps she was correct with her initial thoughts on the Hunter having a son.

He nodded at the crossbow. "I take it you're not an arcane."

She dipped her chin at the trunk. "I take it you're a Hunter."

His smile was crooked as he stretched his collar down, exposing the brand of the Hunters' crest etched into his skin: an arch of the moon cycle, the smooth lines pale in comparison to his dark tones. Erika shifted her coat aside, revealing her matching mark awarded with the completion of her trials years ago.

They lowered their weapons. The gunman blew a relieved laugh.

"What's your name?" he asked. At Erika's frown, he laughed again. "You're the one trespassing, but I guess I'll go first." He waved. "Hi. My name is Alex Arwood. This is my home. Who are you, and why are you in it?"

Erika's cheeks flushed pink. She barely even considered what she'd do if the roles were reversed. "Sorry," she uttered. "Erika Lupine."

"Lupine?" Alex cocked his head. "Christopher's daughter?"

"You know him?"

"Dad does." He glanced at one of the bedrooms—the one with the cookbook—then his shoulders drooped. "Look, I'm all for meeting new people, but why are you here? It's been a rough night."

You and me both. If his struggle was the same as hers, there was no point in lying to him. "My dad is missing. I was led here to find him."

Alex looked around, almost patronising in his manner. "I hate to break it to you, lass, but he's not here."

As if she didn't have eyes. "Clearly. But I think there's another lead here somewhere."

"Why?"

Unlike Dad, *he* was a time-waster. "When the arcanes took my dad, he gave up this address. He knew I was listening. I think he sent me here to find something that could—"

"Hang on," he snapped. "Your dad told the arcanes where we were?"

She didn't even blink. She understood his anger, but Dad's decision was logical and in the interest of the bigger picture. "You've seen them?" Erika said.

"Aye, I've seen them." Alex's brows arched, his lip curling. "When they kidnapped my dad, I mean."

"What did you learn?"

"Nothing, as I was too busy worrying about my dad's safety— which *your* dad compromised."

Erika shrugged. What was this achieving? "It was the only lead he could give me, I suppose."

The shotgun shook in Alex's hand. Erika's finger found the crossbow's trigger.

"That *lead* put my dad in harm's way."

"Arcanes threatened my family," Erika argued. "What would you have had him do?"

"Anything else."

"That's reasonable." Her finger tightened around the trigger. "Maybe he could have taken the whole cult out while at it."

"Don't get clever with me."

"With you, it seems hardly difficult."

Alex pointed his gun—Erika her crossbow.

She groaned her sigh. Alex should have been an ally, not an obstacle, but she'd never trust a stranger enough to disarm herself. "Look, I'm sorry your dad was taken. Blame the cult, not my dad."

"My dad didn't give anyone up." Alex's voice broke. "They cornered him in the car park, tortured him till his nose bled. The screams could be heard for miles. Still, he gave them nothing."

Commendable, Erika would admit. Not to Alex, though.

"Like I said: my family was at risk. My dad made the best decision for *us*." She knitted her brows together, unboxing that judgemental frown she kept secured in her arsenal since the day she was born. Dad's frown; Diana's frown. "Would yours not do the same?"

His eye twitched. For a split second, Erika thought he would yank back the trigger and end her for simply getting on his nerves. Then his scowling lip relaxed into a heavy sigh, his head drooping. "I don't like this… But I'd be an idiot to not at least hear you out."

Not as stupid as she thought, then.

She lowered her crossbow. "Did you learn anything from the arcanes? Anything at all that could help me find them?"

Alex scratched his head, letting the shotgun fall to his side. "No, I—I don't think so."

"When they arrived, where were you?" she wondered.

He swallowed. "Not here. My neighbour saw it all unfold out the window and tried to call the police. She didn't, before you go off on one." Erika shut her mouth. "She's a terrified old woman, bless her. Even if she remembers what she saw tomorrow, no-one will believe her. I did my best to look for Dad, but I'm not the best tracker in the world and lost the trail almost instantly."

It was unwise to follow. Erika debated not admitting anything, to keep the hunt as quiet as possible, but she needed the input of a fellow Hunter.

"The arcanes mentioned a ritual," she explained. "I don't know much about it, but it needs all the Hunters who took part. Or a direct descendant."

"Blood magic?"

She nodded grimly. "Dad's journals are all *painfully* detailed, but this case has nothing on it. He left it out intentionally for whatever reason."

Alex hummed. A tenebrous cloud formed behind him, the scent of ash seeping into the room.

"My dad writes in his journal a lot, too. Every hunt, actually. If he's been doing that for as long as I think he has, then there's got to be something in there. I'll look for them if you—"

"*Duck!*"

Alex dropped. Erika's arrow flew overhead.

She missed her mark. The arcane standing in the corridor—Percy—anticipated the move and held up a hand, halting the wooden arrow.

Thoughts circled her mind. What did he control, the air or the wood? *Aura or Terra?*

The arcane tutted. He answered Erika's question with a whirling finger that flipped the wooden arrow—

Towards her.

Definitely Terra.

She grabbed the desk chair and shielded her torso. The arrow—*her* arrow—pierced the base with a thud, stopping just two centimetres before her abdomen.

Before she reloaded, the chair pulled away, and the oak desk behind her dragged forward with the arcane's power. It knocked her out the door Alex cowered behind, and into Percy's grasp.

His face was serpentine, lips thin and smiling, shrinking his already-small grey eyes. Small hoops pierced his ears, a jewel dangling from each—one green, one black. A Terra and a Shadow Traveller.

Long fingers closed in around her neck.

"You're a Lupine." Percy touched her cheek, then brushed a strand of hair from her eyes. "I thought you would put up more of a fight if I'm honest."

Oh, she would.

She snatched an arrow from her quiver and dug it into his belly. Percy screamed. In his rage, he tossed Erika aside. As she scrambled to her feet, the Terra's magic tore down the wooden doorframe and threw it her way.

Ow would have been an understatement.

The door launched her a few dozen feet down the corridor. She bounced off the carpet, rolling further. The exposed skin on her wrists burned and she wheezed.

Then she charged. Percy's bloody hand pressed against his flesh wound, stitching the skin back together.

Percy's healing was slow. He had the ability, as most arcanes did, but the affinity was not there.

Beneath his shirt, the wound shrank, then Percy raised his hand to cast. Erika kept running and braced for impact, finding none.

Alex threw himself at the arcane from behind, grabbing hold of his throat. Erika launched herself towards him, arrow at the ready to conclude the fight.

She found herself stuck.

The wooden floorboards bent upwards and locked her feet in a cage. She yanked her legs up, but Percy benched her, giving him time to deal with Alex.

Or so he thought. She may have been trapped, but she still had her crossbow.

She had always been more suited to range, anyway.

Percy shrugged Alex off into the wall and, before he could cast, Erika sent her arrow flying. It did not kill him, but that was not the goal. Percy's focus on deflecting her arrow gave Alex time.

Seemingly unarmed, Alex jumped to his feet and swung his sleeve at the arcane, cutting a long strip of red across his cheek. Percy snarled and staggered back, breaking the enchantment on the floorboards.

Erika kicked them away and ran to join Alex. She raised her crossbow, ready to fire the final shot as Alex swung his arm.

With a deafening cry and desperate magic, Percy flipped the floorboards, ripping through the carpet and knocking the Hunters off balance.

He fled to the window inside Room 432 and, by the time the pair caught up with him, he was gone, trench coat billowing behind as he jumped, falling into a vortex of cloudy ash.

CHAPTER TEN

Your Hunter's journal is your guide, your evidence, and your legacy.

Philip Lupine's Journal, Second Edition.

The pair almost fell from the window.

"He's gone," Alex rasped. He scowled at the tendril of fading smoke twisting in the air. "Is he—?"

"A Shadow Traveller, yes," replied Erika.

"Fabulous." Alex scratched his pulsating neck, breathless. "They have a bloody Shadow Traveller."

"They sent Percy to scout ahead," Erika told him. "Perhaps he thought they missed something here."

"Yeah," Alex grumbled. "Us."

If they really wanted spares, why did they not wait for Erika at the cabin? It made no sense to change their minds after giving her up so easily.

Because they caught on to what Dad was really doing.

Aurelia knew Dad well. She must have known he would never surrender that quickly.

"They were testing me," Erika said. "To see if I'd follow my dad's instructions or retreat like he told them I would. They wanted to know if they were being tracked."

"And they are. Cover's blown now."

Maybe it didn't matter too much. Aurelia didn't seem worried at the thought of Erika looking for her father. She was even willing to let Erika live if she didn't prove to be too much trouble.

She would, however, be exactly that.

Alex fell back to her side, rubbing a dark gauntlet around his wrist. Although subtle, concealed well beneath his sleeve, the armour was stitched with thorns and roses hued in bronze under the overcast light from the window.

Curiosity overcame her. "What's that?"

Alex frowned, checking his body before relaxing. "This?" He outstretched his arm. "I made it."

Alex flexed his wrist to release a blade at the top of the gauntlet, needle-thin but deadly sharp. Realising the tip was still coated in Percy's fresh blood, Alex took an old rag from his coat pocket and ran it once down the blade to clean it.

Erika stared in disbelief. She'd never been able to create weapons. *Ever.* The closest she came to success was a jagged wooden arrow whittled out of boredom before a hunt. Dad said few Hunters made weapons in this modern age since they were so accessible from the Watch, but Alex's gauntlet was different. Unique.

"You actually made that?"

"Yeah." He chuckled at her open mouth. "More of a hobby that complements the hunting."

She could already hear the lecture from Dad about how useless her hobbies were: the violin, cocktail sampling, film critiques with Florence…

"That's…" Erika gawked, shaking her head. "Wow."

Alex grinned. "Thank you."

Erika rested both hands on her hips, taking slow but steady breaths. The twins were still in the car, unaware of what had unfolded in the flat. Alfie texted *Are you alive?* minutes earlier that she responded to with a blunt *yes*.

"Are you—?" Alex cleared his throat. "Are you okay?"

In the space of a few short minutes, Erika and Alex had fought and then defended one another.

"Fine," she said. "You?"

Alex released a low laugh. "I'm grand. Only the best introductions end in bloodshed, I suppose. Come on, let's search Dad's stuff."

Erika pursed her lips. Alex dug inside the open trunk, pulling out a few coloured books. Considering his initial hostility, he was awfully trusting of her, but she wouldn't complain.

Then again, she bore the Hunters' mark as he did. They were one and the same, in a way.

The journal covers were dated in metallic calligraphy of either silver or gold.

"One for every year," said Alex. "Perfect!"

Quietly, he handed Erika a pile of books and sat atop the desk to flick through the pages of one dated back to the nineties. Erika leaned against a wall with another.

The ritual took place before either of their births. Neither believed their mothers timid enough to let an incident like this slide unnoticed in the Hunters' journals, so they started even further back. Erika noticed Alex had not mentioned where his mum was now, but she let that thought go, not being inclined to answer the question if it was returned—if he did not know already.

They presumed the search was limited between 1986, when Alex's dad started hunting, and 1995, the year Alex was born. Even as a young man, Alex's father—Thomas J. Arwood—wrote meticulously. Every word was intentional, the whole text written like a novel with descriptions of rich detail. Alfie would get lost in this, Erika thought, but neither he nor she had the time. She rushed every sentence, tearing herself away from the words and skipping chapters lacking arcanes or cults.

"Dad does like his detail," Alex grumbled, though there was some pride in his tone. He turned another page. "I think if it wasn't for the family name, he would have become a writer."

Erika knew the Arwood name was big—mainly for their long line of occult scholars and parapsychologists, which checked out for Thomas, or 'Tommy,' as Alex said he preferred. "And what about you?" she asked.

Alex shrugged. "I've never thought about that, really. Being a Hunter, it's... it's—"

"All you know?"

He blew a humourless laugh, flashing a smile that didn't quite reach his eyes. "No-one needs a legacy quite like a Hunter."

Exaggerating his sigh, he flicked a page. Erika's assigned journal had not mentioned a single arcane by the back cover, so she tossed it aside and picked up another, bound in emerald green, modestly titled: *1992.*

Every hunt was just as detailed, just as dramatised as the first. This year, Mr. Arwood fell deeper into writing the hunts, sensationalising each heroic action, exaggerating every emotion...

In all but one entry.

"Alex. Look."

Erika flipped the book to let him read.

By the order of the Council and per Divine instruction, the Cult of Chimera, hunted in the early Winter of 1992, is to be excluded from this entry in the interest of preserving the stability of the Treaty of the Four Worlds, thereby ensuring the safety of the human realm.

It has been a difficult hunt. I will be forever bonded to the eleven Hunters I accompanied on this journey. For our safety, we are to remain separated. I will miss them all, but losing Chris and Leopold from my life left a hole I fear will never be replaced. I trust they will be happy.

The entry was stoic, written as though held at gunpoint, desperate to let *some* emotion fly from pen to page.

Alex's mouth gaped open. "The *what* of the *what*?"

Erika blinked a couple of times to read the text again. "The Cult of Chimera. I take it you've never heard of it."

"If Dad mentioned it, I wasn't listening." Erika could have rolled her eyes, opting for a deadpan look instead. Some scholar he turned out to be, then. "Bit of an intense name, isn't it?"

Erika leaned further into the wall. Chimaeras were beasts from Ancient Greek mythology—beasts with three heads. Was the Cult inspired by the legends, or simply that old?

"Any ideas?" Alex probed.

"I'll think of something."

He snorted. "That's a no, then."

"I don't see you participating much."

"Lassie, without me, you'd be waiting in the corridor by yourself. Maybe you'd even be stuck in the floorboards, courtesy of that Terra."

Erika scowled and read the paragraph again. "They needed five more Hunters when they took my dad," she said.

"And they need twelve in total, plus my dad. At a minimum, they need four more."

He's a mathematician now, apparently. "Interesting observation." Erika flipped through the next few pages. "Not at all obvious."

"Alright. Don't have to bite."

"Believe me—" she glanced up from the book, "—if I bit, you'd know it."

Alex chewed on a smile and fell back against the wall, spying over her shoulder at the journal. The closeness made her nose twitch. He smelled warm—sweet like cinnamon and brown sugar.

Erika read the pages back and forth, up and down, and, having nothing left to read, almost threw the journal at the wall.

They had two paragraphs to work with. That was all.

She paced away, reaching the billowing curtains, casting her eyes over Edinburgh's rooftops.

Twenty-seven years had passed since this interaction, and now the Cult returned. The Council was involved. *Divines* were involved.

She spun to Alex. "I think the Council should be told."

"And go all the way to Oblivion's Watch? By the time we got there, all twelve could be taken and sacrificed. We don't know who's involved, where it is, or when it'll take place."

"Arcanes are involved, not to mention Divines. If we do something reckless without the blessing of the Code—"

"We'll be rewarded for doing what's right rather than what's easy."

Heroic nonsense. They'd be punished for breaking the rules. Besides, from Edinburgh, Oblivion's Watch was just a few hours away.

"You said this ritual runs on bloodlines, right?" Alex continued. "If that's correct, then this Leopold is needed for them to succeed. If we can get there first, we can prevent that ritual from finishing, and he can give us the crucial information our dads neglected to tell us." *If he was not yet captured.*

Still, Alex had a point. A round trip from Edinburgh to the Watch was around seven hours and who knew where this Leopold lived—not to mention how long the Council would take to sanction their orders. The Council would not like them reacting so quickly on an unauthorised hunt against arcanes, coven or no, but surely they'd approve if it got the job done. This was not one rogue hexing a neighbour—this was a small coven prepared to kill for power.

An arcane, under no circumstances, is to seek power acquired in the exchange of blood belonging to him or herself, or from others, consensual or not.

No Supernatural is to harm, seek out, or compromise the identity of Hunters in retaliation to the maintenance of the Treaty.

The Treaty covered their backs. They had the authorisation—whether the Council realised it yet, or not.

Erika reached back into the trunk. "Have a look in the journals for an address."

Alex took that as her agreement and got to work alongside her.

They found one. Eventually. Leopold Hopkins joined Alex's dad in hunting a djinn close to his home in Chelsea shortly before the ritual. For further confirmation, Alex pulled out his phone and searched Leopold's name. He found his picture in a few articles citing huge charitable donations earlier in the year to children's hospitals, his smile blinding white, skin smooth and untouched by age like Erika's father, hair slicked back and solid brown. In April, at least, he still lived in Chelsea.

It was a loose lead and a tedious journey down there, but it was all they had.

"Good work," Erika said. "Thank you for all your help, but I should get a move on."

"*You* should?" Alex blocked the doorway.

"Yes," she replied. "I should."

He laughed. "You're going to Chelsea alone to track down this Leopold?"

"I'm not a child, Alex. I know how to cope by myself."

"I didn't say that! I just think it would be best if we visited him together. You can't expect me to sit around waiting for a stranger to find my family for me."

She sighed. "Like you said, we're strangers. I don't know you. For all I know, you could be working with the cult, and I can't have you putting my family and me in danger."

He laughed again. Bitterly, this time. She did not *think* he was with the cult, but she could never be sure.

"Brilliant," he said. "You'd put your family in more danger because you're too stubborn to accept my help."

"It's not that I don't want your help, it's that I can't trust that you *will* help."

"I want to find my dad too. And if these arcanes are so desperate to carry out a ritual twenty-seven *years* after they failed the first time, you can bet they're after *a lot* of power."

That put everyone at risk. Their families, themselves, even perhaps the humans ignorant of the reality of basic witchcraft.

She had few leads. The stakes were high. Alex was somewhat experienced. She'd be a fool to allow stubbornness to drown logic.

But he was already so unbelievably frustrating. Combining him and the twins…

"Pack your things," she grumbled before she could change her mind. "I'll wait out here."

Alex's smile ignited the room. Erika rubbed her temples.

"My guess is this is the blossoming of a beautiful friendship." Alex clapped her shoulder on the way to his bedroom, almost winding her. "Just you wait and see, Lupine."

She would wait. And she would see her instincts proven right.

CHAPTER ELEVEN

There are just five rankings among the Hunters: Rookies, Initiated, Generals, Sentinels and, overseeing all, the Council.

The Hunter's Codex, Chapter II.

While Alex carried a holdall of clothes, Erika wrangled a bag of weapons. Alex offered a hand in the corridor, but pride had her swatting him away.

"You could use some of mine, you know?" The lift chimed and they entered.

Alex tapped the button on the wall, closing the doors. "Nah. I'm guessing your weapons are pretty much standard. Aside from that thing, of course."

He pointed at the crossbow. Still, Erika scowled. Her weapons were not modified nor expensive, but they were not 'standard.' It didn't matter, anyway. The Hunter wielding it was more important than the weapon.

In fact, if a fight *had* broken out between the two, she would have won. She overestimated his speed back in the room. He was stronger, yes, but she was quick. One swift kick to the knees and he'd be on his back.

"What are you smiling at?" Alex wondered.

She shrugged. "Nothing."

The doors opened and they swept over the lobby, exiting the automatic glass doors towards the car park, shin-deep in mist.

Erika decided it best to tell him about their other companions. "Two cousins," she said when he pried further. "Twins."

"And their names?"

"Florence and Alfie. My aunt convinced me to bring them. I warn you, they can be a handful."

He chuckled. "I'm sure I can handle them."

"Do you have any siblings? Cousins?"

"Not that I'm close to."

Poor man. Poor, *poor* man. "Then I pity you."

The twins exchanged nervous glances when Erika opened the boot and began loading it up with Alex's belongings. He took the weapons from her and shoved them in while she returned to the driver's seat.

"Any trouble?" she asked both twins.

Florence sat on her knees, craning her neck to see through the rear window. She spun around in her seat as the boot slammed shut. "Who is *that*?"

"Alex Arwood," Erika replied. She started the engine. "His dad's part of the ritual. He's already been taken, so we're helping each other."

Florence expelled a squeal before hushing her voice. "Do you always bring fit men out of strange buildings? Can I come next time?"

Erika did not need to look behind to know Alfie rolled his eyes. "Usually, it's just demon corpses and flesh wounds," she said.

Florence huffed as Alex climbed into the backseat. "You're no fun," she whispered.

Alex fastened his seatbelt. He looked up to find Alfie staring at him through his glasses. He backed towards the window as Alex smiled.

"Hi," he said. "I'm Alex."

"Alfie," he replied.

Alfie wiped his glasses with a scowl. Like Erika, he was suspicious—of everyone, really. Alex seemed tolerable, but the moment he compromised her hunt, he'd be left behind. Her family was the priority. She would do anything to get Dad back and keep the twins safe.

Florence smiled, showing off the dimples in her rosy cheeks, and outstretched her hand over the back of her seat. "Florence Clara Mullein. It's so lovely to meet you."

In the rear-view mirror, Alfie cowered behind his book's hardcover. Alex frowned, looking between the mute and the chatterbox as if wondering whether to leap out of the car while he had the chance.

Ninety minutes into the eight-hour journey, the group stopped at a roadside American diner. The twins skipped through the frosted doors, but Florence held back to let Alex select his seat in the burgundy leather booth first, sliding in beside him, trapping him in. Erika and Alfie sat opposite.

Florence dropped the menu as food arrived in a cloud of salt, oil, and heat. She licked her lips, clutching her knife and fork with vigour while the rest of them waited politely. The waitress asked Erika if she wanted anything else. She didn't, so she left them to eat in peace.

Erika squeezed mayo on the side of her fry basket and dug in while they were still hot. They were too salty, especially sitting on top of the bacon and sausages from breakfast. Still, she ate them faster than intended.

The waitress frowned when she asked for the bill while the others were still eating, but the traffic announcements lighting up her phone were not encouraging. She snatched the receipt from the silver tray and read the contents carefully. Why was everyone so obsessed with service charges these days?

Florence shovelled in the last of her cheeseburger, covering her mouth while she chewed. When she swallowed, she asked, "Where does the money come from? For hunting, I mean."

She aimed the question at Alex, who looked to Erika for an answer. After an hour and a half of tolerating a bombardment of questions on his personal life, Erika imagined he'd had enough for now.

"Hunters get paid by the Order," she explained. "So long as you provide evidence you've been hunting, you get paid a wage for that month."

"That doesn't sound very efficient." Alfie set down his veggie burger. "How do you know people are genuine? Surely some will put in less work than others."

Alex nodded as he squeezed more ketchup. "One of the core values of the Hunters is trust. Trust in the Code, trust in each other. Without it, we'd crumble."

Alfie frowned. "Sounds like a fragile system."

"The more work you do, the greater your reputation among the order," Erika added. "A good reputation moves you up the ranks."

"What about the jobs that *need* doing? The ones no-one wants to volunteer for?"

"That's what the ranks are for," Alex explained. "Rookies are like apprentices where you *need* a mentor otherwise you'd, like, *die*. The Initiated are sort of like freelancers. You pick your jobs, but obviously aren't guaranteed work. Pay's a bit shit as well."

Erika took over to let him finish his chicken tenders. "When you move up the ranks, your pay rises, but the orders become stricter. The Initiated have more freedom with less pay, Sentinels get a lot, but just about every hunt they do is a direct order from the Council. They live to serve them."

"Would you ever become a Sentinel?" Florence asked.

Erika shrugged. Only once had she ever considered it, but she accepted the reality of how unlikely it was with her family's current status. "You need to be nominated as a General for that, and they get the worst jobs anyway—the ones the Initiated won't volunteer for and Sentinels believe themselves above. Plus, you have to do your trials twice to become a Sentinel and fuck that."

Alex forced a laugh, but the smile did not reach his eyes. Most Hunters were left scarred by their trials in more ways than one. Small spaces still made Erika uncomfortable.

Florence's lips tightened around her lemonade straw, eyes bulging while she sipped. "Twice?" She and Alfie shared a glance. "Just how hard are these trials?"

Erika couldn't name a hunt more difficult than her trials. The training left her mind and body exhausted enough, but the trials themselves were a whole other level of nasty. She found herself particularly unlucky with the draw of her second. It took place on the cliffside of Oblivion's Watch in early January with rough seas and the sky heavy with thunder and rain. Even years later, she wondered how she didn't drown.

Her fourth anniversary was coming up soon—for her trials and everything that came with it.

But Erika couldn't tell the twins anything more. By law, the trials remained an Order-kept secret between the Initiated. It was the responsibility of the uninitiated to train for every possible scenario. How could you learn that lesson if you knew what to prepare for?

If the twins were aware of how dangerous they were, they'd run a mile. Depending on their actions on this hunt, Erika pondered scaring them off intentionally.

Judging from the look Alex gave her, Erika figured he thought the same.

"They're hard," he finally answered for her. "You've got to graft well before even requesting an attempt."

Alfie seemed to forget his food altogether as he leaned over the table. "What if you fail? Can you try again?"

Alex hummed. "Technically, *yes*, but we're a proud bunch. It's humiliating to fail, but if you do, there's nothing stopping you from having another attempt, if you can."

"If you can?" Florence echoed. "What…What's that supposed to mean?"

"It means—"

Alex shut his mouth at Erika's nudge. She lowered her leg and shook her head.

What it meant was Hunters never forgot their trials—never forgot the moment their life hung, sometimes literally, by a thread to reach their dream. It meant teenagers lost limbs to complete a trial. It meant some were left too physically and mentally scarred to join the Order, even if they passed. It meant children sometimes died to live up to the legacy their parents laid down before them.

Alex knew this. He cleared his throat, breaking Erika's stare. *Don't scare them yet*, it said.

"Never mind. Forget I said anything."

The twins tucked into the rest of their food without another word. They'd learn eventually, Erika reminded herself, if they chose to follow in the footsteps of their parents, uncle, herself, and the long list of Lupine Hunters born before them. It was the responsibility laid on the shoulders of every generation but if the twins decided not to partake, Erika would bear it for them.

Her stomach growled and she found herself smiling when a chicken tender landed in her empty basket.

CHAPTER TWELVE

The presence of a supernatural brings with it physical symptoms. Look for the signs.

Philip Lupine's Journal, Second Edition.

Back on the road, the sun dipped below the treeline, fracturing golden hour into an angelic kaleidoscope beyond the forestry. Alfie drifted off to the penultimate chapter of his book, and travelling always exhausted poor Florence, who pressed her head against the window, ashy hair covering her face, uncharacteristically still.

Their sleeping tormented Erika. Since leaving the diner, the journey slowed, and her body grew heavy. Falling darkness lured her to sleep. Vibrant headlights and streetlamps stung her eyes into closing for agonising seconds at a time.

Free of Florence, Alex's attention turned to Erika: her home, her hobbies, her family. Dad's warnings bounced around her mind that Alex could very well betray her, as she had not judged him sufficiently yet. He seemed innocent enough to let him know she had a dad and a younger brother. She said they lived up north; Yorkshire was too specific, though he guessed by her accent. When pressed about her mother, she said her name was Emily.

"Nothing more?"

Erika kept a stone face, watching the road. Rumours circled her mum at the Watch. If Alex spent enough time there, he would know of them. Regardless, the matter was confidential by order of the

Council. She'd not allow ravenous crows to pick at Mum's memory again.

She swallowed her words. "I miss her."

Alex looked at his shoes. He expected more. "I miss mine too."

The indicator ticked through their silence. Erika switched lanes, letting an Astra merge off the slip road, then cleared her throat. "Have you got much family?"

"Just me and Dad nowadays," he said. "My mum…" His smile faded and he covered it poorly with a cough and a forced, bitter laugh. "Well. Being a Hunter isn't the safest job in the world, is it?"

Erika bit her cheek. Hunters knew the risks. "Knowing that doesn't make the losses any easier." Uncle Freddie was a prime example.

"No." Alex sighed. "No, it does not."

Erika opened her mouth. She stopped herself from speaking, but when Alex turned to her expectantly, she let her words flow. "For what it's worth, I'm sorry for your loss."

He smiled sadly. "Yours too."

The conversation weighed her head down until she yanked it back up, careful not to fall asleep at the wheel. She blinked rapidly to keep her eyes open. For God's sake, this wasn't like her. The roads usually kept her awake. She shouldn't have been drifting—

"Is this—"

Erika jolted, Alex's words a lightning strike.

"Is this their first hunt?"

Erika nodded her heavy head. They would have been in Chelsea by now if not for the congestion at the border. She knew better than to zip past the side roads at rush hour, yet did it anyway. Her mistake set them back more than four hours.

What was wrong with her?

"It is," she barely breathed out.

"Why bring them?"

"It wasn't my choice," she admitted. "My aunt is persuasive."

Alex snorted. White and yellow headlights ignited the contours of his face: his dimples, his laugh lines, his jaw. His eyes, too. She saw now just how exhausted he was as well. "You mean she ordered you."

Erika scowled. "No-one orders me to do anything."

"I don't think that's true. You're a proper goody-two-shoes, aren't you?"

The twins insulted her enough—she didn't need the onslaught on her pride to become a trio. "I follow the Code and show respect to my father and aunt."

"You mean you do as you're told."

"I…" She squeezed the steering wheel, numbness spreading through her fingers. She pushed the tips further in, sighing as she finally felt leather burn her skin. "I can have fun if I wish."

Alex grinned. "I don't believe you."

"I can."

He shrugged. "You'll have to prove it."

A dare. She liked dares. "Maybe I'll show you one day."

He raised his brows. For a moment, Erika thought he might laugh at her. Then he leaned back, crunching the leather seat. "Maybe I'll enjoy it."

That, too, was a lightning strike.

The adrenaline lasted all of two seconds before her eyes blurred and she yawned. She needed coffee—a lot of it.

Alex yawned too. "You're tired."

"So are you."

"I'm not driving a car."

"I'm—" She yawned again. *Bloody hell.* "I'm fine."

"And if you fall asleep at the wheel?"

"I won't."

"But if you do?"

They'd crash, prolong the hunt, potentially die. She wanted to carry on, but the two sleeping bodies in the back made her cave.

"I'll find somewhere."

"Good." Alex's stomach rumbled. "Let's hope they have food."

Just ten minutes later, Alex's desperate eyes spotted a dull, grey sign through the fog for a quaint hotel on the roadside. Erika signalled off the motorway, following the road with an odd sense of familiarity. She'd never been there before but found her hands spinning the wheel in all the right ways, crunching dirt and twigs and stones, emerging from the mist on an incline towards *Pendle Hill*.

Alfie woke at the handbrake's creak. Florence stayed sleeping.

Erika flung off her seatbelt with a newfound sense of freedom and stretched her arms. A smoky sweetness hung in the air, but the grim environment failed to match its scent.

In the surroundings of lovely pine and oak, Pendle Hill was a vampire. With its unflinching trio of bland blocks of brick and vast car park littered with more crunched soda cans than vehicles, the hotel vacated itself of any sort of life. The windows were wide and low, and the solid blackness within gave the impression of a gaping mouth, the frozen curtains sharp as twin fangs. The beaming rating above the flickering green OPEN sign explained why.

Alex pursed his lips. "Why would you advertise a one-star rating?"

From behind, Alfie rasped, "Are we staying here tonight?"

"It's better than the car," Erika insisted, even though she was considering the four sharing the Fiesta instead of a hotel sharing a name with a famous witch trial. "Flo, come on."

She snored quietly. Erika leaned over and tapped her arm. "Florence. Wake up."

She didn't move.

Alfie sighed and unscrewed his water bottle. "I've got it."

Before Erika could protest, Alfie dumped half the bottle's contents on her head, soaking her hair and t-shirt. She coughed and spluttered, and her brother cackled hysterically.

It was probably *a bit* far.

"What was that for?" Florence snapped.

"We're staying here tonight," Alex said.

Her jaw dropped, eyes igniting with desires that knocked Erika sick. "We are?"

Erika glared. "*All* of us are."

Florence huffed, her dream so visibly spoiled it made her brother snort. "Fine. Then let's go before I fall asleep again."

As they crossed the car park, a sour taste coated Erika's mouth. Her exhaustion dwindled with every step, and a new bout of adrenaline soared through her. She should have been growing *more* tired but she was only…

Panicked.

Rain soaked them through by the time the four reached the reception door. Erika tugged on the handle, grunting as it fought back before inevitably giving in.

"Never known a hotel not want guests," Alex muttered.

"*Shush*," Erika warned. She dipped her head towards the desk and the ancient receptionist behind it.

But he was right. Everything Erika's eye caught repulsed her from the peeling magnolia wallpaper, the broken sofa with springs jutting out of the cushions, to the oak check-in desk clawed by time and human touch. Her gaze followed a line of slimy black mould on the left wall until a brown dot scuttling over the floorboards snatched her attention.

A cockroach. Fantastic.

Florence paled. "I had a nightmare like this once."

"That's a health and safety violation if I ever did see one," Alfie commented.

A rasp from behind the desk made the group shudder. "*Are* you health and safety inspectors?"

"N-no," replied Alfie.

"Then it's none of your business how many violations you see."

"Could always report it," Alex challenged.

"And get this place shut down? Ha! Please do. Send me into an early retirement, I beg."

There was nothing 'early' about retirement for this lady if she were granted it in the next ten seconds. With her bony frame, stone-shaded perm, and crow's feet sinking into her pasty temples, the woman looked like she might crack under the crumbling weight of the hotel. She narrowed watery eyes at Erika and folded a knitted yellow cardigan over her torso. Magnolia, like the wallpaper.

Despite her discomfort—and the cold and the damp—Erika reminded herself she had slept in worse places and forced a smile as charming as she could muster while soaked to the bone. *There better not be spiders.* "We'd like to check in."

The receptionist complied with haste, evidently hoping the sooner they checked in, the sooner they would leave. She had nothing to worry about. Erika was just as keen to get back on the road as the receptionist was to retire.

The receptionist held out two copper keys—one for each of the twin rooms Erika booked. "Check out at eleven. No breakfast provided."

Alex gasped. "Do you have *any* food?"

She shrugged. "Vending machines are by the laundrette."

Alex sighed. "That'll do, I guess."

The receptionist leaned back in her chair. "Anything else?"

Erika read the badge on her magnolia cardigan: *Mrs E. Winston*. At least she had a name to match the old face now. "No. That's all."

Mrs Winston drew a sigh. "Enjoy your stay."

Erika backed off to rejoin the others. She handed Alex the second key, stretching over Florence, who gawked absentmindedly at her phone. "Do you mind sharing with Alfie while Florence stays with me?"

Alfie raised his brows. "You'd leave me in a room with a stranger?"

"I wouldn't leave him in a room with your sister. Who knows what she'd put the poor man through?"

Florence blinked, snapping into the real world. "What was that?"

Erika waved their shared key. "I said we're heading to our rooms."

They exited reception and re-crossed the car park to reach the outdoor staircase leading to the second-floor apartments, 204 and 205 being theirs for the night.

A shiver ran down Erika's spine and she stopped. Despite their isolation among the trees, despite the dissipated fog, she struggled to breathe. There was too much going on, yet nothing at all at Pendle Hill. Anticipation gnawed at her from every angle.

Alex lowered his brows. "Erika?"

She shook off her nerves and tapped her wet boot against the bottom step. Rubber squawked and grating creaked. "Watch your step."

Most were careful with their footing—Florence not so much.

Metal clanged as Alex caught her by the crook of her arm. "You alright?" he asked.

She nodded, cheeks pink in the light of the phone she'd been staring at. "Yeah. Thanks."

Erika groaned. "I told you to watch yourself."

"I did!"

"While looking at your phone?"

Alfie snickered. "Clumsy, much?"

"It's easy to fall down these stairs. Why don't I show you how?"

Erika glowered. "*Florence*. Be nice."

"I've been nice. He's being a dick for no reason."

"Then you shouldn't be in a *mood* for no reason," retorted Alfie.

Alfie shot his sister a smile as she climbed the remaining steps, more mindful of her footing now. She dug her elbow into Alfie's stomach on passing, forcing a grunt from him.

Erika kept quiet.

"Can I have the key?" Florence asked.

Erika handed over the key and watched her stomp into their room. Alfie raised his middle finger when the door slammed in his face.

"Please, can I *also* have the key?"

Alfie accepted the key far more graciously and slipped into the room in silence.

Erika expelled a sigh as the second door slammed.

Florence had always been wild in a way Alfie could never comprehend. Likewise, he spent hours upon hours researching, reading, and enjoying his own company—a way of passing time that Florence saw as torture.

Alex cocked his head. "What just happened?"

Erika tore her eyes from the doors. "Pettiness. They'll get over it."

"Are they like this often?"

She shrugged in reply, blowing out a long sigh. "Damned if I know."

"Damned if you know? You're family. How could you not know?"

"Look, I don't need to be whinged at," she snapped. "Least of all from you."

Erika made to follow Florence inside, but Alex appeared in front of her, hands held before him. "Hey. *Hey*." He reached for her arms, retreating the moment he caught her glare. "I didn't mean to criticise. It just surprised me, that's all. I'm close to my dad, you see. He's all I've got, really. I thought you'd be closer to them."

Erika opened and closed her mouth once, twice, making no sound audible over the rainfall. She considered asking Alex about his dad. *How close are you? Why are you alone?* But that was too personal—and too obvious that she was avoiding giving the response he wanted.

Diana knew why she was never home. With the rising supernatural cases—and the drop in General numbers—orders came flying in by the day. Although of a lower rank herself, Dad could never handle it alone. He needed her. Diana understood, Alfie understood. Florence accepted it. Ollie, however... Well, how could he understand?

She never stopped feeling guilty for that.

"I'm the only child in the family who was taught to hunt from a young age," Erika admitted. "The twins are too much for Dad and—" She reconsidered, then gave in. "And my brother's clueless."

"He doesn't—?"

"He doesn't know what we do."

Alex's eyes bulged. For someone so close to his dad, he likely found it strange for another to keep such a huge secret from his son. "Why? What does he gain by keeping your brother in the dark?"

She'd asked that question a thousand times and only ever got one response. "Dad says it's for his protection, but…"

Alex tipped his head to the side, angling to see the face she turned away from him. "You have doubts?"

She checked over her shoulder and swallowed. "I have doubts."

Erika had been studying the supernatural for as long as she could remember. It was too late for her brother.

Alex laughed. "Look at this." He cupped his palms, filling them with rain. "We're getting soaked out here talking all sad. Why don't we track down those vending machines while the twins cool off? They can make up over Crunchie bars and Pringles."

She hadn't noticed the rain soaking through her jeans until he mentioned it. "Nothing says 'nutrition' like Crunchie bars and Pringles for dinner."

His childish smile made hers grow wider, and his excitement over simplicity charmed her. She joined him at the stairs, the two descending together. Her smile held until his guiding arm arched over her back, leading her on. It hovered over her coat, not touching her at all, but her smile shrank, and she felt herself stiffen.

Maybe I'll show you one day.

Maybe I'll enjoy it.

Too close, she thought. *Too close for a stranger.*

If Alex noticed her pace quicken, he did not say anything.

And if he caught her clutching her quartz, he didn't say anything, either.

CHAPTER THIRTEEN

There is no moment or corner in which a Supernatural cannot find you. Keep your arsenal varied and remain vigilant.

Christopher Lupine's Journal.

Florence's cold fingers tugged on the scratchy burgundy blanket as she propped herself on the edge of the bed closest to the bathroom. If she hadn't checked her phone so often, this wouldn't have happened. Alfie called her obsessed. Maybe she was.

All four of them—her best friends—huddled together, posing for the camera, clad in rhinestone and satin dresses of white, black, pink, and gold. They gathered at Amy's. Florence didn't know she was hosting a party tonight.

As she swiped through stories of the other party guests—all school friends—she came across one that made her pause.

She never *officially* dated Owen, but the ten months of once-or-twice-weekly dates at his house and fate-driven meetups at parties meant something to her. The girls knew this. Amy heard the worst of his inconsistencies and the extent of Florence's feelings on the matter. She hated Owen but if he called, she'd answer.

Amy *knew* this.

So why was he at her house, drinking from her dalmatian-spotted wine glass, hugging her waist… and *laughing?*

Somehow, a slip of her finger sent a snide 'thumbs up' to her *best friend.*

She threw the phone. "Bitch!"

Her hand clamped over her mouth as it banged against the wall. Did Alfie hear? What would he say if he thought she was punching walls and swearing at him from the next room?

It didn't matter. She didn't care. Alfie never bothered to ask about her feelings—ever. He wouldn't listen if she explained herself, so an apology was off the cards. If anything, he should have apologised for his comment *first*.

Erika hadn't followed her, but she'd at least be kinder than Alfie.

As she stood, she wiped the tears from her face and sniffed, then headed for the door.

When she swung it open, she did not come face to face with Erika—or Alex, for that matter. Instead, she locked onto the enchanting eyes of a young stranger.

Florence scoured his slim, six-foot frame up and down, assessing every item of clothing – a branded white t-shirt and loose-fitting black jeans – then every contour. With his head of fluffy platinum blonde, he looked angelic but, even in a world full of supernatural entities, those didn't exist.

He flashed a smile. "Sorry. Hi."

Florence looked back at the room, then at the stranger. "Me?"

He shrugged, letting out a little laugh. God, it was heaven. "I don't see anyone else."

If only Owen had thought the same thing. "Oh."

He blinked. She blinked. "Can I help?" she asked him.

"Oh! Sorry, I—" He ran a tongue over his smile, lost for words in a way that made Florence shiver. "I forgot what I was… Yes! I was looking to borrow a phone charger. Do you happen to have one I could borrow?" He showed her the device—a model compatible with her charger.

Florence scanned his figure the same way he roamed hers. He was pretty. He was interested.

Fuck, he would do.

"I have one in here. I'd rather not give it out, but you could come in for a few minutes?"

From the neighbouring doorway, Florence's more judgemental counterpart looked her up and down. "That doesn't sound like the best idea. Then again, you're not full of them," Alfie said. Florence scowled. "Thought you'd gone off in a huff."

She shook her head. "I'm fine."

Another look: up and down. He heard the phone bang against the wall. *Shit.* "Erika won't like this," Alfie warned.

"Erika's not here. And she doesn't need to find out."

"This isn't safe. You don't know who this guy is. He could be a—" Alfie choked on his word, spitting out a different one. "—*murderer*."

The boy laughed lowly. Damn, he was gorgeous—maybe even better-looking than Owen. "I'm not a murderer, mate, but I get the suspicion. I'm Nathaniel."

Florence rolled her eyes at her brother's glower towards Nathaniel's outstretched hand. A scar ran down his palm, white and deep like an oven burn.

"Forgive me for not shaking it," Alfie said. "Germs and all that."

Dick. "Oh. No worries, I guess." Nathaniel retracted his offer. Florence stirred at the way his knuckles flexed.

Hot anger flooded her for a single heartbeat. "Hey, Alfie." Smiling bitterly, she stuck up a middle finger.

Alfie slammed his door.

Softening her features, she turned to Nathaniel. "A phone charger, did you say?"

His eyes roamed her body. "If you have one."

Silent and smiling, she embraced the rain and threaded an arm through Nathaniel's, pulling his wet body into her room.

Was this the safest decision given that arcanes attacked Erika and Alex back at Parkview? Maybe not. But the arcanes that took Uncle Chris knew him in the eighties. Unless Nathaniel had an *excellent* skincare routine—that she would be taking notes on—that boy could not have been on the cult's side.

The air turned thick when the door fell closed behind him. "So… Florence. Like the city?"

She shrugged. "That's me."

"I've always wanted to visit there."

"Well—" She thought of Owen. His betrayal and Amy's, Alfie's attitude, Erika's dismissal. Then she smiled, teeth clenched with the force of her frustration. They'd scold her for this, but they could all get fucked. "Maybe you will."

In the twenty-four hours since meeting at Parkview, Erika learned two things about Alex Arwood. One: he bounced on his heels like a hare while impatient. Two: he had an *abominable* sweet tooth.

The vending machine broke. It swallowed Alex's cash without remorse and jittered briefly, refusing to give up his chocolate. Erika's appetite dwindled with the augmenting acidic stench, but Alex was distraught. He shook the machine. Again. *Harder*.

The machine's contents collapsed to the bottom in a cacophony of clangs and rustles.

Erika cursed him and helped bag the confectionery, lecturing Alex in his giggle fit until a pitchy voice silenced them. "Excuse me."

They whirred. Alex dropped the crisps to the ground, relaxing upon realising the voice belonged to a young girl and not Mrs Winston.

The girl carried the colours of daytime spring in her sunshine pigtails and periwinkle sundress, her face harnessing Winter. Cold, January Winter.

She glanced through delicate lashes, her voice an empty breeze. "My mum is gone."

"Oh. Where…" Erika looked past the girl, not a body in sight. "Where did you last see her?"

"By the pool."

"You've been swimming? This late?"

She nodded. Slowly.

"Why?"

"*Erika.*" Alex nudged her arm and shook his head. Perhaps it was unkind to question her. She was only a teary-eyed child.

"I thought it would be fun." Her features crumbled like an ancient statue, the sound of her sobs conflicting Erika. "But I'm alone. This… this isn't fun any—"

She broke. Erika froze at her sobbing while Alex knelt, towering over her even while crouched. "Hey, don't worry. We'll find your mum. Why don't I take you to—"

"No!"

She dodged Alex, hiding her face in porcelain hands. Goosebumps prickled Erika's arms. She was so *white*.

"Alright," Alex reasoned. "How about the lovely Erika takes you to the pool?"

Erika raised a brow, but the girl liked that idea more. She wiped her eyes and nodded. "Yes, please."

Erika pulled Alex to one side. "You're not coming?"

"She's scared, and she doesn't seem to like the idea of me going with her. It's better if you go."

"And I'm going alone because…?"

"I'll inform reception. Who knows, the mum might even be there asking about her."

The girl tugged on her coat. "Help me find my mum."

Erika's stomach dropped. The memory of her own little hands pulling on Uncle Freddie's shirt hit her like a rabid lychan. Even so, with her uneasy feeling, she'd rather do *anything* but explore the creepy hotel. "Don't be long," she told Alex.

"I won't let you miss me too much, Lupine."

When he left, the girl took her hand. Erika jolted. *Holy*— "You're so cold," she said.

"We need to get inside," the girl asserted as they walked. "We need to get inside where it's safe."

Safe. Not warm. Not dry.

Safe.

She intended to ask what she meant by that, but the overhead clap of thunder and lightning striking a pine silenced her questioning.

A faint turquoise glow slipped beneath the pool doors in a perfect line. Like the girl, it stood vibrantly among the darkness. With every step, the line grew, expanding into an opaque, glowing rhombus, reaching for the silent pair.

They crossed the threshold into the blue light.

Really, he should have gone after her, but Alfie didn't have the energy to lecture her about both blondie and safety. This was not a party or a school trip. She couldn't just frolic away with any good-looking boy she met like the Lakes retreat—as if that was a safe decision in the first place! Alfie saw the lesions on Erika's neck. She was hurt just entering that Arwood guy's flat. They *all* had to be careful. Spending time alone with 'Nathaniel' was not careful.

But she wouldn't listen. Arguing with Florence about boys was like fighting a wendigo with a revolver. *She's so stupid.* That was precisely why she had her heart broken again and again. One day, the heartbreak would stop because there'd be a fucking dagger lodged in it.

He backed into his bedroom and allowed the door to close behind him.

The room was disgusting. No doubt Florence had already combed through hers, finding it to be less adequate than the standards she was used to. She never cleaned at home, of course, that was all Mum, but Florence liked things to look nice even if she was too lazy to put in the effort herself.

Alfie loosened his muscles and swung back on the bed.

With a crack and a thud, the bedframe snapped, and the mattress fell to the carpet in a cloud of brown dust.

Alfie coughed and spluttered. This place *seriously* needed a health inspection. Hopefully, Florence brought her inhaler inside.

He stretched his arms on either side, pushing himself back up again, only to feel the flimsy texture of paper beneath his palms as they slid off the mattress.

Careful not to rip it, he tugged the newspaper from underneath him.

He sat up and let out a dust-filled cough, adjusting his glasses. The focusing headline latched onto his throat, the printed words beneath sinking in, dragging his heart to his stomach, taking his breath away like—

Like he was drowning.

He launched himself off the mattress to find his cousin.

As a chill caressed her spine, it struck Erika that it did not originate within the acrid air.

It emanated from *her.*

The little girl who walked alongside her, not in the least bit bothered by the rain pounding their backs, soaking them through despite her desperation to reach safety indoors.

It emanated… from her.

Truth did not strike until the two stepped inside.

She was porcelain, deathly pale like an aged doll. The blonde pigtails and smooth perfection of her sundress were too neat, too tidy, for Erika to not notice what she was.

Erika never had a particularly soft spot for children, but something about this child made her throw away logic and rush to her aid at a simple command. She had doubts. Alex convinced her to bury them.

She was stupid to listen. And for that stupidity, the girl would make her pay.

With a ricocheting rattle, the doors slammed behind them.

No, not *them*. Only Erika. The little girl vanished with a squeeze of ice against her palm.

Like a ghost.

Erika swore, yanking and pulling at the handle, throwing herself at the metal until the overhead lights switched off. This was why Dad did the planning! He always spotted the things she didn't. He kept her safe with his instructions. He—

Splash.

Tarnish the Veil

Breath hitched in her throat, scratching her windpipe as it turned dry and cold. The windows darkened with inky rain leaking inside, following the trail of moss down crumbling bricks into the blue lights below.

The water was still, calm, and unmoving—not a single wave or ripple. A solitary lagoon. Something glittered beneath the water; a forbidden treasure reeling Erika in.

Her anxieties eased, drifting outward from her chest like steam from the pool. Glimmering ribbons of turquoise danced along the walls, the floor... her head.

She wanted *more*. More colour. More light.

She could not move back. Only forward. So, she reached out, towards the colour, towards the light.

Towards the deep end.

She leaned over the edge, narrowing her eyes at the glowing iridescence rolling over the room as a wave. It stretched and recoiled the closer she came and morphed into something new. Dark. Skeletal. It—no, *she*—smiled with an outstretched hand, hovering before it broke through the watery veil.

She called to Erika without a single movement or sound, asking for her help.

She needed her. She needed saving.

Erika crouched low and reached for the surface, her fingertips tapping the water as she shook. She blinked at the cool breeze lifting at her touch. The water looked warm. *Why was it... Why was it cold?*

"ERIKA!"

CHAPTER FOURTEEN

A lingering ghost is a reflection of itself. A dwelling demon reflects its host.
Secrets of the Veil by Cassandra Starling, Chapter Two.

Metal clanged. Erika jolted awake as Alex called her name from the open doorway, Alfie behind in the pouring rain. Realisation dawned the moment her wrist burned and a vicious, gnarly creature latched on.

Fuck!

The creature hissed as Erika fought, then freed herself. It tugged on her ankle, knocking her to the ground, dragging her into the deep end.

She fumbled for something to grab onto, everything slippery and wet. She was helpless—almost.

White knuckles gripped the pool's edge, her legs submerged, slowing her kicks against the creature—*a grindylow?* She could maintain a defensive position there, but not an offensive one.

Alfie dropped to his knees, squeezing Erika's arms, fishing her out. "Come... *on!*"

Alex lashed at the creature. It screeched, its grip loosening enough for Alfie to release Erika from the water.

She rolled on her back and scurried away, her eyes glued to the splashing waves, her mind finally clear, along with the water. Not a grindylow, then. Grindylows didn't just *disappear*.

She heaved, soaked, shivering, and breathless. Some 'rest' this turned out to be.

Alfie put an arm over his cousin, retreating at the cold. "Are you alright? What happened? Why did you—"

"I can only answer one question at a time, Alf."

"Right." He nodded quickly, choosing which to ask again. "Sorry, you're right. Alex!"

Erika pushed onto her elbows. Alex stared at the water a few feet ahead, back straight with a deadly grip on an iron crowbar: a weapon against ghosts. Yes, that was it! Alex knew what to expect when he found her.

"Alex!" she wheezed. "Get... get away from there."

Alex scanned the pool, analysing every wave until they calmed, then his body relaxed. The creature had retreated, at least for a short while. It didn't expect a fight.

Alex rushed to Erika's side. "Are you okay?"

"I'm fine. How'd you know something was wrong?"

"Alfie worked it out," he replied. Alfie blushed. "Mrs Winston said she doesn't allow children to stay here. I was walking across the car park when Alfie slammed into me, telling me the bloody place was haunted."

Erika looked to Alfie for his explanation. "There were newspapers left in the room talking about a string of unexplained deaths, all related to drowning, starting with a young girl eight years ago. That, combined with the things I know from Dad's journal, I, uh, worked it out, I suppose."

Despite the circumstances, Erika caught herself smiling. "Well done, Alf."

He wiped droplets from his glasses. "It was nothing. Anyone else could have done it."

Alex brought Erika to her feet. Her eyes wouldn't leave the water.

The ghost fought with the strength of a vengeful supernatural clinging to the wrong side of the Veil. Child ghosts often did this. Cutting innocent lives short while the guilty turned grey was life's cruellest trick.

Erika understood their anger, but the result was not an easy fix for a Hunter on a tight schedule.

"Now we need to figure out how to solve this mess," Alex said. He fired a glance Erika's way.

She sucked in a breath.

"We… are staying to fix this, aren't we?"

Erika shared a look with Alfie, who seemed to accept her logic whether he agreed with it or not.

Chelsea was still miles away, and none of them knew how long they had left to find their families. Stopping at the hotel was a reluctant necessity but a short walk and peaking adrenaline left Erika keen to drive on. If tackling a vengeful spirit ended in injury or worse, their families' lives hung in the balance.

"We can't afford to delay our search any longer," she said. "Our families could be dead in a matter of days."

"This place is damaged, Erika," Alex insisted. "We can't just abandon it, pretending nothing is wrong."

"That is *exactly* what we will do."

His countenance shifted, darkening at the sight of her.

Erika sighed. "This hotel is quiet. How many people do you think will pass through here by the time we find our families? Ten? Twenty? Alfie, how many people have drowned here since this started?"

"E—" Alfie's voice cracked. "Eleven."

"There you go." She let her arms drop. "Eleven people in eight years, I believe?" Alfie nodded. "Less than two victims every year. What's the likelihood there will be another in the next week or so? We can come back once we're finished with the cult and our families aren't depending on us."

She whirled around then turned back again, rolling her eyes at Alex standing stoic.

"There's still a chance there could be another victim. Someone's life could be at stake here. Someone else's family."

"It's unlikely," Erika retorted.

"But there's still that chance."

"Yes, Alex, a *minute*, small chance of just *one* person being harmed! Nothing compared to what the cult may have planned."

Alex raised his brows, looking her up and down. "Just one person?"

"Yes, one person. Finally, you understand."

She turned again and made her way to the doors, gesturing for Alfie and Alex to follow. "Come on, then. Let's grab Florence and get back on the road."

Only one pair of footsteps followed. Erika kept walking, trusting Alex to give in and leave with her.

"*Just* one person."

Erika froze, clenching her jaw and releasing it. He wasn't *listening*. She turned to face Alex, calm and collected. "Against the dozens that will be killed by the cult, yes. It is *just* one person."

Alex laughed, bitter in a way she did not think him capable.

But, then again, she didn't truly know him, did she?

"Is that all people are to you? Numbers?"

"I didn't say that."

"You implied it."

"Don't paint me as something I'm not!"

Erika's tone cut through the room, Alfie flinching beside her. She approached Alex with a tight jaw and squeezing knuckles dripping with pool water.

"If it were any other time, I would gladly stay to take care of this job, but it's not doable now. We're leaving. We can return when my father, *your* father, don't forget, and the other Hunters have been saved."

"And if it were *your* father that turned up here, say tomorrow, and ended up dead? I'm sure things change when it's not *the* Christopher Lupine in danger."

"Things change when your death coincides with eleven others."

"So what happens when you have to choose? When the greater good stands in the way of your dad, or Florence, or Alfie? Your *brother*? Is it just one life then?"

"My family *is* the Order. The Order *is* the greater good."

She gritted out the words, barely moving, while Alex shook his head, fighting to be steady, but his shaking was unmistakable. "Being a Hunter isn't about saving the many over the few. *The shield at humanity's back.* That's what we're told, isn't it? I've never seen a shield pick favourites."

"Don't you *dare* quote the Code to me. I've abided by it since the day I could read."

Alex took a step towards her. Then another. Until he was just short of half a metre before her, casting a shadow before the turquoise light. "Then your interpretation is wrong."

"And yours is right?" Erika huffed a laugh. "Awfully arrogant, don't you think?"

"Because I don't agree with a perfect fucking Lupine?"

His hot exhale brushed her skin, infuriating her further when it itched her neck and spine. He raised his chin, looking down as if she were inferior: a heartless Hunter allowing people to die for her own gain. She was no coward, but no fool either.

Pendle Hill could wait. Dad could not.

She locked eyes with Alex, silently asking one more time: *Are you with us?*

He scowled, confirming her answer.

And just like that, the hot air between them froze over.

Erika backed off. "Come on, Alfie. We're leaving."

Alex snorted. Erika whirred, still backing away. "Is that a problem?"

He bit his lip and met her eyes, sharpening and pointing them like daggers towards Erika.

"When my grandpa was alive, he talked about you a lot during training, you know? He never told me your name, but 'Christopher's girl' was somehow my number one adversary." He tilted his head. "You didn't know I existed, did you?"

She debated politeness. Not for long, though. "Funnily enough, no."

"Your progress was my motivation. '*Christopher's girl just had her first hunt, Alexander. Christopher's girl took out a demon. Christopher's girl passed her trials first go!*' All I could think of while training was how I could be better than *you*. I both admired and loathed you, and you didn't even know I existed."

Erika's eyes betrayed her, giving him a once-over at the flattery. She didn't need validation—not from him—yet her body said otherwise.

"You've heard what the consensus is. People say your family is washed-up and expired, and I disagreed with them for years, but now? Now I see what they mean. You're just like everyone else. Scraping the barrels of glory for crumbs of relevancy rather than doing what's right."

Erika held her breath, along with every impulse to retaliate with enough cruelty to make him shed a tear.

Every bone in her body followed the Code, just as Dad did in the shadows of her grandpa. Her actions would be supported by the Order entirely, while Alex's decision would be deemed reckless, yet she was the one ashamed to stand her ground.

Yet another of Dad's reasons not to get close to people. *He's making you question yourself.*

"Thank you for all your help, Alex Arwood. Sorry I disappointed you."

His features flinched, but no other response came. Erika ushered Alfie out the door, almost having to push him back into the rain, following behind without looking back.

CHAPTER FIFTEEN

Hunters are permitted to hunt the unallied Supernaturals without permission from the authorities, including their own Council. These species include, but are not limited to: ghosts, demons, wendigos, and djinns.

Treaty of the Four Worlds, Section 5, Paragraph 6.

Solving a haunting was like solving a crime. You'd trace the ghost's death to find the anchor chaining it to the wrong side of the Veil. If you couldn't do that, you needed to find and burn the body.

Erika stopped at the top of the stairs to their rooms, turning to Alfie. "Did I make the right decision?"

He shrugged, unreadable beyond his fogging glasses. "You did what you thought was best."

"That's not what I asked." She blocked the stairs. "Do you agree with what I chose to do?"

"I… don't have an opinion."

"Yes, you do," she pushed. "You just don't want to share it with me."

He sighed. "Fine. I… I see your logic in why you want to leave and I agree with it. But we could use Alex on this hunt, and if we leave him now we're never getting him back."

Erika pursed her lips. "Do you think it's worth leaving or helping him?" She trusted her judgement for the most part, but Dad had always been there to reassure her. Failing to recognise the ghost instantly put her on edge.

Alfie scratched his chin. "I don't know. Honestly, I don't."

Alfie knew the cost of hunting down the cult, but he did not trust Alex as much as Florence did. Fear made Alfie more inclined to leave the stranger behind. Alex could take care of himself against a ghost, but were three Hunters enough to take on a dozen arcanes?

Erika reached for the door handle to her room.

It wouldn't budge. Florence had the key. "Flo!" Erika banged on the door.

Beside her, Alfie covered his mouth. "Where's your sister?" Erika snapped.

"She... no, she wouldn't... no way—"

"No way?"

"Some blonde guy knocked on her door asking to borrow a phone charger. I was cramping her style, since he was *mildly* attractive, and she more or less told me to piss off."

"And you're telling me this now?"

"I'm sorry, I was more focused on—what was it again? Oh! The ghost!"

The cult had at least a dozen members, according to Aurelia. Erika had seen less than half of their faces. No-one could be trusted, including this *blonde guy*.

When Alfie saw Erika's face, his mouth fell open. "I... she'll be back soon, right? She always runs off. She *will* be back."

Erika groaned and rubbed her temples. All Florence spoke of this year were boys—one in particular—but Erika imagined she still retained *some* logic in her small mind.

Maybe that was Erika's mistake. Alfie's, too, for leaving her alone with *some guy*.

"If she is harmed in any way…"

"You'll throw me in the pool?"

"With an *anchor*."

They tried calling Florence—Erika five times, Alfie seven—but neither got a response. With no luck in calling from Alfie and Alex's room, Erika and Alfie waited in reception, sitting in the closest thing it had to a lounge in case Florence and 'Nathaniel' appeared or Mrs Winston came off her break to tell them this boy's room number. Erika had cash and a knife at the ready. When it came to Florence, she wasn't fucking around. Alfie chose to sit. Erika paced back and forth, wet shoes whining on the linoleum.

Erika abandoned Alex to get back on the road, yet here they were.

What happens when you have to choose? Alex had asked her.

Anger pained Erika's jaw. "I have it in mind to leave her here."

"You should… but you won't," Alfie replied.

Erika stopped pacing. "Won't I?"

"She's an idiot, yes, but you love her, really."

Erika snorted. "Sometimes I wonder why."

Between leaving Alex behind and losing Florence, the seed of Erika's worry planted upon their arrival branched into several grim possibilities. Florence could have been with anyone, even a cultist, knowing the naivety of that girl, and Alex hadn't the faintest idea of how to solve the haunting.

A glint by the door made Erika blink. She thought it to be the shine of Florence's highlights but it was just a plaque: a polished, golden plaque screwed onto the mouldy, magnolia wall reading *in memoriam*.

She ran her finger over the names. The third, dated eight years prior, captured her attention.

Carly Winston, Age 9, Cause of Death: Drowning.

This had to be the little girl. There were no others on the list. The only other child was a boy.

Her death catalysed others, causing four in the first two months. After one particular name, the drownings paused, starting again a year later.

"Rachel Winston."

Alfie stirred. "What?"

Erika blinked, still staring at the name. She had to check. "Alfie, the name of the girl who died at the pool. It was Carly Winston, right?"

"Uh…" The newspaper crunched while he flicked. "Yes. Carly Winston."

"What about a Rachel Winston?"

He ran a finger down the columns, muttering the names through an inhale.

He exhaled. "She was her mum. She returned to Pendle Hill a few months after her daughter's death and was found dead—" his voice softened and his features laced together in fear, "—in the pool."

Erika stepped back from the plaque. "That's it."

Alfie frowned. "What's it?"

Carly was alone when she died. Surely, she would have been frightened—hell, even adults would've been. She would have called for help. She would have screamed and cried for the person that matters most to any child in the whole world with her last breath.

For the person who did not come.

"She's looking for her mother."

And her living, breathing grandmother.

CHAPTER SIXTEEN

~~*In their early career, relationships are a waste of time for Hunters.*~~ *Bullshit, bullshit, BULLSHIT!!!*

Philip Lupine's Journal, First Edition (annotations by Diana Mullein).

Nathaniel wanted a walk.

A walk was usually code for something else with the boys Florence went to school with, but Nathaniel genuinely seemed to fancy a stroll, commenting on the density of the woods, old folk tales about snowdrops, and things Florence *tried* to sound interested in. Even with the rain, he didn't seem to care. With the way he tipped his head back to let the droplets run down his cheeks, Florence figured he was some sort of nature-lover and decided not to judge, despite her shivers. He was polite in her room, as well, maintaining a few inches between the two of them at all times like a gentleman.

And Florence was *frustrated*.

On their journey down, Florence brushed his hand *and* his thigh as they walked, but the man kept both hands to himself—so much so, she began to doubt his intentions. Were his smiles plain kindness? His laughs only to save her feelings? She debated turning back to the room before he suggested something else behind the pool house.

"There's a bench here," he said. "We could sit and talk if you'd like?"

The pool's metal roofing extended out the back, held afloat by cracked, creaking beams sheltering a lonely white bench. Florence glanced at the dark object nestled in the corner like a sparrow: a camera not blinking green or red.

Her stomach knotted as she sat. Paint flaked beneath her in a spider-web pattern.

Nathaniel slid in beside her. "You're here with your family, I'm guessing?"

He pulled one leg up and relaxed the other. His arms stretched wide over the back and arm of the bench. It was hard to concentrate when he put himself on display like that, his figure golden as a trophy.

"Yes," she finally said. "My brother, whom you've met."

"Any others?"

"My older cousin and—" *A stranger?* The answer was too unusual to share. Alex looked nothing like the rest of them, so calling him family was out of the question. "Her boyfriend," she finished. "My cousin and her boyfriend."

His brows flicked in apparent surprise. They were perfect; groomed but not too neat. Conscious but casual. She always got on Owen's back about plucking a gap between his eyebrows. Maybe that's why he got sick of her.

"Yourself?" she asked.

"Me? Oh, I'm here with my dad. He's back at the room, don't worry."

Air hitched in her throat. "I wasn't worrying. Why, are we… Are we doing something wrong?"

He laughed as nervously as she did. "What? No! No, of course not, we…" Another laugh. "Well, maybe. Perhaps we *are* doing something wrong."

Confidence dipped in and out of him like a dolphin coming up for air. He flirted, he laughed, he chatted, then he submerged himself. All boys her age were like that. They put on a show and forgot their lines. She had yet to meet a boy with genuine confidence.

Metal slammed shut within the pool. "Where are you headed?" Nathaniel asked as if he heard nothing.

Florence rubbed the fright from her arms. *What the hell was that?*

Erika taught her the best way to lie was to conceal it within a truth. "Chelsea," she said. "We have family there."

"Do you?" he wondered. "I'm headed down there myself."

"For?"

He blinked. "Dad's business." His fingers found a shiny plaque on the bench. *Rachel Winston, Loving Mother and Daughter,* it read. "He has a meeting with some members there."

"What business?"

Nathaniel's mouth turned up in a slight smile. A lone dimple sunk into his left cheek as he leaned forward. "You are curious, aren't you?"

She scrunched her nose. "Is that a crime?"

He shrugged. "I suppose not. But you know what they say about the cat."

"Then it's a good thing I'm not a cat."

He blew a laugh. "Not quite."

Florence's eyes found her feet. She swung both legs beneath the bench, listening to the pattering of rain echo beneath the shelter. The conversation dragged on longer than planned. Her mind teetered back and forth on Nathaniel's intentions—and whether she cared about them at all.

"What do you want?" she asked.

His eyes broadened. "Do I have to want anything?"

"Everyone wants something from everyone," she said. "You brought me here for a reason, didn't you?"

He tapped the pile between them. "Can I not fancy a walk?"

"You could have gone alone."

"*You* offered to come with me while my phone charged."

She did. Just like she offered everything to Owen, because she wanted him to have what *he* wanted. Nathaniel would not even tell her what he was after. He just… went with whatever she was doing. Did that make him better or worse?

Florence pursed her lips. Her body vibrated as both legs swung with a greater force, matching the rainfall's quickening pace. She squeezed her hands, letting the water drip, drip, drip from her skin. A breeze drifted through the shelter and she shivered.

Nathaniel exhaled. "So tell me, Florence." The bench moaned under his movement. He shrugged off his jacket and wrapped it around her shoulders like a cape. "What do *you* want?"

She reached for her neck, clutching the denim collar where Nathaniel's left hand lingered. His right arm draped over her shoulder, unwilling to let her look away if she tried.

She didn't try. She wanted to look at him: at his hair, his eyes, his lips.

He neared. And when he was this close, she uncovered more of him. She discovered his eyes were not a perfect shade of green but held an array of muddy specs joining together like constellations. She found his nose slightly crooked, and his lips chewed where skin met teeth. Her gaze fell to his jaw, then neck, then the cotton on his shoulders, and she wanted to explore more.

Soft skin brushed the back of her neck as his arm reeled her in.

Florence closed her eyes—then Nathaniel stopped.

He swore. Florence opened her eyes at the draught. She faced Nathaniel's thigh where he stood over her, angling himself to look around the edge of the pool house.

"What—?"

"*Shh!*"

Rude.

Nathaniel's breath turned shaky. He knelt, pressing a finger to her lips. "Stay here," he said. "Don't move for anything. I'll be right back."

She learned not to question men who walked away from her. They'd still do it regardless. So, she sat, waiting, hugging her knees close to her body until her clothes turned damp and cold like the rest of her.

Tears pricked her eyes, but it was the scream that made her run.

CHAPTER SEVENTEEN

There are just two means of defeating a ghost. 1) Recover the bones and burn them to ash. 2) Assist the ghost in settling its unfinished business, helping it pass through the Veil.

The Hunter's Codex, Chapter IV.

With a lead in hand, leaving the hotel would have abandoned Erika's honour with it. Nathaniel could have been a cultist or Carly—powerful ghosts could shapeshift. If it were the latter, Alex was investigating by the pool and would keep Florence safe. If it were the former...

Shit, her mind was a mess. Erika would kick Flo's arse for being this dumb.

There was still no sign of Mrs Winston at reception—only a vacant red computer chair and half a cup of cold coffee. Erika leaned over the desk, unable to spy into the nearby office. No bell waited to grab her attention.

She tapped her nails atop the oak, wincing when it chipped under the impact, and a splinter pricked her fingertip.

Mrs Winston returned as Erika cursed under her breath. She lowered into her chair, almost tortoise-like, and crossed a knitted cardigan over her wrinkled chest. *Magnolia, like the wallpaper.* The same walls that bound her granddaughter.

"Can I help you?" she rasped. Erika grimaced at her cigarette breath.

"You can. First of all, I'd like to know if you have a Nathaniel staying with you."

"I can't surrender guest information."

Erika slipped a hand into her inside jacket pocket—where her knife waited—but Alfie slowly reeled her arm back to her side.

"What if I told you that I *really* need to speak with him?"

"Then I'd suggest you keep me out of whatever spat you two are having. Next question."

She should have just looked at the computer—Mrs Winston had been gone long enough. Still, she had one use.

"I'd like you to tell me what you know about Carly Winston."

Mrs Winston drew a sigh as she threw on beaded glasses, staring Erika down. She stared back. Only Diana or her father could win this match. "Are you one of those ghost-hunting people?"

Alfie's eyes widened but Erika shook her head. She ran into an eccentric pair of 'ghost-hunters' once. They were no longer in business after following her into a haunted cabin, finding the reality of their beliefs to be... *shocking*, to say the least.

"No, I—"

"I've told you people before, and I'll tell you again: we are not *haunted*, okay? Now leave that poor girl to rest, take your camera crew, and go."

"There aren't any cameras," Erika promised. "I read the name on the plaque. Her mother died soon after, didn't she? Rachel, I believe."

Mrs Winston rocked back in her chair, analysing Erika with a sharpened gaze. Erika held her own, begging for a confession of what she already knew. Details made all the difference with haunts.

No matter how long Mrs Winston worked at the hotel, she should have known something was wrong. Even if Erika and the others failed to recognise the haunting, they felt it. The twins bickered, Erika and Alex argued; Erika herself had been on edge since checking in. Paranormal activity had that effect on human minds.

Mrs Winston chewed her cheek. "You don't look like one of those crazies."

She should have seen her car boot.

After a moment of deliberation, Mrs Winston kissed her teeth and slumped her shoulders. "Rachel and her daughter Carly passed through here once a year on their way to visit Rachel's parents. They were a small family, you see? Just the two of them. They had a close bond, and Rachel was very protective. Carly's father, he… he wasn't nice."

And Rachel failed to protect her in the end. That was why she returned after her daughter's death.

"Carly would always ask to go in the pool, but Rachel refused since she wasn't a confident swimmer herself. She told her to wait for Grandpa to teach her, but he was always so busy and couldn't spare the time to take her swimming. When she was nine, Carly snuck out of her room and went in anyway after closing. She… never made it out. No-one was on duty to help her."

"And the hotel never answered for this?" Alfie pressed. He shuffled in closer, nudging Erika's arm and placing his hands atop the desk. "Surely some security measures should have been in place. The doors had to be locked, at least."

"Yeah." Mrs Winston choked on a sigh. "Yeah, they should have been."

"What about Rachel?" Erika pressed.

"Heartbroken. She came back one day to be closer to Carly, but couldn't bear to go anywhere near the pool. She must have changed her mind because the next morning she... she was found."

The desk rattled under Alfie's hands. Erika reached for them and squeezed, covering them from Mrs Winston. "What happened to them after they were found?" she asked. "Do you know?"

"They were taken to a cemetery in Penrith, close to where Rachel's parents lived."

Almost thirty minutes away. "Together?"

"No, separately. The grandmother requested they be buried together, but it was never carried out. She wasn't in a state to... Well, once the request was put in, she turned her mind to other matters, as I'm sure you can understand. They're on opposite sides of the cemetery now."

That answered everything. "I see."

The instructions were there: Erika had to burn the bones. She hated digging up corpses, but Carly would never truly rest until she felt safe.

Just one small detail needed addressing. "How long have you known, Mrs Winston, that your granddaughter has been haunting this hotel?"

Mrs Winston's cracked lips parted, shaking as she fought to respond.

Alfie swallowed. "Erika—"

"Why pretend otherwise?" Erika snapped. "Why tell people nothing is wrong and allow them to stay here?"

"I..." Tears welled in Mrs Winston's eyes. "I told the owner to close, but the tragedies were not enough for him to give up on this place. I've tried to stop people coming, I really have, by making it less appealing, but..." She blew out a sigh. "Some people, like yourselves, slip through the cracks, and I find myself awake all night fearing the worst."

It explained her curtness upon arrival. The facilities were unsatisfactory, the rooms cold and damp. With no food provided, customers were forced to leave within a day.

The old woman let her head fall into her hands and sobbed. "I don't know what she wants. I don't know why she's hurting so many people. It's not like her—I promise!"

Erika's hand hovered over hers. She closed it to squeeze. "Carly is frightened. She needs her mother."

Mrs Winston wiped a tear. Another fell in its place. "Rachel is gone. Carly can't be helped. Please, you all must leave tonight. There is nothing you can do to help her. Just let her be."

Alex wouldn't leave until he solved the haunting. If Erika could speed up the process... "Mrs Winston, I think we can—"

"Please! Just leave us alone. *Please.*"

She whirled in her seat, pretending very poorly to read a notepad of scribbles in front of her. Erika opened her mouth to retort, meeting a silencing, wrinkled hand. She refused to even look at the two Hunters.

Erika sighed. Carly wanted her mother, but Mrs Winston was right: she was no longer around to help her. She could track down the bones, maybe convince Mrs Winston to help her find the graves, but that would take time. If Mrs Winston did not like the idea of burning her relatives' bones, which she imagined she would not, they'd have to scour all the cemeteries in Penrith to find them.

She had to do *something*, at least.

"I'm sorry I brought this up for you," Erika soothed. "But please, if you change your mind…" She scrawled her phone number on the communal notepad and tore it away. "Give me a ring."

Mrs Winston frowned at the paper. "Who are you?"

"Just people willing to help, if you'd let us." Erika nudged her cousin. "Come on, Alf."

Leaving a frozen Mrs Winston, Erika ushered Alfie out the door, stepping into the heaving rain. They crossed their arms at a wintry chill blustering through the flooded, desolate grounds.

Alfie bellowed over the rain. "We're not going to help her?"

Erika shook her head, shouting just as loudly. "She's not going to let us. Either way, we should tell Alex what we know before finding Florence. Maybe we can convince him to drop this for now."

Alfie snorted.

"What?" Erika snapped.

"You just… you seem like you care."

She released a short breath. "He's stubborn and ignorant. Doesn't mean he should be left to die."

Alfie pursed his lips and nodded in disbelief. Erika didn't challenge him. She felt nothing deeper than admiration for Alex's desire to protect. Ideally, however, he'd see logic and divert his attention back to the cult.

Alfie was right. Alex was an asset.

Lightning struck the car park with a threatening roar. At the pool, Erika reached for the handle. Ice coursed through her blood.

"What is it?" Alfie asked.

She pressed her ear to the door. The room—it was too quiet. She imagined some indication of Alex searching within but… nothing.

With a hushed warning to Alfie, she confidently but carefully opened the door and entered, glancing around for any sign of Alex—or Carly.

Nothing?

Nothing but an iron crowbar at the back of the room and something in the water.

It bobbed.

Recalling her first encounter, Erika treaded tentatively, keeping a hand behind to grab Alfie, if needed. She craned her neck to look beneath the surface, spying a figure drifting at the deep end. It was not gnarly or frightening, but well-built and far larger.

Alex.

CHAPTER EIGHTEEN

The Veil is a tethered blanket separating the living and the dead. It is sheer, unveiling an array of monsters and demons unable – or unwilling – to migrate to the next world. Creatures scratch and pull on the threads, hungry to feast on the living. Sometimes, they get through.

Secrets of the Veil by Cassandra Starling, Chapter One.

Erika bolted. Alfie screamed as she threw off her jacket and dived in.

Both needed to be out before Carly had a chance to react.

Alex's eyes were closed, his mouth open. Water rushed into his lungs.

Erika pushed through, nearing him with every stroke. She yanked him by the collar, locking her arms beneath his broad shoulders, and kicked off the floor, powering towards the surface.

Aim for the light. Aim for the light...

She spluttered and sucked in the chlorine air, forcing her head above the surface while carrying Alex. Still unconscious, he couldn't swim for the ledge, but Erika couldn't make it there with him in her arms.

"Alfie!" She gagged, swallowing a mouthful of water. "Alfie, help him!"

He stepped forward, then froze. His eyes fixed on the water.

"Alfie, please! Help us!"

He didn't move.

Scowling, Erika heaved Alex's torso onto the tiles. Arms burning, she pulled herself up. They shook under exertion, but she managed to drag Alex a few strides away from the water.

She dropped and listened to his chest. *Nothing.*

She ripped Alex's jacket open and placed the heel of her hand on his chest, beginning compressions as Diana trained her.

After several, she checked his breathing. Again, nothing.

"Come on, Alex."

She started again, but nothing worked. She put her lips to his and exhaled twice, struggling to breathe herself.

No.

"Come on!"

She cursed and tried again. After another dozen, she exhaled again. Once—twice.

Alex coughed and hacked water into her mouth. Erika spat and fell back while Alex rolled onto his front, water pouring from his pale lips.

She sighed, chest pulsating, pushing oxygen towards her pained muscles. The pain was worth it to see Alex open his eyes, wide and brown, stained red from chlorine. "You came back?"

Erika wiped water from her eyes, then met his. Their connection was short, a mere flicker of candlelight, broken by Erika looking towards the doors. "You owe me petrol money."

Alex laughed. His smile pulled on Erika's lips. Laughter almost fell from them.

Instead, she screamed as she slammed into the back wall and dropped into the water below.

Carly had woken.

Erika kicked off the pool floor and sank back down at the hands of a deathly creature. In a bubbling frenzy, Alex appeared, shoving her head above the surface, fighting to hold on against Carly's grip.

The pool doors slammed and Alfie disappeared. *Fucking coward.*

Alex strained against Carly's grasp, but he would not give in, clenching his jaw and bruising Erika's arms in a stubborn grip, digging his other palm into the pool edge.

He would not let her go.

The doors burst open again; a new figure in the doorway. "Shit!"

Florence gawped from the entrance, eyes bulging like a deer in headlights.

The spirit screeched. It slashed a watery tendril at Florence, flinging her to the opposite wall. She grunted, hissing as she slid down the bricks.

Carly released Erika and rose from the water, landing delicately atop the tiles. She skulked towards Florence, barely acknowledging the more experienced Hunters in the pool.

The grasp on Erika was not human nor monstrous, but an invisible force of nature that whipped her beneath the chlorine waves.

She burst through the surface in Alex's arms. "Florence! The crow—the crowbar!"

Her eyes widened but she did as told, scrambling for her weapon. She swung the iron towards a watery tendril. It splashed to the ground on impact and Erika's muscles slackened. She shared a look with Alex—Carly was weakened.

They swam for the edge. The creature snapped around. With a single scowl, the water fought back, but not as strong as before. They were not the main targets now. Florence was.

Unprepared, inexperienced Florence.

Water whipped the Hunters' faces. Erika reached the pool's edge—another wave propelled her back. Carly divided them, intending to pick them off one by one.

Florence took a breath and gripped the crowbar, knuckles turning white. "Come on, then," she hissed. *"Come on!"*

Florence blocked Carly's assault, clumsy but perceptive. She ran for the ghost herself, weapon held high, and swung in a vicious movement.

She collided again with the back wall as Carly shrieked. *"Don't... hurt... me!"*

Carly brandished her palm and engulfed Florence in a massive watery orb. Erika yanked herself over the pool ledge—an underwater force tugged her back down. Alex secured his grip and grabbed her hand.

Erika's hands turned white in Alex's. Beyond the ledge, Florence choked underwater. An enraged Carly threw her power around the room, ready to kill, starting with Florence.

"Let go of me!" Erika snapped. "Help her."

Alex shook his head, scowling and tightening his grip.

"Let go!" Erika ordered. "Get to—get to Flo!"

Between Erika and Florence, one of them was not making it out alive. Alex had the chance to escape if he timed it right, but from the look on his face, he would not take it.

He would not leave her.

"CARLY WINSTON!"

A booming, maternal cry stilled the water.

Mrs Winston slouched in the open doorway, a photo frame hanging at her side, with Alfie behind her. "Would your mother approve of this?"

Erika's surely fucking wouldn't.

Carly didn't move. Her orb, her tendrils, and her pool held their ground, holding the Hunters to ransom. Somehow, the ghost girl paled, features ridden with the guilt of a child who stole too many sweets.

"You're afraid, my darling, I know," hushed Mrs Winston. "You miss Mummy, don't you?"

Carly squeaked and her anger broke into sobs. Erika *despised* the sympathy in her heart. She was not maternal, but Carly was a lost soul.

She missed her mum.

"I...I need to find her."

"I know you do, darling, but please listen. You need to let these people go. They don't want to hurt you. They have done nothing wrong."

"But—"

"Carly Winston. Let them go."

Carly hesitated but, with a forlorn sigh, let the water splash and settle. Florence escaped her orb, spewing up water, and Alex and Erika were free to clamber from the pool. Alex lifted Erika out and the two fell on their fronts.

Florence was okay. Alfie was okay. Alex was safe.

"My dear, this isn't you," said Mrs Winston, approaching her granddaughter. "Be calm. Go to your mother."

"But I don't know where——" She broke down into tears. "I don't know where she is, I... I can't remember what she looks like!"

Mrs Winston smiled sadly and held out the photograph. Erika pushed onto her knees to get a better look. A young blonde woman smiled cordially at the observer—at Carly.

Rachel Winston.

"She's with you, child," Mrs Winston explained. "She's always been with you. Just as she said she would be. You remember what she said, don't you?"

Carly smiled back and touched the paper. "Thank you."

She glowed. Then her blonde pigtails were threaded in gold, and her pale skin shimmered like glass beneath the sun. Her drenched dress dried to ironed perfection, transforming like the sky turning from night to day. She turned curiously towards the exit—towards a melodic voice calling, *"Carly. Carly. Carly..."*

Angelic joy beamed from Carly as she skipped towards the smiling woman in the doorway. She leapt into her arms and giggled.

The room ignited to a blinding white. Erika squinted, watching two shadows be consumed by the light until it faded, carrying them onto the next world.

Through the Veil.

Erika slumped to the tiles with a long exhale. Alex gave her a hand to rise. "Thank you," he said to Mrs Winston.

She shook her head. "No, thank *you*." Her eyes fell on the doorway and the void within it—within her. "I hope that they—that *we* —can rest now."

Alfie gripped the wall, pale and sheepish, while Florence slumped in the corner, shaken, but alive and found, strangely wearing an oversized denim jacket Erika had not seen before. Alex stood behind Erika. His laboured pants stroked the back of her neck.

A cloud lifted from Pendle Hill and, with it, a spiritual weight fled Erika's body. Lonely silence drained her. Her body ached. Her eyes stung. Her hands prickled, red and raw.

"I'll refund you for your rooms," Mrs Winston assured. "Feel free to stay as long as you need."

Florence snorted. "Not long, I hope."

Erika shot her a look. "Just the night will be fine."

"You don't want to leave now?" Alex wondered.

"I don't think I can manage to open the car door at this point," she admitted, rubbing the back of her neck. "We should get some rest before setting off first thing in the morning, as planned."

With a nod, Mrs Winston left the Hunters alone.

Florence hid in the corner, head dipped low as she sucked on her inhaler. Alfie glared as Erika stormed over.

"Erika. I... I—"

Erika launched, hugging her tightly, ringing water from their clothes and hair into a puddle between them. "Are you hurt?"

Florence shook her head. "Not really. Bruised, but I'll be fine."

"Good."

Erika's embrace turned into a fierce grip. Her cousin's face fell as Erika smiled. "Now explain where you were and convince me not to send you home right now."

She filled her in promptly. The second she confirmed she met a boy, as Alfie said, Erika started to call Diana. Florence flirted with him, followed him, and he still left her alone.

"You're *relieved* he abandoned me?"

"I'm relieved he didn't do anything else!" Erika showed Florence her phone screen. "Don't do anything like that again—especially on this hunt—or I press call. No going anywhere without my say-so. Got it?"

She pointed at Florence then at Alfie. This applied to them both.

"Got it," Florence said.

"Understood," Alfie added.

"It's for your protection," Erika explained. 'Hunting is a dangerous profession, as I'm sure you learned tonight."

Florence nodded, messy, wet curls hiding her sad face. "I know. I'm sorry I worried you."

Erika sighed and hugged her again. Florence willingly wandered off with a complete stranger, while Alfie, on the other hand, ran away when others needed him most. He did a smart thing in finding Mrs Winston, but Erika saw his face when she jumped in to save Alex. If Alfie found Alex alone, he would have left him. That wasn't the Hunter way.

Tarnish the Veil

Hunters didn't run away from monsters. They faced them head-on with courage and a will to survive the night. *The light in the dark.*

CHAPTER NINETEEN

Possession is somewhat permanent. You must report happenings of any person, place, or object to the Council within one month for the records.

The Hunter's Codex, Chapter IV.

Terror startled Erika awake in the early hours before dawn. Horrid dreams conjured Dad alone in a woodland clearing, throat slashed, fear stretching his eyelids wide. Erika screamed over and over, cemented to the grass by rope-like roots, Aurelia standing behind her. As the rogue arcane raised the knife, Erika woke stuck to the sheets.

Florence didn't stir as Erika climbed out of bed—the girl snoozed through storms and even a break-in once. One arm under the pillow, the other hanging off the edge of the bed, she slept.

Erika checked the time: 5:30. Not as early as she thought. With hardly any reason to go back to bed, she glanced through the curtains. The rain had stopped.

She grabbed her coat from the radiator and headed outside.

Her legs swung back and forth from where she sat atop the stairs, resting her arms on the railing. The metal cut like ice, but she didn't mind. The lingering raindrops were her coffee this morning, and she found herself more alert in the brisk, fresh air at their touch.

Anticipating sunrise, the sky transformed into a muted blue. The balcony served as good a place as any to watch the colours, even with the brownish-grey stain of Pendle Hill.

No person, place, or object ever fully recovered from possession. Repairing tears struck by a vengeful spirit left scars in the Veil. Once haunted, anything or anyone became a beacon for the unknown. Erika would hear of other happenings in this place again. She hoped they would not take so many lives next time.

Her insides tangled with dread. Pendle Hill almost took Alex. If she hadn't sought him out, what would have happened?

He'd be dead. Erika swore against attachments while hunting. Yet somehow this man—this heroic, inventive Hunter with a ghastly sweet tooth—made her eyes well at the thought of him drowning in the water, never getting to enjoy sweets, tinker a weapon, or see his dad again.

Possessions did funny things to people. Pendle Hill needed burning down like Diana's shed.

The stairs creaked behind her. "Sorry." Alex held up his hands when Erika made to stand. "I came to say good morning."

The room was dark and quiet behind him. Alfie still slept.

Alex squeezed Erika's arm, lowering himself beside her, letting his legs fall through the gap. "Up to watch the sunrise?"

Gold silk threaded over the horizon's hilltops. "I couldn't sleep."

"You're worried."

She almost laughed, but instead nodded and rested her chin on the railing. More rest was needed, but temporary respite had to be enough. Waking herself up was simpler than slipping back into a nightmare.

Alex's hands landed on the railing beside hers. "You don't sleep much, do you?"

Even without nightmares, she was a light sleeper. She kept her eyes locked on the views ahead, smiling at a pink pair of clouds drifting over the skyline. "No. Not really."

"We see a lot as Hunters. There are a few jobs I know I'll never forget."

Arcanes, lychans, vampires, demons. Erika saw pain, death, and destruction, and felt it within as all Hunters did. It was the price they paid for the boon of living such free lives. They walked the world with no ties, imprisoned only in themselves.

"Most hunts don't bother me," Erika started. "But things like this, the hunts that mean something, they… they make me think."

"About?"

About whether her soul was settled enough to pass through the Veil. She was too strong to be possessed—she knew the risks and avoided them—but Erika's will to hunt, to redeem her family name, to keep them all safe…

She'd do everything it took to achieve those goals. *Everything*.

"About how much I love my family," she finished. "Everything I do is for them."

Alex smiled. "That's as good a reason as any."

"And yours is…?"

He shrugged. "I like to protect people."

"To be their knight in shining armour?"

He mirrored her laugh. "Oh, believe me, that image helps, but… I don't know. It's just right, isn't it? A natural instinct to protect people."

Erika glanced at the two doors behind them. "It's innate."

"I've seen how much the supernatural can devastate this world if not kept in check," Alex said. "If putting my life on the line with this job can give even one person a dozen years of ignorant bliss, then so be it."

The shield at humanity's back. He didn't have a grand goal like she did. He just counted his wins.

Still, Hunters were people. People wanted things. "What about *you?*" she wondered. "Where does Sir Knight Alex Arwood find reprieve?"

He nudged her arm playfully, shooting goosebumps up her cold arm. "My interests are so mundane it's almost embarrassing for a Hunter to admit to them. Music is important to me, of course."

"I wondered who the keyboard belonged to."

"Nosy! But yeah, it's mine. I'm big into rock, jazz—"

"Tchaikovsky's jazz now?" Erika laughed when his throat bobbed. "Don't pretend you're not a romantic."

"Says the woman who gave me the kiss of life. Should I swoon over my protector?"

"I…" Her cheeks heated. *Fuck.* "It was CPR, it had to be done."

"Forced proximity, darling. I've watched rom-coms."

"I'll let you drown next time, how about that?"

"I was surprised you didn't!"

Erika's heart dropped. His words flooded back into her lungs, her chest. *You're just like everyone else.* "Alex, I—"

"You didn't disappoint me, Erika."

Alex read her mind. People weren't supposed to do that. "But you said—"

"I said your family was washed-up and I shouldn't have. I was angry and convinced I was right so…" He blew out a sigh. "I've been known to say things I don't mean when I'm cornered. You cornered me because you were right."

"I abandoned you," she croaked. "I abandoned Pendle Hill."

"You came back."

"Because circumstances changed. My mind didn't."

"Because you knew you were right." Alex breathed a laugh. "Ouch, that hurt!"

Erika tilted her head. Something about him irked her in the right way. "You're a stubborn arse, aren't you?"

Tension released from her neck, her shoulders, her chest when he laughed. She was right to leave. Chance allowed her to stay and resolve the issue. Alex's decision to stay came from a place of goodness. A place of love. She chose the greater good and the assertion of cold, cruel calculus. For their partnership to work, they had to understand each other. She worked so well with Dad because she wanted to be like him—because she had to do as she was told. She and Alex were different, but maybe that could work.

"So, we're good?" she asked him.

His eyes gleamed. Through the orange glow of sunrise, his hand appeared. "Truce?"

A shadow loomed over the metal between them. "Truce."

They shook on it. Alex gripped her hand, securing the image of their intertwined fingers before letting go. "Sun's coming up."

Golden light lifted above the hills in the distance and stretched through the skyline, melting into the hotel. A house of remembrance, not sorrow, now. Damaged but not broken.

Alex must have thought the same thing, for his contagious smile widened in the amber glow, marvelling at the rising sun.

CHAPTER TWENTY

We do not hunt for wealth nor power. We hunt because there is no other option for the enlightened.

Mattheus Hopkins' Journal, 1854.

For hours, nothing but rubber rumbling against tarmac and Alex's low hums broke their silence. The twins barely spoke since the incident at Pendle Hill, with only Alex there to offer smiles of reassurance that they'd made the right decision. The group reached central Chelsea mid-afternoon—despite the Fiesta's engine warning light flashing on and off—and, after a short bathroom and coffee break, headed for the address provided in Tommy Arwood's journal.

The house situated itself in Chelsea's outskirts through a winding, narrow road off the motorway, surrounded by walls of heather and thorns. A gaping iron gate wedged itself within the bushes, and Erika drove by it once before she clocked where the online map was taking her. She braked and spun beneath the bushy arch. Tarmac turned to gravel, and heather collapsed into a massive lawn of luscious green stripes.

Three floors of white stone and full-length windows stacked atop one another at quirky angles like children's building blocks, defying gravity at the outstretched third floor. The roofs were flat, their trimmings painted obsidian to match the windowpanes and patio door. Hopkins was no millionaire, but possessing this much land in an affluent area signified he was more than a retiree—more than a Sentinel or even a Councillor. His wealth was sourced beyond the Order.

They crunched to a stop on the gravel behind a silver seven-seater BMW.

Florence pressed her face against the window, gawping at the house. "*This* is where the Hunter lives?"

"*Ex*-Hunter," Alex clarified. "Though most choose retirement homes humbler than this."

White daylight ricocheted off the house like a glimmering trophy.

"This——" Erika opened her door, "——is the opposite of humble."

They clambered from the car, passing a framing flower garden of pinks and reds to a white, temple-like patio constructed of marble threaded in silver. Atop the steps, Erika spotted an alternate back entrance: a narrow driveway of sandy yellow leading into the bushes towards wilder country roads.

Alex pressed the doorbell while Erika thumbed her crossbow through its pocket. Dad's old friend or not, Leopold Hopkins was still a stranger. *He could betray you.* For the sake of building trust, the others left their weapons inside, apart from Alex's gauntlet.

The door opened a fraction.

An old man, short and round, elegantly moustached with a shiny, white combover to match, stared them down. "I am sorry, but Mr Hopkins will not be accepting visitors today."

Alex wedged his foot in the door. "We need to speak with him. It's urgent."

The old man's eyes widened in challenge. "No exceptions. Could you move your foot, please, sir?"

Florence pushed to the front. "We drove for two whole days to meet Mr Hopkins. Can he at least give us five minutes?"

Erika raised a brow at the old man. His frown deepened the crease between his brows. "I do not care how long it took you to get here. No. Exceptions."

"Not even for us?"

Erika tugged down her collar, along with Alex, showcasing the fleshy Hunter's brand. If this was some sort of doorman, butler, or even a personal doctor for Mr Hopkins, surely he'd recognise the symbol.

If not, she had a backup excuse of getting group tattoos on a wild night out. She *always* had a backup.

But even the aged features of the old man softened. "Names?"

"Erika Lupine," she replied. "This is Alex Arwood, and Florence and Alfie Mullein."

He blew a defeated sigh. "Come in."

Their footsteps chorused in the entrance hall. Erika circled as she walked, tipping her head back at the bronze chandelier draping down from the second floor like wilting willow branches.

Alex whistled. "Damn."

Alfie cleaned his lenses. "How does Mr Hopkins have the money for a house like this?"

The old man stilled. "Leopold has his ways."

When no-one responded, he continued, "I am Robert, by the way. Leopold's butler."

Florence beamed. "Nice to meet you, Robert."

He raised his brows. "Hm."

Alright then. The twins were not articulate by any means, but Diana taught them basic manners, at least.

Robert gestured to the staircase. "If you will."

Erika clutched the cold, silver banister and climbed, the smell of burnt incense augmenting with every step—jasmine and basil.

Abstract art bursting with eclectic colours and patterns littered the clinical-white walls. Robert led their squeaking, echoing boots over the landing and through a long, narrow corridor, passing two doors, a discreet spiral staircase, and glass cabinets of pristine books and obsidian ornaments of birds and bats, but no photographs. Erika peeled her eyes to examine the books' spines. His interests resided in celebrity autobiographies, cookbooks, economic 'how-to's, and a single dictionary.

Robert halted them with a short order to stay put at the end of the corridor. He squeezed between the gap of double ebony doors, careful not to reveal the scene within.

"He can't be a Hunter," Alex whispered. "He... he can't be!"

Erika lowered her brows. "For an *ex*-Hunter, he's certainly doing well for himself."

Diana retired later than Leopold and her wealth hadn't prospered as well as this. It was almost unheard of for Hunters to amass such luxury. It infuriated Erika to remember Diana transferring her savings to afford the weekly food shop while Leopold thrived. This was not a Hunter's pension.

Alex danced on his feet. "There's doing well for yourself, and then there's this. I don't like it." He flexed his right arm, loosening up the gauntlet.

"So, he has money." Florence shrugged. "There's nothing wrong with that. In fact, it's a bonus."

Alfie sighed. "If anyone sees her gold-digging, step in."

"Mum would be proud."

"I'm sure she would be."

Erika shushed them as the door drifted open. The movement was smooth. Quiet.

Erika reached behind and tugged Florence's sleeve, urging the others to follow through a scented cloud.

White marble walls, columns, and floors twinkled gold under sunlight's impending gaze through the incoming wall of glass. Before it, circled by incense dishes as smoky as a blown-out brazier, casting a broad shadow shaped like a wildebeest, bathed a luscious, scarlet loveseat of velour. Lazed atop, a far smaller shadow dangled a comically large wine glass over the back. The silhouette glanced over his shoulder, his surprise splashing maroon onto the pristine marble. The red accents in the room teased the star of the show: a ruby piano in the far-left corner, positioned suggestively in front of the minibar. Alex flexed his fingers.

Mr Hopkins leapt to his feet and strutted towards the group.

"You!" He pointed at Erika, the flared sleeve of his burgundy robe wafting like a flag. "*You* are Chris's girl." Then he beamed at Alex. "And you, sir, are Tommy's."

Exchanging uncomfortable looks, the two forced polite smiles.

"We are," Erika confirmed. "And you knew our dads."

He was lean for a Hunter, not built with experience like Dad or even Alex. "You both look so much like them! What's your name, good man?"

Alex cleared his throat. "Alex."

"*Alex.*" Mr Hopkins nodded as if approving the name. "Alexander the Great! You *are* a handsome one, aren't you? Just look at them shoulders!" He whistled. "Tommy trained you well."

Alex shifted his stance. Erika angled herself towards him—he was being examined like a fucking show pony. "Thanks," was all he said.

Mr Hopkins chuckled. "And look at *you*."

When he clasped her face, Erika reached for her crossbow. She relaxed her hand at Alfie's humoured snort.

"Ashy hair, pretty face, blue eyes, and—oh! That glare. That's it!" He threw his head back, letting Erika go as quickly as he'd grabbed her. "Chris and Emily's daughter for sure. Erika, right?"

She nodded, touching her jaw. The eyes came from her mum, the glare was all Dad. Few spoke of the lost Emily Lupine. Few dared to.

She reminded herself to remain pleasant. "We're sorry to drop in uninvited, Mr Hopkins."

He waved his free hand. "Please, call me Leopold. And don't apologise. Tommy, Chris, and I go way back."

At his instruction, the group piled onto the loveseat. Alex and Erika centred the twins while Leopold crouched before a stool tucked beneath the piano and dragged it through his knees, sitting himself ahead of the Hunters with just a glass coffee table between them, the sun at his back.

"Now." He slapped his knees. "What can I do for you?"

Alex looked to Erika for an answer. She had to speak wisely, now. Clumsy words could have broken the second-hand trust gifted by their parents.

She held a breath, then released it. "Chris and Tommy, among others, I assume, have been abducted by arcanes. A cult, not a coven, headed by a woman named Aurelia. *The Cult of Chimera* is what it's called. We have reason to believe you were involved in a ritual of some kind that they are interested in. You're our only lead."

Leopold slipped both hands into his gown's pockets. The silk slipped down his shoulder, exposing his Hunter's mark. It was different from Erika's, crossed out with a second branding.

"I see," he croaked.

"We don't know anything about this ritual," Alex continued. "And, honestly, we're desperate. Anything you can tell us would be a huge help."

Flashes crossed Leopold's oak eyes in a series of blinks making him sweat. He snapped from his daze when Florence coughed. "Robert, would you get us some tea?"

From the doorway, Robert lowered his brows. "From downstairs?"

"Please." He swallowed when Robert didn't move. "The fine blend, if you will. The one in the purple box?"

Robert rolled his shoulders back. The edges of his blazer were sharp. "Of course, sir. Right away."

Erika didn't want tea but, to be polite, accepted. Florence scrunched her nose and tilted her head at Erika. *Are we staying long?* she silently asked. Florence recognised the stare she gave in return, warning her not to speak. If anyone played the game incorrectly, it would be Florence, and the consequences could be dire.

Florence dipped her head in understanding.

"He'll just be a minute," said Leopold. "You'll have your tea soon."

Alex didn't try to mask his frown. Leopold avoided the topic far too desperately, whether he did not wish to relive the ritual again or had something to hide.

The twins knew to keep quiet, and Alex spent too long debating what to say, so Erika took charge again.

"Leopold, thank you, but we didn't come here for tea. We're on a countdown that's getting shorter by the minute, and lives are at stake. Our parents' lives. We're here because we don't even know what we're up against. I mean, look at us. We just want to find our families."

She gestured not to herself, but the twins. The innocent, youthful twins in search of lost relatives.

Leopold closed his eyes and exhaled. The wine glass shook violently at his side.

Then he stood. Both hands secured the glass. "I don't know anything about the ritual. I just did what Katia and Chris told me to do."

A lie. An obvious, rehearsed lie. "Katia?" Erika pondered.

"She led the opposition against the cult," Leopold explained. "I was barely involved. I didn't know anything."

"Then why move away?" Alex challenged. "If you knew nothing about the ritual, why leave your friends behind? Friends you cared *so* much about?"

Erika held her composure. *Risky move, Alex.*

Leopold gestured to his surroundings: the loveseat, the piano, the minibar. "*This.* I'm better suited to business. Ask your parents, I was a god-awful Hunter."

How, in twenty-seven years, did he manage to evolve from a lowly, aspiring Hunter to a successful businessman? As curious as Erika was, his private affairs were not relevant.

Leopold shakily sipped his wine. "I left hunting behind long ago. Honestly, I never thought I'd hear from the Hunters again after you were born." He pointed to Erika with his glass.

She frowned. "Dad told you when I was born?"

"Oh, yes. The truth is, I was hoping to be godfather." He shrugged, scrunching up his nose. "Freddie Mullein was gifted that honour, but never had the chance to fulfill the duties, I suppose."

Florence's hands balled atop her leg. Hunting accidents were common for the Order, but Uncle Freddie's death crushed a family already in the mud. Dad was mid-transition from searching to grieving over Erika's mum, Ollie was just a toddler, the twins still children, and Erika's training had not yet officially begun.

Freddie's death did not just leave the twins without a father. It left every Lupine vulnerable, especially when Dad was away. Things got easier when Erika started hunting, but not by much.

Erika thanked the gods of all creeds for Robert's timely return, signalled by a rattling silver tray. "Tea?"

Robert set the tray on the coffee table with a clang and backed away. Erika poured herself and the others a cup each. Alex filled his with three teaspoons of sugar—enough to make Erika's teeth hurt.

"Don't judge," he whispered with a wink.

Leopold ran his hand along a stubbled chin, vacant of a single speck of grey or white. Despite their 'old' friendship, he was far younger than Erika's father, and presumably Alex's as well. The ritual may have been one of Leopold's first ever hunts and the trauma disturbed him for life. If the ritual involved as many deaths as this one may have, she didn't blame him.

Leopold watched her as if wondering the same. "How many hunts have you been on, Erika?"

Alone? One. The rest, she counted. The numbers stumbled into one another when she reached her six-month anniversary as an Initiate.

"I've lost count," she admitted.

"How many alone? Without a mentor?"

She paused for a beat and, not wanting to appear weak, answered, "A few."

Leopold turned his attention to Alex. "And you?"

He shrugged. "Same answer."

Leopold's eyes glazed over the twins. "You're so young." He put down the wine glass and took Erika and Alex's free hands. They quivered, hot and clammy. "Please... just drop this. Take these two and get somewhere safe. Get as far away as you can."

Erika narrowed her eyes, her heart thrumming within her chest. Leopold wanted no part in this. He left this life behind a long time ago, yet it came back to haunt him.

If Pendle Hill taught Erika anything, it was that hauntings could not be wished away so easily. With only two ways of solving one, Erika had a feeling she may be digging up a grave or two of Leopold's.

"From what?" she asked him. "What are you afraid of?"

He didn't even breathe. "Her."

"Aurelia?"

"No, not her."

"Then who?" Erika pushed.

"I can't say."

"You—" Erika's head spun. She sipped her tea. Sweet lavender tickled her tongue, yet the honey-silk texture failed to relieve the dryness in her throat.

Alex caught her unease. His hand found her knee, which spiralled her further. "What do the arcanes plan to do?" he asked Leopold, still watching Erika. "How does the ritual work? How do we stop it?"

"I…" Leopold's gaze hopped from Robert to Alex. "I don't know."

"You're lying."

Alfie, who kept to himself since they entered the room, glared through hazy lenses. "You know what this ritual is. You just don't want to tell us."

"Now listen here, young man—"

"Don't call me 'young man' to undermine everything I say. You're hiding something."

Alfie may have been fearful of spirits and demons, but the experience of one was enough to disintegrate any anxiety towards a simple, single man. Mortals were nothing when compared to the Supernatural.

Which the Alliance *loved* to remind the Hunters of.

Alex clenched his jaw. "You never answered Erika's question. *Who* are you afraid of, Leopold?"

Erika sipped her tea. Another tingling sensation ran across her jaw—a feeling she would attribute to the first gulp of liquor before a big night. Her throat opened wide. Every breath reeled in freezing air. Leopold watched her wince and crossed one leg over the other.

He dismissed Alfie and Alex's criticism and cocked his head, his interest directed towards Erika. "How old is your brother now?" he asked her.

She didn't anticipate Leopold knowing about Ollie, but older Hunters knew what happened to Mum, and Ollie's birth was a huge part of that. Perhaps ex-Hunters got word of it, too—especially those close to Dad.

"Fifteen," she answered.

"Not old enough to stay on his own, I presume. Who's he staying with?"

"Diana."

What the hell? Erika's stomach plummeted. She hadn't meant to say it—it slipped like butter from her tongue! Florence's jaw dropped, and she mouthed: *What are you doing?*

Erika had no answer—it was simply the truth.

Leopold smiled. "Diana, of course. Now, Erika. Dear, sweet, Erika—"

"Don't call me that."

Alex's eyes bulged but Leopold only laughed, tilting his head before asking another question. "Where would Diana's address be?"

Fuck, no. Erika's head grew heavy. She couldn't reveal this—not to him – not to anyone! She clenched her jaw, clamping her eyes shut, focusing on the feeling of Alex's thumb circling her knee.

Until the pain grew unbearable and she told him.

The words fell from her lips, escaping her throat as routinely as air. She astonished herself more than the others. Panic contorted Alfie's features. Florence squeaked.

Of all the information they were given, Diana's address was the most sacred. It was their safe house; a place to rest and replenish without a second thought to the darkness outside their front door.

And Erika broke the lock.

Leopold slouched back on his stool and grinned. "I now possess the location of your brother, and I know he is guarded only by Diana. Has he been trained yet?"

"No." *Shut up, Erika!*

Leopold nodded, laughing. "Good."

She looked at the twins—to Alex. He didn't know how sacred Diana's home was to them, but Erika figured he had a good enough guess, judging by their faces.

"You best watch your words for the next few minutes, Miss Lupine, because I've got you by the scruff of your neck. You never know what else you might give up."

Leopold's eyes gave it away. He looked into Erika's teacup to check she had finished the contents. She'd heard of truth serums but never experienced or used one.

Evidently, they were powerful.

And Erika was fucking *livid*.

She launched the cup at the window, deciding only at the final moment to miss Leopold's head. As much as she desired nothing more than to give the man a taste of his own serum, he knew where Ollie was. Harming him would harm her family.

But the anger had to go somewhere. "Bastard!"

"That's not watching your words."

"You *drugged* me."

Alex scoffed. "That's not very godfatherly." He placed his full cup back on the tray far more delicately than Erika. Florence and Alfie shared a nauseated look and did the same, their drinks untouched.

"You'd drug us?" Florence exclaimed.

"I would drug strangers who have entered my home uninvited, yes."

"But we've been honest with you!" she cried. "What more can you want?"

Leopold shook his head. "You don't know what you're doing with this ritual. Go home. All of you."

Erika scowled. "Not without our parents." An honest answer she'd have given with or without the serum.

"Your parents are dead. There's no way you can stop this."

"Please," Alex begged. "Just tell us what you know and we'll leave."

"Your own life is in danger too," Alfie warned. "We're trying to protect you as well as our families."

"I…"

Leopold's countenance broke, and fear slipped through its cracks. Erika followed his eyes to Robert, who frowned at the ex-Hunter's hesitation. They were both worried.

Robert barely whispered, "Perhaps we should discuss this more."

But Leopold would not give in. "Get out of my house," he said.

Florence paled. "Please—"

"For your brother's sake, get out," Leopold snarled at Erika. "Remember: I know where he lives. I have contacts that can deal with him."

Erika did not need 'contacts' for what she would do to him if he were to touch Ollie, but she had no counterargument to give. Their hands were tied for Ollie's protection.

And now they had no leads.

"Alright." Erika sighed, holding up her hands. "We'll go."

She nodded for the others to follow her out the door, keeping a close watch on Leopold for any sudden movements or change of heart. Erika had to come up with another plan.

"Essence of Candour only lasts fifteen minutes," Leopold called from the piano stool. "You should be able to lie your way out of anything you please after that."

God only knew how he managed to swindle Essence of Candour. The serum was reserved only for the highest Supernatural authorities. You needed a warrant for it.

Alex glowered and put a gentle hand on Erika's back. "What a prick," he said as the door closed behind them.

Erika glanced over her shoulder—neither Leopold nor Robert chose to see them out. "They're scared," she muttered, more to herself than anyone else.

"Of 'her'?" Alfie pondered, closely following his cousin down the stairs.

"No, of—"

A black spot in the entrance hall turned. It was a subtle motion—Erika was lucky to catch it—but the others were oblivious. On the way up, she'd been so distracted by the grandeur of the house to spot it.

A camera. It rotated to focus on them.

Erika narrowed her eyes at the lens and urged the others downstairs and out the front door. She was unsure if the camera had voice detection, but they were definitely safe outside.

Florence frowned. "Erika, who—?"

Erika pressed a finger to her lips. She'd not answer until they reached the car, for prying eyes were watching, attentive ears ready to collect the answer Leopold told her without uttering a single word. With the serum still in her system, she could not trust herself to keep her mouth shut for even a second if asked a simple question, fearful of revealing anything that could let their enemies know she figured out their game.

The cult got to Leopold first.

CHAPTER TWENTY-ONE

The extent of a witch's power is determined by their training, environment, access to power sources, and creativity with their affinities—not just the magic in their genetics.

To Know a Witch by UNKNOWN, Chapter I: Origins.

Erika held her tongue until the car doors shut.

The twins gasped but Alex only nodded. He admitted Leopold appeared *off* but figured he was just paranoid.

Florence shuffled forward from the backseat. "How could they get to Leopold first? Arcanes can't teleport… can they?"

Alfie groaned but Alex replied, "Some can, but it's rare. Most arcanes are born with different gifts. Affinities, they call them."

"And Shadow Travellers teleport," Alfie said. "Don't they?"

Erika nodded. "And they have one. Percy. He attacked Alex and me back in Edinburgh and was at the cabin when Dad was taken. I imagine he's been scouting for them."

"So, the Shadow Traveller likely arrived here long before us," Alex suggested. "Maybe he came here as he left Parkview."

"It's a possibility," Erika replied. "Though I can't imagine he'd have the strength to take down Leopold and Robert post-battle with us. Shadow Travelling from Edinburgh to Chelsea would take a toll."

"Either way, the cult has Leopold. They've been two steps ahead of us this entire time and now they know *all* our faces."

"And they set a trap for us," Erika added.

"Excuse me?" Alex replied.

"If you think about it, Leopold is being watched. He stalled for a while but all of a sudden had a change of heart and ushered us out of the building as soon as possible."

"You think Leopold was the bait?"

"I'm almost certain he is, but he changed his mind. And I'm sure we'll soon see a—"

"Duck!"

Erika and Alfie lowered below the windows at Alex's command, the latter having to drag Florence to the car floor.

"Duck?" she whispered.

Alex pointed up.

A Mercedes of midnight black spilt smoothly over the yellow driveway. It came to a sudden, silent halt, and out stepped an arcane: the youngest of the women present at Dad's abduction.

Her tall, lean figure cast a long shadow that stormed across the gravel. She whirred to drink in the surroundings, her dark, sleek ponytail whipping around a slim waist covered by a billowing beige trench coat. Erika held her breath—the arcane chose the back entrance nearest to the yellow driveway, failing to catch sight of the car.

Alfie released a breath. "Was that—"

"An arcane," Erika finished. "One of the cultists."

Likely there to see the ignorant Hunters caught in her trap. She'd be furious when she found Leopold and Robert alone.

Leopold was not the friend Dad once thought him to be. Her father hadn't spoken of him before, but she refused to believe Christopher Lupine would associate himself with someone so cowardly as to abandon hunting and sacrifice children to save himself. But, as much as she wanted to leave him to his fate and not risk the twins' safety, she had to intervene. Leopold's death was useful for the cult. She could not allow them that advantage.

"We go after her," Erika stated. She nudged Alfie to move. "Come on."

The Hunters equipped swiftly. Erika unfolded her crossbow; Alex flexed his gauntlet and slung his shotgun across his body. The twins eyed the boot of weapons as though choosing what to have for dinner.

"What are you best with?" Erika pushed.

Florence paled. "We've not used any of them."

"You've never—!" Erika sucked in a calming breath. *One, two, three…*

She imagined the twins had been given weapon training by Diana, but perhaps that was too much to hope for. Guns were difficult to train with without attracting attention, after all, and crossbows were uncommon. Knife training was too dangerous to undertake without practice dummies and a safe environment.

"How did you train?"

Florence raised her fists. 'With these."

Something, at least. Erika handed her a small blade for good measure. "Hide this somewhere in case you're cornered. Alfie, what about you?"

He flushed white, lips pressed together as if holding in vomit. "I don't… I've never—"

"Alfie here figured reading about hunting was better than actually training for it," Florence tutted.

"Well, you don't even know how to use any weapons, so don't talk to me about—"

"Forget it." Erika tossed Alfie a gun. He juggled it briefly. "Only shoot if you have to, and stay behind one of us."

"How do I shoot?"

"Here."

Alex took the gun from Alfie to demonstrate, showing him how to load it afterwards and flip the safety on and off.

"Only if you have to," he stated.

Alfie nodded. "Only if I have to."

Erika led them to the patio. Alex tapped the door with his shotgun, letting it fall open. Erika angled herself around the frame, noting the empty entrance hall.

The arcane hissed from the upper floor. "You let them *leave?*"

Leopold's blubbering could be heard from the base of the stairs. Erika lifted her crossbow, her lips brushing the arrow's feathers.

She pointed ahead with the weapon and the others followed. The stairs didn't flinch beneath their weight. Alex stuck his blade in the camera as they passed it.

As she reached the landing, Leopold sank into the loveseat, his back to the Hunters. The arcane towered above him, her hand clawed and ready to cast.

"Tell me why I shouldn't break those spindly little legs of yours, Leopold."

"I—I didn't know what to do! Please, Vivienne. There were four of them, I—"

"Four *children*, you mean."

"T-they were—"

"Here."

Before Vivienne's black eyes locked onto their presence, Erika seized the moment and fired an arrow into her chest.

Vivienne flung it away with a snarl of magic. The arrow landed at her feet like the mass of the iron tip outweighed its wooden body. Vivienne's affinity was metal. They were dealing with a Ferreus.

In a modern house.

Erika darted for the lounge.

Vivienne brought her hands together, bending the silver banister to her will. Erika almost made it, but the bars caged the Hunters against the bookshelves with a crash.

She trapped them—all except Florence.

She rolled beneath the makeshift cage and stood. When she glanced behind at Erika and Alex trapped, and Alfie left on the stairwell, she paled, then sprang into action without another thought.

Shit, she needed Erika's help!

On the arcane's approach, Florence swung, swinging again when her initial shot was blocked. With Vivienne's magic focused on the older Hunters, little energy had been reserved for fighting Florence, and she was left with no other choice but to spar the Hunter way.

Divide and conquer. That was her plan.

They were completely stuck, wedged between bars and shelving. Vivienne snarled and twisted an arthritic hand, tightening the cage when Florence made a misstep and stumbled in the wrong direction.

"I can't move!" Alex cried.

Erika fought back against the bars, realising herself to be in the same predicament. She gasped for air as her ribs caved in and her legs fell off balance.

Ahead, Florence's arms locked around Vivienne's neck, squeezing her tightly. "Let... them... *go*."

Vivienne bit her hand, making her cry. Florence threw her away like a vicious animal then charged like its predator, fists balled, one of them bloody.

Vivienne swung a palm, unleashing her magic across the room.

Florence dropped to her knees, her mouth open as she choked. A Ferreus *and* an Aura, Erika noted. Dual affinities were common. Blood boiling, she kicked, punched, and clawed at the banister.

"Alfie, where are you?" she called.

"Back here! I can't get by!"

No matter how much Erika and Alex fought against the metal, neither their own nor the combination of their strengths were a match for arcane magic. Yet, she kept at it, knuckles bruised and stinging.

Vivienne paused. Upon closer inspection of Florence, she seized a moment to compare her face with Erika's, focusing on the latter's narrowed, blue eyes and the former's doe-eyed, green ones.

"It's *you*," she said to Erika. Then, back to Florence. "*You're* disposable, then."

Over my dead body.

With an anguished cry, Erika bolstered herself against the wall and pushed with both legs, fighting and fighting and fighting.

Under all her efforts, the bars moved less than a centimetre, squeaking like a mouse.

The sound made Vivienne turn.

She missed Florence's hand slip towards her belt and flick at the arcane's abdomen.

The blade skimmed Vivienne's skin—not fatal but deep enough to drain the energy needed to maintain her hold on the banister.

Erika and Alex dropped to the ground and kicked their way into the brawl.

Erika got there first.

She and Vivienne rolled once, twice, until Erika grabbed her by the shoulders and slammed her into the marble. Alex was at her side in an instant, pressing his blade to Vivienne's throat.

"Enough," Erika hissed.

Vivienne's eyes, deep with rage, darted around the room from the Hunters, to Leopold, to his butler in the corner.

"We are going to ask you some questions," Erika declared. "And you are going to cooperate fully."

Vivienne spat at her face. When Erika opened her eyes, she found Alex's knife angled closer to the arcane's throat. This was no passive follower of the cult—Vivienne was an honorary member. Evidently, her plan was for Leopold to stall the Hunters until she arrived.

To take them. Hand them over. Sacrifice them.

Erika glanced at Florence and Alfie. *Children.* She wanted to sacrifice *children.*

She lifted herself off the ground as Alex pressed Vivienne's arms behind her back. He hoisted her up, Erika pointing her crossbow at Vivienne's temple.

At Erika's order, Alfie retrieved a dining room chair from downstairs. Alex shoved Vivienne in it and bound her with zip ties from his pocket, ensuring her palms pressed tightly against the wood, keeping her magic restrained.

"Essence of Candour," Erika directed at Leopold. "Where do you keep it?"

"She made me drink it," Leopold said grimly.

Erika raised a brow. "All of it?"

"All of it," Robert answered for him.

Erika's stomach pitted with dread as she realised what had to come next.

She took a few strides back, spine straight and poised to radiate confidence as Dad taught her. Alex mimicked her stance—he must have been taught the same. Erika had watched Dad interrogate a lychan once. It wasn't pretty.

She raised a brow. "Vivienne, isn't it?"

Vivienne sighed. "Yes."

"Why did you come here, Vivienne?" Alex asked. "Specifically."

Silence. Her expression was bored. These were no Hunters— merely children playing detectives. Erika curled her lip. She would not be humiliated for her age and her merit ignored. Yes, this was only her second hunt unsupervised. Yes, she lacked her dad's guidance this time. But she was a good fucking Hunter, and she would not be viewed as an amateur.

"Answer the question, Vivienne," she said. "We don't have all day."

"Neither does your father."

Erika's face was stone. Dad would not be killed tonight—not without Leopold. As far as she knew, the Hunters did not have to be sacrificed simultaneously for the curse to break, but rituals required power. The more blood spilt at once, the more power they drew.

Alex scowled. "We're not playing your games. Why did you come here?"

She snorted. Alex gave Erika a nod.

She fired a bolt into the chair's headrest, splintering the wood inches from Vivienne's skull. She gulped.

Leopold gasped. "My chair..."

"Why did you come here?" Alex repeated.

Vivienne looked between the four Hunters. "For *you*."

"And you knew we'd be here. How?" Erika wondered.

"We have sources."

"And they said..."

Vivienne cocked her head. "That you would be here for Leopold. Certain *abilities* allowed me to get here first."

"We know of your Shadow Traveller," Alex declared. "We're not stupid."

Vivienne only laughed.

Percy could have found the same journal Erika and Alex did. He brought Vivienne here the first time but let her drive the second. What preoccupied him now?

"Why set a trap for us?" Alex asked through Erika's silence.

"Your fathers are not cooperating, and neither are you. You are spares, sure, but we are deliberating whether the parent or child is more difficult to deal with. The others, well—" She chuckled. "If the others kick up a fuss, we've been given the order to put them down. Nothing will threaten our cause."

A cruel move, Erika thought. She wanted to make the twins stir—get a rise out of Erika to prove she still had power in this dynamic.

And she did. Enough to make Erika's jaw clench.

Arcanes could be nasty, if desired. They were clever—notoriously cold in maintaining tradition—but threatening *children?* Erika reminded herself that this was a rogue group. They did not reflect the inner mindset of the Seven Covens.

"How many Hunters of the twelve do you have?" she asked.

Vivienne pursed her lip, finding a spot on the floor to focus on—a spec of blood from Florence's knuckles. She looked at Erika as if she were a child, yet she wielded juvenile tactics to escape questioning.

So, Erika would fall to her level, crouching down to match her sitting height. "How. Many Hunters. Do. You. Have?"

Vivienne's nails proved more interesting to the arcane.

The senior Hunters locked eyes. Alex gulped, aware of what was coming, but displayed no signs of acting. When Erika's lips parted, he gave her another nod, asking her to take charge.

Already nauseated, she removed an arrow from her quiver, twirling it before Vivienne's eyes. They fixated on the pointed tip, glinting.

"How many Hunters of the twelve do you have?"

Vivienne swallowed. Erika stared at her weapon, wondering—and fearing—what she would do with it. *Stop shaking*.

She raised the arrow.

"T-Ten," Vivienne admitted. "We have ten."

"Including Leopold?" Alex pushed.

She shook her head. "With him, eleven."

"Shit." Alex fell back on his heels.

Eleven. *Eleven* out of *twelve*. It was a race to the final Hunter, now. He or she could have been anywhere—perhaps they'd already been found.

Starting a search now was a huge risk, considering they were yet to find a name. The priority now was finding out as much as possible about the ritual to gauge any way of stopping it. Leopold could provide the names of the Hunters now he was in their hands and drugged up with Essence of Candour. Justice had been served in that sense, at least.

"Where are you keeping them?" Erika pressed.

Vivienne chuckled. "As if I would answer that "

"You would if your life was on the line."

"What good is that? You'll kill me either way."

"If Erika promises to keep you alive, she will," said Florence.

Erika didn't blink. Vivienne was *not* leaving this building. She was a powerful Ferreus and an Aura—a weapon of the cult—and too committed for repentance. Erika knew that. Vivienne knew that. Everyone seemed to realise that except Florence.

"Erika." Florence knitted her brows together. "You'll do that... won't you?"

Her heart broke knowing the inevitable.

Vivienne tutted, shaking her head. "You're naïve, aren't you, child? You Hunters may abide by a strict code, but one little loophole and your conscience is clear." She chewed her lip, looking down, then up. "All rules are off the table for witches."

Witches. Not arcanes. Why?

Alfie frowned. "This isn't the sixteenth century. We have laws in place."

"To serve your best interests," Vivienne reminded him.

"To serve us *all*," Alex corrected her. "To *protect* us all from people like you."

"You never answered my question," said Erika, breaking the digression. "Where are the arcanes? Where are our fathers?"

"The ritual has to take place in the same area as last time," Leopold answered. "Bekker's Forest. The Hunters must be kept nearby. A Shadow Traveller can't take a dozen people far at once."

Erika flicked her brows at Vivienne, who looked away silently.

"Thank you, Leopold," said Erika. *Bekker's Forest.* She'd never heard of it.

Leopold could tell her anything about the ritual. She had to pick her questions for Vivienne wisely. What would Leopold not know?

"Which Hunter have you not found yet?"

Vivienne scowled. "If you're so smart, you figure it out."

She laughed, trying to make it as patronising as Vivienne's snarky chuckle, but she couldn't conceal the nerves running through it. "It would make my life *so much* easier if you would just tell us."

"Then I guess I'm keeping my mouth shut."

"Vivienne, I can make this as pleasant or unpleasant as you wish."

"I'm not saying another word to you," she spat. "I'm done."

Vivienne slouched back in her seat, flexing her fingertips over the arms of the chair. It was solid ebony—barely an inch of metal aided its construction. She could not bend it to her will, but she could control her silence.

Erika blinked. This was not the way she wanted this to go. Dad's instructions rang in her mind. *Do what you must.*

She clutched the arrow. "Fine. If you want to be like that…"

She slammed the tip into Vivienne's hand.

Her scream shook the windows—and Erika's gut. Blood dripped on the white marble like rose petals against snow.

Florence's knife rattled to the floor. "Erika!" she cried.

Alfie gasped. "The hell…"

Erika dug the arrow in further. "Tell me the *name*."

"Go to hell!"

"Original," Alex tutted. "So, very original."

Erika scowled and twisted the arrowhead. Vivienne's projecting cry cracked and shook the room. Erika's stomach turned with the wood. "Tell. Me. *The name.*"

She twisted again, again, again, taking a deep breath for the nausea to subside.

It didn't.

The arrowhead turned and tore through Vivienne's flesh and bone, cracking and crushing under Erika's control. Her eyes welled, but no tears fell. Any signs of weakness were tools for the arcane to use against her. Dad always did this part of the job. It was horrible enough to watch.

Turn off the tears. Reject your emotions. They're getting in the way again.

Another turn.

"Martin!" Vivienne screamed. "Wyatt Martin. Now, please, stop it!"

Erika stumbled backwards, the bloody arrow in her grip. She hoped to see Wyatt Martin again one day, but not like this. She was aware of the past friendship between him and Dad, but *un*aware it stretched back so many years.

Then again, their friendship was how she *met* Wyatt. And Pete.

Florence furrowed her brows, noticeably paler. "Wait—"

"Where is he?" Erika interrupted. She didn't need questioning from Alex just yet. If he noticed Florence's confusion, he didn't say anything.

"I don't know, I—I seriously don't know."

Vivienne had little left to lose. She thought the Hunters too weak to even touch her outside of battle, but Erika proved her wrong.

She would do so again. "Then we're done here."

Silent, Alex surrendered a knife. Erika twirled it between her hands. It was tiny—small enough to fit in her palms—yet big enough to pierce a heart or vital artery. This was *her* knife, she realised. The one she gave Florence, twisted in bronze vines.

That was all it would take to end this. One flick and it was done. Arcanes were weak when parted with magic. When it all came down to it, she and Vivienne were equals: two women fighting for opposite causes.

But they were not equal. Here Erika was, standing above her, armed to the teeth with weapons, while Vivienne was... bound. Unarmed, aside from the magic tied down to a chair.

Was this... fair? Was this honourable?

"You can't, can you?" Vivienne taunted. "Surely Christopher Lupine's daughter has killed a witch before."

Erika met her eyes for a second. Just one. Then Vivienne realised. "You haven't... have you, child?" Erika's shoulders tensed. "You've slain demons and dark creatures but never something so human." Vivienne tilted her head. "I should have known. You've been treading on eggshells from the moment I sat in this chair."

Erika swallowed. "You're an arcane. Not a human."

"We're the closest thing to it in the supernatural world. You think us monsters, but that's not true."

"*You're* a monster," Erika corrected.

"Because I believe in a greater world? A world spared of human sins of greed and lust and pride? The humans who ruined the land and hunted us to near extinction? The Morrigan will shatter the shards of this broken earth to create a better one. Sacrifices must be made for peace, my dear. 'Tis only in the agony of a roaring flame will we be purified."

Arcanes burned their dead to cleanse their soul for the afterlife. "And if that price was *your* family?" she challenged. "Suddenly it's no longer worth it, I imagine."

"I have lived and loved enough. I committed myself to a cause knowing *exactly* what I was letting myself in for. Can you say the same, huntress? Did you imagine yourself an executioner, as well?"

The knife turned to butter in Erika's grasp. Execution sounded so daunting—so final. She did not think twice while hunting whether to kill the beast or not. If it was her life or the beast's, she would choose to save herself every time. Her life was not on the line, here.

What would Dad do?

Vivienne snorted as if hearing her. "Miss Lupine, how can you expect to lead a team when you are so busy looking for instructions?"

The thought made her sick. "I'm not a leader," Erika assured.

"Someone has to be." Vivienne nodded at the twins. "Princess and Petrified are clearly inept, and your handsome fellow doesn't want to get his hands dirty." She cocked her head. "So, what will it be, huntress?"

Erika looked to Alex, begging him for an answer. He glanced at the knife but did not make a move to take it. "Our dads would tell us to do it," he said.

Half an instruction. She could have sworn, thrown the blade at the wall.

Yet he was right. Her father would have told her to end the traitor there for the sake of the Treaty and the family. It was the best decision, but every instinct warned her against it.

But what she wanted didn't matter. She couldn't ask Alex to do something because she lacked the spine for it.

With closed eyes, Erika dug the blade deep into Vivienne's chest, trying to make it as clean as possible with shaking hands. Warm blood mixed with the sweat on her palms. Erika's broken gasp inhaled the burnt scent of draining magic.

She opened her eyes. Tears fell from Vivienne's. *"Child."*

Erika left the knife as she staggered backwards.

She had killed before: demons and monsters and beasts so savage the world was better off without them. She tried to see Vivienne as that —a monster threatening to kill her family—but found her gaze latched on the arcane's. Already, Vivienne's eyes turned graveyard brown.

She was right. This was an execution.

And Erika was the executioner.

CHAPTER TWENTY-TWO

The goal is to feel nothing. Killing gets easier.

Christopher Lupine's Journal.

Leopold emerged from behind the mini bar, unfazed by the corpse before him. "Thank you for your help there."

"What happened?" Alex turned his back on the arcane. "When did they find you?"

Leopold huffed, then rolled his skinny shoulders. "A few hours before you did. That one and a Shadow Traveller said to keep you here until they arrived so they could—"

"Kill us?" Florence raised a brow.

"Yes. They wanted Erika and Alex for the ritual. As spares, as she said. The youngest were to be killed if they got in the way."

"And you would sacrifice children for what?" Alex spat.

"They were going to torture me! I… I thought if I gave you up, I would be given time. Time to stop the ritual."

"But you let us go." Erika folded her arms. "Why?"

"Because you… look like your parents." He sighed in defeat. "Chris and Tommy did a lot for me. If I gave you up, I could never forgive myself."

Erika resisted a scowl. Alex didn't. "We're all *thrilled* to know your guilt has been spared."

"It's *something*," Leopold hissed. "Be grateful my conscience kicked in."

Erika clenched her jaw and sat down on the loveseat, turning away from Vivienne's body. It needed to be dealt with sooner rather than later. Already, she felt queasy, but they needed information first. On the ritual—on *The Morrigan*.

"What can you tell us about the ritual?" Erika asked Leopold. "You were there. What happened?"

He rubbed a bead of sweat from his forehead. "That damned ritual made me quit hunting altogether."

"We know."

"Your father told you?"

"We guessed," said Alex. "We didn't know about you until reading my dad's journal."

Leopold looked at his slippers. "I see."

Alfie stepped forward, leaving his sister's side. "The arcane mentioned *The Morrigan*. I've never heard of it. Can you tell us what this is?"

Leopold shuddered. "Be careful of speaking her name, boy. It's a legend, almost a secret, held tightly within the Seven Covens."

"Why a secret?" Florence wondered.

"It gives the arcanes a bad name. You see, she was not just a powerful arcane—or witch at the time, I suppose. She was an *immortal* one."

"That's impossible," Erika argued. "Arcanes can't be immortal. They're almost human." She glanced at Vivienne.

"Exactly why this legend is kept under wraps. Ever wonder why they moved away from the *witch* stigma?" Erika paled. "*Yeah*. No-one knows how she gained immortality, but she did. Some think she made a deal with a demon; others believe she was *actually* a vampire. Either way, she gained immortality while an active monarch."

Erika could see why the Divines contained this knowledge within Stryga's borders. "So, if she is actually immortal," she started, "at Bekker's Forest is—"

"A *live* witch, buried in a coffin sealed by a curse. More powerful than any who ever walked the Earth."

"Then who put her there?" asked Florence. "Surely, they're more powerful in that case."

A fair point. "Again, no-one knows," said Leopold. "It's believed among the arcanes that the successive monarch sealed her inside, managing to weaken her long enough to send her into a vegetative state. If The Morrigan is given enough magic, she can escape that state."

"Which is why the Hunters will be killed," Alfie finished. "The sheer amount of blood is enough magic to wake her up."

"And killing the Hunters breaks the curse that sealed the tomb." Erika blew a sigh. "God."

"Not sealed," Leopold corrected. "*Resealed*. With the death of the one who sealed it, the spell wore off, leaving a vulnerability not exposed until the group of '92."

The year Dad helped seal it back up.

"So, the coffin is protected by blood magic?" Erika figured.

"The Divines helped cast it, tying it to the bloodlines, *not lifelines* this time, of the twelve Hunters left alive so the spell can never naturally break." Leopold rubbed his stubbled chin. "It was Katia Starling who discovered what the cult was doing. She was obsessed with them, researching their history for years until she pieced together what they were after. Turned out, Aurelia was part of this cult. Her involvement got Chris, Tommy, and me roped into all of it. Ruined our damned lives, that girl."

No doubt, Dad blamed himself for it.

Leopold swept a hand over his hair. "We teamed up with Katia's group, arriving at Bekker's to discover they'd laid a trap for us. Their plan was to execute us for their queen's life energy, i.e., blood magic. To focus the magic so they didn't kill everyone, they used an artefact: a blade called Horizon's Edge. Enough of the group was killed to allow the queen to wake, strengthening her enough to fight back. She was awake for no longer than three minutes before Katia stabbed her with the blade, trapping the queen's life force within it, creating an extra step should someone try again."

Meaning the blade was crucial for the ritual to work. The Morrigan was *in it*.

"Like I said, the Divines helped us seal the coffin tighter than before with blood magic, keeping the events strictly under wraps. If we or our children, or grandchildren, die on the burial site, she will be freed so long as she has Horizon's Edge. No-one *needs* to be stabbed with it, but all that power needs a syphon."

"But nothing can happen if the Hunters still have the blade, right?" said Florence. Leopold was uncannily silent. "Right?"

"The blade was... stolen," Leopold confessed. "The Divines took the artefact back to Stryga. Somehow, I managed to swindle it back into my possession, then I..." He mumbled beneath his breath.

Erika's stomach knotted. "You... what?"

"I lost it."

Her eyes bulged. "You *lost* it."

"Look. Not my finest hour, okay? I made a bad call in a supernatural poker tournament after one too many Johnnie Walkers."

Alex scoffed. "You really are a piece of shit, aren't you?"

"Tommy said that once. Though your father's tone was more jovial than yours."

This was an issue. No-one who acquired an ancient artefact would be so inclined to give it back willingly—not without a price.

"Who has it?" Erika asked.

"A human, in fact. The Collector."

Florence pursed her lips. "'The' is a funny first name."

"*The Collector* is not his name, you stupid little—"

Erika raised a warning brow. She'd been looking for an excuse to lash out.

Leopold cleared his throat. "*Sweet, sweet child.* The Collector is an alias. He lives and breathes supernatural relics, acquiring them as trophies. He keeps himself relatively hidden from Alliance command—God knows how considering he flaunts his wealth like a damned peacock. *And* he's a gambler. If you challenge him to a poker game, his own arrogance will have him offering up the relic if you push for it."

Erika sighed. She had many poor habits, but gambling was not one of them. "Can you play?"

"I'm afraid I'm under probation with The Collector. No gambling on his grounds for another two years."

Curiosity nipped Erika's thoughts, but his ban was irrelevant in the immediate moment. Instead of questioning him, she blew a sigh in acceptance. "Anyone else know how to play?"

Florence raised her hand.

"Play *well*, Florence?"

She lowered it.

"Alex?"

He shook his head. "Hell no. I've lost way too much money playing that game. I take too many risks."

"I can."

The room turned, stunned at Alfie's offering. There was no way. He was too timid for gambling.

"Surely not," said Alex.

"I *can* play," Alfie urged.

"When do *you* go to casinos?" quizzed Erika. He turned eighteen only eight months ago.

"Not casinos, no way. I play online. Been using the money to save for a car."

"It's true," Florence added. "He's far better than me, anyway."

Alex crossed his arms. "No matter how good he is, how do we ask for a match?"

Leopold glanced behind Alex, and the group turned around, spotting Robert in the corner, still behind the ruby piano as he had been this entire time.

Creepy. Very, very creepy.

"The Collector hosts a party every other Friday to see what wares he can have his associates gamble away," Robert explained. "They are dreadful affairs. Distasteful. Overcrowded. *But* he accepts anyone with a wallet to join his table."

"He won't let you have it," Leopold insisted, dragging the back of his hand over his sweating forehead. "It's been sought after for years. They'll get to it first."

By 'they,' Erika assumed the cultists.

"It won't do much harm for the children to try," said Robert. "Calm yourself, Leopold. Have a little faith."

Leopold's features contorted with reluctance. Yet, he agreed.

The Hunters gathered around to discuss their options. Erika wanted to leave the blade and find Wyatt first, but a warning from Alex made her recognise the importance of this blade. No Hunters would be killed without it. Even without Wyatt, Dad and the others may have been sacrificed at the first opportunity.

All they had to do was attend the party and demand a match against the gambler. Winner takes all: a blade containing the essence of an immortal witch.

There could be only one winner, and that was the young, untested Alfie Mullein.

CHAPTER TWENTY-THREE

Greed is a deadly sin. Be cautious it does not consume you.

Uncited Prophecy.

The Collector resided in a castle-like manor atop a hill twenty minutes north of Leopold's home. The ex-Hunter gave little away, showing the group a few online images from newspaper articles delving into The Collector's generous donations to London's museums. *Fitting*, Erika thought, given his hoarding of Alliance artefacts. The journals were no help. Neither Erika nor Alex's dads had come across the man once in their long careers. Both focused their efforts on the north—the denser hunting ground.

The Morrigan fared similarly, having no mention in either journal, thanks to the Divines. Horizon's Edge, however, proved more substantial with research.

Alfie surrendered one of his books: Gamlen's Guide to Magical Artefacts. Within was a section dedicated to the blade. If the weapon ended a life, the soul became tied to it and could be drawn upon for power for all eternity by the wielder.

At least they knew how it worked, now.

Getting rid of Vivienne's body was the difficult part.

"By the Code, her Divine should be told of her death," Erika decreed, standing over the body. Vivienne was still bound to the chair, slumped forward. Erika had already closed her eyes.

"In the eyes of the Treaty, she is no longer part of a coven for getting involved with the cult," Alex reminded her.

Erika nodded. "I see."

So, she was buried in the garden. A shallow grave until the Divines were told and she could be burned at Stryga. Leopold insisted it be deeper, but he was not the one with a shovel in hand.

Erika showered instantly, scrubbing her hair from the scalp to the tips, harshly rubbing soap into her skin and watching the soil and blood fall to her feet in a puddle of black and brown. The hands were always the most difficult to clean. No matter how long she spent grooming them, she always managed to find a rogue speck beneath the nail bed.

She switched off the waterfall shower and stepped onto the bathmat, naked and cold in the wide, white bathroom, most of it unfilled space apart from the colossal shower behind her, a sink and toilet in one corner, and a free-standing bathtub. To the left were the windows: nothing but blindless glass walls offering everything to onlookers. None passed by, but she still felt seen.

She rolled the Egyptian cotton towel around her torso. Completely white—until it touched her skin. Somehow, the soil of Vivienne's grave still lingered.

She vomited down the toilet and stepped back into the shower.

While they waited for Robert to return with formal clothing, the Hunters milled about the manor. Erika left the twins and Alex to explore, choosing to spend the next few hours of her afternoon in the upstairs lounge. She did not care to flatter Leopold by gawking at his house any further, but she was curious about the locked room upstairs.

Dressed in one of Leopold's spare robes—overpriced midnight silk that was far too big for her—Erika slouched in a beanbag before the daunting walls of glass, a book from Leopold's shallow collection in her lap while Vivienne's words picked at her mind like an axe.

Did you imagine yourself an executioner?

Was that what she volunteered for? Were all her trials to prepare her for what must be done? Did it make her weak to hesitate? Or human?

The beanbag beside her sank. "Hey."

Alex.

"Hi," she replied. Alex's hair was wet, his dark skin glossy with moisture. He'd borrowed another of Leopold's robes; ivory silk that barely reached his knees. Erika tugged her gaze away from the riding material.

Alex craned his neck over the open pages of her book. "What are you reading?"

The Art of Italy. "A cookbook." The shirtless chef on the cover alluded to a *different* kind of art.

"Oh. You cook?"

Did she hell. "Nope."

"Then why—"

"There was nothing else." She slammed the book shut on a page dedicated to puttanesca. "For its size, Leopold's *mansion* doesn't hold much regarding entertainment."

"You could borrow one of Alfie's books."

"And stop him from reading four at once? I wouldn't want to impose."

He laughed lowly. "We can't have that, can we?"

Erika returned to the cookbook, reading the blurb again, analysing every word for the third time. For all its focus on cooking, why were the descriptions so... *suggestive*?

She felt Alex watching her. "What's on your mind?"

She flipped the book. Alex snorted at the cover, but Erika was not in the mood for laughing. "Have you put any thought into what Vivienne said about the Hunters?"

He chewed the inside of his cheek. "A little. It stuck with you?"

"She said I was an executioner."

"You *did* execute her."

"Alex."

"Well, you did."

She frowned at his tone. It cut through her like she was at fault. "I didn't see you volunteering."

"I know, I'm sorry. Looking back, I feel a little... I don't know, ashamed? I should have taken over, but I couldn't."

"Why should you have taken over?"

"So you didn't have to hold that weight. Because what she said to you unsettled me. We didn't sign up to be executioners, yet here we are." He relaxed back into his bean bag. "*But* we don't do these things out of enjoyment. We're not executioners, we're enforcers. We trust that we're doing the right thing by following the Code."

Erika *did* follow the Code. It was not always easy, but it was right. Perhaps the difficulty of the decision proved its righteousness. The Council would approve, as would Dad and Diana. She took no pleasure in blatant execution—not like her grandfather. The Code covered her morality.

"You're right," she croaked. She cleared her throat. "I needed to hear that. The twins wouldn't understand."

He shrugged. A dimple in his left cheek sunk with a ghost of a smile. "They're new to this. You said they're not initiated yet?" Erika shook her head. "Then I guess you've got me if you ever need to talk."

"I'm not into 'talking' that much, if I'm honest."

"Well, if you ever need some company while brooding…" He gestured to himself. "I'm your man."

"Are you, now?"

"I could fill that role, if you'd like."

"I may just take you up on that."

He pulled at a thread on his jumper, delicately looping the wool around his fingers. His hands were large, strong, but possessed a craftsman's care. They'd take care of her. Protect her.

The thought made her look away in shame.

"I'm sorry you're holding that weight," Alex said. "I knew it was coming, and I imagined I'd step in, but when it came down to that decision, I… I just couldn't act. *You* acted."

"Because we had to," she assured.

"Because you had the drive to make that decision. You had the Code, you had Vivienne. You made the best decision you could with the information you had. If I took charge, she'd still be alive because I was reluctant to get my hands dirty." When Erika opened her mouth to protest, he silenced her with broadening, determined eyes. "This is why *you* need to lead us."

She'd left him at Pendle—then backtracked. "Alex, I can't—"

"You can make the hard calls. Better still, you know they're hard. You test the weight and you carry it still."

Because she had to! She wasn't a leader—wasn't Dad or Katia Starling or even Aurelia. She wasn't experienced, heroic, or passionate. There were others better suited.

"I made the wrong call at Pendle," she insisted.

"No. You made the right call. If I packed up my pride, we could have reached Leopold before Vivienne and none of today would have happened." He reached for her hand. She held her breath when their skin touched, the calluses of his craftsmanship igniting her palm. "And like a good leader, you came back for me."

And if she made the *wrong* call? Dad's logic was already screaming at her to reassess their plan. It was too brash—too reliant on an untested Alfie—but what other choice did they have? "I can't do it," she whispered.

"This is my first hunt alone," Alex admitted, releasing her hand. "Without Dad, I mean. I tried once and the old man had to rescue my careless ass. I... lied earlier."

Shit. At least Erika had Dad's instructions on her first. Hell, leading Alex and the twins didn't feel right, but at least she'd been out *once* on her own.

Thank God she had Dad's journal.

Alex's head fell into his hands with a sigh. "I don't know if that makes you look at me any differently. I bet you've been out plenty of times on your—"

"This is my second."

Alex cocked his head. "What?"

She didn't even think when she confessed it. "I lied, too. The day my dad went missing, I completed my first hunt alone. He gave me the location, identified the monster, and sent me into town for a lead. He made all the decisions. He planned it all pretty much down to the kill. I was confident, having Dad's advice, still being instructed by him, I suppose, but now…"

She reeled in her legs, locking her hands around her knees. Dad sent her to Edinburgh then… that was it. She didn't know what the fuck she was doing with this hunt—who could prepare for arcane cults and ancient curses?

Dad could.

Alex rested a hand atop her knee. Her jeans' fabric suddenly tightened. "Now…"

Her eyes trailed Alex's hand, up his muscular arms, and landed on his handsome face. Stubble shadowed his dark, angular jaw and outlined soft lips Erika tore her gaze away from.

She forced a smile. "Now I'm alone, but it's fine. I'm fine."

"You're not alone, Erika. For what it's worth, I've got your back. I'll follow you through this hell because I trust you'll carry us through it."

I could fill that role, if you'd like.

Maybe I'll enjoy it.

Dad's warnings reverberated in her skull. *He'll betray you. He'll change you. He'll—*

The warnings fell silent at Alex's crooked smile. "I know what might cheer you up."

He gave her knee a knowing double tap and led Erika to the scarlet piano bathing in daylight's golden hour. "The red is a bit much for me, but I have no doubt the quality is gorgeous."

A laugh jerked her body as she approached. "Is this where you show me your jazz rendition of Tchaikovsky?"

"You *did* call me a romantic." He winked. "I've played since I was young. Though I only had this echoey, second-hand electric keyboard from a car boot sale. When I was in school, I used to sneak into the music classroom during my lunch breaks to borrow the teacher's piano. He caught me once. I thought he'd go ballistic, but he offered to teach me properly."

"You must have been a prodigy."

He half-laughed. "I'm an amateur, trust me. I usually don't go anywhere without my keyboard, but…" He shrugged with a long sigh and slid onto the leather stool. "I don't know. I guess I'm getting withdrawal symptoms or something."

Effortlessly, his fingers drifted over the keys in a simple but perfect C Major. *Show-off.* "Do you play, too?"

"Violin," Erika croaked. As if she could even say that anymore when the strings dulled, and the spruce gathered dust in the garage.

Alex snorted. "So a nerd, then?"

Erika scoffed. "You gave up your lunch breaks to practice piano."

"*And* eat a couple of KitKats. Music isn't my only love, dear Miss Lupine. Good music, at least."

"The violin *gives* good music. It's not just a 'nerdy' instrument."

He kissed his teeth. "I've never been a string fan, to be honest. Not my cup of tea."

"You just haven't heard someone play it correctly. Done right, the violin is the most versatile instrument there is."

Alex raised a brow. "You should prove me wrong one day, if you're so confident."

"Oh, I am," she replied.

"Then you know what to do, in that case."

Her cheeks tightened. "So call me when you want to be enlightened."

Alex dared to let himself smile. "You *are* a confident one, Erika."

Strong fingers drifted over the keys, releasing a soft melody into the room with loving eyes and a gentle touch. Like summer air, it was warm. Then the tune sprang into action with a string of high notes that danced like spring flowers. Pressure on the keys increased, and the song grew cold, shallow like a looming snow cloud.

Erika concealed her awe behind crossed arms. "Now you're just showing off."

"Am I? I told you: I'm an amateur." He cocked his head innocently.

"Don't act cute. You're *decent*."

"Decent?"

"Now where's that humility gone?"

He chuckled, eyes lighting up as they fixated on her smile. "Now you."

"Oh no. I'm no pianist."

"Nor am I a model but…" He shrugged. "Here we are."

God almighty was he arrogant. Wrong? No. But arrogant? Absolutely.

"Come on," he taunted. "Have a go."

"I don't think I—"

"You can."

He shuffled aside and tapped the empty space on the stool beside him. Before him was a set of sheet music Erika recognised as the intro to Beethoven's *Sonata Pathetique*. She performed a violinist's adaptation for an exam.

"You play the melody. I'll handle the bass notes."

She slid in beside him, her silk hissing against the leather. She said she could have fun if she wished.

So they did. Alex's bass notes were perfect, flowing so effortlessly as if the sound originated from his mindful fingertips. Erika's melody was not so pristine. They were in time but rough, slightly messy as Erika struggled to reach the highest note.

Alex only smiled. "That was good."

Was it? "It needs work."

"Everything does. You know the notes, at least."

"I've played before. I'm just clumsy with it."

"You'll build confidence," Alex encouraged. "Have faith."

He punched her arm in a way that rendered a funny look from Erika, which flushed his skin. He had such high expectations of her.

He thought her a great Hunter before their first meeting—now he anticipated a budding pianist.

She laughed through her nose and shook her head. "How do you stay so positive all the time?"

He shrugged. "I didn't think I was."

"Compared to most of us, you are. Now's not the time for fake modesty, Mr Model."

He huffed a laugh, but his body slouched, dragging his smile down. Darkness flickered in his eyes as he pressed a D flat.

A low sound filled the room.

Before she could think, Erika reached for his hand. "Alex." He released the key. "Are you alright?"

His smile returned. When he raised his hand, his knuckles grazed her palm. The touch didn't seem to bother him. "Of course."

Air hitched in Erika's windpipe. He switched back and forth so quickly as if readjusting a mask. The most shamefully curious parts of her wanted to tug on it to find the truth, but she buried that desire deep down out of respect. She wouldn't want him digging into *her* history—or her heart.

Mostly.

"Ahem."

The two spun. Leopold slouched in the doorway, still in his robe, looking between the Hunters. Erika followed his line of vision and shuffled to the side upon realisation she was leaning into Alex, closer than anticipated.

"You should get ready soon," Leopold said. "I've had Robert leave some clothes for you in separate rooms. Unless you'd prefer to share."

Erika scowled. "We're fine separate, thank you."

"Then hurry along and get dressed. We have two hours before we should leave, and, looking at the state of you both, you'll need every minute to fix yourselves."

CHAPTER TWENTY-FOUR

With lessons learned, blood magic will henceforth be banished from Stryga and beyond. I pray you all do not make the same mistakes as I.

The Last Queen of Stryga, 1851.

Makeup and hair presentable, Erika and Florence stood beside one another before a free-standing mirror, two dresses in each hand.

"You see, the blush is cute, but the black is also sexy."

Alfie groaned through the door.

Erika preferred the blush and, admiring the mesh, beaded sleeves, tapped it with her coat hanger.

"That one."

"But I'll look like a kid."

"You *are* a kid. And it's not childish—it has a plunging neckline your mother would gasp at."

Unsure, Florence set down the dresses on their shared bed for the evening. With only one more spare room, Alex volunteered to take the sofa, leaving Alfie with a room to himself: a reward for volunteering to gamble tonight, Alex claimed

Erika pulled her short, sand dress up over her hips and waist. It was a tricky one to get into for its corseted bodice, but, once on, it became unwavering. The layers of tulle, threaded in warm glitter, were loose and malleable, enabling a quick getaway, while the corset bones and off-the-shoulder straps added delicate luxury to distract wandering eyes.

Florence whirled a commanding hand and Erika spun around to be zipped up. "How do you get over someone?" she asked.

Diana once told Erika that the best way to get over someone was to get under someone else. Of course, that advice didn't work for either of them, and Diana would *murder* Erika for relaying it to her only daughter.

"Why do you ask?" Erika digressed.

"Me and Owen are finished. For real this time." Erika raised a brow. "No, *really*. I think he's with Amy."

Was that why she ran off with Nathaniel? "Isn't she meant to be your best friend?" she asked instead.

Florence nodded. Erika scowled. "Then fuck him. Fuck *her*. People worth keeping around don't treat you like that."

"But what if I don't find someone else? What if Owen was the best guy I could ever get and I ruined it?"

It broke Erika's heart to hear her say those things. Did Florence really think so little of herself? "Flo, you're beautiful. You're kind, funny, sweet, and you took on an arcane without a second thought today. Can Amy do that? Can *Owen* do that?" Flo shook her head. "No. They can't. There's no-one like you, Florence, and that is a good thing."

"Doesn't that make me weird?"

"Everyone's weird. Getting with your best friend's ex is *weird*. Don't waste time thinking about who's going to love you when you haven't even found who *you* are yet."

"You're eighteen, Florence. There's a world waiting for you. You don't need someone weighing you down."

"Did Pete weigh you down?"

Erika shook her head. "Never."

"Then why do you no longer speak to him?"

Erika reached for the quartz around her neck. She held it twice today, feeling only the mineral's biting cold in her palm. "When you become a Hunter, you'll understand."

Before Florence could press further, Erika shook off her feelings and fluffed her hair. "Anyway, getting over a guy? A bottle of wine and nineties romcoms."

"Not *again!*" Florence exclaimed. "You were too into those films."

"It's my new favourite genre, what can I say?" Erika shrugged. "Sometimes all you need is a good laugh and a few tropes."

Florence reached for one of the dress hangers on the bed: the blush tulle piece reminiscent of her old ballerina days. "Promise me wine and nineties romcoms when we get through this."

Erika flashed her cousin a smile. "I'll get the wine.'

The Fiesta was not classy enough for Leopold, so the Hunters crammed into his seven-seater—because *that* screamed wealth. Erika scowled between the twins in the middle seat, Alex with Leopold in the back, while Robert drove.

"Why do you even have a car this big when you live alone?" Erika snapped.

"Don't forget about me, Miss Lupine," Robert reminded her from the front.

"Respectfully, you don't span three seats."

"I play golf," Leopold replied. "Need to put the clubs somewhere."

"A boot, maybe?" Florence replied.

"My dear, if you had Callaways, you'd be careful too. Those clubs are worth more than your life."

Erika pulled a face and focused on forcing her purse closed.

"What on Earth have you got in there?" Alfie wondered.

"Just lady things, you know? Lipstick, perfume, foldable crossbow…"

Florence choked. "You didn't?"

Erika grinned and proved it.

Her cousin giggled. "Amazing."

"You're bringing a weapon to The Collector's house?" Leopold snapped. "Are you looking for an early grave?"

Leopold's eyes ignited. Erika met them with a cold stare. "Do you think I'm going in there unarmed? With these two to protect?"

Leopold shook his head. "If he sees that weapon—"

"If he catches us trying to rob him, which he probably will, a weapon will prove handy," Erika argued. "How many crossbows do you know of that can fold into a purse? He won't suspect it."

Thoughts ticked behind Leopold's eyes. "Leave it in the car."

Erika snorted, squeezing the weapon through her purse. "No chance. This stays with me."

With another disfavouring headshake, Leopold silenced. All afternoon, the ex-Hunter avoided the group, showing his face only to address the evening's plan of action and what to do with Vivienne's body. Tension lingered between them after the tea incident, but given they were now working together, Erika assumed Leopold would be curious to know more about herself and Alex, considering he regarded Dad and Tommy as his 'best friends' for a time.

She had to know more.

"After you sealed The Morrigan—"

"*Don't* say that," Leopold warned her. "Saying her name gifts power for her to rise."

Superstitious nonsense. Alfie thought the same. "Arcanes are powerful, but they can't hear us from hundreds of miles away— especially considering The Morrigan is comatose."

"Shhh!" Leopold smacked his nose with a finger. "I ask you to do one thing and you—!"

"Chill out, mate, or it'll be my name you'll not dare speak," Alex bit. Erika warmed at his defence of her cousin and gave him a grateful nod.

"This witch," said Leopold, "allegedly fed her power through all sorts of demons and blood magic in her youth. Magic like that weakens the Veil, as you well know. *That's* why it's banned. Plenty of these demons beyond the Veil are *thankful* she did that—and that's if they're not bound to her already! Even in her slumber, they serve her because she is what anchors them to this world. If they hear you plotting against or disrespecting their queen…"

Alex laughed. "Demons don't have an excellent track record in their encounters with Hunters. We'll be fine."

Erika bit her cheek. "I'd say the same, but we'd be silly to get cocky."

Alex gawped. "You don't believe this superstitious bullshit, surely?"

"I don't. But we take any precautions necessary. No speaking her name in vain. Agreed?"

Florence nodded quickly, as did Alfie and even Alex. The average demon didn't frighten her, but she'd never underestimate one's desire to crawl through the Veil. They craved the human world as a vampire did blood, as arcanes sought power—as lychans desired a mate.

"What about Aurelia?" Erika went on. "Who is she?"

"An Aura arcane," Robert replied from the driver's seat. Erika blinked at the response, not expecting a word from the butler.

"That's it?" Florence wondered aloud. "Leader of a cult, and she's *just* an Aura."

"Possessing one affinity is growing common," Robert reminded Florence.

"Because the environment is fucked," Alfie explained. "That's right, isn't it?"

The leather of Robert's gloves stretched over contracting knuckles around the steering wheel. "Our world is suffering beneath the weight of a rising climate, squeezing around the globe, forcing magic from its cracks swifter than the melting of the ice caps. You may not care, Miss Mullein, but that is our reality. Arcanes may be weaker than they once were, but you'd be a fool to forget that Auras are powerful affinities, despite their numbers. Especially when harnessed by an intelligent arcane."

"And is she?" Erika quizzed.

"Is she…?"

"An intelligent arcane?"

Robert sighed. Erika shifted to view his eyes in the rear-view mirror but found no luck. The angle of the pathetic shrivel of moonlight betrayed her.

"From what I have heard, Aurelia Hemlock is more emotional than intelligent."

"I suppose passion is what leads a group," Alex figured.

Erika shook her head. 'Only externally. True leaders *have* to be intelligent. She must have something about her."

"She *is* passionate," Robert assured them. "She has been ruined by Treaty loopholes and coven ideals, losing family members to the pandering of vampires and suffering beneath restrictions on magic."

"Restrictions on blood magic," Alfie corrected. "Evil magic."

"Blood magic has its uses, boy," Robert hissed. "You'd be surprised at just how many fall into that trap out of desperation. But I'm not condoning it, know that."

Erika pursed her lips. *His* tone sounded emotional. Personal. Erika glanced at Robert's hands. They were sweating.

She locked eyes with Alfie and subtly shook her head. *Don't be alone with him,* she wanted to say.

"So, Aurelia joined a cult because she hates the system," Florence summarised. "And the cult wants a factory reset."

"That's pretty much it," said Leopold. "I didn't know Aurelia well —not as well as Chris, at least—but she seemed like a typical anti-Treaty activist. Finding out she was a cultist was a bit of a shock, though."

Erika found it strange that Dad would fall for someone described as an *anti-Treaty activist*. "And the cult's goal," she started, "is to bring back their queen to…"

"Revive the time before the coven system," Robert answered. "A return to the monarchy – especially with a monarch so powerful—would topple the contemporary structure and crush the Treaty's value within the arcanes." Which was why the cult called themselves 'witches.'

Take away one card and the house collapses. The other species would soon follow, no doubt, leaving the Hunters without a purpose.

Alex cleared his throat. "We can't let that happen."

"Obviously," said Erika. "If we want to carry on living in relative safety, we need to stop this queen from reviving."

Leopold's gaze slipped to catch a glimpse of the waning gibbous. "And to do that, we need that blade tonight."

Yellow lit Leopold's irises as the twins gasped, a castle panning into view over the hill.

No, not a castle. A *mansion*.

The Collector's mansion.

CHAPTER TWENTY-FIVE

Outside the confines of the Hunters, humanity is not to be made aware of the supernatural. Knowledge of any breaches in this law is to be reported to the Sentinels and issued with punishment. Failure to do so will also end in punishment.

The Hunter's Codex, Chapter IV.

Four towering floors of explosive light and sound ignited the hilltops enough to shame the sun. Music roared, spotlights shot like stars through the night sky, while cars and limousines compacted with ardent party guests orbited the rolling grounds.

Robert nabbed a free parking space atop the grass between a navy BMW and a sleek, black Range Rover. An eager Florence reached for the door, having it slammed back in her face by the Mercedes' passengers as they spilt vivaciously onto the grounds, sprinting and bottlenecking at the grand ebony doors behind them.

The six stepped onto the vibrating tarmac and approached the ivory towers.

Shielding the twins, Erika took the lead, peeling her eyes and ears for any signs of danger. She found a lot of it. Nothing you wouldn't find in your average nightclub, but danger, nonetheless.

Feral sounds broke through the temple-like walls as they ascended the patio.

Florence peeked over Erika's shoulder. "This looks... mad."

"He's held worse gatherings," Leopold replied. "I once attended a full-moon party—" He leaned towards Florence, "—with drunk lychans."

She gulped. "At least it would have been wild."

"Wild," Leopold echoed. "*Feral.* The bridge between humanity and the dark world—the *real* world—is nothing short of feral."

"A bridge?" Alfie quizzed.

"A lot of young Alliance supernaturals, mainly arcanes and lychans, tend to break free from their duties at least once in their lifetime to find freedom among the humans," Erika explained. "Likewise, humans aware of the supernatural will turn to them for a wild time."

Alfie glowered. "And the vampires?"

"They're beasts from the moment they're turned," Alex said with a shudder. "They only find release in feeding."

"But they were people once," Florence argued. "Surely that connects them to us."

Alex huffed. "You'd think."

Erika led the group across the gravel and up the grand patio steps. A partygoer slammed the door shut before them. Erika reached for the vibrating handle while Alfie's breathing grew heavy behind her.

"Are you okay?" Alex asked him.

Alfie wiped his glasses with the sleeve of his tartan blazer. Even in Leopold's second-hand Burberry, he looked like the teenager he was. His sister was a confident young woman elegantly making her debut in the adult supernatural world. He was a child anxious about his school prom.

He swallowed, coughed as he choked, then forced out, "I hated house parties in school. They were always so loud, and messy, and this one looks…" His wide eyes scaled the four floors of madness. "I don't know what's in there."

Erika put a hand on his shoulder. "Alf…"

"Don't think about it," Alex said with a reassuring smile. "You'll be fine. Stick by me if you feel comfortable."

"But the poker game, I—" His feet cemented to the ground. "Oh god, I can't do this."

"Alfie," said Erika, "just take a breath and—"

"I can't do it, Erika! I'm panicking too much. I won't be able to bluff, or read the cards, I—'

"Hey!"

Florence parted Erika and Alex and took her brother by the shoulders. She squeezed the pads in his jacket down, exposing how he drowned in the polyester. Erika opened her mouth to tell her to lay off him, but she only rubbed him gently, comfortingly, staring into his matching emerald eyes.

"You're doing this because you're the most capable. That means you'll succeed. I know you will. Now breathe like Mum tells you to. One. Two. Three. Four…"

He shut his eyes and took a long inhale… then released.

Florence smiled. "You good?"

He nodded, his breathing fast but slowing. "Yeah. Yeah, I'm good. I will be."

"Do you want a minute outside, Alf?" Erika asked. "We'll wait for you."

"Ahem." Leopold coughed. "In case you are forgetting, we are on a schedule. We don't have time to—"

"We'll wait for him," Alex asserted.

"But—"

"We'll *wait*." Erika glowered at Leopold. "Go inside if you wish. We'll find you."

Leopold stammered, looking between each of the Hunters, then to Robert. His butler shrugged. "Bloody children," Leopold spat. He brushed past the group, Robert in his shadow. "If you need me, I'll be at the west-wing bar."

The four that remained sat on the steps in silence for a few minutes, doing their best to ignore the multitude of commotions behind them for Alfie's comfort. Erika accepted the moment to survey the area, instead finding herself laughing at a tanned blonde in a canary two-piece twirling on the grass, already far drunker than her exasperated friends. Alfie spotted it too and chuckled.

He was the first to stand. "I'm ready."

Family behind her, Erika opened the doors to an explosion of wild extravagance she hadn't witnessed in years.

The entrance was an ocean of guests clad in sequins and sparkles, most dressed in their best, some Erika hoped was their worst. Overhead lighting dimmed upon entering the living room, then snapped into a spectrum of cyan and magenta that struck the swaying dancers. It was a living room once, but the sofas and coffee tables had been removed in favour of a vast space for strangers to let loose. The only signs of home were the gaudy fireplace and the Grecian vase of yellow roses atop it.

Alex leaned in close and yelled, "I wonder where this poker game is."

Erika couldn't see the faces of a single dancer. Reading cards was next to impossible. "Certainly not here. Let's find Leopold first."

They pushed through the crowd. Spotting light beneath a door to the right, Erika urged the twins to hug the wall, muttering 'excuse me' and 'sorry' to anyone she bumped shoulders with.

They opened the door, relieved to find the bar, and Leopold propped on a stool, bourbon on the rocks in hand. Erika narrowed her eyes at the glass.

"We're working," she warned.

"We're at a party!" he exclaimed. "Have what you like."

Erika grabbed Florence's hand as she reached for the bar. "We need clear heads."

"Come on, Erika, it's just one drink," Florence whined.

Leopold pointed to Florence. "She gets it."

"I hate saying this, but he's right," said Alex. "We'll blend in more. The two of us just need to make sure we can still drive if things go sour."

Erika sighed. "Fine. One pinot."

Leopold snorted. "It's an open bar."

"Sauvignon Blanc."

The group ordered: Alex a beer, Florence champagne, and Alfie a cider for his nerves. Erika took no more than a sip of her wine.

"The poker room," she said.

Leopold rolled his eyes. "Can you not sit down for one minute?"

"When our families are found and the cultists are dealt with, then I will sit. For now, show us."

Albeit reluctantly, Leopold gestured for them to follow. They re-entered the realm of bright lights and feral dancers, crossing the floor to exit the building out the back.

Glass patio doors led to a whole other world within the party. Green grounds of dispersing guests stretched far, its edges trimmed with rose bushes and pine. Such an open, liberating space found itself enjoyed by guests, particularly the stripped man running naked towards the trees... at eight o'clock.

He wouldn't get far. Beyond the trees, a nine-foot fence surrounded the property, painted white and topped with curling barbed wire. Erika suddenly felt more trapped than anything else in the open air.

Robert watched her staring.

"The Collector's possessions are of high value," he said. "Security is his topmost priority."

Erika grimaced. "And yet he invites hundreds of strangers into his home."

Leopold shrugged. "He's a gambler. What do you expect?"

The poker room separated itself from the house in a hexagonal conservatory in the centre of the garden, the walls glass to allow for more onlookers, Leopold explained. Gamblers stared as the group entered. They were too young to be there. Even with some being of a similar age to Erika and Alex, they were still too young, naïve, new to the trade. Erika was lost, entirely reliant on Alfie's skill for this to go well. Her only use tonight was the group protector.

So, she maintained that role, keeping her head held high as they waded through the crowd, realising just how haphazard this plan was.

But with time ticking on, they had no other choice.

Leopold paid to deal Alfie into the game, who stretched his fingers. "I've got this. I've got this. I've—"

"Leopold Hopkins, is that you?"

Leopold stiffened, almost grimacing. His face twisted and contorted into a counterfeit smile as the rest of the group spun to find the source of the voice.

"Mr Collector, sir! Pleasure to see you again."

His low, clear laugh rumbled through Erika's body. "I wish I could say the same."

The Collector's smile was enough to make Florence, and even Erika, blush. "And who might these be?"

In Erika's imagination, The Collector was an old man. A dull, old man thriving off the company and culture of others to fill his lonely void, but he was not that at all. He was far younger, perhaps early-to-mid thirties, and significantly more attractive with his groomed, golden hair, sunset tan, and pearly, perfect smile. His suit was Brioni; his martini the only dirty thing about him.

Leopold draped an arm over Alfie's shoulder. "This here, is Alfie Mullein. He's entering the game tonight."

The Collector snorted, the action revealing a pair of dimples flanking his smirk. "Good luck, son. This is for high stakes, you know?"

Alfie nodded. "I know."

The Collector raised an eyebrow. "Do you? Then I wish you well, Mr Mullein."

Erika held her stare as The Collector sipped his martini, meeting her eyes over the rim of the glass.

"And what of you, angel? Do tell me your name."

The twinkle in his eyes made her swallow. "Erika."

"Erika…?"

She glanced at Leopold, who nodded for her to respond. "Erika Lupine."

The Collector threw his head back and whistled out a laugh. "Lupine? That's a *big* Hunter name. How is it carrying that weight around?"

She shrugged at the jovial tone. "I can manage."

Another flash of white between his lips. "I'm sure you can."

Erika was not the type of woman to succumb to a handsome face, but The Collector drew her in. His stare was intoxicating—and not in a good way.

"You know," said The Collector, "a Hunter with a name like yours would appreciate some of the artefacts I have on show upstairs."

Damn right she would. "What kind of artefacts?"

"*Many* artefacts. I don't want to give too much away, but I have buyers from across *all* factions drooling over my collection, *gagging* for a private tour."

Diana's voice chanted in Erika's mind, telling her to play along. "Do your tours run into the evening?"

Alex nudged her from behind while The Collector smiled. "They run all night long, if that is what you wish."

She ignored Alfie's mortified look. "I am actually leaving Chelsea tomorrow."

"Then it's a good thing I'm here all night, so long as you are."

Looking up between her lashes, Erika gave her best closed-lip smile.

Leopold coughed.

"Accompanying us is Alex Arwood and Florence Mullein—Alfie's sister."

"A pleasure." The Collector shot the others a polite smile. Florence turned cherry-red while Alex forced every muscle in his face to smile back.

The Collector whistled a sigh. "It truly has been a delight to see you, Leopold, but I really must—Who is *that?*"

Robert blinked. He kept silent during the conversation, hiding in Alex's shadow. "I am Robert, sir."

"You're a little old to be in this group. Even for Leopold." The Collector floated towards the butler. "Who are you?"

"My… my butler," Leopold croaked. The Collector cackled.

"A *butler?* Can you not wipe your own arse anymore?"

Erika met Florence's wide eyes as she fought to contain a laugh, then looked to Leopold, who didn't find it so amusing. They had to keep The Collector sweet for now so the ex-Hunter showed no signs of retaliation, and Leopold took the disrespect like an obedient dog.

As if to save some shred of dignity, he replied, "It's nice to have some help at the manor. You have your own, right?"

"Five maids, four gardeners, two chefs, and a chauffeur—to be exact." He winked at Erika. *So arrogant.* Alex groaned behind her.

"See," said Leopold. "It's perfectly normal."

"Oh, but you don't really need the help, do you?" He swaggered towards Leopold and leaned in close. "All that money, all that empty space in that glass box you call a home… and no-one to share it with. So, you pay someone to be your friend."

Erika and Alex shared a weighted look.

Leopold stuttered. "That's not what I—"

"You can argue all you want, Hopkins." The Collector backed away, his spine straight and posture perfect. "I know what you are. You're a loner. A nobody in a world of somebodies." He outstretched his arms, gesturing to his wild kingdom. "You don't belong here, and you know it. This world is entirely different to any other. You are either born into greatness or you take it, and if you're not willing to do the latter, you can be left to the dogs."

He sighed at his empty glass. "I should make the rounds. See you soon, Erika." He winked. "And I'll see you at the match, little Mullein."

Even at the opposite end of the conservatory, The Collector was still the biggest person in the room.

"What a dick," Alfie hissed.

"Can we just talk about how you were acting?" Florence began. *"Do your tours run in the evening?* Talk about making it obvious!"

"He's far too slick," Alex added. "And the way he was looking at you like you're a bloody meal he just—" He shook his head, clenching his jaw. His coolness evaporated. "He's shady! Why would you—"

"Chill out, both of you!"

Erika froze as the bouncers guarding the conservatory tuned in to listen. She smiled to avert suspicion and signalled for the group to come closer.

"I saw an opportunity and I took it. If Alfie fails at winning this artefact, I may be able to get it instead."

"Are you deluded?" Leopold spat. "You can't steal from—"

"Shush! Do you want to get us thrown out?" Erika snapped.

His features darkened. "Oh, he won't throw us out. He'll keep us in this maze of a house till we're begging to leave, one way or another."

Florence blinked. "That wasn't ominous at all."

Erika motioned for the group to step back into a less-conspicuous stance. "So, we're all in agreement? I step in if things go south." It looked like she didn't trust Alfie to win. The truth was, she didn't trust *anyone*. Alfie was too nervous, The Collector too slick—even Robert was too quiet.

She was more experienced than the others. She needed to catch them if they fell.

Alex groaned. "This is too risky for my liking. You, alone with him, is dangerous. We won't be able to reach you if you need help."

Erika laughed. "I've managed just fine without you for years, Alex. I'll cope alone."

Alex chewed his lip. "Fine. Since you're in charge and all."

She frowned. "What's that—"

"Erika's right," Alfie interrupted her. "Even if she doesn't get the artefact, she can pinpoint its location. Having a backup plan never hurt anyone."

"Thank you!" She sighed.

"Just be careful," Leopold warned. "He may look charming, but The Collector will skin us alive if he catches us disrespecting him in his own home."

She dealt with 'charming' men often. "I will."

Glasses clinked, signalling silence across the conservatory. The Collector stood at the head of the poker table, a fresh martini in hand.

"If you haven't yet paid your way in, you've lost your chance. All players, take your seats."

Alfie's glasses frosted and he froze to the spot.

In school, he was an outcast. He dedicated his life to reading, studying, and playing video games by himself. He was content with that.

Tonight, he had to grow up. As far as Erika knew, the kid hadn't ever seen so many people in one place before. His hands trembled, sweat beaded and trickled down his forehead. These people were older, more experienced, and well-versed in the tactics of one another. They knew each other's strengths and weaknesses, but nothing of the eighteen-year-old stranger making his debut against the best of the best. *This* was his advantage, and he would exploit that with everything he had.

He was still a child. He was still an outcast. But with his school textbooks, he read journals. Hunter's journals.

Deep down, Alfie Mullein was a supernatural Hunter. And tonight, everyone would see that.

CHAPTER TWENTY-SIX

Supernaturals are intoxicating. To be in the presence of one as a human is thrilling. To accompany many is euphoric.

Freddie Mullein's Journal (unfinished).

Texas Holdem. Basic. Simple for Alfie to play under stress—which was a good job.

The first two rounds breezed by with fortunate hands: four queens then a straight flush, knocking out two other players with poor cards and even poorer bluffing skills. They were better than most of his online opponents, he realised, but not good enough to lie their way out of a bad hand. He had been lucky so far. This would not last.

He knew his own tells well. He scratched the back of his neck with every bluff. So far, he had not done so, and he was conscious not to reveal himself when the time came, but, as Andy always said, the impulse was too much for him. That tell always gave his friend the upper hand back home. He hoped no-one at the table would catch this and exploit it throughout the game.

Andy *always* caught it.

"You're doing well for a child, Mullein," said The Collector.

This was the first time he'd addressed Alfie directly during the game. "I… thank you."

The sound of cards sliding across the table always relaxed Alfie. He picked up his dealt hand and dared to look at The Collector, who smiled.

"You remind me of myself when I was your age. My father had me play for hours every Thursday evening until I mastered it. Do you know what it meant to master it?"

Alfie shook his head.

"I had to beat *him*. *He* was the master. Did your father teach you?"

He looked at his hand: four of hearts and three of clubs. Not great. "Sometimes."

"Afterwards, I'll teach you a few tricks my old man taught me. How about that?"

He remembered what Leopold said about The Collector's charm and reminded himself not to be naïve. The man knew how to play him already, but he followed Erika's example.

"I'm always willing to learn more," he replied.

The Collector approved his answer, and the reaction gave Alfie an idea.

Already, The Collector held a pre-conceived notion that Alfie was shy—even gullible. He was, in part, those things, but being in the box The Collector put him in gave room for defying expectations. He pretended to be submissive and gained The Collector's approval because he thought he could control him. If he revealed his tells, just subtly, and used them as a weapon to confuse The Collector, maybe he had a shot at winning this.

First of all, he had to *prove* he was naïve without costing himself the game.

"Mr Mullein," said the dealer. "Your bet?"

It was a risk, but he scratched the back of his neck. "I raise."

Alfie astounded Erika. His focus matched only that of study season—even when he made a sloppy raise that handed a dozen chips to a sympathetic Collector. Alex and Leopold flanked him the entire time, but he did not once turn to ask for advice. He knew what he was doing, which was why Alex encouraged Erika and Florence to explore the party.

She warned her cousin to stay close, ignoring her grins at the prospect of meeting her future lychan lover in the smoke and lights, as if they turned into fluffy Alsatians and not raging monsters during a particular time of the month. Florence giggled and twirled upon reaching the edge of the crowd on the west side of the dancefloor.

Her joy faltered when they stepped into the next room, where she thought the VIP lounge would be.

Somehow, this room was darker than the last. Nothing but an overhead red light offered guidance against the pillars marking the four corners. This was a private, converted theatre, where audience seating was now a dancefloor, ripe with feral couples thrusting against one another to the rhythm of hypnotic music.

Erika raised a hand to stop an overzealous young man, no older than Alfie, from falling into her, too drunk to stand.

She pulled it back to warmth and wetness.

Blood. Fresh blood.

Fangs glistened in seductive scarlet within an ocean of ecstatic, smiling vampires. They swayed and danced with victims just as frenzied as themselves and gorged on their necks. Bile stung Erika's throat and Florence held her arm.

"Are they—?"

"Vampires." Erika nodded. "Yes."

Florence's jaw trembled. "They're just… they're just—" The silhouette of her shoulders lifted and fell rapidly. "Can we go back? Please."

Erika put a hand on her back and shielded her, guiding her to the exit. She was just as eager to get out.

As she turned, a figure captured her attention. A vampire, veiled in platinum hair reaching his waist, leaned over a balcony on the third floor, overlooking the chaos beneath him, eyes red at the sight of the sinister dance.

He smiled from his perch as he caught sight of Erika, who ushered her cousin from the room.

Florence walked into a bouncer. "You two vampires?" he boomed.

Erika guarded Florence. "Human. We were just leaving."

"That's alright, ladies," he excused. "I'm just stationed here to enforce the feeding. You're both safe to go."

Erika frowned. "Enforce?" There was nothing 'enforced' about this.

"Yeah. No killing, no unwilling hosts, and no newbie vampires."

"Why's that?" Florence wondered.

He almost laughed. "Let's just say the young ones get a little too enthusiastic about the feeding room. Even just the sight of blood turns them feral, so we keep them away from here. Keeps the hosts safe."

Florence's brows arched. "This isn't feral?"

Erika had seen 'newbie vampires' in action. There was a reason Hunters nicknamed them 'Ferals.'

The bouncer shrugged "Part of The Collector's policy. He caters to *all* his guests." He scowled and pointed at the crowd. "You! Get off her!"

The bouncer charged at a vampire with his fangs two inches deep into a screaming girl's neck. She clawed until the bouncer shoved her assailant back into the crowd, leaving him to be dealt with by the more dominant members of his kind, who pushed him to the floor, baring their fangs in warning. Erika glanced up at the balcony, the blonde vampire nowhere to be seen.

Other vampires tutted at the crying girl being escorted out by the bouncer.

"Always someone spoiling the fun," one muttered.

"Some just *have* to take it too far."

Florence rubbed her eyes. Erika wrapped an arm around her. "Let's go."

She looked back as they reached the doorway, witnessing a flash of platinum sink into the sea of bodies as the assailant vampire's pleas reverberated over the eclectic melody.

They stopped. But the dance carried on.

Florence shook like a leaf, even when they reached the garden, silent as a mouse. She took one long breath. Then another.

"That scared you," said Erika.

She nodded, lips quivering. "I've always known what vampires are, but that..." She pointed back at the door, through the thrusting bodies, through the theatre. Her body jerked as she reigned in a sob. "That was horrible."

It was common knowledge of what vampires drank to stay alive— even to humans who believed them only horror stories or fictional love interests. In Erika's few years as a Hunter, she'd come across many who pushed the boundaries of the laws allowing them to feed.

"Not to rub it in," she said, "but what did you expect?"

Florence shrugged, hugging her body. "I don't know. Something tamer, at least. I thought they'd be reluctant."

"They're wild, Florence. They always have been and always will be. Especially the younger ones."

With a sniffle, she threw her arms over Erika and squeezed. "Sorry," she said, stepping back just as fast. "I needed that."

She gave Florence's shoulder a comforting clench. "I know."

Florence glanced beyond Erika to the glass double doors and hushed her voice. "Who was that man on the balcony? He was watching you."

"You noticed him too?" Florence nodded. "I don't know. I saw him leave to intervene with the young vampire. Maybe that's his Master."

"Like the arcanes' Divines?"

"Sort of. The Masters are more relaxed than Divines in enforcing the Treaty."

"In what sense?"

In all kinds of senses. "Vampires are simply told not to expose themselves to humanity. If they stick to that rule, they can roam free, feeding as they wish so long as humans don't turn up dead, but accidents happen."

Florence gawked. "Sorry? 'Accidents happen?'"

"The Treaty accounts for one-off accidental deaths. They're especially lenient towards new vampires since their urges are so strong. Arcanes, on the other hand, are far stricter. Any defilement is cause for instant exile. Or execution."

Florence put a hand over her mouth, pushing a finger against her lip in thought. "I didn't realise. But does that mean the Divines might help us if the cult is using blood magic?"

The Havens of the Alliance factions were kept secret from outsiders. Only the Council had access to the Divines' Haven, and making the trek to Oblivion's Watch to contact Stryga was far too time-consuming to undertake. Calling them was out of the question. One of the few things Supernatural leaders could agree on was humanity's desperate need for surveillance.

"They might," Erika answered. "But we don't have the time for that. If we're desperate, it's an option."

An indoor crash startled them into running for the doorway. The girl in yellow from the front drive stumbled towards the fireplace, knocking over the Grecian vase, shattering it. Yellow roses crumpled under the trampling dancers.

"Oops!" she exclaimed. A red-haired boy grabbed her by the arm and escorted her to the sofa, clearly exhausted by her.

"I hope The Collector doesn't mind losing a vase," said Florence.

Erika shrugged. "I'm sure he can afford another one."

Her eyes skimmed the garden, squinting at the conservatory. Alfie was still in the game, Alex leaning over him, glaring protectively at the other players while Leopold and Robert shadowed them. The sight made Erika shiver.

"Florence?"

Erika whirred at the scent of pine to meet a teenager: a blonde, green-eyed, tall teenager. Florence's ideal type.

Florence's ideal type.

Without thinking, she pointed. "Pendle Hill."

He didn't move but Florence nodded. "Nathaniel."

He flinched beneath Erika's scowl. *Good.* "I—I'm sorry, I don't think we've met. You're…"

"My cousin. Erika," said Florence. "Nathaniel, what are you doing here? You said you were going to Chelsea, but *here*?"

The odds of Florence stumbling upon him again were next to none.

Erika raised her chin and crossed both arms, brushing her fingers on the lock on her bag where her crossbow lay in wait.

Nathaniel took a half step back, then sighed. "Honestly, the reason I approached you in that hotel… The reason I was there, I… Although I didn't mean anything bad by it, was I… I—"

Oh, fucking hell. "You, you…?" Erika pushed.

"I know you're all Hunters. It was obvious. No-one normal stops at hotels as shady as *that one.*"

Florence tilted her head. "You approached me because I'm a Hunter?"

Uninitiated. That meant he saw the car. "Yes. I know it looks bad, but I've had a hell of a journey on the road, and I didn't dare to trust anyone."

"Why tell us now?" Erika wondered. "You don't know us."

He swallowed. "Because I'm desperate. Benjamin Patrick, my dad, was taken by the cult."

Erika flicked a brow. She was not aware of a 'Benjamin Patrick' nor a Nathaniel of the same surname, but, then again, she knew only a few names of the Hunters involved. Tommy Arwood, Leopold Hopkins, Wyatt Martin, and Katia Stirling were the known examples.

"You know about them?" asked Florence, astonished.

"My dad talked about his past. A lot. Even when he wasn't supposed to." He touched the back of his neck. "I saw the big, bald arcane take him from our home and knew instantly what was happening."

The big bald arcane. Felix.

Still, Erika frowned. "If you knew we were Hunters, why not speak to us at the hotel?"

He exhaled a bitter laugh. "My dad had been kidnapped *two days* earlier. Do you really think I'm going to trust a stranger?"

"Alright," Erika admitted. "Then why abandon the hotel when it was haunted?"

"I said I knew *you* were Hunters. I never said I was."

"But your dad—"

"Is a Hunter, yes, but I've never wanted this life. I finished school, I started university just last month. A normal person learns there are ghosts in their hotel and they run. I'm sorry I didn't stay to help, but I saw the weapons you kept in your car." Erika should have known he was there, watching her, watching all of them. "You seemed perfectly capable of handling it yourselves."

Florence's eyes met the floor. "But... at the bench—"

"I know, I know. I heard hassle and snuck off to investigate. I left you there because, well, because I thought you were safer there than with the rest of them at the pool."

He was right, Erika realised, but wrong for abandoning her in the dark. "Don't go into the west wing of this floor," Erika warned him. "And be careful."

Florence grabbed her wrist as Erika bypassed Nathaniel. "Where are you going?"

"*We* are going to check on your brother. Come on."

"I didn't like it in there," Florence admitted. "I don't want to go back in."

Erika sighed. She hadn't mentioned this before, but she did look uncomfortable. "I can't leave you. It's not safe."

"I'll wait at the bar," she said. "Nathaniel could stay with me... if you wouldn't mind?"

A small smile played on his lips. "Of course."

No. Way.

"Florence, you don't know him. He only *just* told you he's been lying."

"And for good reason. He's just as cautious as us. That's a good tribute."

"A good *attribute*. And he's still a stranger. No offence."

Nathaniel shrugged. Florence pulled her cousin in closer, out of earshot.

"I'm giving you a chance here," she whispered. "The Collector wants to give you a tour. He won't do that with me in your shadow, and I don't want to stand awkwardly with all the gamblers in there. They make me uncomfortable."

"You'll be with Alex and Alfie out there."

"They're busy," Florence argued. "Even if they take a break, I'll be left out. I'll be fine, I promise. I can take care of a teenage boy if I have to."

Erika glanced over her cousin's shoulder and assessed Nathaniel. He appeared innocent enough, but no-one could ever be completely trusted—especially on the first meeting. He had some build about him but, in the fight against Vivienne, Florence proved herself to be strong enough to face an enemy alone.

When she'd ensured no-one was looking, she slipped an arrow from her purse into Florence's palm.

"Keep it hidden and stay safe. Think twice before doing anything stupid. I'll try and make this tour as fast as possible."

"Not too fast." She winked. "A woman needs time to work."

"Florence!"

"Joking, I'm joking! I'll be good. Now go be sexy." She pushed Erika towards the conservatory and laughed. "And… be careful."

Erika confirmed with a nod and headed inside. She fluffed up her curls and applied a fresh sheen of sparkling champagne lip gloss. She reached for the door handle and the conservatory's light ignited her smile in the most radiant of glows.

Radiant enough to make The Collector's thoughtful lips turn in the most sinister, knowing smile.

CHAPTER TWENTY-SEVEN

Hunters are proof that humanity is a force to be reckoned with. Reinforce this, but never forget it—ever.

Philip Lupine's Journal, Second Edition.

Four remained in the game when Erika returned: The Collector, an elderly woman with purple glasses, a blue-haired man in his thirties sucking on a cigarette, and Alfie. The air turned thicker, warmer, carrying with it nicotine, spilled, sweet cocktails, and wine.

The boys had their backs to her, facing the table, but The Collector spotted her figure at the door and aimed a crooked, seductive smile her way. Alex looked over his shoulder to identify The Collector's interest and blocked his line of sight to approach Erika first.

"Erika." He almost sighed out her name. "Everything okay in there? Where's Florence?"

"She's fine, I'm fine. I'll explain later."

Telling Alex that she planned on wooing The Collector into revealing the location of Horizon's Edge did not seem appropriate to announce ten feet away from the man himself.

"How's Alfie?" she asked.

"Well," Leopold butted in. "Very well. To be frank, I'm actually quite impressed."

Alfie rumbled his throat and the group turned. All eyes fell on the youngest player commanding the room. "I want to raise the stakes."

The room rearranged itself as onlookers exchanged whispers.

Alex leaned into Erika. "Medium or well done?"

She elbowed him in the gut.

The Collector chuckled at Alfie's gall and threw one arm over the back of his chair. "You want to raise the stakes?" He cocked his head. "To what? What do you desire, young man?"

He took a deep breath, harnessing every ounce of his courage to announce, "I want Horizon's Edge."

The conservatory gasped.

This was too brave. Too much.

From her spot, Erika surveyed the room for any cultists after the artefact themselves. She found none. None that she recognised, anyway.

Her gaze fell back on The Collector.

His smile faded.

"*You*... come into my home. You drink my refreshments, sit at *my* table, play *my* game, and demand one of the most precious supernatural artefacts to ever grace the Earth? You *dare* to think I would risk a piece that took me *years* to acquire? That I would risk it all for a silly little game?"

Alfie closed his eyes and stiffened. His shoulders rose, stilling at the height of his jaw.

They fell with his exhale. "I do."

Every head in the room angled towards The Collector. Erika's hand touched her purse, eyes on the bouncers closing in.

The Collector snorted. "You've got balls, kid. I'll give you that."

Silence broke into polite laughter. The bouncers stopped in their tracks.

Erika let her hands fall to her side, feeling faint.

"The only problem is," The Collector continued, "you need to match my bet."

Alfie frowned. "This is poker. I raise if I want to raise."

"You raise if I say you raise!"

The Collector's chair dragged back against the wood and the room jolted. He forced a laugh to settle his audience and lowered himself into his seat.

He sipped his martini. "I'll gamble Horizon's Edge if you put forward something just as valuable."

Alfie held his breath because they had nothing. Nothing The Collector wanted, anyway. All they had were the clothes on their backs and a boot full of weapons and old journals.

Erika looked to Leopold. He had more than them. Their success tonight would save his life, too.

"Well, little Mullein," teased The Collector. "What will it be?" He swung back on his chair and grinned a feline smile. "Will. You. Raise?"

"What do you want?" Alfie asked.

He targeted Erika with his smile. "I don't suppose your cousin is up for a gamble or two?"

The crowd whistled.

He liked her impertinence, so long as it stayed behind a line. "You forget my skillset. Talking to me like that is a gamble in itself."

The crowd shuddered. Meanwhile, The Collector hid his grin like a blushing schoolboy. Poor manipulation from him. It was hard for a thirty-something-year-old man to act innocent.

"I like you. I mean no disrespect, angel, I hope you know that."

"I don't," she said plainly.

He ran a tongue over exposed, perfect teeth. "Then I shall apologise to you in due course."

Alex turned rigid beside her and touched the crook of her arm. She flinched at the gentle fingertips on her bare skin.

The Collector exhaled an awkward laugh. "Look, I don't know you, boy. I don't know what you have that I could want."

"What about a crossbow?"

Erika's neck yanked towards Leopold.

The Collector was almost in hysterics.

"A crossbow? Oh, Leopold, you really are funny! What could I possibly want with a crossbow beyond the satisfaction of shooting you between the eyes?"

Leopold ignored the insult. "It's a prototype. One of a kind, designed by Gamlen."

Gamlen? The author of Alfie's book?

The Collector pursed his lips. "Go on."

Leopold shot Erika a look and nodded at the poker table. "Erika, your crossbow."

"No."

The boys took it in turn to frown at Erika. They were close to the dagger, now, but that crossbow was more valuable to her than anything else she owned. It came only second to the clear quartz hanging from her neck.

"No," she said again. "We never discussed this."

"Something the matter, Miss Lupine?" The Collector taunted.

"Erika, we need this," Alex pleaded. He thumbed the part of her arm he'd been holding. "We can get you a new crossbow."

"I don't even know who 'Gamlen' is. I can't ask for a new crossbow *exactly* like this."

"He destroyed the plans," said Leopold. "It would be impossible to get one."

Leopold was doing a *remarkable* job of convincing her to hand over the greatest weapon—the greatest *gift*—she'd ever received in her hunting career. She looked at her purse where the weapon lay. What about this crossbow made it so special to anyone besides sentimentality? It was a solid weapon, sure, and the swiftest little thing to reload, but how great could a crossbow really be?

One of a kind.

That was enough to make The Collector crave it like a magpie with silver.

Erika opened her purse as a courtesy and unfolded the weapon to a crowd of *'oohs.'* Perhaps the mechanism was what made it so unique.

Even The Collector seemed impressed. "It's so small."

Erika stroked the ebony edges. "I've taken this thing everywhere with me for the past five years."

"It's a weapon," Alex said bluntly. "I know it hurts to part with it but if we lose, it can be replaced."

She shook her head. "No, it can't."

But neither could her father. He needed Horizon's Edge more than she needed her crossbow. She acquiesced the weapon. Leopold handed it to The Collector without a second thought.

Alex's hand slid down her arm to hold her by the wrist. The limb might as well have been floating beside her because she could no longer feel it.

The Collector turned it over in his grasp. His money-hungry, greedy grasp. Erika's fingers twitched as he reached for the trigger.

"Extraordinary. Marvellous. Exquisite... I'll take it!"

"You'll *gamble* for it," Alex corrected.

"Yeah, yeah, of course," The Collector replied, setting down the weapon in the centre of the table, knocking over piles of chips. With the tone he used, Erika gathered he did not plan on losing.

"So, we have a deal?" said Alfie. "You'll bet on Horizon's Edge, and we gamble Erika's crossbow."

He smiled. Not the charming, pearly smile he gave Erika outside, but a devilish grin. Feline. Crafty. Like this deal was doing him a favour. "Of course."

He sipped the final dregs of his martini and straightened his jacket. His eyes fell on the two remaining players beside himself and Alfie.

"Look at us go, Mullein. It's almost as if the boring ones are no longer here." He looked over the rim of his glass. "They might as well leave."

When the players remained still, The Collector cleared his throat. The bouncers took a single step forward and the players left without haste, abandoning their winnings and any remaining chances.

The Collector chuckled and brought himself to his feet. "We'll recess before continuing."

He abandoned the table and chatter commenced. Immediately he spun to discuss something with security, pointing at the blue-haired poker player.

Alfie rose and rushed to Erika, knocking his chair into the one behind. "I am so sorry, Erika, I didn't know he was going to do that."

"I just gave you a shot at winning the blade!" Leopold spat. "Don't be ungrateful."

"I had it under control!"

"And what were you going to bet on? My Burberry? He'd use that to wash the windows."

"Anything but the crossbow would have been nice!" Alfie cried. "It means a lot to Erika."

He was there when Diana gifted her that crossbow. He was so in awe of the weapon that he did not dare to even touch it. On Boxing Day, he argued with Florence for opening and closing it over and over, telling her she would break it.

"It's alright, Alf," Erika assured, albeit begrudgingly. "I know it's not *your* fault."

Leopold scowled. "You Lupines are spoilt shits, you know that?"

Among all of Leopold's riches and material possessions, evidently, he did not understand sentimentality.

Alex nodded to the glass doors and nudged Erika's arm. "Can I talk to you outside?"

Beyond his shoulders, Erika spotted The Collector hounded by a swarm of young women. They kept their heads tilted towards him the same way Erika did in his presence, their lips pursed, backs slightly arched. The Hunters had to keep an eye on him to ensure the game was not rigged in some way, but she could spare a single moment for Alex.

"Sure. Alfie, watch *him*."

A curtain of platinum swung by as they stepped through the doorway. Erika followed the locks to meet the pale, angular face of the vampire she and Florence saw at the theatre. He appeared young, only years older than Erika, but carried himself with the wisdom of a hundred years and the burden of bloodlust. He smiled in acknowledgement and made a beeline for Leopold, guiding him away from Alfie's ears. Youthful vampires flanked him, licking their lips, hungry gazes locked on Erika and Alex.

She made a note to ask Leopold about this when they left the party—when she quizzed him on Gamlen.

Erika crossed her arms, hiding the goosebumps running down them as they strode away from the conservatory's heat. She needed air a moment ago, but the late-night breeze sent November's chill beneath her dress, into her heart.

Without asking, Alex shrugged off his jacket and hung it over her naked shoulders. He rubbed the arms twice before letting go, giving her warmth.

"Thanks." She forced a laugh. "Picked a bad dress for today."

"No, you did not."

Oh? Erika raised a brow and Alex swallowed, looking away sheepishly. At the silence, the two of them laughed.

"I'm just saying it suits you. You look good in gold."

She let herself smile. "It's champagne but—" She shrugged, "—thank you."

"No, it's gold. I see you as gold, anyway."

Her smile faltered and she stared back at his solid gaze. Reflections twinkled in his eyes: stars in the black sea of space.

Goosebumps submerged her.

"The dress," he corrected. "I meant the dress."

Her smile broadened. Then she remembered why they came out here. "You wanted to talk."

His throat bobbed. The stars in his eyes shrank to blackness. "I know what you're thinking. Don't do it."

"Alex—"

"Please. I don't like the thought of you alone with him."

"I can handle men like him."

"There are no men like him." Tension released in a sigh. He wet his lips. "Look, I think Leopold talks out of his arse more than anyone else, but you saw his face when The Collector spoke to him. You saw *everyone's* faces when he snapped. Everyone here is scared of him, Erika. Why aren't you?"

She frowned, then forced a nervous laugh. These were civilians, not Hunters. Not Lupines. She took out a *wendigo* alone, for Christ's sake! No-one else here could say that. "These people aren't me."

"They aren't. But this is his battleground. His game. For all you know, he has a maze upstairs and he's ready to toss you in it."

"All mazes have an exit, Alex. I'll find it."

He fell back on his heels and dragged both hands down his face, groaning.

Erika snapped, "If you don't think I can handle it, say so."

His eyes widened. "I know you can handle whatever he throws at you. I just don't *want* him to throw anything at you, if you get what I mean."

He was being protective. It was not his right. She fought wendigos, lychans, ghosts, and ghouls. What was a man compared to a monster?

"Thirty minutes," she said. "Give me thirty minutes before you come looking."

"That's thirty minutes too long."

"*Alex.*"

Any sooner and he could ruin the rapport she built with The Collector. Or worse, blow her cover and get them all killed.

Hesitantly, he nodded. "Thirty minutes."

The conservatory doors opened and Erika found herself smiling fictitiously at The Collector's swaggering posture.

"Erika, angel! How about that tour?"

Alex rotated to be at her side, his hand loosely on her arm covered by his jacket. He leaned in close.

His words stroked her ears. "If he tries anything, my blade goes through his skull."

Erika glanced at the gauntlet visible only a millimetre above his cuffs and fought a smile. She wondered how he would have reacted if his hidden blade had been offered up as leverage instead of her crossbow.

She offered a crooked arm for The Collector to lead the way. "I'm keen," she said.

He liked that. Alex did not.

The Collector locked eyes with Alex as he brushed the jacket from Erika's shoulders. He caught it with two fingers and swung it out for Alex to snatch away.

"She won't be needing this. Thank you for keeping her warm for me."

For me. Everything was for him. His entitlement tied Erika's stomach in a thousand knots. She took a breath to release them.

Alex clenched his right fist, but no blade emerged from his sleeve. Not yet, anyway.

The Collector all but stole her from Alex with a single touch on her back and left him alone on the lawn. Erika engaged in pleasantries with the gambler but ensured she caught one last look at her companion before turning a corner and stepping into The Collector's eclectic jungle.

Prosecco exploded when she laughed into her glass.

Florence clamped a hand over her mouth. She kept her cool until Nathaniel started googling cereal box jokes to pass the time. They were all terrible, but each joke grew funnier with every sip of wine following a huff of laughter. Now, she turned pinker than her blush dress.

"Oh my God," she said through her fingers. "I am so sorry."

She reached for the rosé prosecco she'd spat on Nathaniel's shirt and started to wipe. As past house parties taught her, she was awful at hiding wine stains.

"Florence, I think you're—"

"Just hold on a second." She bit her tongue, continuing to rub his chest with her sleeve, and the ridges beneath the cotton. It was cheaply made and left very little to the imagination.

The stain wouldn't budge. "I think I'm... actually making it worse. I'll stop."

"No, please." Nathaniel smiled when she stopped rubbing. "Continue."

Florence glanced up to meet his eyes and froze at the vortex of colour. The earthy browns, vibrant greens—even flecks of lilac winked in the chandelier's light.

She gulped. She always did this. She could initiate conversation, flirt, keep someone's interest, but when that intrigue triggered something inside of her, she turned awkward, unsure.

Recalling why she was on the road in the first place, she thought perhaps they would be better suited as friends.

For now.

His groomed brows furrowed. "You have some... uh... I'll get it."

What is he doing?

He brushed a thumb over the corner of her mouth, and she panicked.

Stop!

No. Keep going!

All she could do was stare.

Nathaniel's eyes didn't leave her lips when he dragged his thumb to the centre. It hovered for a moment, his forefinger beneath her chin. His skin was velvet.

She hadn't been looked at like that for a long time. Not since…

Owen.

With a quiet breath, she moved away.

Nathaniel pressed his lips into a fine line. "Sorry," he said. "Too much to drink, I think. You make me a little nervous."

"Don't worry about it."

Florence harnessed a hollow laugh. Her gaze darted around the room, anxious to find a distraction for them both. When it landed on Nathaniel's arm atop the bar, she pondered, "What is it?"

It was a tattoo, obviously. She could see only black shapes poking over from his unbuttoned cuffs.

He yanked back his sleeve, smiling. He wanted her to ask this.

"It's an oak tree." He drew a finger along his left forearm and up his bicep. *As if he didn't want me to swoon anymore.* "See the roots?" His finger moved up. "The trunk, the branches…"

"The leaves look different," she noted. They were smooth. Floral. "Is that—?"

"A lotus flower."

"What does it mean?"

Florence debated tattoos since turning eighteen. Despite being old enough, her mum begged to be consulted before she altered her body in any way. She approved of the ear-piercings—she and Erika had the same—but all of Florence's tattoo suggestions had been shut down. She wanted one that meant something to her, but was yet to find anything of significance that Mum didn't view as too 'hasty.'

Nathaniel's smile was like sunshine.

"Lotus flowers grow in unusual conditions. Harsh conditions. They spend their adolescence submerged in water. Only the ones who have the strength make it to the surface where they can bloom. I suppose I relate."

Florence's lips parted in a gasp. She was no lover of poetry, but his casual verses enthralled her. "And the oak?"

"Strong foundations," he said. "I wouldn't have got to where I am without those."

"Your family?"

"Correct."

She thought of her father. He was always closer to Alfie, but he made her feel safer than anyone else had. *He* was the foundation of their family.

Not having him in her life anymore grew easier, but there was always that wave of silent grief that rushed everything else away whenever he was mentioned. "You must miss your dad."

He stiffened. It was swift, but she caught the glance at the scar on his hand. "I do."

Grief seemed different when the fate of who you lost was unknown. Do you mourn the person missing? Or is hope the better option—even if it causes more pain? She wondered what went through Erika's mind every time Aunt Emily was mentioned. She never brought her up with Florence, and she followed suit. Mum warned her against it.

"We'll find him, you know?" He looked up from his palm. "I'll do whatever I can to make that happen."

His brows tugged together, surprised. "You're... a good person."

She laughed. "Did you expect me to be anything else?"

"No, I..." His eyes ran up and down her figure, his mouth hanging open. "I don't expect *people* to be anything else. Just... Thank you, I guess."

She frowned and smiled at the same time. He was different at the hotel. All that confidence and extraversion shrunk into a shy yet sweet man. Quiet was not her type, and yet...

She called the bartender over and politely requested two more glasses of prosecco rosé. Nathaniel thanked her and the two drank cordially. Florence rarely averted her eyes from the doorway, however, cautious of why they were truly at this party.

And of the Adolescents in the next room.

CHAPTER TWENTY-EIGHT

Alliance-bound supernaturals are to acknowledge one another as equal. All individuals, laws, customs, histories, and relics are to be upheld with respect.

Treaty of the Four Worlds, Section 1, Paragraph 2.

The Collector grew up in London, born into the elite. His father worked overseas in a business he wouldn't disclose, training him to swim amongst the seven seas of capitalism. He learned how to swim, then built a boat on which to sail.

Erika yearned for more. Was he secretly a Hunter? Did a relative marry into a supernatural family? He wouldn't say. He found her questions flattering, of course. A Hunter of her calibre *should* be interested in him. His attitude uneased her, but arrogance was simple to exploit.

Music drummed in her ears while The Collector escorted her through the red sea of vampires. They parted for the pair, wild yet domesticated enough not to bite the hand that fed them.

The food itself stumbled and fainted in their predator's arms. Pungent iron stung Erika's nostrils, the floor noticeably stickier than before.

Even alongside The Collector, Erika averted eye contact and kept her neck covered with hair.

They reached what she imagined was once a stage door and let out a sigh.

"Do they frighten you?' The Collector closed the door, latching it tight. Behind them was a dimly lit staircase to the second floor.

"I've seen worse." Flashes of the wendigo's hiker, of countless vampire prey, of warped, possessed souls, crossed Erika's mind. The victims of the creatures she hunted were not willing like the ones in the theatre.

"It's sickening, isn't it?" The Collector grinned. "How people thrust themselves into danger for nothing more than a rush of adrenaline."

He signalled for her to follow the staircase. She cringed at the tackiness of her heels leaving the floor. *Blood. Wet and dry. Old and new.*

"You're hardly different," she said. "Throwing countless parties with creatures more powerful than yourself, letting them run riot, feeding as they please."

She humoured him, she realised. Or perhaps he humoured himself. She had to know. "Why do you do it?"

Erika turned on the landing to watch him ascend the stairs, resisting the nerves running down her neck as he waited to reach the top to angle in close. "For the thrill."

He outstretched an arm towards the corridor. "If you will."

He dedicated the second floor to his collection, alongside a handful of spare bedrooms and storage cupboards, the tour breezed by. Like its exterior, the floor spread out like a museum, every archway flanked by ivory columns, the panelled white and gold walls gently illuminated by candelabras and hanging gothic chandeliers. Erika inhaled, the air a blend of pottery and roses.

Each room had its own tribute: one for the vampires, then lychans, arcanes, Hunters, and even the most unusual of supernatural creatures like demons and angels. Despite her true reasoning for strolling the shrines, Erika couldn't help but marvel, particularly at a stained-glass window taken from Valour.

"I thought humans couldn't get to Valour," she said.

The Collector chuckled. "I did not retrieve it myself, if that's what you're asking. Someone gifted this to me three, maybe four, years ago."

The art depicted a flower—no, a sun. A blood red sun igniting the white-tipped mountain Valour concealed itself within. The only sun a vampire would ever see following their transition.

And The Collector stole it to be locked in a private room. A trophy for a capitalist to woo women with.

Out of respect, she resisted touching the glasswork, astonished to think the creature that created this was part of the same kind gorging downstairs on human flesh. "It's beautiful," was all she could say.

She felt The Collector step beside her. "Yes, I suppose it is. They have lots of windows like this at Valour, I heard. I had another, but—"

Erika stiffened at the way his tone darkened. "But...?"

"It was stolen." His voice cut through the room, echoing over the arches. "It truly was a marvel. The vampires and lychans fought for that piece for decades."

The species shared very little in common. Although not at war anymore, it was difficult for Erika to imagine the two sharing similar art tastes.

"Why is that?" she asked.

"It depicted a hybrid beast. A legend, or a prophecy of some sort. Apparently, no-one could agree on whom the art belonged to. The artist was unknown, of course. The vampires held onto it for years, but

I found it in my possession alongside the *Blood Sun*. Then it was stolen. Less than a year ago, actually."

Erika frowned. It was strange to take one and not the other. If that was so, it was likely a lychan. Surely, a vampire would have taken both that and the Blood Sun.

She reminded herself not to think so hastily in a world she knew so little of.

They moved on. The final room—again, flanked by eminent, candlelit columns—was the most vacant of all.

The arcanes' shrine was meagre in comparison to the rest of the museum. Erika could smell the emptiness; the age of the tapestries hanging around the room. Only a couple of mahogany stands displaying artefacts marked the centre of each wall, many of them referencing 'witches' not 'arcanes' in the descriptions. If the Divines knew of this, they'd burn it to the ground for sure.

Unworldly energy drew her to one of the tapestries.

It fell seven feet tall, possessing a multitude of colours and tiny stitches only a marksman possessed the capability of threading. Depicting a scene of a lone arcane, the tapestry showcased the affinities of magic: Ignis, Aura, Hydres, Terra, Ferreus, Shadow Traveller, Soul Searcher, and Lightbringer. Among the Tractatori, the raven-haired arcane healed a wounded starling. Beneath her, roots descended into ebony soil where gnarly skeletons clawed their way to the surface, eager to touch her blood-soaked palms.

Necromancy—then blood magic. Was this normalised before the Seven Covens?

Erika dared to reach out but neglected a touch. The hours this would have taken…

"Amazing, isn't it?"

For all his flaws, she was glad to see The Collector could appreciate the art. "Yes, the stitching is—"

"Not the stitching." He stroked the shadows of the tapestry with his fingers, sending it rocking back and forth. "The magic. Bringing someone back to life."

Never mind. "It's illegal," Erika reminded him. "The Treaty dictates—"

"You think I give a flying fuck about that Treaty?" His hand dropped to his side. "You've seen my party, my museum, and you think I care that *necromancy* is illegal?"

She shouldn't have—not for a second. He didn't care for art or history. Profit and power are what crafted his collection, which still wasn't enough considering the way he ogled the arcane in the tapestry. The world was his oyster, and he would not hesitate to snatch the pearls for himself, sacking off the Treaty despite the lives it saved.

She couldn't say that, not without sacrificing the mission, so she smiled to ease the tension. "If you're interested in eternal life, I'm sure the vampires downstairs would be happy to satisfy you."

But he did not laugh. "I enjoy my freedom of movement, thank you. I would be nowhere without my yearly retreats to the shores of Bali."

Wouldn't we all? The image of Diana counting coins and flicking through bank statements had her jaw clenching.

Erika flinched at The Collector's arm looping around her waist. "I'll be back," he whispered into her hair.

He backed out of the room into the shadowed corridor. Erika clocked the empty martini glass flashing in the candlelight.

This was her chance.

She scoured the museum in search of Horizon's Edge, careful to rein in her urgency should The Collector return. 'Keen intellect' was more favourable than 'lying thief.'

It had to be in this section. It belonged to the arcanes.

She turned a corner, gasping as she came face to face with a woman.

Not real. Thankfully.

The woman acted as a centrepiece for the largest painting in the section. With amber eyes, she glared at Erika with an upturned nose, black hair cascading in ringlets behind her. A crimson gown fell to the foot of the artwork, spilling like blood. Warmth radiated from the canvas as Erika raised a hand.

At a spark, she drew it back.

"What are you doing?"

She whirred. "You were quick."

The Collector followed her into the room, two glasses of champagne richer, the martini glass abandoned. "I have a bar upstairs," he said. "No bartender, so, of course, no martinis, but I assume *Dom Perignon* would suffice?"

The internal battle lasted two seconds before she accepted the drink. She had to save face. *Give a little trust, you get a little back.*

"Does she intrigue you?" he asked, referring to the woman in the painting.

Erika sipped from her flute. She looked like the arcane in the tapestry. "Who is she?"

The Collector shrugged. "I'm not sure. Although I always find her stare captivating. She entrances you, though she is only a painting."

Magic, indeed. The woman's amber eyes made her shudder. She could smell the magic—the peppery smoke.

Behind her, The Collector cleared his throat. "Your cousin wants something from me."

Men like him basked in being the smartest person in the room. He liked her intelligence but preferred to best her, still.

So, she played dumb. "It's some sword, isn't it?"

He chuckled at her insolence. "Not a sword. A *blade*."

An unwanted hand on her back escorted her to the far end of the room. Erika grew eager for the artefact—she had to see it to know what she was looking for if Alfie was unsuccessful.

The Collector's hand lowered, further and further until it rested on her waist. If she had not grown sidetracked by the painting, she could have seen the dagger and made up an excuse to leave by now. His touch unnerved her.

"There she is."

Illuminated in its glass coffin, Horizon's Edge was something to behold. Despite its rumoured age, the blade remained immaculate, holding immortality in its jewelled hilt. The silver glinted a heavenly white and the jewel a hellish red; a perfect balance for something so unworldly. Something that bled magic into the room—bled an immortal arcane once, trapping her inside indefinitely.

"It's…"

Beautiful was the wrong word. It was trashy, ugly, and a vessel for death. Majestic was better suited, but Erika was more frightened than amazed by the weapon. No word could match the dread and nausea she felt looking down at Horizon's Edge. Somehow, it looked back.

Her mouth dried. She wheezed a rumbling cough.

"*Now.*"

A hand wrapped around her throat.

She gasped, reaching for the solid grip, but her fingers turned numb. She was faster than this. Her reaction time slowed.

The drink.

This was the last time she drank with strangers. Leopold's tea should have been enough warning.

The Collector's lips brushed so close to her neck she thought he might bite. A thousand possibilities ran through her mind, telling her to run.

But she couldn't.

"Let me go," she warned.

A low laugh made her shiver. "Do you know how many whores like you try to steal my collection?"

When she did not answer, his grip tightened. "*At least* one a month. Do you know what I do with *whores* like yourself?"

She choked, unable to find the air or words to reply. She stumbled back and The Collector let her fall. She did not feel the impact, but she would eventually.

"Strong champagne, isn't it? It's a brand made for vampires because, bloody hell, their tolerance is off the charts. However—" He bent down and craned his neck to smile at Erika, "—it *is* enough to knock the most seasoned drinker off his feet. A single sip is all you need."

She tried to move, but her limbs weakened by the second. It was agonising just angling herself to follow the footsteps rattling the floorboards against her skull. The Collector towered above her, casting a shadow over her stilling body, a pointed object now in hand.

He twirled Horizon's Edge. It blurred in a flash of silver and scarlet. "I'm going to take this blade and shove it down your cousin's throat. *Both* of them. Then your boyfriend is next. Then you."

She tried to push herself up. Her cheek smacked against the floor.

The Collector laughed. "Sweet dreams, angel. May they be kinder than your reality."

CHAPTER TWENTY-NINE

We are the shield at humanity's back. Let them look onward into the light while we strive in the dark. We must not fail them.

A Speech from Henri Lupine, Date Unknown.

Erika's face turned raw as she woke. Her eyelids itched. She groaned and rubbed them viciously, squeezing tears onto her knuckles. Her chest and belly ached, but her neck hadn't stiffened. She can't have been unconscious for more than a few minutes.

She hoped, anyway.

She woke on a carpet and opened her eyes to find colours of her makeup smudged into the white fibres. Her head throbbed. She couldn't decide if she was still horrifically drunk or hungover from the vampiric wine.

The vampiric wine.

Horizon's Edge.

The Collector promised to use it tonight. "Alfie…"

She fell back on her knees and banged her head against something hard. She slumped down and reached for her scalp. The impact shattered her vision, so she fell forward and threw up. It'd stain the carpet. *Good.*

Her eyes squinted to reorientate herself, noting the walnut bedpost behind her, the pearl, gossamer drapes before French windows…

This was a bedroom.

Panicked, she touched her thighs. Feeling returned, and she didn't sense any pain down there. *One thing to be calm about.*

Knees knocking, she gripped the bedpost and dragged herself up. She tried to think, but thoughts were agonising. Knowing her family was in danger was all the more painful.

Assuming she hadn't moved, Florence was at the bar with Nathaniel, making her the safest of them all. Alfie had Alex, but she was not prepared to put him on the line either, or count on him to protect her cousin sufficiently.

Alfie was at the poker table. He had to be the first target.

The earth trembled beneath Erika's feet as she walked, limbs exhausting themselves with every movement. A migraine hounded her, and her back stung with the impact of her earlier fall. The Collector could end her in a second in this state, but she would not leave her family.

Lupines would never be left alone.

In her daze, she stumbled down the dingy, elongated corridor. She had been drunk before—*very* drunk—but vampiric wine was a different ball game. If it made vampires tipsy, it was a miracle she was conscious at all.

A screaming sob froze her. Erika felt her surroundings, squinting for any signs of danger, but the cries came from further down the hall. She backtracked, searching for the source, then fumbled with a brass doorknob to witness a scene that reinstated the taste of vomit.

Erika recognised her from the grounds. The girl had been frolicking around, drunk, since the moment she set foot on the property. She *was* horrifically drunk but had done no harm besides knocking over a vase.

Yet here she was. Broken. Mangled. Shattered and bleeding like roadkill because that was all she was to The Collector. *Vermin*. And because she got in the way, he ran her down.

Ran her *through*.

"Help me," the girl cried. "Please. Before he comes back!"

Erika staggered. She fumbled with binds at the girl's wrists, quietly conscious of her rope burn. The Collector had been sitting at the poker table since she last saw the girl. *Did he pay someone to do this?*

She wept as Erika scratched her skin. "I'm sorry," was all she could say. Her vision was still an abstracted mess, her mind a chaotic canvas.

"He…" Her head swayed sluggishly. "He hurt me."

"I know. He's—"

Erika's palm froze over the wound.

The Collector had stabbed the girl in the stomach at least four times, each of the wounds gaping but not fatal.

At least not instantly.

The cuts were calculated: meant to kill eventually, but not immediately. He intended for her to bleed out, alone, in pain. That was more satisfying to him than the kill.

Erika had not seen this brutality from a human before. Not one that hadn't been corrupted.

Tears pricked her eyes as she applied pressure to the deepest wound through her buttery outfit. "Can you stand?"

"I… I don't…"

She blinked. Her eyes stayed closed for a second. *Two. Three…*

"Hey!" Erika wiggled her shoulders. "Come on, wake up."

She woke. Barely.

"I'm getting you out of here." Her voice slurred from the drink, but she was steadying. She could do this. "We're going to make it out."

She oscillated in a drunken nod.

Erika threw the girl's arm over her shoulder and forced them both to stand. Her legs trembled under the weight of her and the vampiric wine, but she managed. She thanked whatever god watched from above that the girl was far more petite than herself.

The walk was a battle. Her muscles ached and groaned beneath the weight of her steps, and her skin sweated through the satin she wore, turning the material rough and uncomfortable against her body. She reined in pitiful sobs every time the poor girl's feet caught on the rug.

As if from nowhere, Erika spotted the dim archway leading to the stairs.

Almost there now. Almost there...

The girl turned limp.

She slumped down Erika's side.

"No. No, no, come on, we're nearly there."

She flipped her on her back and tapped her cheek. Her eyes remained still. A trickle of blood slid down her chin.

Erika put an ear to her chest, then two fingers to her neck. "No."

Erika fell back to sit beside her, covered in blood. Now that she was close to the girl, most of the wine wearing off, she could see her features. They were youthful. Bright but dimming. Her attitude at the party reminded her of Florence, in a way.

That was only an hour ago. Now, she was dead. Killed for having too much fun.

Erika's lip quivered as she gently removed feathery hair from the girl's face. It rusted with drying blood. "I'm sorry. I'm so sorry."

Because she was not quick enough to save her. If she had been faster—if she hadn't taken the wine—the girl may have lived another day.

If she did not underestimate The Collector.

Carefully, she drew down the girl's eyelids and got up.

Christopher Lupine would never have let her make the mistakes she had tonight. Accepting drinks from her enemies, leaving her family downstairs—she messed up one too many times. This death was on *her*. Nothing about her actions inched close enough to perfection.

Her feet fell from under her on the stairs. She tumbled until she reached the bottom.

She choked and heaved, her ribcage battered, but Erika reached the door to the theatre and into the vampires' frenzy.

None of the vampires saw her stumble into the crowd, drenched in blood and weak enough to be an easy picking. They pushed and shoved her mindlessly. One vampire yanked her towards him with a fanged, lustful grin, while another helped her away without a second thought. The tide tore her towards the door, where she launched herself into the smoke and neon lights of the dancefloor, knocking her temple against someone's shoulder.

"Erika?"

She squinted. "Nathaniel?"

She followed his arm to a concerned Florence curved against his body. Her jaw dropped at the state of Erika's chest, hands, and dress. "Erika, the blood—"

"It's not mine." She hated how it offered her comfort. "I'll explain in a minute, we need—" She grimaced at the pain in her neck, swallowing more vomit. "We need to get to Alfie."

Florence shook her head. "You can barely stand!"

"Bar," said Nathaniel.

His assertion made Florence take Erika's arm and lead her to the west wing bar. She pleaded with her cousin to return her to Alfie and Alex, but she wouldn't listen until Erika was sitting on a barstool with a pint of water in hand and an ice pack against her neck.

"He knows," she rasped between gulps. "He knows we want Horizon's Edge."

Florence blinked. Her eyes followed a water droplet falling off Erika's chin. "Oh."

"Yes, oh."

"And the blood?"

Erika's eyes welled at her failure. She took another drink. "A girl's." *From an innocent girl who looks like you.* "The one who broke a vase. The Collector…" She gestured to the excess of blood down her body. "Well, I'm sure you can guess what he did to her for that."

Florence swore. When Erika downed the rest of her drink, she nudged Florence and beckoned her and Nathaniel to follow.

The girl was lost to The Collector, now, but Alfie and Alex would not be.

They sped through the party, out into the garden, and burst through the conservatory doors to a choir of 'oohs.'

The Collector grinned from his usual seat at the head of the table, one arm hanging laxly over the back of his chair. "Good game, little Mullein. Such a shame you didn't get the… dagger."

The room followed his eyes to gawk and gasp at Erika: the blood, her dishevelled figure, her scowl. The scowl saying *screw you and screw your wine*.

Even if she still felt like absolute shit.

Alfie paled, Leopold stiffened, and Alex darted for her.

He gripped her shoulders. "Erika, what—?"

"Erika, angel!" The Collector leapt to his feet. "Had a bit of fun with our vampire friends, have you?"

Erika raked over Alex's face—his panic, his care—then his shoulder to meet The Collector's cordial smile. He raised his glass to her, splashing the rose martini on his Royal Flush, and took a sip. Around him, a dozen vampires laughed, some drooling at her. Nearby, the blonde vampire held up a warning hand. They were Adolescents; Ferals leashed by their Master.

She felt Alfie's defeated eyes on her, saw his rolled-up sleeves and yanked-down tie.

He lost the game.

"I imagined you perfectly capable of winning tonight, Mullein, but your cousin hurt my feelings. Other arrangements had to be made to accommodate."

The Collector swaggered around the table, unwavering in his stare. He reached into his pocket and out came the scarlet glint of Horizon's Edge.

"You see, everyone, she—" He pointed with the dagger, "—tried to trick me. Whispered an evening of sweet nothings just to lure me to my collection and *steal* from me."

His broadening audience laughed either through agreement or fear. Erika spied her crossbow on the table—too far to reach.

The Collector's ocean eyes glazed over the closer he got to her. "She toyed with my heart. Now, I'll play with hers."

Alex took one look at Horizon's Edge and positioned himself in front of Erika. A quiet gasp left her lips—he didn't even think about it.

The Collector rolled his eyes. "Security?"

Bouncers jumped Alex in an instant. He thrashed and swung, but two burly men built like mountains gripped an arm each. "Harm a hair on her head and I'll break your fucking jaw!"

Erika's heart raced but she didn't intervene. She knew what The Collector valued. She knew how to play him. Alex had to trust her.

Even if some part of her wanted to see just how true to his word Alex was.

The audience silenced with anticipation. Even the Adolescents were still.

The Collector's arrogance to throw parties with open-invites was satisfied with its mass attendance. These numbers were only achieved by a single thing.

Trust.

People trusted The Collector to throw a good party. They *trusted* him to have vampires feed off their necks, but let go. They trusted him to acquaint them with death, yet wave goodbye at the morning sun.

With Horizon's Edge in his grasp, the tip aimed at the arch between Erika's collarbones, The Collector would bring death, and death would party on.

The knife touched her skin. The Collector applied the tiniest of pressure to pierce it.

"Go on, then," she whispered. "Do it."

She was certain he could feel the reverberations of her heart through the knife. Adolescents licked their lips at the sole drop of blood pooling on the cool blade.

"Let them watch. Show them how you *really* tend to your guests. Your greed. Your pride. The consequences of your cold wrath. Show them how to *really* dance with death."

She had to be right. If she hadn't outwitted him now, it was over. She could feel the sweat on the back of her neck, the ache of her spine, the blood trailing down her chest.

Teeth bared as if he would bite her ear, The Collector leaned in. "Oh, angel…"

Behind him, something stirred in the darkness—a flash of auburn and an outstretched palm…

A white syphon shimmered like moonlight.

"They already know."

CHAPTER THIRTY

It is an insult for a witch to be born with just one affinity. They are a symbol of diluted power and breeding with the mundane

The Last Queen of Stryga.

The windows caved in. A lethal blizzard shot the guests to the ground.

Erika's knuckles and shoulders took the brunt of the falling glass, shielding the more vital parts of her body. Already, wet blood slid down her spine.

When it was safe, she dared look up and met eyes with The Collector, who was just as baffled as she was.

Florence and Nathaniel were in the doorway, Alfie still at the poker table with Leopold and an unscathed Robert, and Alex on the ground by the two bouncers who restrained him earlier.

All were safe. Scraped and shaken, but safe.

Sniffing made Erika shudder.

A few guests were already standing, their injuries healing quickly as their eyes swirled into a deep, copper-red.

The vampires were Adolescent, their features darker than their Master's at the back of the room. Animal instincts kicked in. Fangs elongated over curled, wet lips. Gluttony possessed them. One wrong move and the monster would take over.

Erika held her breath. Her family had the sense to do the same.

"Ambrose…" The Collector panted at the platinum-haired Master. Strands of blonde slipped out of place, covering The Collector's eyes. "Keep your Ferals at bay!"

Ambrose paled—even for a creature of the night. His blonde brows knitted together while his wild followers stalked the more disorientated humans in the room. Sudden movements or clumsy footing would make them charge with supernatural speed. The urge to follow their master was strong—the pull of blood stronger for the newly turned. Their obedience hung on a thin, thin thread.

He did not order them to resist.

The Collector sensed this conflict in the Master. "Ambrose. Do something!"

The vampire's reddening eyes skimmed over the ocean of possibilities. *So much blood. So much pleasure. So much temptation…*

His ruby, longing gaze landed on The Collector's neck and, near silent like a twilight breeze, told him, *"No."*

On cue, the Adolescents indulged.

Screams shattered among the carnage of fangs and blood. Erika ducked out of the way of a mad vampire, catching The Collector backing towards the table to snatch her crossbow.

She scowled. *Mine.*

Erika ran for him—for her weapon—as he raised it to eye level. "How do you… How does this thing…?"

The Collector grappled with her crossbow, unable to unlock it in time to dodge Erika's whack. She caught the crossbow in her left hand, swung an arrow at his cheek with the right. Something clanged on the floor.

Horizon's Edge.

The two scrambled around the tiles to catch the blade. When Erika seized it, a pair of desperate hands covered hers.

"This is *my* artefact!" Blood from his new scar soaked their locked fists. "You have... no right!"

A figure from behind brought The Collector to his feet and loosened his grip on the blade. Erika fell back, holding it and her crossbow, with solicitous strength.

Ambrose's mouth dripped scarlet as he looked down on The Collector.

"Vampire. I swear, you—"

His eyes darkened to a controlled crimson when he bared fangs and sank them into The Collector's artery. He screamed and thrashed as Erika backed away beneath the sea of running legs.

The Collector's limp body slumped to the ground before Ambrose's feet. "I'll have that artefact now, my dear."

She loaded up her crossbow.

Ambrose sighed. "Disappointing, Lupine. But nonetheless..."

Her bolt struck him in the neck, and she darted. The wound was not fatal, even with a wooden arrow, but it gave her the opportunity to run for the door and blend into the crowd. *Everyone* was bleeding. Ambrose's senses would have been a mess.

Among the masses, not one person tried to save The Collector in his own home.

Beyond the conservatory, she saw nothing. *Someone* broke the windows. The Adolescents' response was anticipated.

This was no accident. This person wanted chaos. She could have sworn she saw...

A tug made Erika point the dagger.

"Erika, it's me!" *Leopold*. "You have the blade?"

She glanced down at the knife, her hands as red as its jewel.

Breathless, he nodded "Okay, good. I know another way out of here, away from the crowd."

"No, I need to find—"

"Robert has them! He's been here before. He knows the other way out."

Before she could respond, Leopold tugged her out of the way of an oncoming object.

A... fence panel?

Behind them, a statuesque woman strutted through the ground with her arms outstretched. Fence panels tore from the dirt around her and fired like javelins towards the house. The resistance blew a curtain of red behind her.

"Aurelia." Leopold tapped Erika's shoulder. "Let's go."

She would have gone after her—cut the head off the snake and be done with it—but Erika knew where her sights lay. From across the lawn, scarlet and silver glinted in Aurelia's eyes.

They made it through the doors before the panels fenced them in.

The screaming carried on inside.

Erika tailed Leopold, near blind among the neon lights and the bodies shoving and tripping her. Already, she smelled the rust.

A male feral launched at a girl bolting for a side room. Erika shoved Horizon's Edge in Leopold's arms to raise her crossbow and fire.

The wooden arrow struck the vampire in the heart. His skin paled and shrivelled like drying clay, the body collapsing in a heap on the dancefloor.

Erika and Leopold made it to the west wing bar, then beyond a door behind it, through the kitchen, and towards what she assumed was a pantry.

The Collector could have fit a whole catering company in his industrial-sized kitchen. For a second, she wondered if he ever thought to cook for himself or someone else. *Probably not.*

Leopold grunted, and the aluminium pantry door slid open. Not a pantry, she realised: a corridor.

He flipped a switch to turn on the overhead lighting. "His staff used to sleep down here before the weekly parties. Now I believe it's just storage."

"Where's—"

"I told Robert to press on. He's waiting for us on the other side."

Storage it was. The corridor—narrow enough to make Erika stiffen—had been left so plain and dingy that it was a wonder anyone lived here at all in the last decade. Doors had been left open carelessly to side rooms that were once bedrooms. Many were crammed with boxes, one had a dusty library, another cleaning supplies, and another—

Vases. Rows upon rows of identical, Grecian vases.

Fucking monster. At least wendigos and vampires hunted to survive. The Collector was—

Dead. Good riddance.

Erika's body lightened without Horizon's Edge. Despite its size, it was *heavy*. Not physically, but the feel of a weapon in her hand always felt natural to her, and Horizon's Edge was not. It whispered things—things she did not want to hear right now.

But relying on Leopold to care for it, after he lost it the first time, felt even more unnatural.

They neared a darker, wider space. Something easily could have jumped out at them. "Can I have that back, now?" she asked him.

"I don't have a weapon," Leopold uttered.

Erika snorted. "Then you should have brought one. Hand it over."

"I'd feel safer if—"

"Leopold."

She spun to face him. His features were grave.

"*I* have a weapon," she said. "That thing is what we came for and is not to be used lightly."

"So, I'm to be defenceless?"

"You have *me*."

"I'm keeping this blade."

"No." The gap between them closed. His face was stone, ready to crack. "We can't go waving that thing around and risk losing it. Imagine if Aurelia gets it?"

He didn't move. He didn't speak. The weight of his silence filled every inch of the corridor.

Then he crumbled, his features softening like the eroding features of the feral on the dancefloor.

Erika hollowed. Leopold retired early, but this man was raised by Hunters, nurtured under the Watch's Code. Honour and loyalty ran through his veins until they didn't.

This man could have been her *godfather*.

Erika curled a finger around an arrow and steadied her voice. "But that's what you want… isn't it?"

His shoulders dropped in a sigh. He didn't want to do this, but his life came first. If only he were comprehensive enough to realise the cult could not carry out its work without him. He had no children.

"It is."

Leopold's arms seized Erika in a headlock, Horizon's Edge pressed to her throat. The feminine voice caught her off guard, and now her hand that clutched an arrow pointed at her own back.

She saw the syphon first, then Aurelia stepped into the light.

Leopold's gulp ran down Erika's spine. "One more step and I'll kill her!"

Aurelia didn't flinch. "I kept my end of the bargain. You, however, did not."

"I… Robert kept an eye on me the whole time! He knew I could get the dagger."

"And Vivienne had to die for it." Her tone lashed through the corridor. "Now Samson is after blood."

Robert kept an eye on me. A spy for the cult. Erika didn't see him with Dad at the cabin. How long had Aurelia held her claws in Leopold?

Had they got to Wyatt already?

Whoever Leopold worked for no longer mattered—both sides rejected him now. He used Erika's family, grooming them as gifts to the cult with fancy wrapping in the shape of Horizon's Edge. To save face with the Hunters, he allowed one of Aurelia's devotees to die. From the sounds of it, she was not too pleased with the notion.

Leopold stammered. "You… You don't need me. You found Lucie, right? *Right?*"

If Leopold was so desperate to find her… If she could replace him in the ritual…

Erika's jaw dropped. "You'd sacrifice your *daughter?*"

"I didn't know she existed until Aurelia said so!"

"She's still your child! She wasn't involved in the ritual. She's *innocent*."

"How can I love someone I've never met?" he snapped. "I know myself and I'd save me any day."

Arrogant. Self-centred. Spineless…

Erika didn't know Aurelia—not beyond watching her at the cabin—and Aurelia did not know Erika. Yet, the two mirrored their disgust for the slimy little man desperate to save his own skin. Aurelia had a son, Erika remembered. If she could respect the cultist for one thing, it was that she would never see her son pay the price for her decisions—just as Erika would for Ollie.

Just as her father would for her.

The silence between them was broken only by the faint hum from the blade at Erika's neck.

Aurelia exhaled a sigh, then smiled. "Lucie does not exist, Leopold."

Leopold slackened his grip. Erika tightened hers on the arrow. "But—"

"So fickle with the lives of others, yet greedy for your own pleasures. 'Tis a wonder your desperation is yet to draw a demon of your own. But, then again, you're not much of a host, are you?"

Erika felt Leopold's drive drain and took a chance.

She dug her arrow into Leopold's abdomen, snatching the blade, and throwing it at Aurelia. The arcane stumbled into the wall before her magic could charge. Erika grabbed and brandished Horizon's Edge before her chest.

Aura magic threw her down the corridor, back the way she came. She groaned on impact but recovered quickly and ran like hell, still clutching Horizon's Edge in a white-knuckled grip.

She screamed her family's names as she bolted around the house. Over half the guests had made it out already, but stragglers were left shrieking under the coup of vampires chasing and biting them. Erika checked every body, followed every cry, putting down four Ferals on her way outside. A small part of her felt guilty. They didn't know what they were doing, but they were out for blood. She saved three innocents by the time she reached the patio, including a friend of the girl in the canary dress. She wondered if the girl who died would have saved her friend or left like the others.

"Get me that blade!"

At Ambrose's orders, Erika scurried through a window. He didn't see her, but her shoulder—the injury from the wendigo—roared at the impact on the grass.

The first thing she spotted in the garden was Alex, on his knees, bleeding from the eyes, nose, mouth, and ears under Robert's clawed hand, dripping with his own blood.

Blood magic.

"Now," Robert hissed, "stand."

Alex moaned in agony as his legs straightened up, striking Erika to the core. She had never seen blood magic in use before.

She could see why it was banned.

"Walk."

Alex did, his movements stiff with resistance as he marched into the arms of an arcane who'd sacrifice him in the place of his father.

If Erika was not there.

She fired an arrow as she ran and swung another at Robert's throat. Vampiric wine had the first miss its mark. Robert dodged the second and shoved a bloody hand in Erika's face.

She cried with the anguish of an oncoming migraine under the stench of iron. It lasted only a second before she heard the slice of flesh, and the pain subsided.

Robert fell before Alex's hidden blade.

Alex paled at Robert's limp body. Fresh blood dripped from his wrist as the marks on his face dried like paint. "I guess blood magic is no joke."

"Yeah." Erika crouched to dig through Robert's pockets, pulling out his car keys. "You know, Leopold—"

"Erika!"

Her neck twisted at the speed she followed Alfie's voice. He called to her from across the lawn, waving and sprinting as fast as his skinny legs would allow him. Apart from a few specs of blood, he was fine. Florence was not with him—neither was Nathaniel.

"Here, Alf!" Alex shouted.

Alfie smiled and picked up the pace. Erika kept her crossbow raised, eyes peeled for any oncoming vampires.

Instead, she found the ultimate target.

Aurelia marched across the lawn, Leopold in chains behind her between a blonde arcane—the one from the cabin—and Felix. The blonde whirred, scowling at Erika, revealing three long scars down his left eye. The Shadow Traveller, Percy, approached the trio and pushed the scarred blonde ahead, snapping inaudible instructions until he moved on.

Erika was a good shot. She could do this. If she timed it just right…

At the click of the safety latch, her arms swung in the air.

"What are you doing?!" she cried at Alex.

He pinned her arms behind her back. "The hell are *you* doing?"

"She's right there! Let *go!*"

"Have you seen the state of you? You miss and—"

"I won't miss."

"I've seen you shoot," he hissed against her neck. "And I've seen you miss several times tonight. I don't know what happened upstairs, but you've been out of it ever since."

His voice cracked, but she fought his grip. Aurelia had Leopold now. Only Wyatt was left, along with Horizon's Edge, then it was game over.

"She's—"

"Getting away. And so are we."

Before she could retaliate, fire shot in a humongous ball across the garden, stemming from the fingertips of the scarred, blonde arcane.

It headed for Alfie.

NO!

Arrows were useless, so they called his name. Only, he did not run.

He *froze*. White and frightened.

But the fire did not thaw Alfie.

Flames engulfed the body that shielded him. It took Nathaniel's screams for Erika to realise it was Florence. She bolted to her cousin, firing an arrow at the blonde on her way. He disappeared in a mass of smoke along with the Shadow Traveller.

And Aurelia. And Leopold.

Florence thrashed and cried on the ground. "It hurts," she whimpered.

"I know, I know." Erika lifted the blush fabric of her beautiful dress and hissed.

"Is… is it bad?"

Fire singed from the top of her ribs all the way down to her hip bone. She was no doctor, only aware of basic first aid, but identified it as a third-degree burn.

She pained a smile. "Not bad at all."

"Oh." Florence flicked her brows. "That's good."

She made to stand then screamed.

Nathaniel knelt beside her. "I'll carry her."

"Zero chance," Alex bit. "Shift."

Alex apologised frantically—softly—as he lifted her. When she was secure, he gave Erika a nod.

Time to go.

Robert's car was left unscathed outside the manor. Guests and vampires dispersed over the grounds, the cries of the dying and the undead breaking through the hills.

After he laid Florence in the back, Erika tossed Alex the car keys and slid into the passenger seat. Alfie positioned himself by his sister while Nathaniel stopped at the door.

Erika groaned. "Get in."

Alex slammed his foot down before the door closed. He drove over the lawn, dodging vampires and guests and a girl face-down on the grass. She lifted her head as they passed, showing confusion, red eyes, and a newfound hunger.

The vampires were not just killing the guests—they were *turning* them.

As the distance between the car and the manor grew, so did the silence. With that emptiness came the realisation that Erika's ears had been ringing this entire time. She winced at the pain that came with it as adrenaline drained from her body and she rested her head against the cool window.

CHAPTER THIRTY-ONE

If you cannot be brave, quit.

Philip Lupine's Journal, Second Edition.

With the extent of her injuries and the blood that covered them all, Florence could not be taken to a hospital. Questions would be raised and, even if they could spout some believable lie, police would involve themselves and cut what little time they had left to stop the ritual.

Erika unlocked Leopold's front door with Robert's key—likely Leopold's, since he'd been kept under house arrest with the cultist. Alex rushed Florence upstairs to the bathtub, ordering Nathaniel to fortify the building and Alfie to find bandages and towels. Erika had been burned before while hunting a particularly nasty fury demon with Dad. Although not nearly as serious as Florence's wounds, she found solace in cool water.

She okayed the temperature before Alex lowered her in, clothes still on but shoes kicked onto the black and white tiles.

Florence shrieked when she submerged. Her burns sizzled.

The sound sent Erika into shock.

"I know, I know, I know," Alex soothed. "It'll pass, it'll pass…"

She clenched Erika's hand, turning it white, then released it with a sigh. Tears slid down her red cheeks. Her burns calmed. Still, Erika needed to undress her.

"Alex, could you…?" She motioned a circle and he turned around without question.

"You need this dress off," she uttered to Florence. "Can you turn?"

She nodded grimly, her lips pressed into a fine line as she rotated a little to the left. It looked *agonising*, but nothing but a small wince escaped her, God bless her, as Erika unzipped and discarded the ruined outfit. Florence eased when it slapped against the tiles.

"Thank you," she rasped. "Can I… can I stay in here for a while?"

Erika brushed a strand of hair from Florence's face. Clammy roots clung to her forehead with sweat. She'd never seen her so dishevelled, but the glint never left her tear-filled eyes. "As long as you need."

Without turning around, Alex left the bathroom while Erika squeezed Florence's dress into the sink. She tossed it in the aluminium bin by the door.

"I'll be right outside if you need anything."

When the door clicked shut, Alex squeezed Erika's shoulder. "Will she be okay?"

The burn was manageable. It looked horrific, and Florence would be in pain for a while. She needed a dressing, painkillers, maybe even a doctor to check for infection. The skin would scar. She would not be too pleased with that reality.

"She—" Her throat closed. She *would* be okay, but Erika never anticipated Florence getting hurt. She knew the possibility was there, but she could protect her.

Until she couldn't. In the same way she failed the girl in yellow, she failed her family.

Alex tilted to see her eyes. She found somewhere else to look as they welled up.

"Erika?"

"She'll be okay," she croaked, nodding. "She'll be okay."

He closed the gap between them, finally meeting her glassy eyes. "And will *you* be okay?"

She always hated that question. When anyone felt the need to ask the dreaded '*Will you be okay?*' the answer was always obvious.

Dad would be disappointed—the Order even more so.

Alex saved her from answering when he curved an arm around her torso, the other gently pushing her face into his shoulder. Erika wasn't one for hugging strangers, but Alex held a warmth about him that made her hovering, shaking hands coil around him. Her eyes stung, so she clamped them shut.

"It went so wrong," she whispered into his shirt. "So fucking wrong. I should have come up with a better plan. I knew it was risky and still—"

"We got the blade," Alex reminded her.

"But Leopold…" Erika started. "Dad trusted him once, so I thought I could… and Florence, she—"

"We knew there were risks. If we sat around waiting to think of something better, what would have happened?"

The cult could have taken Horizon's Edge without challenge. Their families could have been dead by the morning. With a ticking clock, action came at the cost of caution, just like it did at Pendle. If Erika did nothing then, Alex would have died.

But what if there was a better way? A plan that led them to success without so many innocents dying—without Florence almost being burned to death.

Dad would have thought of another way. Erika wasn't ready.

She jerked with a restrained sob.

"Just let it out," Alex whispered.

"I can't."

"You can—"

"No."

She pulled away, still gripping his arms, unwilling to completely let go. She loved how sweet he smelled—like cinnamon and sugar—a release from the pungency of blood, alcohol, and magic.

In the vortex of violence, his embrace was home.

The fact that he didn't try to reel her back in shouldn't have stung. "Stay here," he said. "Watch over Florence while I get the boys in line."

"The manor needs—"

"Fortifying, I know. I'll go grab some weapons from the car. Alfie is finding some bandages for Florence."

"And we need—"

"Blankets, food, fresh clothes. I'll take care of everything. Florence needs you, and you've been—"

Colour drained from his face. All attempts to force optimism vanished. Alex glanced at her unwavering grip on his arms and she swiftly let go, suddenly feeling empty.

"I don't know what he did to you, but you've been *off* ever since." It was not an accusation. A dozen questions lingered on the tip of his tongue that he knew she wasn't yet ready to answer. "Take it easy."

"I c—"

"You *can*. That's an order, Lupine."

Despite it all, she laughed. She caught a smile from Alex at that. "I don't remember voting you in charge."

"Someone has to take the reins when you're pissed out your mind!"

"That's unfair!"

"So was walking into the conservatory looking like that. I didn't know—"

Neither dared to breathe when the air grew devastatingly heavy, the weight carried by a paper-thin space, but holding her breath knocked Erika dizzy. She swayed forward, hoping to brush his lips when she did, and reminded herself that vampiric wine jumbled her thoughts. She trusted her logic as much as she trusted her aim right now.

Erika broke their standoff first when she buried her thoughts in her bag and surrendered her keys to Alex. Despite everything, he smiled. Of course he fucking did.

He was kind—kinder than Erika imagined a stranger could be. *He could betray you. He could change you.*

She didn't have to worry. "Alex?"

He stopped at the stairs and leaned back over the railing.

"Thank you."

He did not ask what for because he knew. She needed a moment to breathe, and he was her ventilator.

His response was a smile. Genuine. Effortless. Defined cordially by twin dimples.

Something in her chest leapt. Something that made her slide down the bathroom door once he descended the staircase. She hoped he would be out of sight, out of mind, but Alex claimed an extended residency in her head.

And somewhere else, she feared.

Alfie tugged on the back door handle for the fifth time before his anxiety eased. He ran over the list in his head: back door, front window, kitchen window, living room window, spare bedroom window. The bottom floor was complete, bar the front door, which Alex took responsibility for once he left for the car to grab supplies.

Did he really lock the kitchen window?

Of course he did. He pulled on the handle to ensure it.

One more check couldn't hurt.

He brushed by Nathaniel in the downstairs living room. He seemed... *different* to how he was at the hotel. Quieter, sure. But far more relaxed, he realised. As content as one could be considering the circumstances, at least.

Alfie's stomach had dropped when he saw his sister throwing herself in front of him, taking the fire in his stead, writhing in anguish because he was too slow. The feeling had not yet subsided.

Stupid. Florence had always been so bloody stupid.

And brave. Perhaps he needed the flames to get him to move next time.

His hands shook, imagining it all. On the grass, he felt the heat emanating from his sister's wound, heard the skin scorching, smelled it burning, saw it blistering. He didn't want that pain. Ever.

Tears stained his glasses when he remembered Florence had felt it. His *sister* would have been equally as frightened, but she didn't think. Instincts made her protect Alfie ahead of herself.

Stupid. *Stupid, stupid, stupid.*

But he envied her.

Tonight was his moment. He was to match The Collector at his own game and use his talents rather than pretending to have someone else's. Wit was supposed to *win*.

Strength won tonight. The vampires won because they overpowered the humans. The cultists won Leopold because their magic allowed them to. Erika won Horizon's Edge because she was fierce enough to fight for it. Even Florence won the respect of everyone there because of her actions.

It was only Alfie who did not win. Not the match, not Horizon's Edge, not the respect of his cousin.

He lost.

He stepped into Leopold's obnoxiously sized kitchen that stank of bleach. Most of it was just sterile, empty space, emphasised further by the white walls, white tiles, and white marble countertops—nothing like the cluttered chaos of home. His leather loafers dragged dirt in behind him as he avoided the footprints he left the first time he came in to lock the window. He checked the lock five times again, but the knot in his chest did not release him.

Erika looked *mad* at the manor. She thought she hid it well, but he caught the subtle disappointed glares she let slip. She'd not mentioned what happened *yet*. After her warning at the hotel, he had no doubt a lecture was coming.

One he deserved.

He jolted when a cupboard door slammed behind him.

"Sorry, Alf," said Alex. He never moved gracefully, but somehow managed to slide into the kitchen unnoticed. Alfie *should have* noticed him.

"Hey." Alex squeezed his shoulder. "Sorry I scared you."

Alfie rolled his eyes. "You didn't. It's fine."

Alex blocked the doorway before he could escape, brandishing surrendering hands, a bag of sweet and salty popcorn in one of them.

"I know tonight was terrible, but your sister will be okay. Erika's looking after her."

"She shouldn't be!"

Shit. Too loud. Too loud.

Alex's eyes broadened. That was the loudest he ever heard Alfie speak. It wasn't like him.

Alfie cleared his throat. "She's *my* sister. I should be the one to do that."

Alex frowned. "We can show you how to do the dressing, but I think Erika is—"

"I don't mean the dressing." When Alex's confusion deepened, Alfie sighed. "My mum told me to look after Florence because she can be a little… hasty, I suppose." Alex laughed at that. Alfie didn't. "Now look where we are. Florence was hasty, I was afraid. I can't… do this."

"Everyone has their bad days, Alf. You just need to—"

"Every day is a bad day! Every single day, I have somehow managed to mess something up. I know the theory, inside and out. I can tell you how to solve a haunting and identify an arcane's affinity. I can recite the Code *and* the Treaty word for word, but none of that has helped me! I'm not brave like Florence or Erika or you."

Alex dropped the popcorn on the counter. Alfie worried he might hug him, but Alex lowered his arms as he approached. He clasped his shoulders, forcing Alfie to look up.

Dad used to do the same thing.

"We've all got bravery in us. Some more than others. Some have too much to the point of being idiots, like me or Florence. Others are more mellow, like your cousin."

"Erika has no fear," Alfie argued.

"She does," Alex retorted. "Why do you think she wandered off with The Collector tonight?"

Alfie shrugged.

"Because she was scared of losing you. You were in the limelight tonight. You were the one The Collector was looking at. As much as she wanted to get that blade without violence, she knew that man wouldn't give up something so precious to a teenager. She took him to one side to suss him out. It got her hurt, but she chose that because she was frightened he would hurt you."

"Does that make her brave? Or scared?" Alfie wondered. Fear, like any other negative emotion—wrath, jealousy, greed, pride—drew demons towards the Veil's edge. Feeling any of them was a risk.

Alex only smiled as if the risk didn't matter. "It makes her a human being. One that loves you."

He picked up the popcorn and sidestepped around Alfie to rummage through the cupboards some more. When Alfie reached the doorway, he paused. "Alex?"

Alex stuck his head out of the cupboard.

"Is Erika angry?"

The sigh gave it away. Of course she was. "Like I said: she's human. But angry or not, she loves you."

"She loves Florence too."

"Which is why she's angry."

Alfie removed his glasses to wipe his eyes. When he turned to leave, a bag hit him in the head.

"Nibble on this," Alex ordered. "It'll make you feel better."

Alfie picked up the bag. "How is sweet and salty popcorn going to make me feel better?"

"It always makes *me* feel better."

"That's you, Alex."

"Which makes it an accurate statement, if you want to be pedantic. Have a munch."

Alfie rolled his eyes, but he could not deny the smile this strange man caused. He was odd. Very odd. Then again, all five of them spent their evening playing poker, drinking, and dancing with hundreds of supernaturals while undertaking the world's worst heist.

They were *all* odd. *Very* odd.

CHAPTER THIRTY-TWO

Be careful who you let inside your heart. Your father never listened, but you should.

Philip Lupine's Journal, Second Edition.

Erika checked on Florence three times before her cousin threw bathwater her way. The fourth time she entered, she waved a white towel ready for her when she was finished bathing. She left it on the radiator, warming it as Diana did.

Downstairs, the boys set up camp. Already, a healthy dinner, defined by Alex as popcorn, crisps, cereal bars, and salsa, had been laid on the glass coffee table behind the L-shaped sofa: red to match the loveseat upstairs. Beside the food, a first aid kit waited, and Alex chose comfortable clothes for each of them. She noticed two piles of Alfie's and figured one was for Nathaniel to lend.

Nathaniel followed her into the room, mismatched pillows from all the bedrooms in his arms, stacked high.

"Where are your things?" Erika asked him.

He dumped the pillows in the middle of the room. The wild, blonde strands of his fringe matted to his forehead. "Back at my hotel. I couldn't bring it all to The Collector's."

"We can go get it tomorrow, if you'd like," she offered.

"No, thank you," he replied. "I left in a hurry, so I didn't have much with me, anyway."

"No weapons or anything?"

He shrugged. "Literally a blunt pocketknife still on me. I'm not a Hunter, remember?"

Right. What reason would he have to carry around crossbows, daggers, and guns like the rest of them?

Erika circled the sofa and helped Nathaniel toss the pillows atop it. For safety, they'd all be sleeping here tonight.

"Speaking of The Collector," she began, "how did you know he had Horizon's Edge?"

"Dad let slip a little more than he should have about his past. He warned me about The Morrigan as a kid, I think to try and scare me into eating my vegetables or something weird like that, and told me about the dagger she was trapped inside.

He was not afraid of her name as Leopold was. "But how did you know The Collector had it? If it was common knowledge, the Divines would have reclaimed it."

"The Collector has—well *had*—influence with the vampires. I don't know how my dad discovered he had the blade, but once he did, he became a target. Dad feared for his life and mine if he admitted what he knew to the Divines or the Council."

It was an understandable excuse. Selfish, but understandable. "At least The Collector only wanted to lock it in a case to gawk at."

Nathaniel laughed. "Such a waste, isn't it? To have something so powerful, to go to the ends of the world to get it, just to shove it in a box."

Erika nodded knowingly. "Powerful things make people think they're invincible."

"But it doesn't *make* them powerful."

"No." Erika tossed a cushion at the sofa—harder than she intended. "But it makes them dangerous."

"What does that make the cult? Powerful or dangerous?"

She met his eyes for a second. Ivy green and unblinking. "Both. They have followers, influence which makes them powerful."

"And the blade—"

"Makes them dangerous as well. They won't kill our families without it. They have it and we're doomed."

"So that's how you see power? Not strength, but... influence?"

Both paused as they reached for the final pillow. "As much as I prefer to work alone, I cannot deny there's strength in numbers."

"But surely one powerful individual could overcome, say, ten weaker ones." *Like The Morrigan.*

Erika shook her head. "Not always."

"Okay then, what would you rather fight with? Five—" He opened his left palm. "Or one?" He closed his right fist and made slow punching motions with both.

Erika sighed and took his left hand. She shoved it onto the fist and forced his fingers to clamp around it tightly.

"Numbers to overwhelm." She dug his thumb and little finger in to form a gap in his fist. "Everyone has a role. And if we play our role correctly..." She used her three middle fingers to open up the fist, twisting his wrist to expose the palm. "The weaker side can win."

She released him, leaving him bewildered as she took the last pillow and tossed it onto the far end of the sofa.

"But... surely not. If The Morrigan rises..."

"Why do you think *humans* are the ones responsible for maintaining order over the supernatural?" Erika challenged. "We're certainly not the most powerful faction. We don't have magic or immortality or a monster form. We train as individuals, learn our strengths, and our Order calls upon our Generals and Sentinels when and if we're needed. United, we're powerful."

He pursed his lips and made his way to the first aid kit. A deep scratch ran down his neck below his left ear.

It looked *nasty*.

"Were you hurt?" Erika asked him.

"Hm? Oh." He touched the wound. "No, no. It's just a scratch."

She angled to look at it. "That looks quite deep. Do you want it dressing?"

"No. I'd rather save it all for Florence."

"It's really no—"

"We don't have a lot." He opened the first aid kit to prove it. Either Leopold was constantly patching up wounds or he didn't care enough to restock it. "I'll survive. She needs it more than me."

Memory of Florence's burn had her surrendering, and she pushed by Nathaniel to take the kit upstairs.

Erika dressed the burns as best she could, offered Florence painkillers for an easy night's sleep, and brought a t-shirt and some joggers for her to change into. Florence struggled descending the stairs alone and expelled a sob on the final one. Erika made a bed for her on the sofa, giving her the most room to stretch out, and tucked her in with one of Leopold's fur blankets before heading back upstairs to get changed.

Erika scrubbed and scrubbed in the shower, only now conscious of just how much blood and dirt she was covered in. The dirt came off with ease, but blood from that poor girl clung beneath her nail beds. Every time she closed her eyes, she saw Florence dressed in yellow, dying in her arms at the top of the stairs, inches from freedom.

Alfie didn't move. He watched it all unfold and he *didn't. Fucking. Move.*

Her skin wrinkled by the time she stepped out of the shower, smelling of Leopold's bleachy body wash, but clean. When she reached the bedroom she left her clothes in, she picked up the phone and made a call.

"Erika!" God, she needed to hear Diana's voice. "Is everything okay? How are the twins?"

"I can't do this, Diana. They're not ready."

She paused. Erika pictured Diana's face twisting in thought. "Tell me what happened."

She told her everything: Percy and Vivienne, the lead to Wyatt, The Collector, Leopold, meeting Alex. Diana gasped, learning of Florence's injury, and sighed at the cause.

"I was afraid it would be like this."

Erika tensed. "Alfie is a coward, Diana. I'm sorry, but he is. And Florence is brash. Both have nearly gotten us all killed at some point." Erika had not been perfect, but she blamed her part-time babysitting duties for that. Every moment was spent wondering how she could keep the twins from imminent danger.

"I knew their weaknesses before they set off, but… I thought…"

"They're not ready."

"No, they are!" Diana insisted. "They needed training at some point, and you needed support."

"I would have been better off leaving Ollie with them and you coming with me," Erika replied.

"You know I would have if I could," Diana said sadly. "I could always—"

"No," Erika snapped. "No, I only trust you or the twins to watch over him." She wiped her eyes. She craved a hunt with her aunt and despised side-lining her. She'd be an asset.

"Speaking of which, how is he?"

"He's Ollie," Diana replied. "Maybe a bit more snappy than usual, though."

"Is he giving you trouble?"

"No, no. Nothing I can't handle."

Erika laughed. "You've handled lychans, ghosts, vampires—everything."

"Yet raising four children is somehow more difficult."

Erika snorted. Even at eighteen, the twins were difficult. They meant well, but good intentions only seemed to make things worse.

Erika lowered herself to sit on the bed. Alex left his clothes there while he showered.

"Talk to them," Diana urged. "Tell them what they're doing right and wrong, but give them space to grow. Within reason, of course. I don't want any more injuries on this hunt."

"This isn't a camping trip!"

"It's not too dissimilar to the ones your grandfather took Chris and I on." She shuddered. "Our careers started *early*."

Erika sighed through her nose. It was too late to send the twins home now. With Leopold captured, it was a race to Wyatt Martin.

"So, what about this 'Alex' guy then?"

Erika crossed one leg over the other, wincing at the pain. Those stairs hurt more than she realised at the time. "He's nice. Why?"

"Come on, you have to give me more than 'nice!'"

Erika frowned. "Why'd you ask?"

"Flo's been texting me."

"Saying?"

"That the two of you have been, you know, *friendly*."

Erika blinked. "*Friends* tend to be *friendly*."

"Oh, so that's what you are? Friends."

"Yes! Friends."

She snorted a laugh. "Heard that one before."

Just once. Diana had always been suspicious, but she knew better than to reference Pete. Erika reached for the quartz around her neck. *Silence.* "I'm going now."

"No, no, wait! Is he cute?"

"Bye, Diana!"

She ended the call, Ollie at the forefront of her mind. Was something bothering him at school? Or was it—

It was her. Her absence, her loose promises, her secrets.

Anger was better than nothing, but anger paved the way for possession. She *needed* to make things right with him.

The quartz twirled between her fingers. "Pete," she whispered. "Are you there?"

The crystal stayed cold in her shaking grasp.

Once dressed, Erika stormed out of the room, her hands landing on a hot, damp chest.

"Oh!"

Erika averted her gaze from the towel wrapped tightly around a dark, water-speckled waist and up six deep contours to meet Alex's stunned features. His hair was soaked, the curls ebony-black. He, too, smelled like Leopold, but through all that musk she found his sweetness.

He smiled. "Hi, friend."

"Eavesdropping on me now, Arwood?"

"I was just about to knock. My clothes are…" He pointed over her shoulder towards the bedroom.

"Oh." She nodded. "I see."

Silence. Nothing but the drip, drip, drip of the shower water running down his calves, off his shoulders, along his jaw. So many ridges, so much muscle, so much—

Alex raised a brow, chewing on a smile. "Can I…?"

His eyes—dark and deep—flicked to Erika's hands—the ones still on his chest.

She yanked them away, spraying water. "Sorry."

"No, it's fine. You can touch them again, if you'd like?"

Her heart stopped. *I can have fun if I wish.* "Why would I want to?"

He gestured to himself, and the towel fell dangerously low. *Please no.* "Why *wouldn't* you want to?"

Erika tore her eyes away to hide the truth, her face heating as she let herself imagine what was beneath that towel. Why, *why* would she do that? "Put some clothes on."

"But you can't feel the mighty force of my chest through the cotton."

"Clothes. *On.*"

She kept her back to him as she trudged down the stairs, unsure whether she was biting back a smile or nausea.

The echoes of his cackling laughter tugged at her lips.

Downstairs, Alfie made his bed in the corner, a fur blanket tucked under his chin, glasses folded up by his side. Erika needed to speak with him, but not now.

Florence and Nathaniel chatted on the far end of the sofa, the latter's arm draped over her cousin, with a blanket covering their laps.

"Too much touching," Erika warned them.

Florence didn't budge. "He's just being friendly."

She knew what 'friendly' meant to her, and her mother. "Five inches. I want to see five inches between the two of you."

Nathaniel retracted his arm. "Erika, this is completely—"

"Five seconds to move five inches."

Florence's jaw dropped. "Erika!"

"Five."

They didn't move. She reached for her crossbow. "Four."

She loaded her weapon.

Nathaniel flung himself off the sofa, landing with a thud. Erika thanked him and made up her own bed, ensuring a satisfactory view of the doors.

"Would she have actually shot me?" Nathaniel whispered.

Erika heard the cogs ticking within Florence. Considering what happened to her ex, Ricky, after his cheating scandal…

Florence shrugged. "Not *fatally*."

Smart girl.

Alex slotted in beside Erika as she plumped up her pillow, greeting her with a jovial *Hi, friend*. Everyone settled into their sleeping positions as he turned off the final lamp.

Soon Florence snored while Nathaniel's breathing turned heavy. Alex positioned himself so his head almost touched Erika's, their bodies miles apart.

He rolled over. "What did the Collector do to you?"

She sighed, her head ringing. "Do we have to—"

"Please. I can't sleep thinking about it."

She considered telling him to turn over and try, but the desperation in his eyes was visible even in the dark. He thought the worst.

And despite the remnants of The Collector's fingerprints on her neck, it could have been a lot worse.

She kept her voice low, out of earshot of the others. "He knew we planned to steal Horizon's Edge. He spiked me with this vampiric wine, and I woke up in his bedroom."

"His *bedroom?*"

"Nothing happened," she said quickly. "Really. I have a headache, but I'm fine."

He reached to touch her chin as if her face held the truth. "But the blood…"

"Not mine," she croaked. "There was a girl, she… she broke a vase and The Collector punished her for it. She was in a room close to me, bleeding out. I tried to save her and she…" She bit back a whimper. "We were so close, and—"

"Hey." Alex's hand stroked her jaw and cheek, incredibly close. A finger almost touched her lips. "You did what you could."

"And it wasn't enough."

His gaze slid down the bruising on her neck. His touch followed it, retracting as she winced.

"Are you sure he did nothing else?"

"*Yes, Alex.*" She laughed at his persistence but warmth soared through her, blocking out the pain. "Though I do appreciate you asking. Thank you."

His mouth curved into a half smile, a breathy laugh escaping. "Stop it. All of this *friendship* is making me blush."

She rolled her eyes. "And here I was being grateful. I won't thank you next time."

"You turned this conversation into mush."

"You're the mushy one."

"Right, I forgot. You're the cold, heartless Hunter, aren't you?"

"The empty crevice in my chest makes men shiver."

He shrugged. "I'm quite toasty."

She put a palm to his forehead and turned it over. *Warm.* The feeling made her chuckle. "Then you're an idiot."

For a moment, they just looked at each other, wondering, frowning; their hands touching one another with gentle hesitation.

Both cleared their throats when the air turned heavy.

"I think it's time for bed," Alex proclaimed.

"Yep." Erika adjusted her blanket. "Sleep it is."

"Time for… sleeping."

Erika rolled onto her back. She could never sleep in such a position, but she had to face something other than Alex.

It took ten seconds for him to speak again. "Do you think we can do this?"

Erika tore her eyes off the ceiling. "Sorry?"

"Save our families. Stop the cult. We have Horizon's Edge, sure, but that witch-queen, that *Morrigan*, sounds powerful."

"I don't doubt that she is, but we're not stupid. If we work efficiently and get to Wyatt Martin, the seven of us can work together to get our families back."

"I know, but… seven?"

She blinked. "I meant six."

To her relief, he brushed off her mistake. "Thank you for not leaving me alone in Edinburgh. I wouldn't have come this far without you."

"Of course you wouldn't have."

"Your humility is striking, Erika."

"So I've been told. However, I…" She rolled back over. "I suppose I couldn't have done this without you, either. If I left the hotel and someone ended up dead, I could never forgive myself. I was harsh."

"Do you think you would have managed better alone? No me, no twins?"

She licked her lips and shuddered when she caught Alex looking at them. "I thought, if I could tick off a solo hunt, I could do anything. That I could wrangle my cousins into some kind of team; that I could beat every supernatural standing in the way of success, but I…"

As it turned out, she couldn't control them all. Florence ran off, Alfie wouldn't move, and Alex's mindset was different than hers. Dad's advice prepared her for monsters, not mayhem.

Despite it all—despite her lack of a real answer—Alex gripped her hand and squeezed. "You don't have to do everything alone, Erika."

"I'm not alone," she said quickly.

"But you try to be. You sideline the twins, create back-up plans without consulting us… Why did you take a tour with The Collector?"

"I—"

"Because you didn't trust Alfie."

She held her breath because he was right. She didn't trust Alfie to win Horizon's Edge, nor did she really trust Florence to stay safe with Nathaniel. In the end, she was right. Alfie failed, and Florence never would have been burned if she were close enough for Erika to yank her out of the way of the arcane's firing line.

Alex's voice lowered to a breathy sigh. "Do you trust me, Erika?"

Her body paused, everything suspended apart from the deafening thud of her heart.

He pulled Percy away from her. He dragged her from the pool. He carried her away from Aurelia, kicking and screaming.

"With my life," she answered.

"And with the hunt?"

That was a different matter. But he wasn't a Lupine. He wouldn't *get it.*

He forced a sad smile, squeezing her fingers so hard she felt his racing pulse. "Trust that we'll get through this *together*, Erika. Trust me the way I trust you."

Echoes of his smile lingered when he let go. Alex was an attractive man, evidently prone to the attention that came with such an asset. He had the kind eyes, strong arms, a smile of sunshine—but his soul was golden. Everything he did was to keep people safe. By all accounts, he was one of the superheroes Ollie idealised. His father would be proud, but Erika dreaded the moment they reunited out of fear she'd never see Alex again.

Dad's argument against the notion reverberated in her skull, his three reasons shattering her heart and drowning the shards with guilt.

Their backs almost touched as they rolled over. Erika felt Alex's heat but, despite shuddering under a draft, did not move closer.

"Sleep well, Erika," he said.

Her chest tightened, and a feeling stirred within. She pulled the blanket up to her shoulders with a frown, covering all inches of bare skin.

She wished him goodnight but did not sleep until mere hours before dawn.

CHAPTER THIRTY-THREE

Dreams are just dreams—until they are not.

Secrets of the Veil by Cassandra Starling, Chapter Three.

Over twisting overgrowth and arthritic, pointing branches, Erika barrelled through the forest, choking in the blanket of night. Candlelight blinked in the distance, but she did not follow—she fled. Her limbs weighed heavy. Her feet dragged until she reached a clearing.

Not here. What isn't here?

"Erika…"

She expelled a pained breath. "Ollie?"

He shouldn't be *here*. He was home, tucked up in bed in the loft above Diana, where he was safe. This place… this was not safe.

The candlelight caught her.

Braziers ignited in a tormenting circle. She followed the emerging pattern, gasping when the trees disappeared, clearing the grass, letting her see him.

Ollie knelt on the earth, tears silver, reflecting a blade at his neck. Aurelia gripped him tightly. Her skin turned scarlet among the fire and the wink of Horizon's Edge

Erika's feet stuck to the ground, latched in a cage of roots ascending her calves.

She called his name. She called Aurelia's. She begged and cried, dislocating her fingers to reach her brother.

Almost there now. Almost there…

Aurelia drew her knife across Ollie's throat.

The roots released her as Ollie's body slumped to the ground. Her scream shattered the silent sky when she threw herself over him. When she opened her eyes, she was atop a staircase, sitting beneath an archway lit poorly by a chandelier of dying embers.

Erika woke in a cold sweat, scanning the room for any signs of danger from the sofa.

No Ollie. No Aurelia.

Alex snored quietly beside her, and she calmed. No-one else was awake—no-one but Nathaniel.

She reddened at him catching her in such a state.

"Are you alright?" he asked. He'd shuffled closer to Florence in the night. Their heads rested beside one another. "You look like you haven't slept."

Unfortunately, she had. She wiped the evidence from her tear ducts. "I'm fine. Just a nightmare."

He raised a brow and tilted his head. His injury was just a scratch, it turned out. It was barely visible now. "What did you see?"

Alex stirred before she could object to answer. Nathaniel forgot the interaction as he angled towards Florence's morning smile. Even through her optimism, Erika saw how strained it was from the pain.

After a swift breakfast of chocolate cereals, the group packed their things and made haste in getting back on the road.

Erika frowned at the large bag slumped over Alex's shoulder as he strolled up to the car.

"What is—"

"Leopold's Callaways." He spun to show off the golf clubs.

"And you're bringing them because…?"

"Because he pissed me off," he snapped. "He has to pay for it somehow."

She wanted to remind him of what Leopold potentially faced from the cult, but she only grinned and climbed into the driver's seat without another word.

They wouldn't shut up.

Florence was a social hurricane, and poor Nathaniel had whiplash. From listening to every one of her boybands to smiling at pictures of her art awards' dress and eight-year-deceased hamster. Nathaniel—in all fairness—took it in his stride. Erika kept her ears peeled for any mention of Ollie or their address, but Florence was more careful than she imagined.

Neither she nor Alfie gave any hint of knowing the Martins.

"It was the next left," Alex said as Erika turned off the motorway.

"This way's quicker," she replied.

"It is?" He zoomed in on his phone's GPS and frowned. "How do you know?"

She flicked off the indicator. "Farmer's entrance. He forgets to close the gates all the time."

"And you know this…"

She held her breath. The quartz at her collar grew heavy. Alfie tore his eyes from his book to meet hers through the rear-view mirror. "Because I've been here before."

Alex didn't mask his confusion one bit. "Why is that?"

"Dad and Wyatt hunted together a fair bit. By default, I came along. As did Wyatt's son, Pete."

"Oh. I see."

Thoughts crossed Alex's mind that Erika couldn't read. Despite her curiosity—despite her *guilt*—she didn't push to hear them, wondering instead why the thought of Alex meeting Pete filled her with such dread.

The Martins situated themselves on the far end of a quaint campsite in the Midlands. Surrounded by forestry in the middle of nowhere, it made for a cheap yet safe refuge for the two of them. Unlike the Lupines, there was no 'Diana' to hold down a more domestic fort for the Martins. A two-bedroomed log cabin had to do since Pete's mother left them.

Erika drove between the familiar gap in the walnut trees and smiled at the unchanged cabin. The fence was finished, she realised—still wooden, much to Pete's disgust. *We need wire, not wood*, he insisted.

Wyatt replied with *wire is ugly*, and thus the fence was built from the surrounding trees.

With the group behind, Erika knocked on the door. "Pete!" she called. "Wyatt? It's Erika."

She tried the door. The ominous creak as it opened sent her stomach down to the foundations.

Pete's cabin resembled Alex's flat. Papers littered the floor, as did shards of glass and stuffing from the furniture.

Florence didn't see the state of the apartment in Edinburgh, but she knew what this sight signified. "We're too late. They've found him."

"The cultists have definitely been here." Nathaniel shadowed Erika into the living room and crossed his arms. "But what if they left in time?"

"A good question," Erika pondered. Pete's silence through the quartz failed to reassure her, but there could have been a good reason for that.

She hoped, anyway.

They filed out to investigate the cabin. The twins, Nathaniel, and Alex tentatively tip-toed around the building while Erika strode through the living room, her gaze panning in on Pete's bedroom door. The hallway painting of the late Mittens was torn in half. *Monstrous bastards.*

Pete's room fared worse than the others. Erika took that personally.

The space had not changed much since Pete was a teenager: the ocean-blue quilt, the same dusty, outdated gaming console underneath the television cabinet, a dozen patched-up coats and worn jackets hanging on a metal rack by the bed, and a collage of colourful photographs on a pinboard. Erika lingered by them for longer than she should have, realising she was still in a couple of them.

"Find anything?"

Erika backed away as Alex appeared in the doorway. "Not yet."

She couldn't resist a second look at the photographs, specifically the one of Pete laughing, blinded by flash in the middle of a nightclub.

That boy better be alive.

"They were looking for something," Alex said. He, too, looked at the photo wall. "My flat wasn't torn up nearly as much as this."

"Neither was my lodge," Erika replied.

Perhaps they *had* got away. Everywhere else was nearly destroyed in the cult's plight to get what they needed, but their desperation was most evident here. Erika opened a few drawers to check her theory. Barely any clothes remained.

She didn't notice Alex leave until he called her from the next room. "Erika, I think they left! There aren't any phones or chargers here."

"And no clothes." She pushed the drawer shut. "They must have gone." *Thank God.*

"Then we need to get to them before the cult." Nathaniel entered Pete's bedroom, flanked by both twins. Florence clutched her abdomen, leaning slightly forward.

"If they left in time, they must know something," Alex figured. "They'd be good allies to have."

"But where do we look?" Nathaniel wondered. "If they had enough notice, they could be anywhere in the country by now."

"Or out of it," Alfie added.

"No." Florence shook her head, looking at Erika. "They wouldn't leave. Not when they have friends in danger."

"What choice would they have?" Alfie exclaimed. "They're the last ones! They'd be logical to get away."

The group deliberated on and on while Erika backtracked to the pinboard, her head cocked to one side.

Pete *loved* photography. Every outing was scored with groans and complaints from her for how often he stopped to capture anything he deemed beautiful. All his images were focused, sharp, scattered with detail and hidden meanings carefully crafted by the artist.

Why, then, did he choose to put the most chaotic, blurred photograph of him and Erika at the centre?

She'd been shot better than this by Pete. In fact, she didn't even remember this being taken, courtesy of the cup of vodka in either hand. The print was even *creased*. He was no perfectionist, but with his photos…

She unclipped the photograph, a gasp leaving her lips as she turned it over.

If you're still out there, find us.

Pete.

The symbol he drew below was obvious to all Hunters because it had been branded onto their skin the moment they chose this path forever, the second they passed their trials; an emblem to commemorate the commitment.

"They've gone to the Order," Erika declared. "They've gone to Oblivion's Watch."

CHAPTER THIRTY-FOUR

To coexist equally, we supernaturals require sanctuary. This Treaty proclaims Stryga, Valour, The Labyrinth, and Oblivion's Watch as our honorary Havens.

Speech at the Signing of the Treaty of the Four Worlds, Author Redacted.

Since Initiation, Erika opted to make the gruelling journey to Oblivion's Watch only for the seasonal festivals, if work permitted. The Winter Solstice was always her favourite, though she visited more half-heartedly as of late.

The Hunter's Haven remained almost empty for most of the year, housing the Council, Sentinels, and Hunters with nowhere else to go. They could train, study, or simply wind down, protected by the Curtain. For almost two hundred years, it remained their heart, their mind, their refuge.

And it was *very* far away.

"…now that it's one hundred and sixty years since the War of the Four Factions. Do you know why it's called that?"

Erika wouldn't have blamed Nathaniel for sighing or even hitting Alfie in the middle of the shop, but he resisted. "Because it was a war. Of four factions."

"Correct. Now…"

Erika headed down a separate aisle. Since Florence split from the group to ogle at the new collection in the dress department, Nathaniel was stuck listening to Alfie's history lesson. Erika and Alex held up the rear end of the group, headed for the scarves.

"Of course, the only thing to split the two of them up was dresses," Alex mused.

Erika snorted, scanning the racks for outerwear. "My aunt said that once?"

"About you or Florence?"

Erika cocked her head and scrunched up her nose. "Hazard a guess."

"I thought I had a strong impression of you, but you surprised me at The Collector's. Seeing you in that gold dress was…"

"A dream?"

He pointed a finger so close it tickled her nose. "*Surprising*."

"Surprising?" Erika reached for a set of violet gloves.

"I didn't expect the woman who dragged me from a possessed pool and stabbed an arcane to scrub up like a damned supermodel."

Like a… what?

Her mind and hands stumbled when they latched onto Alex's, who beat her to the gloves. "Sorry," Erika said. "I thought they'd be good for—"

"You."

"Florence," Erika corrected. "I was going to give these to her."

"Oh. Yeah, of course."

Spotting Florence already in possession of a scarf in a similar shade, checking that it matched with Nathaniel's denim jacket, Erika rushed away with a new sense of urgency. She made for the till, catching up to her cousin, and turned around only once to steal a glimpse of Alex staring downcast at his phone with sparkling eyes and a tear rolling down his cheek.

It was an eight-hour trip to Scotland's northern coast, so the Hunters stopped for sandwiches and to stretch their legs twice at the insistence of Alex and Florence. The older Hunters swapped roles halfway through the drive so Erika could rest. It did little to help. Every time she dozily dipped her head, images of the poor girl from the manor fired through her mind.

Alex caught her the third time this happened.

"Are you okay?" she asked before he could.

He blinked and locked his eyes back on the road. "Yeah. Why wouldn't I be?"

She sucked on her dry bottom lip. She finished her water bottle an hour ago. "You look tired."

He scoffed. "Should see yourself!"

Scowling, she yanked down the sun visor and slid open the mirror. *Christ.* Not a second later, she slammed it back up. "Wow. You really know how to compliment a woman, Alex." She rubbed her eyes and yawned, muffling Alex's words.

"...tired, not ugly!"

She made a noise mid-way through her yawn that resembled an owl. "You think I'm ugly?"

"I never—" Alex slapped the steering wheel. "When did I say that?"

"You implied it."

"I really didn't."

"Yes you did."

"Erika, you're beautiful, for God's sake. End of story. I'm too tired for this argument."

Unsure whether it was the words or the sleep deprivation, it took Erika a few moments to compute what he just said. "You think I'm beautiful?"

He turned to stone. "I—"

Florence's head appeared between the car seats, headphones in hand. "Heard that one, Alex."

"No, you didn't."

"Yes, I did."

"No, you didn't. Put your pop shit back on and be quiet."

"Stop it, Flo." Erika grinned at Alex's rosying cheeks. "You're making him blush."

"I don't blush!"

Erika laughed. "That's not what you said last night."

Florence dropped her headphones. Alfie's book slammed shut. Even Nathaniel captured sudden interest in the conversation.

It was Erika's turn to blush. "That's not... That isn't what I—"

"Erika!" Alex grasped his chest. "I never knew you thought of me like *that*."

She scowled at his knowing wink. Was it hot in this car? She could smell smoke.

Nathaniel frowned. "Wait, I thought you two were a thing."

"No!" Erika exclaimed. "Why would you—" *Florence.*

Alfie's lips twitched, almost reaching a smile. "Erika, you look pink."

He already stood on thin ice. "Thank you, Alfie," Erika sighed.

Alex chuckled and tapped Erika's knee. "It's cute, don't worry."

Erika's frown deepened—as did the hole Alex was digging them in. The conversation was innocent enough. *This* interaction was not.

Alfie narrowed his eyes, Nathaniel fought to rein in his laughter, and Florence leaned back in her seat, crossing one leg over the other like a supervillain, grinning maliciously.

"Now this—" Popcorn appeared in her palm and landed in her mouth. "*This* is the content I love."

The car was fucked.

Erika blamed Alex's driving; Alex said the car was a piece of crap, anyway. Either way, smoke choked the five of them, and Erika and Alex wouldn't stop arguing over the danger.

"It's probably fine!" he insisted again.

Erika wasn't sure. Since leaving Pendle Hill, the car had *stunk*. She swore upon leaving Leopold's that the vehicle was not driving as smoothly as before. She knew her car. It felt different.

Twenty minutes of debating later and she turned on the air conditioning. A wave of smoke blew through the fans, and she swept into the hard shoulder, both twins panicking.

"What are you doing?" Nathaniel cried.

She didn't answer. She leapt from the car and swung open the bonnet. She coughed at the sweet but sooty black cloud that rolled out of it.

Alex choked as he propped up the bonnet. "The hell's wrong with it?"

"I don't know." She winced, her eyeballs raw.

They let the smoke clear before Erika turned on her torch to investigate the car. The problem was clear.

Tiny black seeds littered the machinery, trapping themselves between the pipes and the engine's exterior.

She reached to pull one out and swore as her fingertips singed against the metal. She sniffed the seed: sweet then sharp with oil. The ones burning in the engine caused the smell.

"What are they?" Nathaniel asked.

"I have no idea," she confessed. She handed one to Alex, who smelled it as well.

"Neither do I," Alex added. "They're so burnt I can't tell what they're supposed to look like."

Alfie took a look himself. He crumpled away the seed's outer shell. The entire thing collapsed against his thumb.

They cleared the car as best they could on the hard shoulder without burning themselves. It needed cleaning up—carefully—so as not to damage the car. But in a few minutes, they reached a point when they decided enough was enough and it was time to leave. At Alfie's request, she dropped a few in one of the tiny glass jars she kept alongside her weapons.

In the final hours of their journey, Erika's body replenished its energy, her mind awake and active like a weight had lifted from her shoulders. She could not help but wonder over the likelihood of those seeds being planted by something more than a moulting tree or an overzealous breeze.

Alfie burst from the car the moment the engine shut off. He knew he would not catch sight of Oblivion's Watch without passing his trials, yet somehow found disappointment at not spying the basalt walls and pointed spires of the East and Western towers. Instead, he stood on gravel, with only sky in the distance.

"Oblivion's Watch has a car park?" Nathaniel wondered.

No shit, smartarse.

Alex laughed. "Where do you think we put our cars?"

"There's a dog walk in the opposite direction," Erika explained, pointing to a gate slotted in nearby wilderness. "That way, it doesn't look strange for so many cars to be parked in the middle of nowhere."

"Does that mean we have to walk there?"

Of course *Florence* would ask that.

Alfie laughed at Erika's grin. "Oh yes."

Florence growled. "Bloody cardio."

She stomped by, sucking on her inhaler, and Alfie soon followed. He noticed Erika trailing behind and turned to find her eyes wandering over the cars, trying not to look as if she were lagging. She caught up with a downcast expression.

Giddiness rose as fog tickled Alfie's ankles. It rolled in from the hills, bringing with it the sound of crashing waves and sea water kisses. According to the arcanes who cast the Curtain, the fog acted as a reminder that the magic still remained. Alfie's teeth ached from the breeze catching his smile, but it did not falter. They were close—he could feel it.

He knew it was so when Erika and Alex turned their gaze upwards. Alfie mimicked them, unable to see a thing.

One day, Dad said, he would cast his eyes over the wonder that was Oblivion's Watch. One day…

He looked to Erika, hopeful, but she only stared at Florence when he found her eyes. His chest hollowed as he heard the screams, smelled the burning flesh, saw his sister fall. After Alex's conversation with him in the kitchen, he worried his cousin would never forgive him for this.

Erika saved face all of a sudden and loosened her scarf to talk.

"Name?" Alfie heard, but the source of the voice was nowhere to be seen. It came from in front of him.

"Erika Lupine," Erika said—to thin air, apparently. She pulled her collar down and revealed the key: the Hunter's brand. How much did it hurt to receive? Though Alfie supposed the branding would be the easy part.

Alex identified himself and introduced the three youngest, including Alfie.

"I'm responsible for them," Erika added.

Following her nod was the rattling of chains and clanking of metal, and with it, the shroud over the fortress unveiled itself.

The latticed gate stretched at least three floors, but even that was minuscule when compared to the enormity of Oblivion's Watch. Obsidian bricks stacked high into walls defending the spiked, purple watchtowers housing the Sentinels, the East and West, as he anticipated, reaching towards the heavens. The fog still lingered past the Curtain, concealing the northmost tower, which supposedly dug into the cliffside.

A dark-skinned female Sentinel smiled at him as he stepped into the courtyard. "I take it this is your first time?"

Alex laughed. "Can you tell?"

Alfie staggered over the cobblestone. A wilting flowerbed centred the courtyard while evergreens lined the arches leading to the many corridors of the Hunters' Haven. Ivy climbed the walls to an overhead chorus of gulls, forcing his gaze further upwards, knocking him dizzy as he captured the magnitude of the watchtowers from a closer angle.

"This is… There are no pictures that… I can't—"

He inhaled the air: salty like the sea yet, somehow, burnt. Was it magic running through the cracks in stone like saltwater streams below the foundations? What lurked beneath these cobblestones? What did the—

He almost fainted. "Can I see the library?"

"We have a job to do," Erika reminded him. "If we—" She looked at Florence again, focusing on the area her burns touched beneath the layers of clothing. "When we finish our task, I'll take you."

"If it's as amazing as this, I think I might have to go, too," Florence replied. She laughed at Alfie's open mouth. "You've been dreaming about this since birth."

"You've always wanted to—"

"I know," she stopped him. She closed the gap between them to hush her voice. "And I'm glad we're both here."

Mum would be ecstatic. Was Dad smiling down on them?

The pair rushed inside when they realised they were the only ones left in the courtyard.

In tribute to the Scottish monarch who last owned the castle, Oblivion's Watch maintained a similar interior to what Alfie imagined to be the epitome of seventeenth-century tastes, with teak, panelled walls decorated with Renaissance paintings and portraits. He recognised very few of those they passed, though some names inscribed below rang bells from his supernatural history module at college.

He crossed his arms, wrapping his scarf around them. Bridgette Bishop's *Crossing Oblivion* claimed the hold was freezing, but Alfie figured central heating had been installed since the book's release. Thundering shivers down his body made him homesick for Mum's hot chocolates.

The entourage turned a corner and approached a desk: dark wood to match the rest of the interior. Erika signed them all in using a fountain pen and a green leather book.

"Is it always this cold?" Florence wondered. Nathaniel's gloved hand snaked around his sister's waist. Alfie glowered.

"In the corridors, yes,' Erika admitted. "The rooms are a lot warmer. They have heaters, and most have fireplaces as well."

Alfie had to ask. "Does Oblivion's Watch have installed heating?"

"Of course it does, we're not animals!" Alex exclaimed. "But, to save money, the corridors and lower levels aren't heated."

Alfie turned up his nose at the sour mildew.

Florence angled towards Nathaniel. "Then I'm definitely not going down there."

Alfie, desiring to ask what was in those lower levels, soon lost his voice to Nathaniel's arm urging Florence further into him. He glared at the stranger, who picked up on his distaste, though he did not let go.

Erika either did not see the interaction or chose to ignore it, and ushered them on, her mind distracted by someone else.

Erika said the assembly hall remained open most days outside of events. It being early December, the Winter Solstice Festival had not yet begun, making it one of the quieter times for Watch residents or visitors while working Hunters scrambled to get as much work in as possible before a long rest. Alfie pushed to know more about the festivities, but all Erika and Alex could offer were snickers about the volume of alcohol drunk and the masses of food eaten.

They reached the mouth of a broad corridor, headed towards a set of arched, wooden doors. A heated argument snuck beneath the doorframe, as did sounds of scraping chairs and swearing Hunters.

"You said you knew Wyatt Martin," Alex said to Erika.

Alfie's cousin said nothing for, if luck permitted, Alex would see just how familiar she was to him.

Or, at least, to his son.

Tarnish the Veil

The doors boomed open, and a voice cried her name.

CHAPTER THIRTY-FIVE

When you pass your trials, to walk freely among the Watch is a reward in itself.
The Hunter's Codex, Chapter IV.

Pete took off into a sprint. Erika's voice broke into sobbing laughter as he lifted her off the floor.

"You're alive!"

"*You're* alive!"

Her hands stroked the fuzz on the back of his neck as he hugged her. *Warmth.* Electric warmth. *Real* warmth. She breathed in his scent: unchanged from his refreshing mint and earthy sandalwood.

He squeezed and shook her side to side, then set her down with the utmost care. His hands reached her face, forcing her to look at his.

Pete was here, alive and well. Not a single scratch on him despite the tears in his oaky eyes. Her thoughts reflected in him, she realised. They had no contact since the abductions started. He likely assumed she had been taken, too.

But the photo…

He held onto hope.

"We've been worried sick." said Pete, gesturing to the other Hunters. Half a dozen, including his father, gathered at the fireplace where Pete stood as they entered, watching the new arrivals. "When we heard Hunters were being taken, we came straight here. I wanted to contact you to see if you and Chris were okay, but… Dad said no."

"It's fine, Pete," she assured him. Her own father would have made the same call. "But the cult is almost finished. They only need one more Hunter."

Pete swallowed. "Dad?" He sighed at her nod. "Deepest shit we've been in, right?"

Despite the circumstances, Erika managed a smile. "A few other things come close."

"Unfortunately, the wrath of Chris Lupine doesn't come close to what Aurelia wishes to unleash." Wyatt Martin appeared behind his far-taller son, his countenance grave yet inviting. "It's good to see you, Erika."

After a brief hug, she introduced the duo to the more unfamiliar Hunters who joined them.

"Glad to meet you both," Pete said to Nathaniel and Alex. "Wish it were under better circumstances."

"How many are here?" Alex asked, looking past Pete to those gathered by the fire. "The families, I mean."

"Twenty-two," Pete replied. "They're mostly kids, but there are some spouses and siblings eager to help. I thought Dad and I were alone at first, but coming here, we found others already gathered. None of the original Hunters, obviously."

"We met one of your old friends," Alex said to Wyatt. "Leopold Hopkins."

"Judging from his absence, I take it the cult got there first," Pete responded.

Alex's brows furrowed. For once, he looked strangely… hostile. "The cult got there first."

"He betrayed us," Erika clarified. "He thought offering up Alex and me would spare his own life. In addition to—" She stopped herself, conscious of what she might give away. Horizon's Edge buzzed in her pocket. "Something more," she finished.

Florence pushed through Alex and Alfie to get to the front. "But we managed to get—"

"Not here," Erika silenced her. Even in their stronghold, they had to be cautious. Another 'Leopold' could be lurking anywhere. Like him and Nathaniel, not everyone here was sworn to the Code.

Pete tapped her lower back. "Then follow me."

Their group expanded as they exited the assembly hall, accompanied now by the relatives of those lost.

Casual chatter rumbled the narrow corridors on their descent to the war room. The lowest chambers dug down deep into the cliff, as was evident when bricks blended into carved stone. Crashing waves echoed on the walls, and frigid moisture nipped the air.

Rarely did Alfie's voice extend over his sister's, but his multitude of questions managed that.

Pete laughed. "Still haven't lost that curiosity, have you, Mullein?"

Alfie composed himself, cheeks raw. "I like to know what I'm getting myself into."

"Well, we're safe here, don't worry. Arcanes can't Shadow Travel through the Curtain, and no-one but the Hunters knows of these tunnels."

"I thought arcanes built this stronghold?" Nathaniel wondered.

"They did," Wyatt replied from the head of the group. "But *we* built these tunnels with the help of our lychan friends. We decided their existence should remain secret when the Watch itself was built."

In case the Covens ever rebelled. An unlikely scenario, but it was good to be prepared. Especially since a select few revolted that very second.

"*And* I'd like to see them get past our Sentinels," Pete added. His laughter reverberated through the tunnel. "They can kick arse, as Erika and I know."

From their training days. Erika was almost certain the bruise on her backside never truly healed. Trainer Lucien was a prick.

Wyatt dipped into a side room. It was far smaller than the assembly hall in both length and height—poor Pete almost touched the ceiling – but large enough to fit the twenty-something Hunters cramming around the stone table in the centre. Unfortunately, the air remained just as brisk as it did in the corridor thanks to the three empty arches standing in as windows against the merciless ocean.

Erika shuddered against the breeze.

"Need a jacket?" Pete teased.

He had no ground to stand on. He shook like a leaf even during summer nights. "You'll be needing it," she whispered.

He cackled, yet when he shrugged his shoulders to take off his jacket, she stopped him. "No," she simply said.

The jacket went back on—not before revealing a glint of silver hanging around his neck that pulled the air from Erika's lungs.

She chugged the relief and pain like a handful of pills.

A Hunter a little older than Erika, with raven hair and eyes of ice, stepped before the crowd. "Should we not be contacting the Divines?" she said.

"That would be unwise," Wyatt replied.

Erika added, "We've been betrayed by our own kind. Who knows whether the Divines can be trusted?"

"That's pessimistic," a nearby blonde said, shutting the door behind her.

"But *smart*," said the dark-skinned woman beside her, her hair braided into four. Erika recognised her from her training years: Lily. They passed their trials the same month. "Considering what is at stake, we must be cautious."

"And fast," Alex added. "Consulting the Divines will only slow us down."

"Then we are in agreement?" Wyatt combed the room. "No Divines. Not yet."

The room nodded.

"The whole Council is here today," he went on. "Whatever we dictate we do, I'll consult them tonight to ensure we have the legality to press on."

Another hurdle, but hopefully a small one. The Council had to see just how many lives hung in the balance here.

Pete smacked the table decisively. "Now, then. All we need is a plan."

Erika snorted. "That's all?"

Wyatt conveyed everything he knew to the Hunters. *Everything*.

Much to Erika's relief, Leopold's intel proved fruitful. A woman named Katia Starling, who turned out to be the raven-haired girl's mother, led an investigation against the cult decades ago. Wyatt was part of that team, only they realised far too late that the cultists had caught onto them, leaving a trail of breadcrumbs so the Hunters believed they could kill The Morrigan while she slept. Thirty Hunters joined the entourage. Only twelve survived.

With the deaths of their comrades and the anchoring from Horizon's Edge, The Morrigan possessed enough magic to burst from her coffin, entwined in a vortex of what Wyatt described as 'blood-soaked flames.' She resurfaced only for a matter of minutes before Katia landed the killing blow with the blade that revived her.

A scarlet-eyed Wyatt brandished the blade that Erika surrendered.

"This weapon is not only a magical anchor. It holds the souls of the dead. If the twelve perish and, God-forbid, the tomb opens, the cult need only stab the slumbering body of their queen, and her soul will return."

"But," said Alex, "if she's trapped inside, would that not mean she'll *stay* dead if we destroy the blade?"

A fair point—if not a hasty one.

Wyatt grimaced. "Breaking it may do more harm than good," he said. "For all we know, her soul may linger rather than pass on."

"The last thing we need is an immortal, vengeful witch-queen parading about," Pete joked—*half*-joked. Erika's stomach looped at the prospect of having said queen in her bag for the last two days.

The room turned silent, everyone's eyes on the blade, minds on what would be unleashed if it fell in the wrong hands. Erika's own ticked on.

They knew *how* the ritual worked, *what* it was for, *where* it would take place… But, without knowledge of where the Hunters were kept, a rescue attempt was an impossible feat.

Unless…

"What are you thinking?" Pete asked.

She cleared her throat. "They need only two things to complete the ritual: Horizon's Edge… and your bloodline."

He pursed his lips. He always looked good when he did that. "Go on."

She swallowed, knowing the risk of what she was suggesting. "We can lure them out with the blade."

"Out of the question," Katia's daughter objected. "That blade has their queen inside it. Without it, even if the twelve are sacrificed, she cannot be revived. It must remain *here*."

"Vanessa's right." Erika frowned at Pete's agreement. He folded his arms tightly, sucking in a breath. "And in that case… I'll offer myself up."

"Again, out of the question." Erika retorted.

Wyatt sighed. "I'm inclined to agree. You are right in what you say, Erika, but the blade cannot be given up." The room stirred at his pause. "Neither can my son."

Pete stepped before him. "I can't let you—"

"I won't allow a son to pay for his father's mistakes. Especially not my own."

"Dad, it wasn't your fault."

"We sanctioned *blood magic*," Wyatt hissed. "If we did not do so, eleven of our own would be safe and well."

Wyatt's voice-crack pained Erika. She realised, then, just how much the man had aged in the few months since she last saw him. Grey streaked the front sections of his outgrown curly hair, curiously whiter at the front than the back. She wondered if Pete's would turn the same unique style when he grew old.

"I will be the bait," Wyatt decided. "When I'm captured, I will drop false hints as to where the blade is so they take us to Bekker's while they wait for someone to fetch it. You will surround the clearing and attack on my signal."

"What if they wait longer?" Lily unfolded her arms from the back of the room. "We could be sitting there for days, weeks, even."

Wyatt smiled. "Tomorrow is a full moon, my dear. They will carry out the sacrifices tomorrow if they can. That way, their queen will wake at maximum strength."

Making it all the more crucial to succeed.

"And the signal?" Alex pressed.

Instinctively, Erika and Pete's eyes locked. With no-one else offering a solution, Erika gently lifted the silver chain from around her neck. The dangling crystal winked in the ribbons of light from the archways, tinting her cheeks pink.

"I noticed you still have yours," she said to Pete, failing miserably to be nonchalant. Then to Wyatt she added, "Hold it tight and you can talk to Pete through this."

She shivered at the nakedness that came with surrendering the necklace. She glimpsed its twin watching from Pete's chest and wondered just how much he wore it. She kept hers tucked away in her bag every day since they ended things, just in case they needed each other again.

Just in case.

"Where did you get these?" Wyatt asked Pete.

"Just a friend." Pete's eyes shifted between the space on Erika's neck and a spot on the stone table as he coughed. "But she's right. These will work well, and the cultists won't suspect a thing."

"It's settled then, I guess." The sharpness in Alex's tone startled Erika. "Wyatt hands himself over, we stand by at the ritual site, save the Hunters when they arrive, and then…?"

"The cultists are restrained," Wyatt declared. "And we call on their Divines to attend their hearings."

Vanessa groaned, so Erika reminded her, "Cornering and killing arcanes without the go-ahead from Divines will only cause a diplomatic incident."

Deadpan, Vanessa bit back, "I'm well aware of the Code, thank you, Erika."

Then the attitude was unnecessary.

Erika looked towards Pete. "As much as we'd all like to get our own back on the cultists, we must hold back. Restrain as much as you want—they're a powerful bunch, so I encourage it—but I don't want to see any unnecessary cruelty."

"Is it cruel if it's simply getting even?" Alex cocked his head, awaiting an answer. Erika thought of the burns covering Florence's skin and resisted voicing her agreement.

"In the ideal scenario, no-one dies tomorrow," Pete replied. "Enough suffering has happened thanks to this cult, don't you think?"

He did not say it, but Alex's silence showed compliance.

"I will speak with the Council," Wyatt declared. "If they authorise the mission, we leave by ten tomorrow morning. Convene here fifteen minutes prior for any last-minute arrangements and technicalities."

His gulp echoed while his eyes cast over the room.

"Get some rest," he begged. "I have a feeling we'll all need it."

CHAPTER THIRTY-SIX

Built on the ruins of King James I's private hunting residence, Oblivion's Watch provides shelter and warmth despite the monarch's misguidance.

A Hunter's History by Alexei Arwood, Chapter Two.

Alex left for the check-in desk alone. Nathaniel and the twins waited with Pete and Wyatt in the dining hall, while Erika headed back to the car to grab the overnight bags.

Hurried footsteps made her whirl as she reached the doors to the courtyard. "Alf?"

His face was already red and damp with sweat. God, he needed to take up running. "I wanted…' He wheezed. "I want to—sorry."

Erika reached for the heavy iron handle. "I did want this to be quick."

"I know, I—I wanted to say I was sorry."

She raised a brow. "About?"

He swallowed. "The manor."

This conversation had been hanging between them like a brewing storm cloud. Alfie wiped his glasses. "I froze when I shouldn't have. I do it all the time, I know. Back at the party, at Pendle Hill… I don't know why I do it, but I realise there are consequences to it. Serious ones. Florence could have—"

He couldn't even bring himself to say it, but Erika *saw* it—saw Florence burn and scream as if she were as close as Alfie right now.

"You're right," she said. "*That* could have happened, and it almost did."

"I'm sorry."

"It's not me you should be apologising to."

Air dropped from his lips in a sigh. "Considering what tomorrow may bring, I should talk to her tonight."

Erika almost cursed. She waved an arm, signalling for him to follow her to the car. He could help carry the bags.

"About that," she said as the doors boomed closed. "I've been thinking—"

"You don't want us to come," he finished.

She could have sugar-coated it, but that was futile with Alfie. "No."

"Because we're not ready."

Sentinels smiled as they allowed the pair through the gates. Alfie staggered to stare at the evaporating castle.

"No. After the hotel, the manor… There've been too many instances where I've had to compromise the job to keep you two safe. Even then, I've not achieved much in that department."

"You got us here."

"Poor Florence is held together by bandages and optimism. I can't protect you both *and* complete this mission. There's too much at stake."

Her dad, the Treaty—the hunt's damned success—all hung in the balance.

The sun bled into the quiet cliffside as they sauntered down the grassy hill. Erika picked up the pace, fearful of what nightfall might bring. Oblivion's Watch was well-guarded and sufficiently concealed, but having cultists on their tail for days on end left her anxious.

"I understand," Alfie said as they reached the car. "Florence won't, but I do."

Erika huffed a laugh. He always was the more logical one.

When Alfie grabbed his books from the car—*Potions and Poisons for the Novice Hunter*—Erika realised that was who he was. He was a poor Hunter, sure, but that kid had one hell of a mind beyond those thick-rimmed lenses. He was weak but intelligent, cowardly yet logical. He picked up where Florence fell short.

Perhaps she'd been too harsh on him. If this was who he was, she would not fight to change him.

He was trying. The guilt for thinking otherwise knocked her sick.

Then Dad's words echoed in her mind. *Hunters cannot ever live in fear.* If he could not change, did that mean he could never be one of them?

"You scare me when you do that."

Erika frowned. She grabbed her own and Alex's bags. "Do what?"

"There's this *look*. I can't explain it, but you look like you're standing in a library, skimming countless titles, deciding which one to pick up."

"Oh yeah?" She slammed the door shut and locked the car, fully loaded with luggage. "And why does that scare you?"

Alfie took Florence's bag from her. His steps turned into strides as he overtook her stroll. "Because you look like Uncle Chris. And that makes *you* hard to read."

The phrase made her stop, left alone with the empty wind in her ears as Alfie headed back to the Watch without her.

At dinner, Erika handed Alfie his bowl with a nod to signal their fight was over. His parting statement unnerved her, but she opted to ignore his words in favour of undertaking tomorrow's mission on good terms. She was similar to her father in *some* ways, though it never seemed to be a bad thing outside of his broody nature.

Alex nursed his beef stew, his mouth only opening for the occasional spoonful.

From the opposite seat on the bench, Erika shot him a playful smile. "Not a fan of the stew?"

He stopped twirling his spoon. "I'm not hungry."

She frowned. He was *always* hungry. "What's wrong?"

"Nothing's wrong." He reached for the bread loaf and sawed a slice off.

"You *are* unusually quiet," Florence said, shuffling in next to him.

"*Uncharacteristically* quiet," Alfie added from beside Erika.

Alex dropped his cutlery. "Can we stop?" he snapped. "We've got a big day tomorrow. I'm just thinking."

"That's dangerous," Alfie muttered.

Alex sighed and rose to his feet.

Nathaniel beat him to it.

Covering his mouth, Nathaniel fell from the bench and sped towards the exit. His spoon clattered on the table.

Erika checked his bowl—almost untouched.

Alfie slurped a heaped spoonful of vegetable soup. "This is why you go vegetarian."

"It wasn't the stew, dumbass," Florence bit. "He's barely eaten any of it."

"Is he nervous?" Erika asked.

Florence slowly nodded. Maybe Erika should have followed him out, but she barely knew the boy. Unlike the twins, he was not even a rookie Hunter, and *they* were staying behind for their own safety.

She wondered what poor Nathaniel would think if he discovered Florence wouldn't be there with him. She didn't approve of any sort of relationship between the two, but when you find your anchor, it can be hard to detach.

His reaction left her with newfound sympathy for the boy. "He just wants to find his dad," Erika said, pouring a glass of iced water from the decanter. "He didn't sign up for cults and magic."

Florence glanced over her spoon with a grateful twinkle in her eye.

Alfie grinned into his. "Maybe Flo can keep him company. I'm sure she'd love to—"

Florence elbowed her brother, who dropped his spoon. It splashed in the broth, hitting him in the chin and sloshing over the table. Erika snorted into her glass while Alex finally let out a delightful laugh.

Alfie dabbed his chin with a napkin. "That was uncalled for."

Florence pointed her spoon accusingly. "It was provoked. Now we've got beef."

"So has the table," Alex replied. "Look at the mess."

"*Vegetarian*," Alfie corrected. "No dead cows from this bowl, thank you."

"Honestly, can you stop calling beef dead cows?" Florence whined. "It puts me off my food."

Alfie leaned in towards his sister. "I don't know if a D in biology enabled you to know this, but beef *is* dead cow."

"No shit, Sherlock. I thought I heard it moo!"

Chaos erupted for a split second before Erika dragged Florence back on the bench and gestured for Alfie to sit. "Down, *down*. Bloody hell, it's like having kids. I don't know how Diana's done it for eighteen years."

"*Does* it," Florence corrected. "There's still Ollie."

Erika nodded gently, finding solace in her broth. What would Ollie think of Oblivion's Watch? Would it frighten him? Excite him?

He would love it. All his life, he held an affinity for the outdoors: sports, hiking, nature, animals, sleeping under the stars. Twice a year, Diana took the kids camping, sometimes to the Lake District, other times to Western Scotland. The timing often aligned with Dad's most dangerous hunts, so he would never come. Erika often wondered if Diana chose to do that solely for the children or partly as a distraction for herself. Until Erika and the twins came of age, Erika's dad was the only non-estranged adult family member Diana had left.

But, as the family grew older, the trips subsided, and Ollie was forced to live out his childhood alone.

"At least your mum gets a break when Chris comes home," Alex figured. When he saw the Lupines' faces, he gawked. "Doesn't she?"

"Ollie lives with us," Alfie replied, checking with Erika to see if his answer was appropriate. "Erika and Uncle Chris are always working."

"Surely, he goes home when someone's there to mind him. Right?"

Erika set down her cutlery, no longer willing to eat. "Diana's *is* home. Dad and I are always on the road. No point renting or getting a mortgage if we're not there to use it."

Alex's brows pulled together, his eyes softening. "You… don't have a home?"

Not a house or a place to stay—a *home*.

She shrugged. "I guess not."

Her home was a two-storey detached house on the far end of the quaint little street just a twenty-minute drive from Diana's. Erika was only young when her and Dad moved out after Mum's disappearance, but she remembered it vividly: the cinnamon fence Dad built and painted himself, the rounded front lawn her mum mowed into stripes every weekend in the summer, the nineties carpeted stairs Mum was desperate to change once Erika reached an age where she would stop dropping spaghetti on them. It was not expensive, nor particularly beautiful, but it was, what she considered, a home.

Erika swallowed the lump in her throat and checked the time on her phone. *After ten*, she saw. She often stayed up later, but she needed rest before the day ahead, as did all of them.

At least, *some* of them did.

"So," she began. Florence's big, eager eyes stabbed a knife in her chest. "Florence."

"Yeah?" She beamed. *She's going to hate this.*

"I've been thinking about what we have to face tomorrow. And…"

She almost reconsidered. Considering her bravery in taking on Carly, Vivienne, and defending Alfie from the flames, she was a true huntress. Then she spotted the burns on her knuckles, remembering the scars on her abdomen.

"Alex, Nathaniel, and I are going tomorrow. You and Alfie will stay here."

Florence's throat made a noise. "But... But I've worked really hard! Nathaniel isn't trained like we are!"

"I know, I know. But you're injured, and Nathaniel is not my responsibility. He can stay if he wishes, but I have a feeling he won't."

"I'm *fine*!" Her insistence strained the burns on her torso. She hissed through her teeth, fighting to keep the noise at the back of her mouth.

"Flo," Alfie soothed. "She's right."

"But we're ready."

"We're not." He said it so assuredly even Erika flinched a little in surprise. "Imagine what it would do to Mum if you got hurt?"

Erika did not let it show that she caught onto his own omission from the statement. If Florence noticed, she didn't react either.

"My decision is final," Erika declared. "I'll tell your mum I've left you here where you're safe. When this is over, one of us will come and get you."

Florence slouched in her seat. "Will you two be okay?"

Alex smiled. "Your cousin's with us. It's the cult you should be worried about."

Erika warmed at his compliment but, beneath the surface, caught his worry. Their plan was loose and swift, relying on too many coincidences. Their skillset had to be enough, tomorrow, or else they'd fail their families.

"I think it's bedtime for me." Erika stood, knocking her calves on the old wood. Alex joined her.

"I'd like to take a look around if that's alright," Alfie said. "Maybe see the library since we're staying."

"I'll go too," Florence added.

Erika nodded. "Alright, but not too late. You know where your rooms are?"

Another round of nods.

"Just watch out for trainer Lucien," Alex warned, backing out of the hall with Erika. "He'll make you do twenty laps around the perimeter just for having the last name 'Mullein.'"

Erika and Alex laughed at the twins' anxious exchanges and swiftly left with ominous 'goodnights.'

When the doors closed behind them, silence hung overhead like an umbrella Erika wanted closing.

"The rooms are this way." Alex said. She took that as a signal to follow.

Emptiness dwindled between them since the meeting. Even now, he kept his silence on their walk.

"We'll be okay," she said, trying to be optimistic—even if the crack in her voice spoke otherwise. "We'll find your dad."

"I know," he said too quickly. "It's just… Oh, never mind."

"Well, you have to tell me now." She tipped her head playfully, anticipating retaliation. "Come on, what is—"

"Why didn't you tell me he was your ex?" He whirred quickly enough to bring Erika to a halt. "Did you not trust me enough to tell me that?"

Her mouth hung open as she gawked. "How do you know?"

"No-one picks up a friend like he did in the hall. The way he was looking at you..." He said it monotonously, but a few threads of emotion slipped through—Erika just couldn't figure out which ones they were. Then he shrugged. "And—"

"Florence?"

"Florence."

She sighed. "Of course."

His voice softened. "Why did you not trust me with this? I thought, after all we've been through, we could confide in one another. You said you trusted me with your life, but not your secrets, is that it?"

Erika clamped her mouth shut when she heard footsteps nearby. Seeing no other option, she took Alex by the arm and dragged him into one of the many empty corridors, uttering an apology as she let go.

"He *is* an ex, technically."

Alex frowned. "Technically?"

"We ended things a few months ago at the instruction of our dads, for the sake of our careers." She forced the words out as neutrally as she could, but the bitterness seeped through, the recital of Dad's words obvious.

"And the crystal things?"

"Charmed by some arcane to allow us to talk to each other. Like a phone but untraceable. We got them on a hunt after things ended."

"So have you..." He gestured to her body as if the answer lay there. "Restarted things?"

Her heart thumped. "We've both been preoccupied."

A glint shone in Alex's eye. He turned away and rubbed his brow, almost ashamed of it. "I see."

"I didn't see it relevant to mention," she insisted. "You can understand that, right?"

She said it more as an instruction than a question because he had no other choice. She wouldn't deny there was *something* between her and Alex, but they'd known each other for a matter of days. And Pete...

They had history. History that kept writing itself further and further into reality no matter how hard she fought it.

Alex cleared his throat. "Right. In that case, I'll stay out of your way."

She held her breath. "Alex."

"No, you..." He gestured to her, backing down the corridor. "You do you. I'll see you tomorrow, yeah?"

Her shoulders dropped when she turned, but she didn't look back. Alex truly was stubborn, but he had no right to be spiteful. She made no promises, no commitments. They established themselves as friends—nothing more.

That was all she needed right now. Because her family was more important than anything that could risk saving them.

CHAPTER THIRTY-SEVEN

Statistics don't lie. Of the last decade, our census indicates a decline in the number of dual-affinity arcanes. What was once deemed 'normal' now attributes to just over half our recorded population. Magic is fading. We are growing weak.

Why do you think that is?

Extract From a Burnt Manuscript Recovered at Stryga.

To hell with the plan and to hell with sleeping. Alfie didn't care that he'd be left behind tomorrow because now he could spend *all night long* in the library with no consequences.

Really, he could have spent months—maybe years—there, reading every tome back-to-back. Florence reminded him that he'd need to sleep and eat eventually, but he was satiated with the warm scent of paraffin, aged leather, and time-eaten pages. Sleep wasn't an option anymore with the thoughts of his predecessors quite literally at his fingertips.

The library at Oblivion's Watch was a three-storey tower of stone walls and ornate bookshelves brimming with every field guide, codex, and transcript Alfie could think of.

He stood on the bottom floor and tipped his head back, seeing through the gaping holes in the second and third levels secured by a pale rowan balcony. Baxter Arwood proposed the design to Henri Lupine for the Order's twenty-fifth founding anniversary. *Did Alex know that?* Arwood said *our knowledge is sacred and we must watch it with the vigilance we guard humanity with.*

The library was shaped like an eye. According to Baxter Arwood's published notes, there would be a jade runner carpet on the second floor (the iris) which, with the blue-hued stone bottom floor (the *inner iris*) and pupil-like obsidian statue in the centre—four shields, each with a phase of the moon, new for arcanes, full for lychans, crescent for vampires, and half for Hunters—resembled the Lupine eyes.

Alfie's eyes.

Florence placed a steadying hand on his shoulder, squeezing before passing beneath the gothic archways, headed for one of the alcoves digging into the circumference of the bottom floor. Some housed tables and plush, green armchairs—the same shade as the upstairs runner carpet, perhaps—but others possessed locked wrought iron doors leading to one of the many archives at the Watch.

That God-awful soup churned in Alfie's stomach when he watched Florence all but fall into one of the chairs, clutching her burnt abdomen.

It was all his fault.

When Florence caught him staring, no doubt paler than the paper on the shelves behind him, she frowned. "Aren't you going to pick up a book or something? Isn't that what you're, like, *meant* to do here?"

If she insisted…

Alfie spent almost fifteen minutes combing the shelves, running his fingers along the leather, cloth, and paperback spines. He recognised a few names – *The Hunter's Codex* had about a dozen editions with several copies of each – but there were so many unexplored titles he was *desperate* to devour not just whenever but *tonight*.

How could he pick just *one?*

Florence winced behind him, and the guilt hit him with the force of a lychan under the full moon. He wouldn't be helping Erika tomorrow; he'd be useless in a fight, but perhaps he could help from *here* in the library.

Alfie grabbed a few books on arcanes, including a slim one so old the leather had frayed, its oak-brown stitched spine bleached with sunlight, the yellow pages thick with dust. That'd be no help—the research was certainly not up to date—but he took it anyway.

He plonked himself in the armchair opposite Florence. Modern miracles permitted electricity to flow through the library—the central chandelier and iron wall candelabras all had bulbs—but Alfie lit the tall, triple candles in the middle of the table, nonetheless.

Florence glowered when Alfie nudged a book her way. "What's this?"

Only the Hunter's Codex—which *everyone* needed to read if they were hoping to pass the Trials, according to Dad. "A start," Alfie said.

"I don't want to read." Flo pushed the book back.

"Just try." He returned it.

Back and forth—twice—they passed the book until Florence gave in and flipped open the hardcover with an exaggerated sigh.

Alfie got to reading. He skimmed the latest edition of *Arcane Understanding*, but, based on the introduction, conclusion, and chapter titles, it was just a rehash of the famous *To Hunt a Witch* without the derogatory language of the first edition—early Hunter-arcane relations were touchy, to say the least. *Arcane Understanding* also wrote, clear as day, how to murder arcanes—it was just more polite about it.

The next book was the same. And the next, and the next. Alfie revised the risks of possession as an arcane, especially when using blood magic—more so without a syphon—but nothing new.

Ironically, the oldest-looking tome of them all was the most enlightening. *Witch Way,* it was called.

This one was different. It wasn't typed by a Hunter like the rest of them—this was an arcane's work, all handwritten, but the author had been redacted. The only hint at the book's origins was the first-person writing style and shitty, allusive title.

The humans take and take and take. Our blood magic? Gone. Our power? Dampened. Now the very earth that feeds us is dying. It withers and decays beneath their concrete jungles and pungent industries. They disable us. They weaken us.

Alfie released a gasp.

"What?" Florence looked up from her book—page five, no less. "Alf, what is it?"

The word barely left his lips. Promoting blood magic, criticising the syphons, denouncing *the Treaty.* "Treason. This book is—shit, where did it come from?"

He examined the cover, the spine, and the endpapers, but found no author in sight. The pages *seeped* with dust, but the author referred to *concrete jungles,* so this couldn't have been more than a few decades old.

Yet they called themselves a 'witch.'

Just like the cult.

He found no author, but Alfie did find a symbol sketched onto one of the blank back pages. A creature with the body of a goat, head of a lion, and a long, coiling snake for a tail.

A chimera.

"Flo, this book came from the cult." He angled the book towards his sister, tapping the symbol with his index finger.

Her lips parted, but no sound emanated from them. *She doesn't get it.*

"Don't you see?" Alfie exclaimed. "Arcanes had their power restricted legally and literally with Treaty terms and syphons. *And* the modern human impact on the environment drained their power supply. This is why the cult wants the Morrigan back. She came from a time before the Hunters checked their power—before the war. The cult wants humans *gone*!"

Worse still, how did what looks like a draft of the cult's manifesto get into the Watch? You needed to be Initiated to pass through the Curtain.

Or invited in.

Florence reached for the bandages on her abdomen, looking like she might be sick. Alfie *hated* vomit, so telling her this revelation was off the cards.

Flo's knees knocked the table when she stood. "Erika will solve it," she declared. "The cult's reasons don't matter because… well, they want to hurt people. Good people. Hunters."

Typical flat thinking from Florence. "Have you not once on this trip questioned *why* the cult is doing this?"

She shrugged. "Power. People do horrible things for it all the time."

"But do they want power for the sake of power, or something else?" Alfie tapped the book's pages as if the answers would rise from the paper. "They don't just want the Morrigan back for power; they see her as the solution to their problem. *Humanity* is that problem—*we* are that problem."

"And that makes them evil," Florence figured. "Honestly, what point is there in climbing in the heads of people who, I'm sure you've noticed, would have us killed!"

"To figure out *why*."

"And if they throw another fireball your way? Are you going to stop and ask *why*?"

He didn't even think when it happened. He was just too slow, too scared.

Florence's face softened. "Alf, I didn't mean… I didn't—"

"If I know why, I might be able to avoid a situation like that in the future," Alfie said. "I need to get into the mind of the enemy."

"What's this about enemy minds?"

Alfie's chair rattled as he stood and spun, positioning the book behind him on the table.

Wyatt Martin sauntered over, already looking worse for wear. It was only eleven, but most of the Hunters heading out tomorrow were holed up in their rooms, grasping at sleep or sharpening weapons. Florence said she found Erika sitting on her bed, counting arrows, looking surprisingly chipper.

A mask. That's all it was. He'd tell her what he discovered as soon as he could.

Wyatt stopped before Alfie and folded his arms. He leaned to the side. "What's that you're reading?"

"The Codex," Florence replied, trying and failing to cover for him because it was quite clear what Wyatt meant.

Alfie surrendered the book without a word, holding it open on the page with the symbol.

"Oh my."

"I found it here, sir, in the library," Alfie explained. Perhaps it was the way Wyatt's face paled that dared Alfie to add, "The cult doesn't just worship an idol. They're politically motivated. Aren't they?"

It felt like he was attacking Wyatt—after all, the Order and Divines *chose* to keep the Morrigan a secret—but, then again, what right did Alfie have to know?

Everyone should have known.

Wyatt nodded slowly. Alfie didn't know Pete well, but he looked so much like his father.

Did Mum think that when she looked at Alfie?

Florence shifted on her feet. "Right… I'm going to… powder my nose or something. Don't wait up for me, Alf."

Powder my nose meaning *knocking on Nathaniel's door.*

"Flo, please—"

"Actually, I was looking for you both," Wyatt said.

Alfie and Florence exchanged a look. "Us?" Florence asked.

"Yes." His lip quirked as a subtle hand reached for the left of his belt where his dagger—no, a satchel—hung at his side. "I have a job for you both."

CHAPTER THIRTY-EIGHT

In your prime, nothing comes before the hunt. Nothing.

Philip Lupine's Journal, Second Edition.

Like the rest of the stronghold, the bedrooms in Oblivion's Watch retained much of their former regal interior, with some modern adjustments, of course. The walls of solid brick kept them warm, courtesy of the electric heaters plugged into every room. Mahogany filled the space in the form of a desk, dresser, a massive wardrobe engraved with flowers and vines, and a four-poster bed draped in emerald with matching bedsheets. Brown furs littered the floorboards, slumbering by the fireplace.

Erika lit a few candles for comfort using matches from the desk and headed for the more updated ensuite to shower and change into pyjamas, opting for the black silk pair Florence gifted for her twenty-second birthday—one of her favourite sets.

She pursed her lips to blow out the first candle as a fist drummed on the door.

A chill rushed into the room as she opened it. "Pete?"

His cheeks turned pink in the candlelight. "Hi." He waved shyly. "May I come in?"

Erika blinked rapidly and stepped aside. "Yeah. Yeah, of course you can."

He walked into the centre of the room, where fiery eyes locked onto the rugs before the fireplace. A smile crept upon his lips, but no words left them. He wore the same pants and boots as he did in the meeting, but changed his top. Pete always wore layers and jumpers at Oblivion's Watch, being particularly sensitive to the cold. Tonight, he garbed only a black thermal—as if he made a last-minute decision and left before he could change his mind.

His shoelaces were untied, tucked into the back of his boots.

"Dad's going back to the house," Pete said, his voice shaky. "To make it less obvious, I mean. He's hoping the Shadow Traveller turns up, then he'll let me know through the crystal when he's been taken."

Erika instinctively reached for her neck. "He'll be fine, Pete."

A muscle in his jaw flexed. He wasn't so sure. "It's good to see you," he said. His eyes cast over her pyjamas, but the sight did not faze him. "Though I didn't think we'd meet again like this."

"We've met here a few times. If you can remember, that is."

"You know that's not what I mean. *But* I think you'll find that *you* were the one who had to be dragged out of bed the next morning."

"Because you were fate-touched in your ability to black out and spring awake fresh as a daisy at seven in the morning." Erika folded her arms, reflecting painfully on the day he insisted on a 'refreshing' jog that had her puking vodka-cranberry over the cliffside. "As you so often did."

"I had to inherit *some* magic from my ancestors! It doesn't help with hunting, I know that much."

Erika snorted a laugh. "It's given you yet another thing to whine about."

"What good did it get me?" He threw his hands in the air playfully. "Another night in the cells."

Erika's eyes bulged. "*Again?*"

Pete's idealism on integration sprouted the moment he discovered his father, born to a family of arcanes, was cast from Third Coven for possessing no magical qualities. Wyatt brushed off his past with ease, but Pete refused to drop the subject. If integration was permitted, he would have known his grandparents. His mother's side left with her.

"I took my proposal of an ambassadorship to the Council," he grumbled, sitting himself on the bed. "Kyran seemed more open to the concept, but Paris and Evangeline?" He shook his head. "Paris is the oldest bat of the lot of them and Evangeline is a bitch."

"*Pete.*"

"She is! *Why on Earth would anyone want that job?*" He mimicked shrilly. "I bloody volunteered, and she still said no."

"And you ended up in the cells because…?"

"Paris ended the meeting with '*the less interference, the better.*' I said they'll start a bastard war if they're not careful, and was shoved into the cells overnight to cool off."

Erika hissed through her teeth. "Bit harsh. What did your dad say?"

"That I'm an idiot," he said through a laugh. "And my cell record is getting embarrassing."

Erika shrugged and leaned against the closest bedpost to Pete. "Everyone's been in at least once, surely."

"Four separate occasions are cause for concern, according to Dad. Commander Riley wanted me in longer as punishment for 'disturbing the peace of the Watch' but Trainer Lucien put a good word in. He grumbled about it, but it was a glowing reference."

Erika tutted. "You always were the favourite."

"All that hard work can't beat my charm, Lupine."

"I know. And it's frustrating."

"You love it really."

She chewed on her foolish smile. "*That* is also frustrating. I hate you sometimes, you know?"

"And I love you too."

"Don't." She waved a hand, ushering him to stop. He played the sentence off as a joke, but she knew better. "Don't say that."

"Why not? There's only us. Nothing you need to worry about."

She followed his eyes upwards as he rose to his feet. Had he grown? She was certain he had.

"You know why. We can't say those things because there's nothing we can do about them."

"But there *is*, Erika."

He rushed her and she backed off—not for fear of Pete but of what *she* might do if he managed to touch her. Their countless run-ins over the past year proved how easy it was for them both to slip into old habits. Separation was for the best.

As agonising as it was.

Pete's face contorted in the candlelight. "When I learned of the ritual, I freaked. All I wanted to do was find you, but Dad wouldn't allow it. We screamed at each other on the driveway until he managed to get me in the car. I knew you'd have a plan. I knew you could protect yourself, but… It got me thinking on why we bother to listen to our dads when it makes us so unhappy."

"Pete—"

"We're *adults*. At twenty-two years of age, we can make our own decisions. Screw the lot of them."

"You're being unreasonable," she argued, even if she wanted to agree. "We're Hunters. Our work comes first, especially at this age. Our elders know better."

"I thought so, too. But the moment I discovered a death note with your name on it, all I could think of was tracking you down and bringing you home to me."

Her lips parted in a silent gasp when his warm hands reached her face. They were ecstasy. Blinding, familiar ecstasy, flushing all reasoning to the depths. She wanted him—missed him.

But suddenly, half a dozen others entered the room: Dad, Wyatt, Ollie, Florence, Alfie. They watched them both with expectations and reminders of who they were.

The guilt of what she was about to say stabbed at her chest. Over and over. She had to take that guilt and crush Pete with it.

His thumb touched her lip. "If anything happened tomorrow, what would you regret tonight?"

Erika choked as the blade dug in deeper. "I can't."

"If you're saying no for you, I understand, and I'll go. But if you're saying no for the sake of others—"

"Pete—"

"Our lives are too short to allow others to live them for us. I'm not my dad, and you're not Chris. Thank God."

She was close enough to see the little quirk in his eyebrow at the comment and smiled. It faded much quicker. "But I'm a Lupine."

Pete stilled. His sigh of recognition blew the loose strands of hair from her cheekbones. *Lupine* was far more than a surname. He knew this.

"I know." His croak flickered a nearby candle.

Pete's chin pointed downward, but his eyes glanced up, green and fragile as sea glass. "For what it's worth, I'm glad to have my best friend back."

She smiled. "It's worth everything to see you again."

Pete enclosed her in his warm arms and torso. A shiver tickled her spine as gentle fingers stroked her hair. She longed to bring him to her bed just to have him do that all night. For the first time all week, she felt truly safe. Weightless.

"I'll see you tomorrow," he whispered into her hair.

"See you tomorrow," she mumbled against his shoulder.

He let go, running his grip down her arm in the hope of a last-minute change of heart. For the sake of her name, she did not give in.

They locked eyes as he backed out of the room. And when the door shut, the closest candle blew out in a wisp of smoke.

Florence spent twenty minutes staring into the bathroom mirror, makeup remover in hand, yo-yoing towards and away from her skin— *yes, no, yes, no.* The cotton pad dried.

She shot it at the bin – horrific miss – then pulled on Nathaniel's denim jacket and charged for the door.

She circled back to slip her shoes on, then returned.

Curiously, Nathaniel's room had been booked *well* away from hers, but he told her the door number before dinner. Oblivion's Watch seemed quieter than what Erika suggested it could be, yet all the rooms nearby had been fully booked, according to her. They were quiet guests—they didn't make a peep through the walls.

She was anxious already that Nathaniel, Erika, and Alex would be hunting tomorrow, but Wyatt Martin's *little job* for her and Alfie only mounted the pressure, even if she would be staying behind.

Take the blade and hide it well. That way, should any of us be apprehended, Horizon's Edge will remain safely at the Watch.

The thought of Erika being tortured for that info almost had her puking in the library's *Supernatural History* section, and the feeling grew with every passing hour.

She needed a distraction.

Her heart stopped when she almost bumped into Alex. "Florence!"

"Alex!"

They stood completely still. Neither spoke.

"Where are you going?" he asked.

Think of a lie, think of a lie…

She gulped. "The library."

Alex fought to retain his laughter. "The… library? Where you've *just* been?"

It was too late, now. "Yes?"

"Right. And I'm off to train at this hour."

Florence nodded. "That sounds lovely, Alexander. I do hope you enjoy it."

She always wondered how Mum knew whenever she snuck out of the house at night.

She didn't need to wonder anymore.

By the grace of God himself, Alex let her be. He strolled around the corner, swinging his arms, whistling lowly.

"Where are *you* going?" she blurted out.

He fell back into the corridor. "Nowhere! Just my room."

"Your room's that way." Florence pointed back the way he came.

His shoulders fell in a sigh. "Erika's." Alex interrupted Florence before she could vomit on the floor. "I need to talk to *someone*. I don't know many people here."

"Those Hunters aren't your friends?"

"No, no. Just strangers."

"Oh." She considered suggesting he pay Pete a visit—he was always kind to Florence—but Alex hadn't stopped staring at Erika since The Collector's party, and Pete set his sights there first.

He wished her a good night and a bid to 'stay safe' before they parted ways.

Then his mock echoed down the corridor. "The library is the *other* way!"

Her heart thrummed in her ears as she knocked on the door.

One thump and it was open.

Nathaniel looked as if he had been rubbing his eyes since dinner. His cheeks were flushed, and sweat clung to his brow. After noticing it smelled like her mum's 'me-time' nights, she peeked over his shoulder and found every surface *littered* with candles.

She'd prepared a speech. "I thought I would—"

He gave her no chance to voice it and smashed his lips into hers.

He pulled her into the room when he felt her return the kiss, clumsy and wild. The door closed behind them, and the noise startled him.

Several candles extinguished, and Nathaniel pulled away.

Florence leaned in for another kiss and frowned when he barely moved.

"I'm sorry," he said. His hands cradled her face, her own blonde strands tickling the skin on her blushing cheeks and nose.

She laughed at his apology. "What for?"

She tried again for a kiss, but he took her hands. "Stop," he whispered. "I can't…"

"You…" *He* kissed *her*, right? Surely, she couldn't have hallucinated it. Had he changed his mind so quickly? What had she done wrong?

He looked as if he would pass out there and then. "I shouldn't have done that," he said.

Florence sighed. "If you're frightened of Erika—"

"No! I—well, I am, but—"

"Then what is it?"

Nathaniel gave her signals. He touched her in the corridor and beneath the table. He told her he felt something when he surrendered his room number so…

There was only one solution. Her mind switched back to the images of Owen and Amy and all their false promises. They all had one thing in common.

"Is it me?"

His face broke. "What? Of course not."

Not again. Despite the lump in her throat, she put on a brave front. "I can go, if you want me to. I don't need to be somewhere I'm not wanted."

She was always the last to realise she was in the wrong place—the last girl at the party dancing when the lights switched on. She turned to leave.

Nathaniel tugged her arm. "Please don't go."

He reeled her into his torso. She weaved her arms around his neck and rested her temple against his chest.

His rapid heartbeat rattled her mind. Nathaniel played her like a yo-yo, and she relished every second. He, on the other hand, looked absolutely sickened.

"I'm so scared," he uttered into her hair. "I'm so scared, Florence. I don't know what to do."

She wasn't important enough for him to be fearful of her opinion. She could be arrogant, sure, but comparing *herself* to what Nathaniel would face tomorrow?

"You don't have to go," she reminded him. "Erika would understand if you wanted to stay at the Watch. You could stay with me."

"I'd love nothing more. The thought of lying here with you while the moon rose and the world ticked on…" He angled her face to look upon his. Before she even processed the sadness in his eyes, he pushed her back into his chest. "But I need to help my family. It's my duty."

God, that was attractive—the drive, the determination, the passion. He loved his family as much as Florence loved hers.

"Will you stay?" he asked. She wriggled her face to meet his eyes. The green in his irises turned dark and glassy, ready to shatter. "Not for anything, just… I like your company."

Now she was baffled. "You don't want to *do* anything?"

"I just like being with you. I don't want anything from you." Then he laughed. "Aside from that smile."

She did as instructed, and Nathaniel beamed like starlight.

He led her to the violet bedsheets and climbed in first. His arm opened up for Florence to find a place in, then enclosed her in his grasp.

On the bedside cabinet lay an array of possessions: a book of supernatural apothecary, a few bottles of toiletries and aftershave, a jar of tiny black nuts, a penknife, and a pencil. She craned her neck to nosey further, but Nathaniel's hand on her waist nudged her towards him.

Without giving into a single lustful thought, Nathaniel began talking —and talking—and talking into the long hours of the night while she listened intently, stroking the long scar on his palm.

CHAPTER THIRTY-NINE

Remember your vows and speak them aloud. They will bring you luck. For in the dark, you may well need it.

The Hunter's Codex, Chapter VII.

Daybreak stretched into the far wall of the war room, forcing Erika's eyes shut. They stayed closed for a moment longer than they should have as she adjusted her position against the stone beside Alex.

"Sleep okay?" he asked her.

She shook her head. Every attempt at rest last night was plagued by images of Dad, Ollie, Aurelia, Pete, and Horizon's Edge. This time, Pete's broken body was the main attraction for her nightmares.

"No," she replied. And that was it.

Alex fixated on Pete as he shadowed his father into the room. He shot Erika a wink. The sight of his bronze curls under the morning light revived her.

Twenty Hunters turned up for the hunt: twelve relatives of the missing, Wyatt Martin himself, and volunteers. Some of the Hunters' family members were too weak, others too young, to participate today.

Wyatt recapped the plan once more, checking every individual for confirming nods, reaffirming how Horizon's Edge would remain sealed within the library, before Vanessa piped up.

"Are we done, now? Our families are counting on us."

Erika rolled her tired eyes.

Wyatt scanned the room, looking into the eyes of every soldier in his makeshift army, seeing their hopes, their anticipation, their fears, and their bloodlust. They were all lone Hunters, bound together by a dark legacy epitomised by him. It was not the inheritance Erika imagined the great Christopher Lupine leaving, but it was the one she and everyone in this room were left with.

"I want to start by thanking each and every one of you," Wyatt declared. "No child should be responsible for fixing their parents' mistakes but, painfully, I must ask that of you all." He looked to Pete. Only Pete. "And for that, I'm sorry."

Pete smiled as if his dad were asking for nothing more than to borrow a penny.

"The cult thinks of you all as nothing more than children," Pete began. "That you're untrained, inexperienced. Weak and naïve. Through being here alone, you have proved to me just how fierce you all are."

The focus he pinned on Erika stirred a fire within her. "Bring that ferocity to the cult. Show them you are far more than just children."

"Hear, hear," Alex praised.

Wyatt clasped his son's shoulder. "Remember your vows. We are the wardens in the shadows."

"The light in the dark," Pete continued.

"The shield at humanity's back," Alex went on.

And the room united as one to finish.

"We are the order of Hunters. And we will endure."

The Hunters dispersed at breakfast. It amused Erika how hesitantly Alex stuffed his face with the fry-up. Evidently, the chef at the Watch had changed since last Christmas. The bacon was underdone, the sausages too herby. Fried bread turned to mush against the pool of oil at the bottom of the plate; somehow, the poached eggs were drier. Erika forced it down for fuel. Afterwards, Alex announced he'd be hopping in a car with Vanessa or Lily and Lucie. Erika called him ridiculous, and the matter was settled: he'd ride with her.

Nathaniel had not turned up, having vomited again after the meeting. Alex made a point to box food for him before they left to pack. Chances were, *this* food would make him worse.

Alex and Nathaniel hounded Erika outside her room, backpacks slung over each of their shoulders. At their sides, Alex clutched a bag of leftover fry-up while Nathaniel adjusted a brown satchel.

The twins were left with orders to contact their mother if the party did not return within two days of leaving—and were reminded to walk *away* from Oblivion's Watch before using the phone. Florence made one last attempt to join the mission, but a stern glance from Erika at her injured torso quietened her down. It had been treated appropriately by a Watch physician this morning, and she claimed to feel much better.

"Then I'll see you soon," she figured. "All of you."

Alex smiled warmly—as did Nathaniel, whose cheeks turned a pale shade of pink at her green-eyed gaze.

Erika welcomed her cousin's embracing arms and squeezed her tightly.

"Thanks for giving us a chance," Florence whispered.

Erika winced. That was all they wanted—a chance. Both of them did. But this was *her chance,* too. The chance to prove that she could solve the hunt Dad left her—without his guidance, this time.

Alfie's head drooped low when Erika pulled away. To her shock, he threw himself at her. "Thank you," he said. "And I'm sorry."

Erika wiped the tears beneath his glasses as she retreated to look upon his wet face. He was sincere. He was trying. "I know."

He debated silently for a moment, pursing his lips. "Poppy seeds. I checked last night, and they were poppy seeds in your car."

Erika nodded. The black circles beneath his eyes were evidence of that. "Poppy seeds. Okay."

"You think it was that Shadow Traveller?"

When treated right, poppy seeds could make you sleepy, even delirious. There was no doubt—they were planted there.

"Maybe," she said.

There was nothing they could do about it now. She hoped to find the truth when the cult was seized.

Beside them, Alex released Florence from a hug, each parting with an understanding nod. Florence dragged Nathaniel by the hand and yanked him into her hold.

Alex clutched Erika's arm at her sharp inhale. "Leave them," he said. "They should be allowed their goodbyes."

Per Alex's wishes, the group left Florence and Nathaniel to have a moment alone. Erika grumbled, Alfie chuntered, but Alex warned them against interfering.

"They barely know each other," Erika hissed.

Alex looked stung. "You can't justify relationships based on the time they've spent together. Who are we to judge a couple of kids for seizing every moment they can?"

Erika swallowed. Her friend didn't speak words from his mind or eyes, but from the heart. His own heart.

Fuck, how did she get into this mess?

Clouds gathered in a miserable umbrella above the cliffside as the Hunters left the open mouth of Oblivion's Watch, armed to the teeth with weapons and faces of war. Erika counted her quiver and felt for the box in her pocket.

"Stop stressing," Alex hissed. "You've checked that thing ten times since we left the gates."

"I'm just making sure I've got everything." She checked her trouser pockets—*car keys accounted for.*

"What would you do without that crossbow?" Alex wondered.

"I could have kicked Leopold when he offered it up," she replied.

"At least we have his clubs as collateral," he snorted. "But who did he say the crossbow was by? Some Ham, Yam…"

"Gamlen," Erika corrected. "I thought you'd know who he was, considering your hobby." She gestured to the gauntlet peeking out from under his grey, fleeced sleeve.

"Hunters don't normally broadcast their talents, as I'm sure you've noticed. Well, unless you're a Lupine."

"I do *not* broadcast my talents, thank you."

"Borderline cockiness, if you ask me," he said with a grin.

"Excuse me, there's a difference between cockiness and confidence."

"Oh, I know."

"First-hand experience?"

"Got me there!"

Erika rolled her eyes but could not restrain the laugh bubbling within her.

The entourage reached the car park and filed into their groups. Erika loaded up the Fiesta with the few essentials Alex, Nathaniel, and she chose to bring to Bekker's Forest, then wandered over to Pete's car, where he packed his own bag into the boot. His dad lingered by his car, ready to go.

"Erika!" Pete beamed and slammed the boot shut. "Everything okay?"

"Fine. I just wanted to check on you and your dad." Wyatt circled Pete's car. "How are you doing?" she asked him. The two had not spoken much since arriving at the Watch.

"Should be good to go now. I'll head back home and wait for this 'Percy' to show up. We'll get your dad back, Erika. I promise."

She was unsure whether Percy would even make an appearance. After all, there were no cultists at Pete's cabin when Erika searched it. She brought it up with Pete this morning, but he reminded her that their options were few and far between.

"I know," she said. "Just be careful when you get there."

Every time Wyatt discussed the ritual, he seemed to age ten years. "This is my mistake. This issue should have been put to bed decades ago. If anyone should be careful, it's you two. I know what you're like, especially together. Don't give yourselves up for the faults of your parents."

"Don't be such a downer, Dad. Erika doesn't want to hear it," Pete teased.

"No, it's alright," Erika assured. "Good luck, Wyatt."

"And you." He smiled cordially, looking between the two of them. "I'll wait in my car. Speak to me before you leave, son."

There was a glint at Wyatt's chest where the silver necklace unveiled itself beneath his shirt.

Pete caught Erika watching and chose not to speak until his dad shut the car door behind him. "So, you kept yours on you?"

"So did you."

"They weren't easy to come by, you know? They're practically designer necklaces in the witching world."

"Pete."

"Alright, I couldn't let it go. After we called things off for the last time, I nearly did, but then I looked at it and... I don't know, I guess I had just a little bit of hope left."

When Erika told Pete their separation was for the best, she'd taken the necklace to a bridge near the campsite she was staying at. She drew her arm back, ready to throw it into the water, but her hand wouldn't let it go, and she dropped the chain into her duffel bag. No-one knew Pete gifted it to her in the first place. It was their secret, just as it was their secret the relationship continued for a while longer after they officially 'called everything off.' Their families didn't need to know when the physical distance between them turned emotional as well.

"You never reached out to me," she said. "I know you couldn't text or call, but… why not use the crystal?"

"I wanted to. I heard you the other night." Her heart leapt. "But when Dad finally convinced me not to drive after you, I realised how dangerous that could be. If they got hold of Dad or me through us, then everything's over. Of course, it doesn't matter now that he's… well…"

"He'll be fine," Erika assured him. "It's risky, I'll admit it, but it's calculated. That kind of risk has always paid off in the past."

"Just not for us."

His sad gaze turned a knife in Erika's chest. There was nothing calculated about what happened between them. It just… happened.

"Not yet," she finally said.

"One day," he replied.

She smiled. "One day we'll put ourselves first. For now, work is the priority."

"So long as it doesn't get you killed," he warned her.

Erika laughed. "You know me. I'm prepared for anything."

"Including sacrificing yourself for the Order."

She would never say it, but he knew. The bigger picture came before them. Although if her family were on the line against the protection of the Order… she was unsure what she would do. The Order was her voyage—her family the anchor.

"Don't," he warned her. "Don't you dare get yourself killed."

"I'll do my best."

"I mean it, Erika. You die, I'm finding a necromancer to drag your ass back so I can kick it."

She sighed. Even if they succeeded, people were going to die tonight, whether that be arcanes, Hunters, or themselves.

She tried to imagine a world without Pete and couldn't.

Seeing her face, he lured her into his arms, offering a moment of safety without having to ask. Maybe she should have let him stay the night. Maybe she would have slept a little better knowing he was there for a few hours longer.

Maybe she did regret letting him go.

He lifted her face by the chin.

"Smile for me," he said. "Go on. Once more."

She could have laughed at how stupid he was. "If you think I'm going to smile now—"

"There it is!" He beamed. The glow lifted her. He was *beautiful*. She was starting to believe that some magical blood found him if he could make her feel the way she did.

Wyatt knocked on the car window, mouthing, *We need to go.*

Pete's face fell. Around them, engines sprang to life. Gravel crunched beneath rubber as Hunters drove off, leaving their refuge— their home.

Pete forced a smile not nearly as genuine as the one a moment ago. "This is goodbye for now, then."

"Have a safe drive," Erika replied. "And good luck."

With one last hug, they pulled away. Both covered their sadness with an eagerness to get on with things, as they always had.

That was the thing about Hunters. Emotions took time to process, and with such relatively short lives, it was better to simply bury them.

"I'll see you later, mate," Alex called to Pete with a wave.

"And you," he returned. "Drive safely."

Erika sighed as she slammed the car door behind her, gripping the wheel tightly as she watched Pete clasp hands with his father before letting him go. Erika started the car and followed, maintaining a safe distance while Alex scanned the map and Nathaniel quietly tapped his knee in the backseat.

She flashed a smile at the rear-view mirror when Pete's car appeared behind hers.

"You worry about him," said Alex.

Understatement of the year. "Should I? We're not together anymore."

His face fell. "Even if you're not with someone, it's only natural to feel like that if you still care."

"We called things off because I *shouldn't* care," she urged. "I've got a job to do and all I can think about is whether he'll be alright."

"You're human," he said plainly. "I'd be worried if you didn't feel anything."

Erika's shoulders dropped as she stared ahead at the road. In a few hours, Pete would watch as Wyatt turned off the motorway alone. "Sometimes I think I'd rather not care at all."

"No, you don't." Alex shook his head, letting a warning glare slip. "Please don't say that again.'

Her stomach twisted. Would it truly be so bad to feel nothing at all? To carry on hunting without a single thought to anything else?

She remembered who all of this was for: Dad, Ollie, Diana, the twins—her mum. They made everything worth it. When she salvaged the Lupine name, they could be proud of her.

"Nathaniel?" Erika called, her voice cracking a little. "Everything okay? You're very quiet."

"Hm?" Nathaniel turned from the window. The glass lowered a few inches, wafting in a wind that whirled his platinum hair into a twist. He looked pale. "Yeah, I'm okay."

"Probably dreaming about Florence." Alex held his attention on the map, even when Erika's glare landed on him. Nathaniel only sighed.

"I can still turn around if you'd like," Erika assured him. "But once we're fifteen minutes in, we won't have the chance. We can't risk missing the signal."

"No, it's okay." He sat upright and rolled up the window. "I'm fine, I—I have to do this."

"It's commendable what you're doing, kid," Alex praised. "You don't have to."

"Yes, I do," he croaked. He sank into his seat. His brows furrowed as he lowered the window again.

"Yes, I do."

Halfway through the drive, Alex hopped into the driver's seat to give Erika's legs a break. They stopped for a swift bite to eat and topped up on petrol. Nathaniel barely touched his sandwich and left for a ten-minute bathroom break, returning very sheepishly to gulp a pint of water.

Nathaniel fell asleep just twenty minutes before they were due to arrive at Bekker's. Erika wondered if Wyatt had been taken yet.

Alex checked Nathaniel was still sleeping before clearing his throat. "Florence didn't come back to her room last night."

Erika frowned. "Sorry?"

"I bumped into her in the corridor as she was heading to Nathaniel's room. Alfie said he heard her come back at around eight this morning before going to the med wing."

Erika's face contorted at Nathaniel's floppy mess of hair in the rear-view mirror. She spun around and opened her mouth. Alex pushed her back in her seat.

"What are you doing?!"

"Don't you yell at him for this."

"He…" Erika gestured to Nathaniel. "…and Florence!"

"And *Florence*," Alex echoed. "It takes two, and Florence was the one to visit *him*."

"And both will get an earful for this," Erika grumbled.

Alex chuckled. "Consenting adults, lassie. You can't control them both."

Erika folded her arms as she sank into her seat. "I'm not trying to control them. It's just too soon. They've only known each other for a few days."

Alex laughed out loud. "You can develop crushes in a matter of hours."

"That doesn't mean you should act on them."

"Oh? And you've never acted on a superficial crush? Not once?"

Erika found sudden interest in the extensive stretch of grey tarmac before her. "I just don't like the two of them together."

He snickered. "Why not? He likes her, she likes him. It's simple enough. If they have feelings, no matter how superficial or small, why not act on them?"

"It's not that simple," Erika argued. "As a Hunter, Florence has to think of more than her immediate wants. Her job, her training, her family—that's what's important. Compromising herself before her career has even begun isn't going to do her any good."

"And is this speaking from experience now?"

She blinked away flashes of Pete smiling down at her from his car's backseat. The sensations she felt, the feelings he stirred. "Maybe it is."

Alex tapped his fingers on top of the steering wheel, composing a nervous beat on the leather as Erika angled herself to look out the door window.

"Do you regret spending time with him?" he eventually asked.

Hunter relationships were doomed to fail. Both were entwined in the supernatural world, full of danger and the unknown. The job came first, at least throughout their youth. This was Erika's decade to make her mark.

"I should," she replied.

"That's not what I asked."

"I don't know." She coped alone just fine, but the thought of never seeing Pete again sickened her.

"You want to say 'no,'" Alex figured. "But you won't let yourself."

When she said nothing, he sighed. "You're not a weapon or a robot, Erika. You're a lovely woman who deserves to feel happy. Please don't give up on everything you are for the sake of a job."

She pondered his sentence before smiling. "Lovely, am I?"

"I can take it back."

"No! No. You're... lovely too, I guess."

He mirrored her smile.

"Look, I'm sorry for last night," he said. "I don't know what came over me. Can we forget it?"

She nodded. Beyond their disagreement, their friendship still stood. "Already forgotten."

His shoulders dropped in relief. He was not entitled to her past, just as she wouldn't expect his, but his acknowledgement of that made her happy to share more, if he asked. He put aside his pride for the sake of their friendship.

"So," he started, "you left the twins."

"I left the twins."

"After all that, they're benched at the finish line."

"It's too dangerous. And…" Erika blew a sigh. "They can't mess this up. They made too many mistakes—they made *me* make mistakes. I can't trust them."

A muscle in his jaw ticked. "Yet, you pushed to have me in the car with you. That means…"

"I trust you."

His brows raised.

"I do. I really, really do."

His breath touched her face. Alex was strong, he knew the Code, and he listened to Erika. She knew it seemed obsessive, but the stakes were too high to charge into Bekker's with an unreliable team.

She trusted Alex—with her life *and* the hunt.

Their silence shattered when Nathaniel woke. "I think I'm gonna be sick."

Erika groaned. "The *one time* I try to be nice."

"No. Really!"

Alex swore and swooped onto the hard shoulder. Erika warned Nathaniel to steer clear of the car and frowned at Alex's glare when Nathaniel bolted to vomit in a nearby bush.

"What?"

"You could try being a little kinder."

"Do you want to drive around in a vomit-filled car?"

He shuddered. "Not really. Might make the cult stay away, though."

"Always a silver lining with you, isn't there?"

Nathaniel returned after a few agonising moments of retching on the roadside, his skin dull and soaked with sweat.

Erika handed him a water bottle and a pack of mints from the glove compartment. "I know I said I wouldn't turn around, but I can book you into a hotel if you want to sit this out."

The cheap water bottle crunched beneath the force of his drinking. "No," he gasped. "No, I'm coming."

"Are you positive?" Erika checked.

"Absolutely."

He shouldn't have come. He was untrained, but she understood his need. "Alright, then. Let's move on."

Alex lowered his brows. "But—"

"He said he's positive. Nothing more we can do."

Huffing his disagreement, Alex climbed into the car last and restarted the engine.

Despite his supposed *engagements* with her cousin, Erika felt for Nathaniel. This was a Hunter's fight, not a child's. Aside from the fact that he wasn't safe, she selfishly worried that he would compromise the hunt.

Failure. Failure. Failure.

Still, Alex was right. Nathaniel's dedication to his family was admirable. Erika hoped his spirit would help him to succeed tonight.

CHAPTER THIRTY-NINE

Bekker's Forest is cursed land. Barely visible to the untrained eye, the trees and undergrowth hold a history of death and ancient magic. There is no real life there. The Veil is alarmingly weak.

Secrets of the Veil by Cassandra Starling, Chapter Four.

From the bird's eye view on the map, Bekker's Forest was a rough, shadowy bullseye—The Morrigan at its centre. The lack of anything resembling a car park or signage suggested even those who lacked belief in the supernatural were prepared to stay well clear of it.

Like Pendle Hill, Bekker's Forest felt *wrong*.

The Hunters' cars trailed one another through a rare opening in the thicket, making it to the largest clearing the maps claimed they would find before the ritual site. After stepping outside and checking her tyres for any bumps or bruises from the undergrowth, Erika headed to the boot to armour up.

She had an arsenal to work with and it still did not seem enough. She checked her quiver was full, even stocking up on a few arrows tipped in iron and silver, ensured her crossbow was up to working standard—as usual, *perfection*—and strapped twin knives to her belt. Alex had his gauntlet and shotgun.

"This feels strange," he said, counting his bullets.

Erika slung the quiver over her jacket, out in the open. "What do you mean?"

"They're so human. And here we are, picking out weapons to kill them."

Erika never thought twice about putting down demons, monsters, and creatures, especially if they harmed her or her family. At Alex's words, her stomach knotted the same way it did when she killed Vivienne.

Dad would have told her to ignore those thoughts. So, she did.

"It's for our families. I don't like it either, but it's for the greater good."

She recalled him digging his heels in at Pendle Hill. He ignored the concept then. Now, he only sighed. "Okay."

"What do I do? I lost my pocketknife."

Nathaniel appeared behind them, apprehensively folding his hands. He'd not vomited again but looked just as unwell, sheer sweat drenching his forehead.

"Take a gun," Alex replied, surrendering a small firearm from the boot. He demonstrated how to use it as he did with Alfie.

"And this," Erika added. She brandished a small blade from the case in her car, its hilt bronze and patterned with branches. It was the same blade she gave to Florence at Leopold's manor; the same one that killed Vivienne. "Just in case we need to be quiet."

He nodded, holding the weapons as if they would poison him. The blade balanced perfectly on his palm, despite the shaking. "I'll do my best."

"That's all we can ask for," Alex assured him. "Come on. We should join the others."

The Hunters abandoned their cars around the clearing and gathered in a group by Pete's bonnet. The trio was greeted with a nervous smile from Pete.

Vanessa sighed impatiently. "Nice of you to join us."

"We had to make a stop," Erika replied. "Apologies for the delay."

"Almost went in without you," Pete joked. "But since we're all here…"

From his pockets, he unfolded a map of Bekker's and sprawled it across the bonnet. He pointed to the far edge.

"This is where we are." His finger dragged until it reached a red, marked circle in the centre. "This is where the ritual took place last time. The twelve won't be kept there—it's too obvious—but they *will* be sacrificed here, likely brought in via Shadow Travel."

The audience of nods let him continue.

"We'll split into groups. That way, we can circle around the ritual site and close in on the cult from all angles."

"Five groups should cover it," Erika suggested. "One keeps back, two cover the sides, and two run ahead from opposite ends to meet up, closing in on the clearing's mouth."

Pete nodded. "Good idea. Dad communicated that he was captured twenty minutes ago, so we should get going soon. At his word, I'll fire three consecutive shots to the sky so, once you're in position, keep your ears peeled. Be on your guard and stick to your teams until mayhem unleashes."

Among the chorus of war cries, Pete quietly rolled up the map.

"He'll be fine," Erika assured him. "Your dad knows what he's doing."

His throat bobbed. "That's exactly what I'm afraid of."

At Pete's instruction, Erika led a group of four assigned to the far-west side of the clearing, aiming to meet Pete's group at the apex. The group had to be fast, leaving her with Alex and two young Hunters, including Lily, and the young blonde from the meeting named Lucie. Nathaniel insisted that he come, but Erika refused since he was too slow. Vanessa agreed to add him to her north-western group.

Lucie headed the pack, Lily just behind, alongside Erika, while Alex brought up the rear.

"Your friend isn't very fast," said Lily. She recognised Erika from her training days, recalling a few harsh mutual interactions with Trainer Lucien. They met up for drinks once as a group.

"For all his confidence, you're not wrong," Erika replied.

"I can hear, you know?" Alex panted behind them.

Lily snorted. "Shocking really, from all the way back there."

"Come on now, Alex," Erika sang. "I advocated for you joining and now you're embarrassing me."

"I've got… muscle mass. That makes… me slower."

Erika's middle tightened at her laugh. "Of course it does."

A whip of platinum blonde from ahead almost blinded Erika. "Be nice, girls," Lucie warned. "It's not his fault he's got low endurance."

"That's not—I give up."

Lucie wasn't wrong, but Alex wasn't alone, either. Erika was a good runner—a marvel at it in school and significantly faster than her peers in training—but pain stitched up her left side, twisting with every thud of her boots against the undergrowth. The other girls, despite their skill, let their mindless chatter drift into silence broken only by rasping breaths.

Eventually, Lucie staggered to a halt and checked the map. "We're here." She wiped her forehead, sweat matting her blonde wisps. "Now we wait."

A smile crept on Erika's lips as she noticed the matching braids of the two girls, Lily's neat, pragmatic, and ebony, Lucie's effortlessly charming and bright.

Foliage crunched behind and Erika's smile broadened. "What about you? Are you okay?"

Alex shrugged. Then stumbled. "Grand. Never been better."

"You could have taken the easier route," Erika reminded him. "Why'd you come with us?"

He frowned, almost offended she had to ask. "You're the leader I chose, remember?"

She snorted a laugh. "I think General Wyatt Martin warrants more influence than me."

Alex shrugged. "You got me this far. I wanted to come with you."

A sound left her lips, but no words formed from it. "You're stupid," she eventually said.

Erika armed her crossbow while the others unsheathed their weapons. With the map in mind, she turned to face the direction of Bekker's clearing.

Soon, her father would be there, minutes away from safety. Soon, this would all be over and they could return home to Diana, to Ollie; to comfortable beds, hot chocolates, and as many terrible films as they wanted. For the first time in months, she could lie in her pyjamas all day, eating homecooked meals surrounded by her family, not a moment dedicated to thoughts of the impending threat of death and immortal arcanes.

If the plan worked.

CHAPTER FORTY

For the love of God, don't plan in haste!
Christopher Lupine's Journal.

Fifteen minutes of waiting amounted to nothing. Lucie got bored and perched herself on an overturned tree trunk. Despite her criticisms, Lily, and soon Alex, joined her. Erika stared into the tree line, flinching at every shadow shifting in the evening breeze.

Something should have happened by now. Erika reached for the crystal around her neck, lonely in its absence.

Lily scoffed from behind. "You could at least do something useful."

Lucie frowned, holding her half-braided hair. "You always tell me I need to make it tighter. What happens when an arcane throws a fireball at me and I'm blinded by hair?"

Despite her argument, she finished her braid and ironically brushed out the front pieces to frame her face. She and Florence would get on, Erika decided.

Lily rolled her eyes, averting her attention to one of her daggers.

Alex dumped his bouquet of torn grass and stood. "We've been waiting too long. Something's happened."

Finally. He ignored her worries only minutes ago. She'd texted Pete, but the poor signal left her message in limbo. "I agree," Erika said.

"Do you think we missed it?" Lucie wondered.

Erika glanced back at the trees. "We would have heard fighting if we missed it. Besides, three shots are hard to miss in a quiet forest like this."

Lily threw her dagger at the ground. "I'm tired of just sitting here."

"Me too." Erika pushed off from the tree she leaned against. "I'm going to look for the others."

"Not alone," Alex assured her. "Are you two good to hold position?"

Lucie and Lily nodded in sync. Erika didn't object, grateful for Alex's company. She was no coward, but trekking into the unknown, shrouded in the looming darkness, did concern her.

"Stay safe, you two." Lily warned. "We don't know what's out there."

Oh, but they did. And Erika prayed it still lay dormant within the forest's heart.

The pair combed through the overgrowth towards Pete's position on the map. No birds or bats swept through the branches; no mice scuttled over their boots. Not even the wind rustled the masses of dead leaves overhead.

The world hovered, coiled in anticipation like an angsty serpent.

"Do you hear that?" Alex pointed a signalling finger that made Erika tune in.

Nothing moved.

"No," she said.

"Exactly."

"You feel it, too?"

"We're in trouble. Stay on your guard."

Not a single organism shifted at the warning, but Erika couldn't shake the feeling they were being watched.

She tip-toed over a root to be closer to Alex. His gaze flicked towards her, but swiftly returned to the path ahead. He pointed his shotgun at the shadows.

Erika lowered it with her index finger. "Too loud."

He sighed but obeyed, checking the functionality of his gauntlet. Its slice through the air made Erika jolt—every sound they made was too loud. Alex kept in step behind her, letting her lead the way with her crossbow angled ahead.

True panic didn't set in until they reached Pete's position.

"They..." *No. No, no, no, this couldn't be happening!*

Erika pointed a shaking hand at the floor as if Pete's Hunters would emerge from the dirt. "They should be here." She spun to Alex. "They should be *here*."

Foliage crunched.

The pair stood back-to-back, crouched slightly with weapons raised, holding their breath.

"Erika? Alex?"

Erika's body relaxed. "Is that Pete?" Alex wondered.

"Pete, what the hell is going on?" Erika snapped. "Where's your group?"

He emerged from the shadows alone, alarmed hands raised at Erika's arrow. "I don't know. We heard a scream, so Ally and I held position while Simon and Brandon ran off to investigate. I left Ally for thirty seconds to look for them and haven't seen her since."

The trio exchanged frowns.

"Has your dad said anything yet?" Erika asked.

"No," Pete sighed. "You don't think the cult caught on, do you?"

Erika swallowed. "Possibly. We should re-join Lucie and Lily, then find where to go from there."

When they returned to their earlier position, the girls were nowhere to be found.

Alex gawped at the log they sat on barely minutes ago. "The fuck? They were here! They were *right here*!"

"They would have yelled if they were jumped," Erika figured. They must have been kidnapped discreetly, if the cult had them. The cultists couldn't have stumbled upon them by accident. "We need to regroup and do whatever we can to—"

"Erika!"

Pete squinted at the tree line. "Who's that?"

Alex took the lead. His brows raised when the platinum mop of hair stumbled towards them. "That's Nathaniel."

"Erika! Alex!"

"Shhh!" the trio hissed.

"Quiet," Erika snapped. "What happened?"

"Vanessa and the others are… She—they—!"

"Spit it out, kid," Alex barked.

"There's a… a…"

The ground shook. Nathaniel whimpered and shielded himself with Alex's body. Erika raised her crossbow, Alex revealed his blade, Pete unsheathed his sword.

A gargantuan bear stalked them through the shadows.

"He got the others," Nathaniel whispered. "All of them."

Erika's lips parted in astonishment as the bear morphed into its true form under the moonlight.

This was no bear.

"Christ," Pete gasped.

Alex gripped his shotgun. "He's… *big*."

Erika saw him before—at the cabin. Double her own height, clad in a trench coat of Grim Reaper black, tattoos winding down white knuckles and up his neck and skull. This was Aurelia's closest guard, her deadliest threat.

Felix.

Pete swallowed from behind her. "Erika…"

"I'll keep him distracted," she ordered. "You two flank him. Nathaniel, cover my back. Don't shoot a bullet unless your life depends on it." The last thing they needed was for others to find their position.

"Got it," they all said.

They ran to their posts.

Before Felix could catch them, Erika fired an arrow. She anticipated his trick— it was getting old now—and fired another as the first returned to her by the force of Felix's magic.

She caught the arrow with ease—the second struck Felix in the shoulder. She grinned at his frustration.

Her smile faltered when he ripped out the arrow with a ferocious growl. Physically, humans matched arcanes. The arrow should have sent him to the ground.

Still, it gave the boys enough time to make their move.

They pounced from behind the trees, slamming their blades down in unison as the arcane unsheathed weapons of his own.

The clang rattled the trees.

Erika reloaded her crossbow as the boys shared their panic.

Alex blinked. "The arcane has swords."

"*Why* does the arcane have swords?" Pete groaned.

Metal scraped on metal as Felix broke defence and slammed twin swords on the boys. Erika fired another arrow, missing entirely with the speed of their movements.

Shit, to avoid shooting her own she had to move closer.

She attempted a stride but remained stationary. She tried again to no avail, almost falling into the dirt.

Her spine strained when she turned, finding her right leg fixed to the ground. Thick, gnarly roots slithered from the soil and worked their way up her ankle, then her shin.

Just like her dream.

She yanked her leg and yelped at the pain. For Felix to subconsciously manipulate the elements while fighting, he had to possess a strength unheard of by the Hunters.

She sawed at the root with an arrow.

"Nathaniel!" she called. "Nathaniel, I'm stuck."

She kept sawing. Alex grunted in pain nearby.

She didn't feel Nathaniel move. "Nathaniel! They need us!"

Then she heard it.

The telling silence.

Nathaniel watched her struggle, a single hand outstretched and shaking, the ring on his little finger glowing greener than his eyes. Erika grimaced at that incinerated firework smell—the greatest indication of a casting arcane.

Nathaniel winced. "Whatever you want to say to me, I already know."

Erika flailed her arms to shrug off the wrangling roots. She barely heard the boys calling her name as she snatched the base of Nathaniel's t-shirt.

She would kill him.

The boys stopped calling when her face met the cold embrace of the treacherous earth.

CHAPTER FORTY-ONE

The Seven Sins are deadly. To proclaim yourself free of all sin is deadlier still.

Recovered Journal from Stryga in 1860, Author Unknown.

Muffled arguing brought Erika to consciousness. She lay in the same position she fell in, face down in the dirt.

"…wrong with the way I handled it!"

She winced, the piercing tone too much to bear.

"…ignorant little child. If she escaped, you'd be dead. Then where'd I be?"

The low baritone rattled in her heavy chest.

She inhaled. The earth clung to her nostrils and she gagged. Her head throbbed. Shit, was she getting a migraine?

"Erika…"

"Erika?"

She couldn't move.

"You hit her hard. What if she's… Holy Morrigan, is that blood?"

The voice melded into focus: Nathaniel. He stood barely a few feet to her right, arguing with Felix.

Ahead, she locked eyes with the voices whispering her name: Pete and Alex, their hands bound before them. A red mark spread over Pete's cheek.

Realising she was the only one free, Erika dug her fingertips deep into the damp, damp soil and pushed.

Her pained groan alerted Felix. "See! Alive. Nothing to worry about."

Erika puffed a curse. She had no chance now. She tried to raise herself from the ground, finding it an easier but more painful feat when Felix gripped her scalp and yanked her backwards.

"Stop that!" Nathaniel whined. "They're contained. Now let's go."

"You're a little shit, you know that?" Alex snarled. "We welcomed you. We saved your life!"

Nathaniel swallowed. With a flick of his wrist, he bound Erika's hands with elastic tree roots from the undergrowth.

Terra. A fucking Terra.

"An arcane..." Pete paled at the dimming syphon glinting from Nathaniel's finger. Erika vouched for Nathaniel, led him into Pete's lodge... and the Watch.

"Can you stand?" Nathaniel asked the trio.

The boys did. Erika fell back to her knees. She clamped her eyes shut, straining to halt them swaying like a pendulum in her skull. *Ow. Ow. Ow.*

"Just walk!" Felix spat.

"She's concussed!" Pete yelled. "Give her a minute."

"We don't *have* a minute. Either she walks or she's dragged. Your choice, sweetheart."

She made to curse at him, managing only a pained gasp. Pain radiated from the crown of her head through the rest of her body, turning to numbness at her fingers and toes. She shuddered beneath a cold sweat.

"Erika." Alex knelt before her. "Come on. You can do this."

His boots multiplied—*two, four, eight…*

"I can't."

"You can."

"No, I—"

He put a pair of bound, cold hands beneath her chin. She stopped swaying and looked at him—the only one of him. "You *can*. You have us."

"Push through," Pete urged from behind Alex.

And she could. Drugged and alone, she weaved her way through The Collector's manor. She killed vampires, incapacitated. She took down a *wendigo* by herself.

She could fight this pain—injured but not alone this time.

Her body opposed, and her mind cried, but she did it.

Pete sighed and smiled. "Good on you, Erika."

Felix shoved him. "Now *move*."

After a few minutes of walking, flanked by the arcanes, Erika's vision stabilised. Her limbs strengthened, sensation soaring through her fingertips, but her hands remained tied. Blood trickled down her forehead, wet and fresh.

"How long was I out for?" she asked.

Pete raised a brow. She hadn't spoken since standing, too fearful of knocking herself sick. "Just a few minutes. We hadn't even clocked onto Nathaniel until big boy had us on our backs."

Erika waited for Alex's joke that never came.

"I'm so stupid," he muttered. "I wanted him included. I thought he could join us after this was all over."

She didn't believe in Nathaniel in that sense, but she gave him the benefit of the doubt. "We all chose to believe his story."

"Because I convinced you to." He sighed. "I'm sorry. And worse, poor Flo."

Erika winced. She'd be devastated.

And Nathaniel was a dead man walking.

"I'm just relieved she isn't—"

"Hang on." Alex craned over her skull, frowning at her hair, inappropriately close.

"I'm not sure if you've heard of personal space, Alex, but—"

"You're healed."

"She's what?" Pete rushed to examine her head, almost knocking her over.

She scurried away. "Can you two stop?"

"How do you feel?" Pete asked.

"I feel…" She turned around, recognition dawning. "…fine."

All arcanes, no matter their affinity, were born with a talent for healing.

Nathaniel lowered his open palm. "Now we're even."

Alex glowered. "Far from it."

Life was not full of transactions. Favours didn't pay for betrayals.

Nathaniel winced and nodded. His hand slid into his pocket then pointed a knife—Erika's knife. "Can you keep moving, please?"

Erika's scowl flickered from the knife to the face that wielded it. She huffed a laugh, spiteful and insulting, and they pushed on, Erika slowly strengthening by the grace of Nathaniel's healing spell. They led the Hunters through a narrow wall of trees which Felix had to shimmy through, and into an area ignited by amber.

Twelve iron braziers surrounded the clearing, every flame eerily still with the rare snap of embers. A dozen scarlet robes guarded the fires while four surrounded a solid stone table at the centre and the bronze coffin atop it.

Watching were another handful of Sentinel cultists—and their sea of sacrifices.

From the grass, every Hunter involved in their operation locked eyes on the trio. Wyatt had been taken, as planned, but so had Vanessa and Pete's groups, Lily and Lucie—everyone. Erika, Pete, and Alex were the final arrivals—the final pieces.

Erika spotted Dad among the masses, ahead of the original twelve, still with his permanent frown and cold eyes that softened ever so slightly at his daughter's presence. He knew she'd be part of this plan. Erika imagined he thought her smart enough to see it through.

He would be ashamed to know it was she who'd let Nathaniel into the Watch.

Failure. Failure. Failure.

The leading scarlet cloak spun at their footsteps: Aurelia. A gold pendant twinkled over her collar—the same one she wore at the cabin. Her syphon.

Aurelia smiled. Before tonight, she needed just one Hunter. Their failure brought thirty-one options.

"Mister Arwood. Miss Lupine." She dipped her head, unable to hide her glee. "How nice it is to see you again."

"A pleasure, really," Alex replied. He kept his cool, but Erika watched his shoulders stiffen at the sight of his dad sitting behind her own.

"And…" Aurelia's lips pursed at Pete. "Mister Martin, I believe?"

Pete waved dismissively with bound hands. "Aurelia."

But the cultist's eyes were on Erika, who locked in her stare. She counted twenty-three arcanes with thirty-one Hunters. They had the upper hand numbers-wise, but one arcane, with powers, matched three trained Hunters.

Aurelia disdained at her silence. "Do you have nothing to say, Lupine?"

She didn't blink. "No."

Aurelia closed the gap between them. She frowned at the blood drying on her forehead and tilted Erika's chin to get a better look, clutching her delicately like a mother.

Aurelia's lips pressed shut in a frown. "She is bleeding."

Erika caught Dad's subtle brow raise, his stone irises locked on Felix.

Aurelia huffed. "Felix, what is this?"

Before he could answer, Nathaniel stepped forward. "He knocked her unconscious. I had to heal her. Otherwise, we'd still be carrying her through the woods."

A smile brought strange warmth to Aurelia's features. "Always so compassionate, aren't you, my boy?"

Erika choked. "Your *boy?*"

"Put them with the others," Aurelia ordered. "Quickly and *carefully,* if you wouldn't mind, Felix."

This was all Erika's fault. She'd spent so long seeking Dad's guidance, placing herself in his past, his thoughts, his journal, that she failed to see the cult standing before her. She should have seen this coming, but Nathaniel's fear and desperation lowered her guard. She tucked him under her wing so he'd be safe until she fulfilled the promise of reuniting him with his family again.

And that family was Aurelia fucking Hemlock.

Aurelia's long fingers choked Pete as he walked by, ripping the quartz from his neck with a heartbreaking snap. "Clever. Morrigan only knows how you acquired *these.*"

As Felix pushed them along, Erika glanced back at Nathaniel, who kept his head down low as his mother dressed him in matching scarlet robes. Erika told Florence of their plan before bed. If what Alex said about their night together was true, chances were she relayed it back to Nathaniel.

That was *exactly* why Erika didn't want her or Alfie involved.

Felix took notice of only one of Aurelia's orders, displaying a greater dislike for Alex with his grounding shove into the crowd of missing Hunters. The gash down the right side of Felix's jaw alluded to why.

Erika lowered herself before Felix had the chance to throw her into the pit of squirming bodies. Feeling watched, she scoured for the source and made eye contact with the same scarred, blonde arcane from The Collector's manor. He narrowed his eyes but averted his attention when Nathaniel leaned in to whisper something. He found someone else to focus on.

Pete scrambled to regroup with his father while Alex beamed at Tommy, reaching his side. Erika found quiet, uneasy joy at the sight of the greying man sitting beside her.

Despite his evident worry, Dad looked well. "Erika."

She rolled her shoulders as best she could with bound hands. "Dad."

"Why are you here?" he asked calmly.

She held her breath. He knew why she was in the clearing. What was confusing him was why she was sitting, restrained and incapacitated, and not storming in, crossbow raised, arrows shooting through the tree lining.

He asked her why she failed.

She brushed off the thoughts and took his words for what they were. "I'm here to rescue you."

Dad's thick brows raised. "I see." Biting his lip, he glanced at the scene: the humming cultists, the broken Hunters, the glowing torches, the rising full moon. "Is this part of your plan, I wonder?"

"Wyatt Martin was meant to be captured."

"And the rest of you?"

She kissed her teeth. "We've had more successful jobs."

Alex appeared behind her, Tommy in tow. "We average at a fifty percent success rate, to put it into perspective."

Tommy scrunched his face. Erika had a feeling he was used to Alex's antics, yet was still amazed by them every day. She and Tommy had that in common.

Dad glowered. "That's not a good rate, Mister…?"

"Arwood, sir. Alex Arwood. I'd shake your hand, but I literally can't feel my fingers right now."

"No need." Dad found a blade of grass. "I will cope without."

Erika absorbed the new faces in the crowd to scan for any she recognised. There were eight men and four women. Some were ecstatic to be reunited with relatives like Lily's presumed parents and Vanessa's mother, but others just looked lonely. Erika could name only a few: her father, Wyatt, Tommy… and Leopold.

He lurked at the back of the crowd, his face frozen with the fear Aurelia burned into him that night in The Collector's cellar. Erika held no sympathy for him. Just seeing him again brought her back to the manor: the girl in the upstairs bedroom, the gluttonous vampires, the fire that singed Flo's abdomen. He didn't cause those events directly, but his selfishness cost a lot of lives.

He grimaced at Erika when he glanced up from his brooding. "Evening, Lupine. Plan went well, I see."

"As did yours," she cut.

"You've met?" Tommy asked. "How?"

Alex laughed cruelly. "If the cultists want volunteers to do the sacrificing, I'm taking Leopold."

Erika answered Dad's confusion with a shaking head. Should they survive this, he could hear the tale.

"Don't trust him," was all she said.

His throat bobbed. "Noted."

Their sub-group shuffled further into to plan: Erika, Dad, Pete, Wyatt, Alex, and Tommy. The Council knew of their hunt, but diplomacy forbade them from ordering the Sentinels to Bekker's. Their only options for saviours were volunteers—unless the Council had permission from the Divines to dispatch them.

"The twins," Alex uttered.

"I told them to contact Diana as a last resort," Erika reminded him.

"We could use that last resort right now," Tommy urged.

Erika shook her head. "It's not an option."

She said to wait another day. That hadn't passed yet.

"But we have time," said Alex. "We left Horizon's Edge at the Watch, remember? They literally cannot get to it without launching an assault on the Council."

Relieved sighs chorused through the crowd.

Dad raised an eyebrow. "You found Horizon's Edge?" Erika nodded. "I'm impressed."

"We're safe." Alex sighed. "We're fine. So long as they don't have the blade, there's time."

Erika's stomach knotted when Nathaniel crossed the clearing. Silver winked as he unsaddled his satchel, a ruby red hilt laughing at their optimism.

Alex shrank. "Me and my big fucking mouth."

Nathaniel was with Florence all night. He had to have taken it this morning, between the meeting and their departure. He was absent at breakfast. How he even knew where to look, she had no idea.

Aurelia called her cultists into action. They ascended with sinister patience, taking agonisingly long strides, enclosing the Hunters in the clearing.

"What do we do?" Pete whispered to Wyatt. He stuttered, slack-jawed—Erika had never seen him like this.

Alex turned to Tommy. "Dad, come on, you've got to have something. Dad?"

"I don't know! I'm sorry, my boy, I... I don't know."

"Erika?"

She almost laughed. "Me?"

"You always think of something!"

Normally yes. But, surrounded by veterans of her craft as confused as she was, she felt lost. Their hands were bound, their weapons dumped in a nearby pile beyond Alex's shoulders.

All but one.

"Alex."

Her eyes shot to the gauntlet on his wrist. It took a moment for him to realise, but then he understood. He tapped the grass in front of him. Erika shuffled within reach, and he began sawing at her restraints.

"Incredible," Wyatt praised.

"His own design," Tommy boasted. "You know, ever since he was eight years old, he's been—"

"This designer will be out of business if you don't lower your voices," Alex hissed. Erika chewed on a smile—those compliments meant more than he was letting on.

Erika caught the branches as they snapped, holding them in position. She switched places with Tommy so Alex could start sawing at his bonds. She counted more Hunters than cultists. If even some could be freed, they stood a chance of catching them by surprise.

Aurelia took her place at the crown of encircling cultists.

The blonde, scarred arcane stepped forward. Aurelia blocked his path with an assertive hand. "Not yet, Samson."

"Vivienne—"

"Will be avenged. Soon. Felix?" Her lackey approached her side. "Find me the first."

Samson backed off, for Felix's smile was bloodthirsty. He patrolled the crowd, humming a tune as he scoured his options for the initial sacrifice. Erika felt Alex rise and swiftly pulled him down. This wasn't the time for heroics—not with only her and Tommy freed.

Felix selected his victim: the oldest and quietest of the original twelve. The frail-looking man accepted his fate willingly, almost breathing a sigh of relief to have been chosen.

He lived a long life. For his brothers, his sisters—

For the Watch.

"Chris," Tommy whispered. "Chris, we need to do something."

Dad's shoulders fell. "We can do nothing."

"We have to do *something*," Alex hissed, now sawing at Dad's ropes.

Dad snarled, "Like getting yourself killed?" He winced when Alex's blade nicked his wrist. "There's nothing more we can do."

Wyatt bowed his head. "Forgive us, Stefan."

Felix led the elderly Hunter to the bronze coffin, forcing him to his knees before Aurelia.

In the moonlight, Horizon's Edge glinted silver and scarlet against her white teeth. "Behold your fate. May you acknowledge your sacrifice in the next life."

Aurelia whispered gently to the Hunter, who stretched his wrinkled neck and smiled. "We... will... endure."

With a single flick, Stefan's long life drew to an abrupt close. The crowd gasped—someone screamed—and a single torch flared brighter than the others the moment his blood touched the grass.

Twelve torches. Twelve Hunters.

"You see!" Aurelia pointed to the brazier with the bloody knife. "It takes but an instant. A quick, painless death as opposed to what, hm? A meaningless life as slaves for the Divines, the Masters, the Alphas. Humanity has destroyed our world, and the Alliance enabled it. You have no future. No security. I guarantee you peace in the next world in exchange for this one."

"Crazy," Alex tutted, moving onto Pete's branches. "Ve-ry, *very* crazy."

Aurelia closed her eyes and inhaled. When they opened, Erika turned cold, overwhelmed with sudden breathlessness.

"*Lupine.*"

Tarnish the Veil

Dad's brow deepened, and Erika panicked. She couldn't take him—not after all Erika faced to save him. Jumping her was a bad move, but maybe it would give him a chance. She didn't care—she needed to save him for the sake of the family.

She flexed her unbound wrists, ready to defend him.

Aurelia floated towards them. "*You*, darling, have been a pain in my neck from the beginning."

Dad scoffed. "If you think you have been so pleasant—"

"How arrogant to think I am speaking of you."

Erika calculated the cruel arithmetic. If she was not speaking of her dad...

Oh.

Oh.

Aura magic from Aurelia's clawed hand yanked Erika from the turbulent crowd, crying her innocence. Hands reached for her legs and feet, but no human strength could match the sheer will of an angry arcane.

"Your pride—your *Lupine pride*—would have made for a fine vessel," Aurelia hissed.

The coffin swelled as Erika neared—as did the flames, the thorns, and the skeletons etched around its perimeter. Despite its alleged age, the bronze had not been tarnished by weather or dust as the eroded stone table had.

This was it, wasn't it? This was where she would die.

"Lia, she is a child!" Tommy cried.

Aurelia pulled Erika back by the scalp. "A child who is not so innocent. I would have left her alone. Until she—"

She choked on a sob. A tear splashed on the tip of Erika's nose from above. Aurelia would relent—not when vengeance and salvation could be taken in one swift motion.

Samson called for her head. Dad threatened to tear him apart.

Erika exhaled a shaky breath. Better her than Dad. "I kill to protect my family."

"As do I," Aurelia said.

"No!" Pete spurred from the crowd. He stumbled into the grass as Nathaniel cast the undergrowth beneath him, wrapping it around his shins.

Aurelia pointed at Pete with the knife. "You just made yourself third."

"Aurelia, *please*!" Wyatt cried.

Erika bit her mouth shut. They had time. If she cooperated, let the cultists calm down, they could get out. The Hunters had a chance, even if she didn't.

Or maybe she did. Just one.

She kept her hands in position, careful not to give herself away. Dad yelled at Aurelia, not looking at her.

Pete roared against the undergrowth, cheek against the ground. Tears streamed from the eyes that fought to see her face. *He cares so much.*

How stupid she was to let him leave her last night.

Her nod gave a silent order, and he calmed. Dad was free—as was Alex, Tommy, and Wyatt. Alex settled upon her stare and shuffled closer to the cultist guarding them.

Aurelia pressed Horizon's Edge against her neck. "Any final words, Lupine?"

She had to be quick. She had just one chance to survive this. She looked into Aurelia's eyes and, for a moment, felt her stomach turn. They burned, almost yellow in the brazier-light, with wrath surpassing her forty-odd-year lifespan. A breath fogged the knife by her lips when obsidian lightning crossed Aurelia's irises.

Ho-ly shit.

Aurelia was *corrupted*—possessed by a demon. She had an idea of which kind, but couldn't be sure.

And Erika did not know Aurelia well enough to pull her from the depths.

She took one shot at it. "I hope your son forgives the pain your anger has caused him."

"I pray the same for your father."

Aurelia drew the knife forward among the shouts and screams of Hunters and readied herself to pull it back.

Then shrieked at the bottle-green pickup smashing through the clearing, charging like a maddened bull towards the ritual site.

CHAPTER FORTY-TWO

Brawn wins battles. Brains win the war.
Philip Lupine's Journal, First Edition.

The driver profusely smacked the horn, scattering panicked cultists over the clearing. Aurelia's grip loosened around Erika's shoulders.

Now.

She twisted Aurelia's wrist and wrangled from the wailing arcane's grasp, clawing for Horizon's Edge. Aurelia pulled. Erika pulled harder. She kneed Aurelia in the stomach and ran off with the dagger.

Alex seized his cue and grabbed one of the cultist guards, flipping him, pressing his blade against his throat. Pete caught Erika's eye, and she ran. She ran for him, for them all, Horizon's Edge in hand, Felix on her tail at Aurelia's beckoning.

Erika staggered into the crowd that dispersed behind her, Pete leading the charge. Without blinking, the Hunters flung themselves at the cultists, keeping them off Horizon's Edge with a roaring battle cry.

She stopped at the pile of weapons just in time for the truck to skirt around it, tyres burning against the earth.

The window rolled down. "Having fun without me?"

Diana beamed brighter than the headlights spotlighting the weapons. Erika laughed. "How did you—?"

"Sur-prise!" Florence shoved her head between the front seats, squishing her cheeks together. Alfie waved from the passenger side.

Erika gawked. "I told you two to—"

"We thought you could use some help," Alfie explained. "So, we called our mum."

"But—"

"We caught on to Nathaniel," Florence said sadly. "Both of us did."

"Poppy seeds, remember?" Alfie clarified. "And, well—"

"Horizon's Edge was gone," Florence finished. "I found the seeds in his room."

Poor girl. She still even wore his jacket. "I'm sorry," Erika told her.

"No, *I'm* sorry." Flo's eyes glazed over. "But now I can make it right."

Erika's stomach twisted. If Diana was here… "Ollie—"

"Is safe," Diana assured her. "Now stop worrying and put that crossbow I gave you to good use."

Erika's crossbow crowned the pile, unfolded, its ammo nearby. She slung the quiver over her back as Alex jogged over, snatching his shotgun, then an extra blade for good measure, its handle diamond-patterned and ruby-red.

"We'll keep the cult at bay," he declared. "You protect that thing."

She'd done it before—she could do it again. The twins voiced their 'hellos' but, for once, Alex didn't respond.

He looked like this before—back in Parkview, back at Pendle Hill. This was a Hunter locked into battle.

"Back of the truck," Diana ordered. "Get in it."

"But the others——"

"We'll manage," Alex said. "You——you're fast. Get it out of here." He put a hand on Erika's shoulder——the same place Pete had squeezed. The same shoulder still aching from the wendigo's wrath. She felt a tinge of wetness at the blood dripping from Alex's gauntlet onto his shaking fingers.

"I'm fine," was all he said. "Now go!"

He pushed her towards the truck's cargo bed. With swift pleasantries to Diana and a smack of the vehicle's body, Alex sent them on their way and dove into the thick of the fighting.

"Such a handsome young fellow," Diana pondered.

But Erika didn't look at him. She stared down at the auburn cultist skulking towards her, two hands clawed, ready to cast.

With the power of a demon, too. Great.

Dad jumped Aurelia, wrapping an arm around her neck. She escaped the headlock by the will of her Aura power and launched a full-blown assault in wave after wave of hurricanes.

He ducked behind the bronze coffin until she slowed. Pete addressed him as "Mr Lupine," and tossed twin blades to his elder.

Dad seized the weapons and sliced at Aurelia. Erika held her breath——ever since their last confrontation with a blood-crazed vampire, Dad's right shoulder had been temperamental. Yet he thrived in the centre of battle, fresh as a young man.

Pete and Alex reunited, the former returned to his longsword, the latter pointing his blade-gauntlet to the sky, a shotgun in his free hand.

With a short exchange, Pete rushed into battle, Alex covering him with the gun. It dawned on Erika, as Diana whisked her away, that the Hunters lacked range.

"Flo." She tapped her cousin's half-open window and dropped Horizon's Edge in her lap. "Take this."

"What are you doing?" she asked.

Erika reached into her quiver and loaded up. "Giving them a hand."

The Hunters all had weapons now and were able to strike against the cultists at their greatest potential. Wyatt and Tommy appeared at Dad's side to take on Aurelia. Lucie and Lily fought as a duo to outmanoeuvre Percy's manipulation of the earth below them. The vengeful pair of Pete and Alex arrived for their rematch with Felix. Alex brandished the diamond-hilted blade as his final bullet missed its mark in a clear but panicked shot.

To the left, a figure flew through the air and winded herself on the ground. A hooded cultist stalked Vanessa, gnarly old hands poised for murder.

Erika shot and succeeded. The bolt struck through the arcane's spine and poked out between his ribs. A dumbstruck Vanessa scrambled to her feet. When she found the source, she saluted her thanks.

"Worth the money, I see," Diana quipped.

But her arrow's firing line drew a path to where they fled towards the trees.

Aurelia's eyes snapped away from Dad and his allies and locked back on the truck. "Felix!"

He didn't need orders. Like a missile, Felix made straight for the vehicle. His magic shoved Pete and Alex away as he broke into a run.

Erika shot. Felix slowed and swung a barrier. She tried again—and again. She wasted arrows to only slow him a few paces.

"Erika." Diana glanced at the rear-view mirror. "What is *that*?"

A fucking monster is what he was. Erika held her breath when Felix neared. Spit expelled between bared teeth like a rabid animal.

"Just drive faster!"

Erika smacked the back window, then fired another arrow—again, useless. "Shit!"

The oncoming earth rose six feet in the air, walling them in the clearing. Dirt spurted from the grass, and tyres squealed, but the vehicle managed to stay on all fours, now driving back into battle.

Nearby, Nathaniel lowered a closing palm. Erika swore she heard Florence mutter a vulgar—albeit creative—insult.

"Mum, we're going *towards* the cult now," Alfie warned.

"Where else do you expect me to go?!"

Erika had to think—quickly. Felix was nearing, Aurelia nearby, one eye on them and the other on Dad. The cultists saw Erika leap into the truck with the dagger…

But they never saw her drop it inside.

She leaned over the edge of the cargo bed. "Keep it safe," she ordered the twins. "I trust you."

She cut short their astonishment when she leapt from the truck, landing in a forward roll, and unsheathed an arrow, still crouched. Felix staggered to a halt, watching her, then the truck, then her again.

Where was the blade?

Erika feigned a careless touch to her jacket pocket. Nothing other than a mobile phone was inside, but he didn't know that.

"Come on then, you ugly bastard."

He ignited a lighter from his pocket and, like a tank at war, fired flaming missile after missile, setting the grass alight. Not good—he needed an active flame to wield his power at range.

Erika ducked and dodged the incoming fireballs and made sure to stamp out what she could on her way. She fired a couple of arrows, which he burned. Strictly, he had to remain at a distance. He could snap her neck in one motion if he wished.

Which she imagined he did.

He was closer, now. She staggered back. A wall of flame boxed her in.

Felix unsheathed his sword and swung, but she had nothing. Time slowed down as the blade inched closer.

"Erika!"

Alex?

A diamond-etched hilt landed in her grip, and metal clanged as her blade scraped against Felix's. Her wrists moaned at the vicious impact, but she held position, Alex's footsteps growing louder.

She slid away the blade and moved to offend. Felix blocked, then swung—she blocked, then counter-attacked as Alex leapt in to assist.

He had no long blade left of his own, but he landed a few decent blows with his shotgun, using it as a club.

Felix blocked and hit and blocked and hit, hoping to crush their defences with his strength. Eventually, they both stumbled.

He disarmed Alex and struck his skull with the butt of his blade. Erika sliced at him, her blow countered with ease as it cut through the air.

The tip nicked her abdomen and she fell to her knees. The sword dropped beside her. Felix hissed and snatched her by the neck, lifting her off the ground with one hand.

Her nails scratched his skin. Felix's grip narrowed. Erika wheezed, her head spinning.

"Where is it?" he growled. "*Where* is the blade?"

She swung her legs at his face, but he was relentless. At long last, she heard a crack and blood trickled from his nose beneath her boot.

"Big mistake, you huntress bitch!"

Tears streamed onto Felix's fists as he squeezed. Erika yanked at his skin, clawing, kicking, and gasping. She would *not* stop fighting. *He* would not stop squeezing.

"You don't have it, do you? But I'll get it. I'll tear it from your family's broken corpses if I must! I'll—"

Felix choked on the blade that punctured through the back of his neck, expelling a spurt of red from his snarling mouth. His grip relaxed and Erika collapsed to the ground, heaving and aching. Alex retracted the blade back into his gauntlet. It was a deadly blow, but Erika could not be sure.

She snatched her lost sword and dug it into the cavern where Felix's heart should have been. "You'll… *what*?"

His limp body slid down the blade and landed on Erika's right with an earth-shattering thud as the air around her turned hot and fire unleashed on the clearing's perimeter.

CHAPTER FORTY-THREE

Fresh blood is a lure for the nastiest of demons beyond the Veil. Keep this in mind before you spill it.

Secrets of the Veil by Cassandra Starling, Chapter Four.

The fireball flung Florence and her family sideways, rolling the car with sickening speed. She jerked side to side until they halted upright. She looked to Mum, to Alfie. A crack spider-webbed on Alfie's right lens, but they were okay, if not living advertisements for always wearing your seatbelt.

And she still had Horizon's Edge.

"Flo, sweetheart," Mum groaned, unfastening her seatbelt. "Give… give that to me."

Mum was hurt. Not drastically, but blood trickled gently down her temple.

Beyond the broken windscreen, figures stretched into view. Arcanes, Hunters—everyone. All came for the silly little blade sitting patiently on Florence's lap, a strange warmth emulating from the jewel. Mum needed time, even a few seconds, to recover. She was stronger than Florence. The Hunters needed her at her best.

She opened the door and she bolted.

Mum and Alfie shrieked and scrambled from the car. Figures closed in on Florence from the trees and torches like ants, but light radiated from the one person Florence yearned for. *"Erika!"*

She tossed her the blade, almost cocking it up when she saw the blood staining her cousin.

Erika caught it. The crowd turned on her.

Red-robed cultists boxed Erika in, who cleverly called to Alex but threw the blade at Pete, who passed it to his dad, then Uncle Chris. Uncle Chris wove between spears of flame before looping around and tossing the blade to Mum, now out of the car.

Mum ushered a confused, near-blinded Alfie out of reach and fled like a spooked doe. Aurelia caught up and, forgetting all her magic, powered her leap by sheer, personal fury.

Florence matched that rage. *Get. Off. My. Mum.*

Aurelia tackled Mum to the ground, and Florence dove in. She grappled Aurelia off her mother, but a swift kick in Florence's abdomen—against her burns—knocked her backwards, crying in agony on the grass.

Mum roared—roared like she never had before. Like a lioness, she grabbed Aurelia's shoulders and pinned her down, then raised Horizon's Edge, wielding its demeaning power for her own, looking so natural grasping it that Florence shuffled back.

Aurelia threw Mum away in a mighty gust as one of Erika's arrows shot through the air.

An incoming rock shielded Aurelia, shattering the arrowhead.

Florence whirred to the source, feeling a punch in her gut as if the rock collided with her and not the bolt. Nathaniel pointed a hand at the scene. When he relaxed it, the rock fell and, with it, his features.

Liar. User. Traitor. Her scowl said as much, so she fled.

Aurelia's magic launched at Mum, who dodged over and over. Until the arcane brandished a lighter, flicked it open with a snarl, and blew with the strength of an Aura's breath, blowtorching Mum.

She dodged it. *Just.* The flames nipped her heels and she tripped. Horizon's Edge hurled at the ground.

Florence threw herself towards it. Her hand stroked the hilt that bounced three times in her palm before she seized a grip on it. Then she ran again.

How long could she keep this up for? She hated running: her chest already ached, her throat dry and sore. She longed for her inhaler.

Mum tackled Aurelia, but other cultists closed in. Erika covered her back, but arrows could only fire one at a time. Uncle Chris homed in—a Hydros beat him to it.

Steps thundered beside her, where Alfie clutched a pocketknife. He came to protect her. He came to protect his sister.

Despite their plight, Florence smiled.

The Hunters caught them first. Alex threw big, broad arms open behind them as Uncle Chris, then Pete, then Erika and Mum, and *all* the Hunters crowded around them, protecting them.

They staggered to a halt. Arcane cultists stood before, beside, and after them. One that got too close felt the wrath of Uncle Chris's swords and slumped to his knees, chest bared open, redder than the torn fabric of the cloak that covered it.

Florence's stomach churned. Was this the reality of what Erika was doing all this time? Was she just as brutal to the people that looked, well, like *them?*

The memory of Vivienne's body told her the answer.

Sound dwindled. Above the heaving pants, shuffling footsteps, and the clicking of weaponry, no-one spoke. Erika weaved her way to the front of the group, a blonde with braids following in tow with a rifle. They pointed their weapons as the cultists formed a wall around them.

"Enough," Aurelia hissed. "No more childish games on our sacred soil. You have one final chance. Hand me the blade, and some of you may be spared."

Aurelia stretched a porcelain hand from beneath her cloak of scarlet red. No magic radiated from her fingertips. Only a promise.

Nathaniel's eyes were on Florence, an ethereal, glowing green under the full moon. They glistened with tears. She wanted to punch the space between them for what he'd done.

"Flo," he said. "You can escape this. You owe them nothing."

She shook her head without thought. He manipulated her. He didn't care whether she lived or died. Alfie was right. That was why he stole Nathaniel's pocketknife from his room this morning. *That* was why he went back after everyone left to examine the jar at his bedside. Poppy seeds—like the ones in Erika's car.

Her only relief was that she didn't make another mistake the night before.

But nothing could match the shame in telling Nathaniel where she and Alfie hid Horizon's Edge. Boasting about the crystal was the cherry on fucking top.

Nathaniel's lip quivered. "Flo, *please*."

Mum's arms opened in front of Florence; Alfie took position at her side. Florence tucked the dagger beneath her jacket—shit *his jacket*—as if the feeble fabric would protect it. "I *am* them."

Nathaniel's sigh blew away the hair Florence had run her fingers through, and she shuddered. Aurelia neared him, standing ahead as Mum did with Florence. "The stubbornness of Hunters is unmatched, my son. Especially with Lupines."

Florence met Erika's eye. She aimed her crossbow at Aurelia—Nathaniel braced himself to protect her.

Aurelia raised her chin. "If you wish to die together, so be it. I hope your camaraderie serves you better in death than life."

Aurelia brandished a clean knife from beneath her robe. Florence frowned, looking to Erika, who appeared just as baffled as herself, muttering to a wary Uncle Chris.

"She's…" Uncle Chris's jaw dropped. "No!"

The knife winked and slid over Aurelia's white palm. She muttered words Florence couldn't understand. The air cracked with heat.

Jagged lines of flaming amber scorched the surrounding air, the dirt, the trees, tearing open holes into God-knew-where. Creatures dripping in shadow, ink, ash, and fire crawled from the depths of their unworldly home and into the mundane world, all possessing a strange array of shapes and sizes and sounds.

"Demons," Alfie whispered to her.

Fuck. "How do we kill them?" Florence asked.

"Well, it—" A bear-shaped creature roared from the flaming doorway, splattering ink over the grass. Alfie gasped. "It depends on the demon."

Florence looked to Mum, who tapped her watch as if it might go faster. *What is she waiting for?* Nearby, Erika shot a wolf-shaped, fiery demon in the skull. Her arrow turned to ash on its skin.

"Behold the true potential of our species," Aurelia's porcelain hands spread in the air. Cultists backed away—even Nathaniel. "Soak in the power which our Divines seek to bottle with your feeble Treaty. You have fought valiantly. But humanity cannot—"

Muggy heat parted with a cold chill; a hurricane of black ash that circled an empty space. More elegantly than the demons entered seven individuals: five men and two women, all clad in business-casual of varying colours and extravagancy. A dark-skinned lady's dreadlocks shone like silver, her suit shimmering as a lagoon at midnight, with the oldest woman standing stock in a powerful pink pantsuit. Florence blushed at the tallest man with dark hair, standing at the end of the line with the most perfect posture she had ever seen, every inch of skin covered up to his sculpted jawline. They exuded godly energy. *Divine* energy.

Mum elbowed Uncle Chris in the abdomen. "You're welcome."

The oldest, a white-haired, bearded man, led the pack, donning navy pinstripes and a pocket watch, and opened his mouth to speak before the presumed second oldest, grey-haired Divine interrupted. "Aurelia."

"Matthias," Mum whispered to Florence. "Her coven's Divine."

"Sir," was all Aurelia said.

Demons hovered overhead, selecting their Hunters, waiting for Aurelia's signal. *"Hold your nerve,"* Uncle Chris urged. Florence tried.

Matthias paced before the Divines. His tailored tweed matched the colours of the surrounding earth. "Aurelia, you have committed an act of treason in defiance of the Treaty of the Four Worlds. You have tarnished your coven's—*my* coven's—name through the enactment of blood magics, attempts at necromancy, and spitting on our sacred customs."

"Not to mention the injustices you committed against the Order of Hunters," the straight-backed Divine added. His voice was quiet, but it swept over the clearing as a chilling gust.

When Aurelia didn't move, Matthias outstretched his hand, and the cult leader dropped to her knees in anguish. Her syphon *hissed*, glowing red, then white-hot. Aurelia sobbed, begging for her Divine to stop.

Florence reached for Alfie to steady herself. *The sound...*

She caught Erika flinch and her eyes combed over the Hunters, who all looked to be as startled as she was. Since when could Divines *control* their arcanes?

"You know our customs," said Matthias. "You know what must be done."

Aurelia swallowed. Her lips pressed tightly together, ceasing her sobs. Florence thought she would cry again. Around them, the dripping demons inched closer, crossing the thresholds of their crackling gateways, ember drifting in like dust, carrying the smell of decay and burnt flesh.

The flaming ones made Florence inch closer to Mum.

Aurelia reached for her neck and ripped the syphon's chain. To a chorus of gasps, she pointed a bloody, shaking finger at the Divines. *"I do."*

Matthias conjured and fired a ball of warped light. It *whooshed* at Aurelia. Her demons unleashed upon them, focusing on the Divines but swooping Hunters in their charge. Florence hit the floor, Horizon's Edge pricking at her ribs. Magic, arrows, bullets, knives, shadow, and ash whipped overhead, blanketed by a tidal wave of fog enveloping the battlefield and obscuring all its soldiers.

CHAPTER FORTY-FOUR

Demons represent all that is negative in the world. Keep a level head, or risk corruption.

The Hunter's Codex, Chapter III.

Fog engulfed her, and Erika lost sight of her family. In the brisk, white cloud, she clutched only her crossbow, eyes peeled for recognition of any demons, arcanes, or allies. Through it all, Aurelia *laughed*.

This was all such a mess. Not only was Aurelia possessed, but the madness of losing her syphon would surely take over soon—as if blood magic and demons weren't crazy enough already!

Erika whirled at a scream. Then came the crackling roar of wildfire and a flash of opaque red. A fireball skimmed overhead, igniting the tawny face of an arcane—a male Divine—and a canine demon shrouded in shadow.

The Divine dodged the incoming fireball, unaware of the demon at his back.

Erika fired. The arrow pierced the demon's chest and it squealed, falling back into a cloud of arthritic ash. At least she could fight the shadow-creatures. Those with fire – the fury demons – were to be avoided.

The Divine spun, straight brows tugged together in a frown upon a sculpted face. Forest eyes softened in recognition of her Hunter status, and Erika signalled a sloppy salute. Dark hair shifted over wide shoulders when he nodded his thanks and turned back to the battlefield.

A cultist threw pathetic Terra magic in a handful of stones. Erika would have laughed, but the Divine did not. Effortlessly, he raised a hand, and the cultist crumbled before him, her eyes turning black as she screamed.

Erika staggered back. What affinity did *that?* When screams erupted once more, Erika buried her curiosity and pushed on, headed for the thickest, loudest fighting zone.

A running body hit her head-on.

"Erika!" Pete gripped her arms. "You're okay."

"Alive and well." He was safe. Blood-crusted and bruised, but alive.

He released a nervous laugh. "You know, if we don't make it out of this—"

"We will."

"But—"

"Pete, this isn't the time for—"

"There never will be a time for this." His eyes turned glassy, desperate. "But I need to tell you, I—"

"Move!"

She shoved Pete away when a shadowed wildcat pounced for the gap between them. It skidded over the dirt, hissing with bared fangs.

Erika twirled an arrow between her fingers.

Pete clutched his sword. "Cover me."

She did as commanded and loaded her crossbow. The wildcat bounded their way, rabid, yapping, spitting inky black foam.

Pete ducked as it leapt. It landed behind him, making a beeline for Erika.

She fired. The wildcat swung a clawing paw.

Erika sidestepped. The tip of her arrow caught the beast. It let out a yelp and scrambled towards her from the left.

Erika jumped to the side. The wildcat tricked her and changed course last minute to launch at her right arm. It latched on, piercing knife-like claws into her bicep.

She ripped away, crying at the pain. The creature knocked her on her back, squealing at the arrow Erika dug between its ribs. Hot, black blood dripped from her knuckles.

It was not enough. To anger it, maybe, but to kill it…

Bloody saliva dripped from its thrashing maw. With every gnash, its jaws grew closer and closer and—

Erika whimpered at the black blade stopping inches from her eyes, elongating from the wildcat's mouth. Clenching her eyes and mouth shut, she turned away from its face and grunted as the full weight of its corpse slumped against her heaving chest.

Pete chuckled and threw off the corpse, offering a hand. "Just like old times, Lupine."

"Don't tell me you miss *this*?"

Erika held back a grin as the tug of his arm brought their chests together.

Pete's lips brushed her forehead. "I miss *you*."

Their heads snapped in different directions as both fathers called their names. God, she never should have let him leave last night.

"Stay alive for me?" Pete said.

"Promise me the same?"

He squeezed her hand and let go in a silent oath.

Erika waded through the thinning fog, stumbling into Diana first, then Dad. Her aunt clutched twin blades at her side, the right one covered in blood.

"Thank God," Diana breathed. "Have you seen the twins?"

Dad swung his head as a flaming boulder skimmed him. Erika swore there were embers in his stubble. "We have greater priorities."

"Nothing takes priority over my children, Christopher!"

Erika found one that did. Just for now.

A great bear, double Erika's height and almost three times her width, charged, encased in red-hot flames. Its jaws opened, ready to gorge on them.

She found herself a step behind Dad. "Any suggestions?"

"Yes." He tapped her arm. "Run."

They scattered. Erika tailed Diana. She ran to the source of Florence calling for her mother.

Erika tripped, almost yanking Diana backwards as an invisible force latched onto her ankle. Diana screamed, reaching for her. Her crossbow hit the ground,

The invisible rope numbed her ankle, reeling her towards a frantic, furious Aurelia. Blood dripped from an outstretched palm, webbing up her forearms in a red-black gradient.

The blood magic, her Aura affinity, the demon—it was all getting too much without a syphon. If she didn't pack it in soon, nature would do Erika's job for her.

"I've had enough of you, Lupine! If you think you're getting out of this, you are mistaken."

Aurelia unfolded a second hand and drew it back, sucking the air from Erika's lungs. Her chest pulsed, and Aurelia's tug swiftened.

Diana backtracked and snatched the crossbow from the grass. "Let her go! I won't ask twice."

The crossbow accepted Diana. It didn't resist her as it did with The Collector.

Erika winced as the bonds on her body tightened.

Diana scowled. "Fine."

She fired an arrow and ran. Dodging the arrow, Aurelia pulled roots from the ground, looping them through the dirt like an army of snakes. Auras were a nightmare. If you could manipulate the air, you could control anything, to a degree. Diana dodged them all.

Aurelia's hold on Erika relaxed, and soon she wrangled free of the invisible pull.

Diana unleashed herself upon the arcane's magic, blocking and parrying the roots with her twin blades until the tip of one scraped Aurelia's shin.

The arcane fell.

Diana shrugged her hair over her shoulder, crossing blades over Aurelia's exposed neck. Her scarlet cloak slipped from her torso, revealing the plain jumper and jeans beneath.

Under the theatrics, Aurelia was just as human as the rest of them.

Aurelia's lip curled at Diana. "You're wasted, Diana. Having children never held *me* back."

Diana retracted her blades, ready to slice through Aurelia's neck, until Matthias' voice boomed over the clearing.

"STOP! She is mine to sentence."

Beyond him, the battle faltered in the Hunters' favour. Arcanes collapsed, some dead, some restrained. Through the dissipating fog, Erika found Alex taking on the bear-shaped fury demon—and winning—and the twins nearby, completely safe. She could not see Dad, Pete, or Wyatt.

"You know the penalty for breaking the Treaty!" Diana snarled. "For what she's done—"

"She will face trial." Matthias approached, sparing not a single glance for Erika as she clambered to her feet, a hand on her raw abdomen. "For now, she is unarmed. Is it not a violation of your Code to end her in such a way?"

Erika bit her tongue. Aurelia could never be unarmed—not when magic and a demon surged through her veins. If her recent trials taught her anything, it was that you could never turn your back on an arcane.

Diana sucked in her cheeks and huffed. "And the others?"

Most of the cultists had been apprehended one way or another. A few survived—barely. Samson crawled across the grass, leaving a bloody streak in his wake. If not for Matthias's orders, Erika would have put him out of his misery and let him be with Vivienne again.

Matthias clicked his tongue. "If they can be restrained, they face the same fate."

Diana's grip loosened, but she did not remove her blades from Aurelia's neck. The arcane deserved it, but ending her life was not worth sacrificing her own freedom. "Fine."

Aurelia's shoulders slumped. Corruption clawed up her arms in her syphon's absence. "Thank you, Matthias."

"I did what I could for you," Matthias snapped. "Evidently, that was not enough."

Aurelia's head dipped low. She disappointed him more than he was letting on. Erika hoped Dad would never look at her the same way.

"She's corrupted," Erika declared. "She may not know exactly what she's been—"

Matthias raised his brow like she was fucking stupid. "I feel no instance of a demon."

Arcanes could *sense* them, Erika heard, but Hunters could identify them. "I'm telling you, her eyes—"

"Have always been this way," Matthias insisted.

The hell? "You're not—"

"Erika," Diana scolded. "She'll get her punishment either way."

And how just would it be? Demons didn't seize their host's autonomy—they emboldened emotions already planted. It was manipulation of the highest degree. Once it corrupted you…

Only the strongest could force it out.

"Mum!" Nathaniel bolted across the clearing. Enraged, he raised his hands, ready to cast at Diana.

Erika unsheathed an arrow, startled when she realised her crossbow was still on the ground a few metres back.

Nathaniel staggered when a pocketknife pressed to his throat.

Florence snarled in his ear, bending both arms back into his spine. *"Don't move."*

Her bitterness encapsulated Diana perfectly.

"Florence." Nathaniel shuddered under her grip. "I'm s—"

"Shut up. Just shut up."

Diana smiled, careful to hold her blades' position. "That's my girl."

The battle ended when Alex plunged his longsword deep into the great bear's skull from above, extinguishing the last of the demons. Flames caught his sleeve, but he was unharmed.

Sweat rolled down his forehead. He smiled when he caught Erika's eye across the battlefield.

Tommy Arwood clutched his son's shoulder. Nearby, Lucie and Lily launched into an embrace, Vanessa and Katia hugged, and Dad and Wyatt patted each other on the back, returning from the tree line, a path of crumbling demon corpses in tow.

Erika caught Leopold's absence, even among the corpses.

Then her stomach knotted, missing someone more important. "Alfie?" She'd just seen him…

Diana's eyes darkened, and she went still—steady enough to make Aurelia gulp.

Florence scanned the crowd, closing the gap between her blade and Nathaniel's neck with every second that passed.

Another second went by.

And another.

"Alfie!" Erika called.

Behind Dad, Alfie stepped into view. Dad swung an arm over his nephew, allowing him to walk in front.

Diana sighed. Florence squealed. "Kept yourself alive, did you?" she teased.

"Barely," Dad tutted. "He's weak, awfully slow, and his aim could do with some—"

"*Christopher*," Diana warned.

Dad blew out a sigh and swung his head back. The sky was clear. Moonlight lit up the silver streaks in his hair and beard.

"But… he has potential. Good work, boy."

Alfie turned to conceal his blush.

But the knot in Erika's body did not subside. Her headcount was almost complete, but one more remained.

She looked at Wyatt. "Where's Pete?"

"Missing me already, Lupine?"

Of course she fucking was.

Wyatt chuckled at the speed at which she took off, polite enough to step aside for her. Hunters and Divines and cultists and corpses drifted by, all irrelevant when she looked at Pete. He beamed, laughing with the same melody as his father, opening his arms and casting his own spell on her.

Bodies moved around them but they did not matter. They'd *won*. They were safe. They could have died tonight. Damn their fathers—damn the consequences!

Erika readied herself to jump, blind to all around her but him.

Blind to the hand that stole Horizon's Edge from Pete's belt.

Blind to the hand that dug it straight into his back.

Florence screamed over the fire that roared from the braziers as Pete's blood touched the grass.

He folded. The world around her stopped, but Erika kept running.

Samson, almost dead himself, drew his arm for another strike. Erika bent back his wrist and pushed the blade into his neck. Flesh squelched, and he slumped on the grass, Horizon's Edge still wedged inside him.

Samson's scarred face broke into a smile. "The pain is nothing. Wait 'til the emptiness... sets in."

For Vivienne. *Shit, no, no!*

Erika kicked him to the side and crawled straight for Pete.

She fell back on her knees and rolled him over, pulling him onto her lap. The wound cut deep, piercing a gaping hole through the other side. Blood gushed from both ends. The two of them were already soaked.

"Shit, *shit*. This can't be—" Erika locked eyes with the nearest Divine, the youngest with silver hair and deep skin. "You can heal him, can't you? Your magic, it... it can help him."

Her lips parted, and she looked to Matthias, who shook his head. "We can't."

The young Divine's jaw dropped. "We could at least *try*."

"No," Matthias boomed. "It is too late for him."

"No, it's not!" Erika's cry echoed through the clearing. "It's not too late, it's—"

"Erika." Wet fingers touched her face. Even in this state, Pete smiled at her. Always smiling. "It's okay."

"It's not, Pete. None of this is okay."

"We…" He coughed, spraying blood onto his chin. "We're…"

His stained and shaking hand reached for his neck—the space between his collarbones. When he felt nothing, he groaned weakly. The quartz was still in Aurelia's possession.

Erika took his hand from the empty space and pressed it to her chest. "I'm here," she said.

His smile broadened as if it didn't pain him. For Erika, it was agony. "You are."

She glanced into his fire-ringed hazel eyes before quivering lips pressed against her own. Warm. Despite how cold the rest of him was. She clutched him tightly, desperately clinging onto every morsel of life, willing her own to filter through him instead as if she possessed magic of her own.

Please, she begged. *Not him. Me. Not him.*

No-one listened.

His wrist turned limp in her grip, energy drained from all but his lips. Erika held the back of his head, her throat closing faster than what Aurelia's magic managed to achieve.

Words failed her.

He coughed down her back and gagged. "Shit, Erika, I don't want to die."

"I know." She rocked him, a sob escaping, but no tears fell. She felt him cry against her neck. "I know."

"Keep your promise. You... promised me..."

He fell still. Light. Cold.

"Pete?" When she angled his chin to look into his eyes, the fire was gone. "Pete?"

Beside her, Horizon's Edge glowed from the jewel, humming darkly.

Before a single sob released, strong arms dragged her away. Wyatt pulled his son into an embrace, crying and cursing.

Erika wouldn't let go. She yanked her arms from the grip that restrained her.

"Let him go," Dad ordered.

"I can't leave him!"

He lifted her by the arms and pinned them behind her. "Don't cry," he whispered through her hair. "Don't let a single soul here see you cry."

"But he—"

"Don't cry."

Diana rushed to her side. She took a gentler hold on her jerking arms. Tears failed to come.

No mourning on the job.

"Give her to me."

Dad retreated and let Erika fall into his sister's warmer hold. She whispered comforts over and over, but all flew over Erika's head, a complete blur in the background of Pete's blood staining her hands, of Wyatt wailing for his son.

Pete never betrayed her. He accepted her nature, never changed her.

But he did break her heart.

It anguished Erika not to cry, but she'd sooner tear out her eyeballs. She had to leave, to go somewhere to let it all out, but her family—

Beyond, Florence bawled against Alex. He gave a silent nod when Erika spotted him. Alfie leaned into his hold. Nathaniel and Aurelia remained in the Divine's care.

The silver-haired Divine locked eyes with another, then stepped forward.

Matthias dragged her back by the shoulder. "We should honour his—"

"Hunters are not our concern," Matthias reminded her. "Collect our dead with the others. Then we take our leave."

Diana's hold on Erika tightened when she tensed. "Leave it," she warned. "Don't say something you might regret."

Erika scowled into Diana's shoulder. Matthias took position beside the well-postured male Divine she'd saved earlier: the one with the strange magic.

He side-eyed Matthias. "This was *your* coven. Don't forget that when it comes to clearing up this mess."

The elder voiced his distaste with a frown and made sure to bump his shoulder, storming towards the stone altar. The right side of his face ignited in an orange cast from the flames licking the bronze coffin.

CHAPTER FORTY-FIVE

Beware the voices.

Recovered Journal from Banstead Hospital, Author Unknown.

Arcanes and Hunters alike tended to the wounded, collected their dead, and scoured for any human witnesses. Amid their scrambling, Erika seized a moment to slip away. Florence called for her to return, but Dad silenced her swiftly. He knew why she left. He knew she needed to be alone.

Torchlight shrunk to distant orbs, and sounds of the wild grew loud. Arcanes possessed a connection to nature unlike any other being, supernatural or not. Aurelia's cultists spooked the natural order at Bekker's. Their absence raised shadows from the trees like rainwater from foliage under heat, giving way to mice scuttling through the undergrowth. An owl hummed contemplatively from the upper branch of a great oak. In a single flash of angelic white, it snatched a mouse from its path.

Death circled her here. Not even something so small and timid as a mouse could escape its wretched claws.

The sky sighed and spittle clung to her hair. Erika wiped her forehead with the back of a cold hand and drew it back to the familiar sheen of blood. Diluted. Pink from the rainwater.

The final remnants of Pete slipped through her fingers. Was this one last cruel trick by the cult? Or did the world deem her unworthy to hold onto him?

They'd already taken his body. Dad and Tommy carried him to Wyatt's car, Pete's father too distraught to even stand. He was to be taken to the Watch, anticipating a General's funeral. An honour, Dad said, considering his promotion was only being debated by the Council. The eldest Divine cloaked the Hunters' bodies the same way their magic cloaked the Watch. No authorities would stop them on their way home, now.

Scuffling made Erika halt. Back in the clearing, two men argued. The distance distorted the voices, but she was certain Dad was not involved in the exchange.

So, she moved on. Completely alone.

With growing confidence in her isolation, her body began to heave. In every breath she swallowed hot pokers, her body rejecting the feelings consuming her more and more with every step. She burned from the inside until she broke down, letting the tears fall in quiet, choking sobs as she scraped down a dying beech, submerging herself among the dirt and petrichor.

No-one could see her here. None could witness a broken Lupine. To the Hunters, the Divines, she was the pinnacle of strength. As strong as the fortress that housed them, the fortress her ancestors built. She would endure. She would.

She killed Vivienne. Vivienne's lover killed Pete. How could she dry her tears when the rain wouldn't stop falling? When the blood on her hands stayed wet?

"Why do you cry, little one?"

She startled, but the forest hadn't moved. The trees were still. Only a gentle breeze caressed her cheek.

"You look so lonely…"

The forest rustled over the sound of her final shaking sob. In a moment of weakness, she hoped it was Alex who followed, but it was not him who tailed her.

The Divine with strange magic stepped over a holly bush, unaware of her presence. She debated slipping away but decided, aware she was unable to do so quietly, to wipe her tears, allowing him to find her.

He looked around with an open mouth, clearly spotting her, looking for something, *anything*, else to focus on. The owl hooted nearby, but it remained hidden.

There was only her.

"I am... sorry," he said. "I came to check for stragglers."

His voice didn't match the one she heard, so she shivered. "None here." Erika brushed a thumb beneath her nose and sniffed. "Just me."

He nodded. His movement towards the clearing made her think he was about to leave but he didn't. He changed his mind and closed in on her.

She shuffled back into the tree and he stopped. He almost looked hurt.

"You have my condolences. I watched your friend in the battle, and he fought bravely. Honourably. The way Samson just..." He sighed, full of regret. "He did not deserve such an end."

His death was a cheap shot. Pete did everything right, apart from one thing.

He turned his back on an arcane.

"He was good." Erika fought back the tears to keep her eyes on the Divine without exposing herself too much. "He didn't deserve *any* end."

The Divine's shoulders dropped. That was the first time she'd seen his posture waver.

"Too many died today. I could not help but notice many of those were innocents. Children. Just two of the original twelve fell despite so much death on your side."

Erika glanced through wet lashes. She wiped away the mahogany tint. "I know."

He wasn't looking at her. Instead, he looked at the grass, reading the earth like Alfie read his books. He made to speak, then stopped. Instead, he approached, stretching out a tattooed hand. The mark was white, reaching from the tips of his fingers and branching down into his sleeve. When Erika noticed his other hand, hanging casually at his side, mirrored the pattern, she couldn't help but wonder how far the marks stretched beyond his clothing.

Despite her curiosity, she glowered at it.

"I will not wait forever," he pressed.

"I can help myself."

"Watching you today, I do not doubt that. Just allow me to—"

"No."

She dug her fingers into the sides of the trunk and dragged herself up. Other Hunters received first aid or healing from the Divines, but Erika pushed the twins in line first and headed for the trees before any arcane could get a close enough look at her tired eyes. She ached. Inside and out.

The Divine clicked his tongue. "You know, Miss…?"

She hesitated, then said. "Lupine."

His brows flicked. Even in Stryga's libraries, her family held space. "Miss Lupine, there is no shame in asking for help. You Hunters are renowned for your camaraderie, are you not?"

She held her lips shut and nodded.

"Good. Confide in them."

And burden them? Show weakness? Hunters were the shield at humanity's back. What good was a shield with holes in the wicker?

Erika pushed against the tree and staggered over the foliage. "I should get back."

The Divine didn't object. "Of course. Just one thing."

She flinched when he made to touch her bicep. His hand hovered. The action flared heat in the wound from the wildcat. Her abdomen stung from Felix's blade. Even bruises from the wendigo prickled along her shoulder.

"May I?" he asked.

She considered refusing out of spite, but her body wailed enough as it was. Considering the sheer amount of blood and dirt she'd rolled in, infection was a grave concern. She didn't fancy losing her arm.

She nodded. The Divine covered the wound with a firm but gentle touch. The contact had her sucking in a breath, swallowing at the weird tickle of her skin stitching itself back together. The Divine closed his eyes, inhaling magic's burnt scent. His was different. Stronger, thicker. *Darker.* Erika swore she saw the tattoos on both arms *glow*.

The pain subsided, and he let go.

"It may mean very little to you, but if no-one thanks you for your service today, I will. From my species and my coven, especially, I thank you. And I swear I will do whatever it takes to uncover the origins of this mess."

An illegible whisper made Erika shudder, and the Divine shut his eyes with a wince. She glanced at the hand that fell to his side, wondering whether to offer a peaceful shake.

Instead, she gave a nod. A *thank you* despite the pain arcanes caused her Order today.

Diana met her with furrowed brows at the tree lining, but Erika stood on something sharp—something *buzzing*. She lifted her boot to a sharp flash of moonlight.

Aurelia's syphon.

Erika crouched to hold the symbol in her hand. The pattern she failed to distinguish was an assortment of swirls blending into an abstract image of a fiery lion head, a vortex of goat horns, and a coiling snake, all blending into one, the translucent syphon jewel etched in the centre where the three animals met.

The chimera.

"Erika," Diana whispered. "What have you—God!"

She grabbed Erika's arm at a snapping twig but it was only the Divine who unearthed from the woodland. Erika closed the syphon in her fist.

The syphon was made *after* Aurelia joined the cult.

"Who was *that*?" Diana whispered as he left.

Erika watched as the Divine re-joined his own kind. "One of *them*."

"Cassius!" Matthias barked. Hunters and arcanes jolted—all but Cassius. His eyes narrowed as he took position in the centre of the congregating Divines, standing between the silver-haired young woman and the elder white-haired male.

Matthias was Aurelia's Divine.

A female Divine, the oldest of the women, with a pink pantsuit and a matching hijab swooped around her head, stepped before the group. "We will be in touch with your Council in the coming days. This disaster cannot be repeated."

Disaster. As if their kind hadn't *chosen* to take part in this. There had to be a reason why. It was her job—the Divines' job—to figure out that reasoning, not the Hunters. *They* held all the secrets, apparently. They certainly kept syphon control quiet.

As if sharing her thoughts, no Hunters replied.

The Divine looked to her right, the rest of her stiff and still. "Cassius?"

Cassius gave another nod Erika's way as if reinforcing his promise. Gale carried ash through the forest, centring at Cassius as he, the Divines, and their traitors disappeared in a vortex of shadow.

The last face Erika saw was Aurelia's, looking at her, not her father. Even though she was possessed—even though her mind was not entirely her own—demons only possessed those who shared their desires. In her silent wrath, Erika made her thoughts known.

You did this. You killed him.

But she did not do it alone.

Through the smoke was a ghost of a smile from the auburn arcane. *"The perfect vessel for pride…"*

Before Erika could question her words, they vanished. And so, the most powerful beings of the supernatural world left them behind to clean up their mess.

Sobs echoed when the wind fell silent. Most of the bodies had been taken already, but others—those without mourners—were left to still be carried. Florence moved to approach one of the lonely bodies, her mother stopping her.

All this death. For what? This was like The Collector's party all over—

Erika's wandering eyes found Alfie, who looked just as concerned.

Before either could say anything, Dad turned to Erika. "Horizon's Edge?"

His question was quiet, but his voice carried through the clearing, lifting over the trees with the midnight breeze. None had an answer for him.

Did the Divines seize control over their lost artefact? Had Wyatt mistakenly stolen his son's murder weapon? Either way, the Hunters were silent, left with nothing but the stench of decay and the weight of mourning as the weather began to turn.

Tarnish the Veil

CHAPTER FORTY-SIX

It is with great sorrow that we remember the fallen. In the wake of our victory, their deaths will not be in vain.

Funeral Speech for the Fallen by Councillor Paris.

The weeks leading up to Christmas dragged. Usually, Erika spent every day until Christmas Eve hunting with Dad, but this year was different. She did a few odd jobs here and there. Dad reminded her that her role in the 'Battle of Bekker's,' as it was soon named, put her next in line for a General anointment. Alex, too, according to his text. So, she went on a few hunts, keeping her name in the loop with a few demons and a handful of ghosts because *Christ*, they were out in full swing before Christmas. Alfie went with her on one occasion, Florence still too injured to join, Diana alleged, but she mostly went with Dad. She said she could handle it alone, but Dad was not convinced. Nearly two weeks before Christmas, Erika decided enough was enough and moved back home for the holidays. Ollie was relieved to see her back so soon before Christmas.

She thought about returning to the Watch for the festivities as a final honour to Pete but the celebrations would be short-lived without him. As she stayed up late on Christmas Eve, watching unfunny comedies with Ollie, Dad, Diana, and the twins, she realised this is what he would have wanted.

Family. Not drowning away her sorrows in the dining hall.

The funeral was lovely, even if it was a combined one. The coffins of fallen Hunters were carried by men and women through the Council Chamber for the ceremony. They listened to readings from the Council, the choir sang high, and the orchestra played to perfection. Erika was not religious. She did not believe in a God, but there must be an afterlife. The ghouls she encountered had to come and go from somewhere.

Pete was buried with an arrow-encrusted medal. The Morris Crest, it was called. The highest honour for dying selflessly in battle. Erika couldn't watch the mud shovel onto his body. It was too finite—too soon.

She left early, returning straight to Diana. Still, thoughts of the Cult never left her. She lay awake for days, examining Aurelia's syphon, her mind struck on the missing Horizon's Edge, the demon possessing Aurelia, and the voice that followed Erika through the tree lining and never came back. No-one else heard a voice and she was met with only confusion from Dad and Diana when she asked what Aurelia meant by a 'vessel' for the ritual. She kept her suspicions of Matthias to herself. With confidence in the Treaty destabilising, questioning a Divine with nothing but a *hunch* was off the table.

Through it all, her mind trailed back to the strange marks on Cassius' skin.

Years of Diana's conditioning had both twins waking Erika up at the crack of dawn on Christmas Day. They dragged a disgruntled Erika downstairs early, Ollie staggering behind her. Dad, who had no other option but to camp on the sofa, was unimpressed by the noise. He was an early bird, yes, but he prioritised sleep during his rare holidays. Rising early for something such as Christmas was a waste of energy, he said.

He still smiled as Florence opened her gifts from him.

Dad watched the kids play their gaming console while Erika helped Diana out in the kitchen, chopping the vegetables she peeled last night.

"You've outdone yourself again, Diana." Erika forced the knife into another potato. "Are you forgetting there's only six of us?"

"It's Christmas," she insisted. She checked the gingerbread men in the oven and straightened up, wiping crumbs on her floral apron. "If there's a time for going all out, it's now."

She did this every year since Freddie died: a silent promise to make Christmas extra special for the twins in their father's absence. Erika noticed, this year, that the food had almost doubled in quantity, the presents rising in value.

"This must have cost a lot," she said. "Are you sure you don't want any—"

"Nonsense!" Diana pointed an oven-mitted finger. "You may be due a promotion soon, young lady, but your work has taken a *significant* drop. Don't think I haven't noticed."

Erika laughed. "Much to Dad's disgust. I told him I wanted time off for Christmas, and he said—"

"Generals don't get Christmas?" Diana rolled her eyes. "Your father means well, but he's no fun really, is he?"

"I made a promise to Ollie," Erika reminded her. "Whether I get this promotion now or in a year's time, I planned on keeping my word to him. He deserves it after waiting so long."

Diana swung open the oven drawer, releasing ginger and cinnamon's hot fumes into the kitchen. "And it means a lot to him. He's happy you're here."

Erika smiled and turned back to her potatoes.

"Don't worry about money." Diana slammed the baking tray on top of the stove. "Because those bonuses the Divines gave us?" She whistled, taking off the oven gloves. "Lifesavers. Our bills are covered for the next year and Christmas is a big one. My God, we need it."

Erika had to laugh. "It's amazing what hush money does."

"*Compensation*," Diana echoed Divine Matthias. "If it pays the bills, I don't care."

A knock at the door almost sent Erika's knife through her finger. They weren't expecting anyone. "Diana?"

Diana shrugged. "Answer it, then."

Erika's stomach knotted but released when she cautiously opened the door.

"I smell gingerbread!"

Alex leapt over the threshold and scooped Erika in a suffocating bear hug that squeezed out a laugh. Tommy approached from behind, a full, rustling plastic bag in one hand, waving at Dad with the other.

"Merry Christmas, Erika. I hope you don't mind, Chris. Apparently, Erika insisted Alex came for Christmas."

Erika's jaw dropped. She'd not texted him for almost a week! "You invited yourself round for Christmas?"

"I did not!"

"Actually…" Diana appeared behind her, carrying spices on the warm hands she placed on Erika's shoulders. "I invited them."

Dad sighed and gestured to the rest of the house, stepping aside. None of them were used to 'guests.' "In that case, do come in. Please excuse the twins."

Tommy frowned, unzipping his coat. "What's wrong with them?"

Dad took a swig of his beer. "Nothing new."

Florence's scream deafened Dad. While Alex introduced himself to an unsure Ollie and greeted both twins, Erika returned to her potatoes.

"We don't do 'guests' at Christmas," she whispered to Diana.

"This year we do," she replied just as quietly. "I thought you could use a friend this year."

"I have you." Her potatoes splashed as she dropped them in a bowl of beef stock. "And Dad, Ollie, the twins—"

"And you're not grateful that he's here?"

Erika glanced over her shoulder, watching Alex converse with her family through the open door to the entryway. His smile was sunlight, his charm entrancing. His presence was a break in the clouds on a rainy day.

Diana awaited her bashful reaction while mixing the royal icing. "I am."

"I invited Wyatt, too," she said. "But he wanted to stay at the Watch this year."

He hadn't left since the funeral. Erika made a mental note to text him before the day ended, though he wouldn't get it until he left the grounds.

Alex skipped into the kitchen. "*Do* I smell gingerbread?"

"You do indeed." Diana shoved the most misshapen gingerbread man into Alex's mouth. "Try!"

He almost choked but the ambrosia broadened his eyes. Erika grinned. She knew the euphoria of trying one of Diana's creations for the first time.

"Diana, this is exquisite."

Erika whistled. "That's posh for you, Alex."

"I've been expanding my vocabulary in hopes of being promoted." He covered his mouth politely then swallowed. "*Divine*."

Erika cooed. "Very nice."

"Outstanding."

"A bit boring."

"Stunning."

Erika snorted. "Now that's a stretch. That's one of the ugliest gingerbread men I've ever—"

"I'm describing you."

Her hands stumbled over the wet potatoes at his words. Diana had already backed out the room, grinning. "I should speak to Tommy. See if he'd like a coffee. Or a beer."

She urged Alex to help himself before leaving.

Before Erika could return to vegetable prep, Alex brandished a gift, hastily wrapped in creased burgundy and gold paper.

"I got you something," he said proudly. "Apologies for my wrapping skills. I work with metal, not paper."

"Alex, you shouldn't have—"

"It's nothing big, don't worry! Just open it."

She wiped her hands then curiously tore the paper, scrunching it in her fist to not let it fall to the floor. When she spotted the shirtless chef on the hardback book cover, she crumbled in laughter.

The Art of Italy.

"How funny."

"Well, you found the book *so* interesting before, so I thought I'd get you a copy of your own. Figured you could learn a thing or two from the English guy that puts cheddar cheese on spaghetti bolognese."

"I'll keep that in mind for when I fancy a self-care night."

She sat the book on the window ledge beside Diana's celebrity cookbooks and personal baking journals. Would the recipes ever be followed? Probably not. But it made her laugh to read it again.

"I never thanked you for coming to the funeral."

Alex met her gaze. The sudden lock of their eyes made Erika's heart leap, then fall, sinking further than ever before.

"I wanted to pay my respects. Pete was a good man."

"He was." Erika gestured towards the living room where Florence and Alfie argued over who won their game, and Ollie overzealously backed up Alfie. "My family are supportive, but I can't really… I can't…"

"Be weak."

"I have to be strong for them. Most knew Pete too and they're hurting."

"But they didn't know him like you did?" She shook her head. "I know. I'm always here, Erika. Hell, you haven't got a choice now. Don't be afraid to rely on me."

"I don't need a shoulder but an arm. I'd appreciate that, if you're offering."

Alex smiled. It did not reach his eyes like always. Instead, those dark, gold-flecked irises pierced her, gathering intel his furrowed brows struggled to string together.

CHAPTER FORTY-SEVEN

I will find her. And if I must kill every single one of them to do so, so be it.

Christopher Lupine's Journal.

Erika was drunk. Very drunk.

The last time she reached such a state was the day after Pete's funeral. She'd held it together all day, reining in the tears and the pain, but the moment she stepped through Diana's front door, she broke. Tears fell as she snuck into the house, greeting no-one. She'd sunk into the kitchen chair, a dusty bottle of spiced rum and a bottle of Coke for company. Diana was furious and sent her to bed. She replaced the friendship of alcohol with a glass of water and herself, holding her until she fell asleep in her arms as she did with Mum before she disappeared.

When she woke, the guilt made her sick.

This was not the same kind of drunk. She was… happy. Floating through clouds while entirely present in the room, surrounded by family.

She would never see Pete again. But knowing these seven smiling faces were safe was enough.

She only wished she had his quartz. Wyatt returned hers, but she often found herself clutching the crystal, anticipating a response. As far as she was concerned, Aurelia still had it.

"Oh, come on, Erika, play us a song," Diana slurred. The turkey dinner cushioned wine's powerful blow, but an afternoon of board games ended in a chugging competition between her and Tommy. If

Erika and Alex were not so stuffed on the meat, roasted vegetables and Yorkshire puddings, they'd have been inclined to join. They slumped against one another on the largest sofa, Ollie on their right, their barely-touched wine glasses at their feet beside Florence sitting on the carpet.

Alex nudged Erika to sit up straight.

"It's been ages since I heard you play!" Ollie, the only sober one in the room, added when she shook her head. Being fifteen had him on a drinking ban by Diana, but a not-so-sly Florence offered a few measures of vodka in his lemonade glass. Erika excused it twice but stole her cousin's flask when the singles transformed into quadruples.

Erika reached for her glass and sipped her pinot grigio. A dry film stuck to the roof of her mouth, and she decided this would be her last. "It's been a while," she said. "I'm rusty."

"Who are we to judge?" Diana exclaimed. "We're hardly Mozarts!"

Alex chuckled. "Speak for yourself."

"You've had greater priorities," Dad reminded her from the armchair. "You don't have time for such things anymore."

"Because she's always working," Ollie retorted. "She needs to save time for the things she loves as well."

Diana's grip slackened on the back of the armchair. Her own words, of course, judging from the nervous glance she made towards Dad sitting in front of her. If Dad knew this, which Erika did not doubt that he did, he didn't let on.

"Time wasted on trivial things is taken away from the those that matter," Dad said in his *I'm doing you a favour in teaching you this* voice.

"What counts as 'trivial,' then?" Ollie retorted.

At Erika's feet, Florence leaned into her knees.

"Hobbies," Dad said bluntly. "The violin, for example, is trivial. Lazing around, watching movies on every day off—" He look pointedly Erika's way. He always complained about her sluggish nature at Diana's. *All free time should be spent training.*

Erika looked downcast as Dad continued. "The phone, socialising—"

"And me?"

The room held its breath. Alfie rotated away from his position at the dining room arch while Florence took a few gasps of her inhaler. Erika shared a glance with Alex in silent apology.

Dad and Ollie rarely spoke directly. Even then, it was just asking for another family member or exchanges threaded with passive aggression neither chose to address. Now, they addressed it. In Ollie's eyes—the blue irises Erika shared as a gift from their missing mother—she saw fire. Not the passionate candlelight of Pete's gaze, but a flashing spark strung to a stick of dynamite, ever-growing, ready to explode.

The string shortened at their dad's silence. "Well?"

"Leave it, Ollie," Erika warned. "Don't be stupid."

Their dad's sigh made Ollie scoff. "Ignoring me isn't going to do anything new, considering that's all you've done for fifteen years."

"Oliver," Diana scolded. "We have guests. *Enough.*"

"*I've* had enough!"

The four panelled walls quaked at his roar. Florence flinched, Alfie shuffled further out the room, but Dad and Diana remained calm. This had been bottled for a while.

Ollie's lip curled. "You're supposed to be my dad and you think I'm trivial."

"I never said you were—"

"No, but you treat me like it."

Erika stiffened at the accusation. Ollie was bolder than her.

He stood, towering over Dad in the armchair.

"You never bother with me, and you never have. Alfie and Florence have been too busy for me since they went away. Only Erika cares enough to talk to me and she's never here!"

The twins had been training since Bekker's, going on early morning runs, visiting the gym, following strict diet plans. While hunting, it never occurred to Erika that Ollie would have felt more alone than ever.

If it was not for his treatment of Diana, she'd have sympathy.

He didn't consider his aunt once in his words. He raged on, ignorant of her sacrifices as Diana played with her hands, sinking sideways into the armchair.

"No-one gives a shit about—"

Erika snapped. "Ollie, that's enough."

He forced a bitter, burning laugh. "But Dad—"

"I don't care what Dad did. Cool off."

"Of course you would defend—"

"Cool *off*. Kitchen. Now."

"But—"

"I said *now*."

Ollie threw his arms in the air but obeyed. He stormed to the kitchen, heat following him, turning the room cold.

Diana wiped her eyes and plastered on a smile.

"Alex, Tommy, I apologise. I'll get you both another drink after I check on Ollie."

"No." Erika handed Alex her wine and brushed down her trousers as she stood. "Sit down. I'll go."

She met Dad's stare on the way out. She wanted to say something, remind him of how little he'd seen Ollie this past year especially, but stayed quiet.

She shook her head. The action surprised him.

Water ran in the kitchen as she stepped inside to find Ollie splashing his face at the sink. Erika paused at the doorway. The kitchen window fogged but he knew she was there.

He dabbed his face with a tea towel. "I'm begging you to please not lecture me."

"I'm not here to lecture you."

She closed the door behind them. Ollie rotated, wet hands on the edge of the granite. "Then why are you here?"

She shuffled beside him, careful of the clean dishes balancing on the draining rack as she crossed her arms. God, he was getting taller. She mourned the days she'd come home from training and lift him to the top of the fridge to steal from the treat basket. He would scoff the strawberry creams and gooey caramels and, even when he grew tall enough to grab them himself, he still saved her the honeycomb crunch.

He didn't need her anymore. It wouldn't be long until she'd need him to reach even greater heights for her.

"You've been off lately." Ollie blew a laugh. "Don't deny it. Tell me what's wrong."

He shook his head. His fringe was matted, his forehead soaked even though he'd just dried it. "I just feel *so* left out of this family. I'm tired of it. I'm a burden to you all."

"No, you're not, you're …" Her heart sank when the reality of his words settled in. The emotions, the implications. "How long have you been feeling like this?"

He shrugged. "A while. But since you left for work last, it's been worse. So much worse. I think Florence and Alfie going with you made a difference. It's like… there's this voice in my head telling me things. That I'm out of place. Alone. Like I don't belong. I love you—all of you. But it doesn't feel right. I only feel at home with you, and you're never here."

His words struck her again. Guilt kept her eyes on the floor. "I'm sorry," she said.

"Yeah, you say that. A lot."

"And I mean it."

"Sorry starts to mean a lot less when it's repeated. Again and again, while nothing changes."

The dishes rattled when Ollie's knuckles turned white. A noise left Erika's throat. Not a scoff nor cry, but something in between. "If I could change things, I would. But work—"

"Comes first, I know." The counter screeched when he pushed himself away. "You're Dad's little angel, aren't you? You won't say anything that didn't come from his mouth first."

"You don't have to be so passive-aggressive."

"You think I'm—"

Ollie clamped his eyes shut and backed away. He looked ill, almost ready to throw up. When Erika made to approach him, he held out a hand, forcing their distance.

"I'm… I'm going for a nap." He pressed his fingers to his temple. "My head…"

"Are you okay?" She tried to reach him again, but he brushed her off.

"I just need to be alone. Sleep will help."

Erika chewed on her cheek. Diana said he could be angry, sometimes even bratty, but her uncertainty in dealing with him was just another reminder of how little time she spent with her family.

"Do that," she replied. "But make sure you apologise to Diana first. Be grateful for what she does for us."

His features softened when he stopped at the doorway, returning to the youthful innocence Erika feared was lost. "I will."

Ollie passed Dad on the way out, but neither acknowledged the other. They scrunched their shoulders like a draft passed through the corridor.

Dad sighed when he closed the door behind him. "What's that look for?"

"He's your son." Erika leaned back against the sink. Dad opened the fridge door, running his hands inside to find another bottle. "I know you're not the most affectionate man in the world, but you need to show him you love him at least *sometimes*."

Dad nudged the fridge door—not hard enough to close it completely. "I am trying, Erika."

"Try harder."

The clink of beer bottles broke their silence as Dad returned to the fridge.

With a dissatisfied sigh, Erika gripped the counter behind to push herself out of the room. She whirled when her fingers sank into the metal.

The draining board had bent, now possessing eight small ridges the size of fingertips.

Ollie's fingertips.

"Erika?" The fridge door closed, and a bottle top cracked. "What's wrong?"

That was… normal, right? Anger encouraged strength.

Hunters were taught to channel their emotions when fighting. Hell, their greatest melee warriors all had underlying issues with aggression. Erika's own temper could get the better of her sometimes, but had she ever caused damage outside of a battle?

No, but she was not Ollie. Erika was *trained* to harness her emotions. Ollie's were untamed.

Erika reached for the quartz at her neck, her chest suddenly tight. "Nothing. I'm sure it's nothing."

CHAPTER FORTY-EIGHT

For Erika,

May you not disappoint me the way most others have.

Keep this journal safe. Keep it hidden.

With love, Grandpa.

Philip Lupine's Journal, Second Edition (Front Matter).

Dad and Ollie's confrontation killed the mood swifter than a knife, and soon the family dispersed. Ollie went upstairs for his nap, Florence stumbled to bed drunk, Dad left for a long shower, and Diana and Tommy searched the new shed for the dusty, old blow-up air mattress for the Arwoods to sleep on. Alfie made a start on his gift from Erika, *A Novice's Guide to Supernatural Botany*, and fell asleep on the armchair, glasses on his chin as he drooled.

Only Erika and Alex were left awake downstairs.

As Erika scrolled through the TV guide, Alex collapsed beside her on the sofa, his third plate of cubed cheese and cured meats in hand.

"You're lucky you do so much exercise," she joked.

"I call it 'Christmas bulking,' dear Erika." He pointed a cocktail stick of smoked cheese towards her lips. "Care to join?"

She'd stuffed herself on turkey dinner, gingerbread men, wine, a chocolate bar, and a cheese plate of her own, but this *was* her favourite cheese. "Go on, then."

She opened her mouth and leaned in. The golden goodness landed in Alex's grinning gob. "Too slow!"

She snatched his plate with a scoff. "Arse."

He cackled when she yanked a chunk of cheese from a stick with her teeth. The laughter faded when a placid Ollie dragged his heels into the living room.

He hesitated before speaking. "Could I borrow your phone charger, please? I broke mine."

Erika smiled. "Front pocket of my bag in the spare room."

"Got it. Thanks."

And that was it.

Alex gave her a nudge when Ollie disappeared upstairs. "How are you doing, really? Things got heated earlier."

Erika expelled a sigh. "I know. I'm sorry you and your dad saw that. There's a lot of tension in the house, but that…" She shuddered at the yelling, the questions, the sink. She wanted to tell Ollie everything, but rules were rules.

Ollie could know nothing. And now she knew nothing about *him*.

"That was a new low for them both," she finished.

Alex took the plate from Erika's lap, setting it on the coffee table. "Diana has a lot to deal with. She does well to handle it all."

"She does, but—" Already, Erika had another glass of wine down her neck and was now regretting it. The dryness, the headache… "She shouldn't have to. She had two children, not four. If Mum were still here… I don't know. Maybe we wouldn't have so many problems at home."

"You never mention your mum."

She felt for her glass, taking another swig. "None of us ever do. She's——" She checked over her shoulder. Water ran from the upstairs shower. "She's a touchy subject."

"So you never talk about her? That's how you move on?"

"I can't move on because she could be alive." Her voice cracked, and she covered her mouth swiftly.

The tale of how Christopher Lupine lost his wife circulated the Watch for years. According to Diana, any utterance of Emily Lupine triggered him into an explosive rage for weeks until the story dwindled to dying embers of speculation. He grew cold after that. Cold as the ashes of a burnt-down home.

She didn't need to repeat the story now. Alex could believe what he wished. "I heard your father's forbidden from tracking her down," he said.

Erika swirled her wine. "He is."

"But you're not."

She took a sip. "No."

He didn't need to ask the question because he already knew the answer.

If any trace of her mother, or the men who took her, was unearthed, she would drop everything to bring her home, Alliance Pack or not.

Everything.

"I'd go with you."

His words startled her, but she laughed. "Alex, I wouldn't expect—"

"I would anyway. You helped me find my dad."

"Because I was looking for my own."

"I don't care. You helped me either way. And, in doing so, in your kindness, you lost someone." Erika averted her gaze to find the floor. His touch, although gentle, struck her deeply when he angled her towards him by the chin.

"If I can help you find someone else that you love, I'll do it."

Several glasses of wine betrayed her in an instant that had her glancing longer at his caressing fingers than she needed to. Silently. Thoughtlessly. She dared look into those dark, dark irises for a moment, relishing the rush of him tilting her head back slowly.

She retreated, catching a glimpse of her distorted reflection in his gaze.

She cleared her throat. "We should watch a film."

Alex rolled his shoulders back. A sigh expelled from his nose. "Sure. What do you want to watch?"

Erika leapt to her feet, remote in hand. She could have thanked Alex for letting the moment fly by. Some part of her wanted it to land—another thought it a mistake. She couldn't afford mistakes with the few people she had left.

She hummed her indecisiveness and tossed him the remote.

It landed in his crotch.

Well played, Erika.

"God, I'm sorry! I—" Shit, he was groaning. That must have hurt. "You pick a film while I…" Erika backed out of the room, pointing at the staircase: her escape route. "I'll change into my pyjamas."

Alex nodded, his mouth pressed into a tight line. "No worries. You… go for it."

The thumbs-up she flashed made her regret being born.

She clambered up the stairs, clutching the banister. This habit of hers? It had to stop.

She was not proud of it, but often her moments of solitude led her to the beds of strangers. It stopped the *thoughts* from coming. It reset her mind, kept her focused.

Those *thoughts* came back when she lost Pete but, unlike the nights following a rough hunt, she did not race into town on adrenaline and anger. She lived off *nothing*. She grew sluggish, unmotivated. Thinking of being with someone else after losing Pete struck her with an immense guilt that kept her at home.

But Alex was *at* home. He was *there*. He was safe—a friend.

And she could never use a friend like that.

She was likely overthinking. Both of them had been drinking, both had been under pressure recently. It was just a moment of weakness.

At least her koala-themed pyjamas, gifted by Florence, didn't offer any bold suggestions.

Erika reached for the door handle to the spare room, figuring it to be shut as Ollie had already taken her charger and gone to bed, but no. He stood before the bed, over her bag, an open book in hand.

A black, leather journal.

Erika stopped breathing.

Ollie tried to speak, but no air circulated the room. No words were enough. No sentences made sense. The Lupine siblings suffocated under the weight of their silence.

Erika wanted to reach for him, to comfort him, but she was stone-still.

Ollie swallowed. "I thought you were on my side. I thought you cared."

Oh, Ollie. "I do, I... I *am.*'

"Then why—" Tears slid down Ollie's cheeks. He held up the journal with one shaking hand, brandishing the scribblings of one of Dad's old vampire hunts. "*Why* did you keep this from me?"

She had no training for this. All reflexes were void, but the marksman's focus on the nails Ollie dug into the leather binding.

"Ollie, we did this in your best—"

She jolted—*jolted* — when the journal banged against the wall beside her head. Paper tore, and a few pages slipped onto the carpet: sketches of lychans and exorcism symbols.

Ghosts, demons, lychans, wendigos, arcanes, vampires—they all existed. The monsters beneath his bed, the shadows at the back of the garden; the ones his guardians protected him from with words of assurance—they were real. Words could not fight against the real.

Ollie had been exposed since the day he was born, left to fend for himself in the shadows of the enlightened watchers of the Veil. Like everything else in his life, he was excluded, alone, unworthy.

And he would not forgive them for it. Not this time.

ACKNOWLEDGEMENTS

I'm going to start with a cliché and thank my mum and dad. Without your support in giving me the best start in life, this book would not be here. I love you both. To add: I'd like to apologise for all the swearing!

I also want to thank my brother for saying it as it is when I've bounced terrible ideas off him at the kitchen table. I'm also grateful to my nana for her unwavering support, and my friend Becky for thirteen years of listening to my ramblings about book ideas. One finally stuck! To the dogs: you are the biggest (and cutest) distraction. I'm especially grateful to the late Chloe for keeping me company during those long writing nights all the way back when I was in school. You were the best first dog and I miss you.

Now for the people who quite literally shaped this book! Thank you to my proofreader Jade for her precision in polishing this manuscript. I also have a big thank you for ambientpixelstudios (Fiverr), for capturing the novel's essence with this gorgeous cover and brilliant marketing materials.

To everyone who beta read this book: thank you. Your critiques and support worked wonders. Thank you to the support of BookTok and everyone who has liked, shared, and commented to spread the word about Tarnish the Veil before I even pressed publish. I also have a thank-you for my old followers on Wattpad (wow, throwback!) who encouraged me to hone my craft during my teenage years.

I'd like to thank the three—yes, three—laptops that carried this book from a page of ideas to a fully-formatted novel.

Most of all, I'd like to thank John. You taught me that my writing is not silly and is a passion worth pursuing. Thank you for listening to my ideas, taking me to book fairs, encouraging me to publish, and for providing me with an endless supply of coffee and chocolate. I don't know what I'd do without you. I love you.

ABOUT THE AUTHOR

C. L. Cross was born and raised in Stockton-on-Tees in North-East England. When she is not drafting her next novel, she can be found reading her endless TBR or walking her two cocker spaniels.

To find out more about her upcoming books, make sure to follow her on TikTok (@authorcaitlinlc) and subscribe to her newsletter!

Printed in Dunstable, United Kingdom